Conestoga Winter

A Story of Border Vengeance

ROBERT J. SHADE

Sunshine Hill Press

First Edition 2013
Sunshine Hill Press, LLC
1610 Nathan Lane
Herndon, VA 20170

Artwork with specific permission:
Front Cover: *Time of War* by Bryant White
(www.whitehistoricart.com)

Map: *Western Pennsylvania 1759–1763* by Stephen Templeton

Conestoga Winter is a work of fiction. With the exception of historical people, places, and events in the narrative, all names, characters, places, and incidents are used fictitiously. Any resemblance to current events, places, or to living persons is entirely coincidental.

ISBN-10: 0615781276
ISBN-13: 9780615781273

Western Pennsylvania 1759-1763

MAJOR CHARACTERS

Historical

Henry Bouquet	Colonel, 1st Battalion, 60th Foot, Commander of British military forces in Pennsylvania
Daniel Morgan	Waggoner from Virginia
James Robertson	Captain, 77th Foot
John Elder	Presbyterian Minister of Paxton
Lazarus Stewart	Captain, Paxton Militia (Paxton Rangers)
Asher Clayton	Captain, Paxton Militia (Paxton Rangers)
John Dunning	High Sheriff of Cumberland County
John Hay	Lancaster Sheriff
John Armstrong	Surveyor who laid out town of Carlisle in 1750, later a Colonel in the Pennsylvania Regiment
Neolin	Delaware spiritual leader, "The Prophet"
Lewis Ourry	Captain 60th Foot, Commander of Fort Bedford
Thomas Stirling	Captain, 42nd Foot (Black Watch)

Fictional

Wend Eckert	Gunsmith of Sherman Valley
Abigail Gibson	Captive of Mingo Indians. Known as Orenda
Joshua Baird	Civilian scout for Colonel Bouquet
Simon Donegal	Discharged veteran of 77th Foot

Robert J. Shade

Arnold Spengler	Corporal, 60th Foot, clerk to Colonel Bouquet
Richard Grenough	Owner of border trading company
Price Irwin	Senior manager in Grenough's company
Mathew Bratton	Freight waggoner of Sherman Valley, undercover operative for Grenough
Charlie Sawak	Conestoga Indian, peddler of tribal wares
Frank McKenzie	Waggoner working for Matt Bratton
Shane Reilly	Trader working for Grenough
Gray Mathews	Trader working for Grenough
Hugh Crowley	Mathews' partner
George Washburn	Tavern keeper in Carlisle
Alice Downey	Boarding house proprietress in Carlisle
Franklin	Former black slave living in Sherman Valley
Mary Fraser	Camp follower and nurse in 77th Highlanders
Paul Carnahan	Minister and schoolmaster of Sherman Valley
Patricia Carnahan	Wife of Rev Carnahan
Wolf Claw	War captain of Mingo band, husband of Abigail Gibson/Orenda
Donovan McCartie	Tavern proprietor in Sherman Mill village
Susan McCartie	Wife of Donovan
Peggy McCartie	Elder daughter of Donavan McCartie
Ellen McCartie	Younger daughter of Donavan McCartie
Frank McClay	Neighbor and lay helper to Rev Carnahan

Sarah McClay	Frank's wife
Elizabeth McClay	Daughter of Frank and Sarah
Thomas Marsh	Gristmill proprietor of Sherman Mill
Hank Marsh	Eldest son of miller Thomas Marsh
Rose Jenson	Indentured tavern maid in Harris' Ferry
Colleen Allison	Tavern maid in York
Charles McDonald	Captain in 42nd Foot (Black Watch), former officer in 77th Foot

CONTENTS

Part I

The End of a Nation

December 1763 – January 1764

CHAPTER ONE

Busy Night at Fort Bedford

The three riders urged their horses eastward along Forbes Road. To their backs lay the hulking Allegheny Mountains, clearly visible in the frigid December air. As they rode, the dense, leafless winter forest pressed in around them, broken only when they passed the abandoned wreckage of hardscrabble farms, the buildings burned out by Delaware, Shawnee, or Mingo war parties during the summer's raiding. All three of the men wore overcoats of the same heavy gray wool to shield themselves from the cold wind which blew through the rolling country. A discerning observer would have noted that their coats were of army cut, with a broad rain flap over the shoulders. The observer would have been excused if he initially jumped to the conclusion that he was looking at three soldiers, particularly since one of the men sported the round, blue bonnet that all His Majesty's highland regiments stationed in the American colonies wore. But then the watcher would have noticed that the other two men wore broad-brimmed hats unlike any issued to a crown soldier and all three of the riders carried Pennsylvania longrifles slung over their shoulders, not Brown Bess muskets.

Suddenly one of the riders in a broad-brimmed hat pulled up and dismounted stiffly from his horse. The tall, rangy man bent down, grimacing slightly as he did so, and lifted the right fore-hoof of the animal. He was in his late thirties and had a scruffy beard on his sharp, craggy, wind-burned face. The other two riders halted their horses and the pack horse which trailed behind and watched as the man examined his mount's hoof and leg. "Damn, Damn, Damn!" He exclaimed, "This ornery critter has come up lame. There's a swellin' right up from the hoof to the knee. He picked a hell of a time, with us not two hours from Fort Bedford!"

"Come on, Joshua, there's never a good time for a horse to go lame." The speaker was the other man wearing a broad-brimmed hat. He was mounted on a powerfully built, long-legged black mare which stood at least a hand taller than the other animals and he was much younger than the man on the ground. The face under the hat brim was clean shaven and stony, revealing little emotion. Only the twinkle of the blue eyes betrayed a mixture of warmth and amusement toward the older man. "To tell the truth, I've been surprised that none of the animals has gone lame before this, what with the way we've been pushing the pace since we left Fort Pitt. You know that if we weren't trying to get back to the settlements before the first heavy snow, we'd have spent more time resting them." Then he swung easily down from the mare and offered the reins to the older man. "Here, Joshua, you ride my mare and I'll lead your horse the rest of the way to the fort."

Joshua reared up and scowled at the young man indignantly. "Wend Eckert, what makes you think I ain't up to leadin' the horse to Bedford? You tryin' to say I'm an old man or somethin'?"

The young man retorted, "Yeah Joshua, you're over the hill, ready for a rocking chair in front of the kitchen cook-fire!" Then he laughed and said, "Come on, Joshua, I'm just thinking of the wound in that left leg of yours. It still hasn't fully healed and you've been even stiffer since the cold weather came on."

The man in the highland bonnet looked down from his horse. "Wend's right, Baird; that hip has 'na finished healing in the time since you took that Shawnee arrow at Bushy Run. And that wee six week hike Colonel Bouquet sent us on through the Ohio Country didn't help it one bit. You need to rest that leg as much as possible if you expect it to get better." He shook his head. "Doc Monro back at Fort Pitt told you to rest that leg in August and you been ignoring his advice ever since."

There was a prolonged silence as Joshua glared at each of his companions. Finally he said to the Scotsman, "Donegal, you didn't have to gang up with Eckert on me. You could've at least just sat there and minded your own business." Then he loudly exclaimed, "Shit!" which was in this case an admission of surrender; he reluctantly handed the reins to Wend and walked over to the tall mare. As he raised his left foot to the stirrup, Wend noticed a sudden expression of pain which the scout quickly wiped from his face.

Once Joshua had mounted, Wend turned eastward and stepped out leading the lame horse. He looked up at the sun which shone feebly through patchy, fast moving clouds. "If we don't tarry, we can be at the fort by mid-afternoon."

* * *

Two hours later they crested a low hill at the edge of the tree line and halted momentarily to view Fort Bedford as it lay before them. The wooden stockade, shaped like an irregular five-point star, was sited adjacent to a branch of the Juniata. The star was further distorted by the existence of a long, roof covered extension of the stockade which ran from one bastion all the way down to the river to provide protected access to the water supply. Outside the stockade, in a great expanse of cleared area which surrounded the main fort, were several smaller log enclosures which acted as camps for visiting troop units or fenced-in pastures for animals.

Joshua said, "I ain't seen this place since we marched through in July with Colonel Bouquet's column. Look at all those wagons parked outside the stockade and herds of animals in the pastures. Busy little place for December, ain't it?"

Wend responded, "Well, while you were in the hospital at Fort Pitt, Donegal and I scouted for several convoys of empty wagons traveling back to Ligonier and here. Bedford hasn't returned to the sleepy post it was before the Ohio tribes rose up in June." He thought for a second. "Bouquet's using it to marshal supplies for the 1764 campaign. They'll be convoyed west to Pitt as soon as Forbes Road is passable for wheeled rigs in the spring."

Donegal cleared his throat. "I'm 'na much concerned with all these little details you two are jabbering about. It's important matters I'm thinkin' of, like where we can get some hot rum and how soon?"

Baird said, "Donegal *does* have a point."

They rode on and in a short time the three had entered the main stockade. Joshua and Eckert went to deliver the dispatches they were carrying from Colonel Bouquet at Fort Pitt to Captain Ourry, the Royal American officer who commanded at Bedford. Donegal stayed behind to look for overnight accommodations.

Ourry's adjutant showed them right into the commander's office. As the two men entered, the captain looked up from his desk, smiled broadly, and then jumped to his feet from his desk to greet them. His voice was heavy in the accent of his native Switzerland. "Ah, Baird, I wondered when you'd be passing through. And here's young Eckert, too. Welcome to both of you." He thought for a moment. "This place is so busy with contractors, waggoners, and all these Black Watch troops Bouquet has stationed here for the winter, it's good to see familiar faces from the old days before the uprising."

Baird nodded to the captain. "Yeah, well I guess nothin's ever gonna be the same since the Ohio tribes rose in revolt last May. Least ways, sir, not until Bouquet marches into the Ohio country next year with a force big enough to make them settle down." The scout walked over to Ourry's desk and laid his leather dispatch case down. "Got some messages for you in there, Captain."

Ourry had watched closely as Baird walked, and concern had spread across his face as he saw the scout's pronounced limp. He pointed to Joshua's left hip. "I heard that you had taken an arrow at Bushy Run. It looks like it's still causing you some problems."

"It ain't nothin', Captain, what some rest over the winter won't cure, proper like. I'll spend some time with the Widow Downey in Carlisle and then up at my sister's place in Sherman Mill. I'll be fit as ever next spring when the campaigning starts again."

"I'm glad to hear that, Joshua. There's no better scout in the army than you, and I know Bouquet is counting on you to guide his march to the Muskingham River."

Then the captain looked over at a side table for a second. "Please excuse me for my manners, gentlemen. You've just come in from the cold. Let me offer you a libation to take the edge off your chill." He stepped over to the sidebar where bottles and glasses were stored and picked up a decanter of amber liquid. Pausing a moment before pouring, he said "I trust this will suit your taste."

They accepted the drinks with thanks and Wend sipped the liquid. It was whiskey, but something much smoother and refined than he had ever tasted. It was certainly not the typical frontier spirits he was used to taking from a corked jug.

Ourry poured himself a glass, then smiled wryly, and looked over at Wend. "Of course Joshua, good a scout as you are, these days you got to keep looking behind you. Eckert, here, has certainly earned a name for himself over the last few months." He waved a hand at Wend. "Young man, all the officers passing through here had nothing but praise for the scouting you did at Bouquet's battle with the tribes at Bushy Run and in the months afterward. And Captain McDonald of the 77th stood right here and told me about how you saved his life with a magnificent pistol shot to the head of a Shawnee who was about to split his skull with a hatchet."

Wend shrugged his shoulders and shook his head. "At that range, Captain, it wasn't anything but instinct and pure luck. I snapped the shot off before I even had a chance to think about it."

Ourry nodded. "That may be true, Wend, but McDonald emphasized how he will always be indebted to you. And the story of that shot and how you took down those two warriors with long range rifle fire the next day has passed like wildfire through the army and border country."

Wend shrugged his shoulders again. "As a gunsmith, I understand rifles and the flight of balls pretty well. And I get a lot of time to practice on my own target range, when I'm back home at Sherman Mill."

Baird said, "That he does, captain. He spends all his time hunched over his workbench or practicing those long distance shots." The scout pointed at the leather case on the desk. "But Captain, I got to tell you somethin' else 'bout those dispatches. Once you get your messages out of there, I got to take that case back. There's a dispatch for Mr. Richard Grenough in there, and Bouquet wanted me to deliver it personal-like to Carlisle, so the commanding officer at the garrison can get it directly to Grenough." He paused, and then said, "I guess you know that Grenough is goin' to be an Indian Commissioner for negotiations with the tribal chiefs next year. 'Cause of that, Bouquet's sending him some plans for the campaign."

Ourry looked down at the case, then back up at Baird. "You'll not need to deliver that dispatch to Carlisle, Joshua. Grenough's right here in Bedford."

Joshua's eyebrows rose in surprise. "Here in Bedford? What in the devil's name would bring him out over the Tuscarora Mountains and Sideling Hill in December? I figured he'd be settled in for the winter in that big place of his over at York, enjoying a warm fire."

"It's the war. He wants to set up a store and a warehouse here. He sat right in that chair yesterday telling me how he figured there will be so many contractors and soldiers here next spring that he'll have a ready market for his trade goods." Ourry waved his arm. "At any rate, he's having dinner in the officers' mess with me tonight. I'll give him the letter from Bouquet then."

Wend was suddenly frozen, his heart pumping rapidly at hearing Grenough's name. For of the three men in the room, only he was aware of evidence that Grenough, one of the biggest merchants in the colony, was also illicitly supplying the tribes with gunpowder, lead and other materials of war. And, in the pursuit of that secret trade, men of Grenough's organization had caused the death of Wend's family and untold pain to people along the frontier.

Joshua was speaking again. "Well, that makes our travel plans a might easier. We can head straight to Lancaster from here without goin' up to Carlisle."

Ourry cocked his head. "You're bound for Lancaster, Joshua? That's well out of your way. Sherman Mill is north of Carlisle." He smiled knowingly. "And besides, the esteemed Mrs. Downey, with all her comforting charms, lives in Carlisle."

Joshua returned the captain's smile. "She does, indeed, sir. And it's a long time since I had the pleasure of the widow's company. But we're goin' with Wend to keep him company; he's got to take the possessions of a soldier, a friend of his who died at Bushy Run, to his mother in Lancaster."

Wend spoke up. "As a matter of fact, I think you know the man in question: Sergeant Arnold Spengler, who was a clerk in Bouquet's headquarters for many years."

"Spengler? Of course I know him." Ourry chuckled. "Henry used to swear about how impudent he was and always said if he hadn't had the fairest writing hand in the battalion, he'd have had him tied up to a wagon wheel and lashed at the earliest opportunity." Ourry smiled broadly. "But I happen to know that the colonel was actually amused by Spengler's wit and impressed with his quick mind. That's why he kept him close at hand."

Wend nodded. "I sort of gathered that myself, from some of the things the colonel said, sir. But more to the point, Spengler and I grew up together and went to the same school. At least until Arnold quit to join the army. He didn't want to be a cooper like his Pa."

The captain nodded his understanding. "I'm sorry you have to carry out such a sad mission, Eckert." Ourry reflected for a moment, then looked up at Joshua and Wend. "I assume you plan to stay the night here at the fort and then ride on east tomorrow. If you speak to the adjutant, he'll get you quarters and provide stable space for your mounts."

Joshua drained the last of his whiskey, and put the glass down on the captain's sideboard. "I appreciate the offer, Capt'n, but we'll be wantin' to leave as early as possible in the mornin'. So, we'll set up camp in one of those open sheds down by the river, so we can leave easy-like before dawn without disturbin' anyone in the fort." He thought for a moment. "And I almost forgot: My horse went lame a few miles back. I'd be much obliged if you'd let me trade him for one of the mounts you keep here for couriers."

The captain waved a hand. "No problem, Joshua. Just talk to the adjutant. And I expect you'll want some oats to feed your animals."

"Thanks, Captain," Joshua responded, "We'd appreciate it." He extended his hand. "I 'spect we'll see you next year when the snows have melted."

Shortly, a sack of oats hanging from the mare's saddle, Joshua and Wend led their horses down to a grassy area on the bank of the Juniata where Donegal had appropriated an empty shed. The highlander had set up a picket line for the horses and was working on kindling a fire.

Joshua looked around for a moment. "This will do, right enough. To tell the truth, the reason I wanted to camp out here was because I can't stand bein' cooped up in a smoke filled barracks with a company of soldiers. At least we'll get a breeze down here, even if it is chilly. We need a good sleep after today, not tossin' and turnin' in some steamy hut, breathin' the stench of sweaty men."

Wend started to pull their equipment and tack off the horses. He looked around as he worked, and saw that they were not alone along the river. Four freight wagons were parked about fifty yards away, their teams made up to a picket line, and the waggoners had set up a camp. However, he could see no sign of the waggoners until he looked over toward the fort. Then, across the wagon track, he saw a small hut, with some trestle tables set up outside under a lean-to. Four or five men sat at one of the tables, laughing and joking, with mugs in their hands. He realized the hut was some sort of a rude tavern and assumed the men were the missing waggoners.

As he was watching, Wend heard the sound of many hooves and the rumble of wagon wheels. He looked up to see three more Conestoga wagons being driven out through the main stockade's entrance and down the road which paralleled the river. They rolled by his position, then the lead driver turned down onto the grass of the bank and pulled up near the river between where the other wagons were parked and the scouts' campsite. The following two wagons pulled up alongside the first, and the waggoners started to unhitch their teams.

Donegal looked up from the fire. "It seems like we're going to have plenty of company tonight, Joshua."

"Yeah, I saw those wagons unloadin' stores while we were gettin' oats from the quartermaster. They must be going to spend the night here before they head back to wherever they're from." Joshua looked around, then over at the tavern, then back to his comrades. "Let's finish gettin' set up, then we can go up to that tavern and I'll let one of you buy me ale—or whiskey if they got it. We ain't seen a tavern since we left Carlisle in July."

They soon walked over to the tavern and took seats under the lean-to porch. It was a ramshackle, unkempt place presided over by a small, balding, chubby man whose appearance matched that of his tavern. A young girl, who looked to be his daughter, waited on the outside tables. Her appearance was even more disreputable than her father. She had dirty, greasy hair, clothing which was only a step above rags, and displayed a grin marked by crooked, yellow stained teeth.

After she had taken their first order, Joshua remarked, "That girl with the snaggle-tooth makes you remember the McCartie girls right fondly doesn't she?"

Wend smiled and nodded. "Sure enough, Joshua: It will be good to sit beside the fire in McCartie's Tavern and enjoy watching them at work."

Donegal shook his head. "I'd appreciate if you two would at least tell me who you are talking about. Who are these McCartie lasses?"

Baird answered, "Donovan McCartie owns the only tavern in Sherman Mill, and for that matter, the only one in the valley of Sherman Creek. Peggy and Ellen are his daughters. Peggy is the oldest; she's about Wend's age. Raven haired and beautiful she is; she'll take your breath away when you see her. And she could wrap her long legs around you an' crush you to death, and you'd be smilin' as you went to meet your Maker. She's smart and cagy, too. The younger, Ellen is about sixteen by now, brown haired and plain as they come." He paused to think a minute. "But they're both hard workers and know how to keep a man amused and orderin' more drinks."

Wend said, "Ellen may be plain, but she has a smile which wrinkles up her face and makes you forget she isn't that comely. And that smile always gives me a warm feeling."

Joshua winked at Donegal. "Yeah, that Ellen gave Wend a ring before he left. He carries it on a string around his neck."

Donegal stared at Wend. "Now wait a minute! Just how many girls you got, Wend? You went on Bouquet's march to Pitt mainly because you was trying to find that Philadelphia lass, Abigail, who was taken by the Mingoes. And then you got mixed up with Mary Fraser, which made every young buck in the 77th mad 'cause they was in love with her themselves. You'd still be with her if she hadn't died from that wound she got at Bushy Run. And now I find out that all along you had some young thing waiting for you back in Sherman Mill."

Joshua laughed. "Ain't I been tellin' you, Donegal, that girls like to wrap themselves around our boy Wend?"

Wend shook his head. "Hold on, Donegal. Joshua is putting you on! Ellen McCartie gave me that ring in memory of a friend of mine, Johnny Donaldson. He was her boyfriend and died defending his family's home from a Shawnee war party. It was his ring; Ellen gave that to me so that I could carry it into the fight with the tribes, sort of as an act of revenge for Johnny. There isn't anything romantic between Ellen and me."

Baird flashed a wolfish smile at Donegal. "That may be true about Ellen. But ole' Wend here still isn't giving you the whole truth. Not by a long shot. He ain't told you 'bout Elizabeth McClay yet. She is a pretty, slim-waisted lass, and he can't no way deny she's set her bonnet for him. Every time there's some get-together she's right there beside him, cuddlin' up, and if any other girl even looks at him, she shoos her away fast-like."

Donegal nodded. "I'm glad you told me about all these lassies. It's about time a man in his prime like me got himself a woman. I'll be thirty before you know it." He thought for a moment. "Now, that black-haired girl you talked about sounds just about right. There's not many a girl can turn down the charms of a highlander. And besides, I'm a man of wealth now, with the Crown owing me 100 acres of land as my discharge bounty, free and clear. Can't be many a man can offer that."

Joshua raised an eyelid at Donegal. "You make a move on Peggy McCartie, you are likely to get that face of yours re-arranged in a major fashion." Baird looked at the highlander as if he was assessing his face. "Not that it ain't been re-arranged a few times before: That nose of yours looks like a creek wandering through a valley."

"And just who is gonna do this particular re-arranging, Joshua?"

"A strappin' tall waggoner name of Matt Bratton, that's who, Donegal." Joshua wagged his finger at the highlander. "Peggy happens to be betrothed to him. And he's a brawler with a reputation all through the Cumberland Valley and Sherman Valley, too. You start movin' in on Peggy and he'll put another bend in that nose of yours in a heartbeat."

Donegal looked between Joshua and Wend. "I'm 'na such a bad fighter myself."

Wend shook his head. "Don't even think about it, Donegal; I've seen Bratton in action. He's got burly shoulders, arm muscles like steel from handling reins all day, and fists like ham-hocks. He'll make short work of you." Wend gathered his thoughts. "You want to stay clear of him anyway. He's the leader of a gang that lords it over most of the young people in Sherman Mill and the valley."

Joshua motioned to Donegal with his mug. "Wend should know. Bratton's been after him since I brought him to live with my sister and her husband back in '59. That was after his family was massacred by the Mingoes at Sideling Hill. Bratton doesn't miss a chance to try and embarrass him. And he's been trying to lure him into a fight since he arrived."

Donegal looked at Wend. "Why is the big man so down on you? You try to make a move on his woman, this Peggy?"

Wend laughed and shook his head. "Me, after Peggy? Not likely. I haven't been able to figure out why he's so antagonistic. I think maybe it's because I'm German, while most of the people in the valley are Ulster-Scots. He calls me 'Dutchman' all the time. My friend Charlie Sawak, a Conestoga Indian from where I used to live near Lancaster, thinks it's because I'm making good money from my trade, which has put me in good standing with business men in Sherman Mill and Carlisle."

Joshua laughed. "Not to mention that you beat him in shootin' matches all the time."

Wend looked around, and saw that the waggoners he had noticed earlier were talking very loudly, obviously feeling the effect of several mugs of libation. He listened to their conversation, and soon picked up that they were from Frederick Town, in Maryland, and had freighted supplies to the fort from that place. As he watched, the men from the second group of wagons walked over from their campsite, joking and laughing as they came. Wend noticed that their apparent leader was a giant of a man who looked to be in his late twenties and who had burley shoulders, large meaty hands, and a rough hewn face featuring a prominent broken nose. The new arrivals sat down at a table next to the other waggoners and began clamoring for service.

As time went on, Wend found himself weary from the day's ride, a feeling which the ale enhanced and further relaxed him. Baird was making the most of the opportunity to drink whiskey, and soon had consumed several mugs to the one of ale which Wend and Donegal had each nursed. The three scouts weren't paying much attention to the boisterous conversations of the waggoners, but suddenly a shouting match erupted between the two groups. Every one of the freighters jumped up and Wend feared a fight was imminent. Instead, the men started laying coins on the table between two men who were obviously going to hold the money for some wager.

Presently one man ran down to the Frederick wagons, and came back carrying a rifle in one hand and a couple of small square pieces of wooden plank in his other. The man with the rifle handed one of the pieces of wood to a second man, who started pacing off a distance along the road which led westward along the bank of the Juniata. He continued until he had measured a distance of roughly fifty yards. Then he shouted back to the rifleman, "That about right, brother?"

The rifleman nodded. Then, with studied casualness, he said, "That'll do," and set about priming the pan of his lock.

Suddenly, Joshua pointed at the other man. "Lord above, do you see that?"

Wend looked at where Joshua pointed, and was astonished to see that the second man had placed the chunk of plank, which was only about four inches square, in the crotch of his legs just below his genitals. Wend was speechless; it was now apparent what the wager was. Wend walked up to the burley leader of the second group of waggoners and pointed at the rifleman. "I take it that he is going to try to shoot that target out from between the man's legs?"

The big man looked down at Wend and grinned devilishly. "Yep, that's the idea. Says he can do it at fifty paces without touching his brother's private parts. 'Course, if he misses high, things are going to get mighty interesting."

Wend studied the rifleman, as he checked out his firearm. It was obvious that he had had more than just a few mugs of ale and was none too steady on his feet. Wend said, "Why doesn't he brace his rifle on one of the tables, or lay down to steady himself?"

The big man laughed. "That's part of the wager. He has to do it without support; just a standing shot." The man looked down at Wend, then over at Joshua. "What's your business here? Never seen you thee fellows in these parts and I run supplies up here to the fort all the time."

Wend motioned at Baird. "We were scouts and couriers for Colonel Bouquet during his expedition to relieve Fort Pitt. But we've been mustered out, and we're carrying dispatches for the posts along Forbes Road on our way east. We just rode in from Fort Pitt today with messages for Captain Ourry." Wend extended his hand. "I'm Wend Eckert, from Sherman Valley in Pennsylvania, and that's Joshua Baird, who more or less calls the army his home. Our highland friend is Simon Donegal, late corporal of the 77th Foot."

The waggoner gave Wend his hand. "My name's Morgan, Daniel Morgan; from a village near Winchester, Virginia. I run a freighting company and got a contract to supply the fort with flour and other victuals." He waved his hand at the other two waggoners in his group. "These are my drivers."

One of the Maryland men raised his arms to request quiet. All the men were now gazing at the man with the target between his legs. Wend looked at shooter, and thought he saw a resemblance to the man holding the target. He whispered to Morgan, "Are those two brothers?"

Morgan nodded at Wend. "Yeah, they must have a lot of trust between them, to try something like this, particularly with the light fading here in the evening."

Suddenly a shot rang out, and Wend looked back at the man holding the target. The piece of wood was gone from between his legs. The man turned and walked a couple of paces, reached down to the ground and picked up the target, holding it high for everyone to see. There was a hole slightly below the center. The Maryland boys cheered and clapped, while Morgan's Virginian's stood around with glum looks on their faces.

Wend looked at Morgan. "That was a neat piece of shooting."

Morgan nodded. "Too neat. Those boys must have been practicing, and I bet they do this all over, making good money at it."

Then Wend heard Joshua's voice. "I'm not thinkin' that was any big deal, not at just fifty paces. Any real sharpshooter could do that at seventy."

Wend felt a cold chill run through his body. He swore silently to himself.

One of the Maryland men laughed at Joshua, who was obviously feeling his liquor. "I suppose you are the man who is going to do it at seventy paces?"

Joshua looked around, laughed and shook his head. "Me? Not a chance. But my friend, Eckert here, he's the best shot in the Cumberland and Sherman Valleys combined. Ain't a man can touch him with a rifle." Baird reached into his pocket and dumped everything in it out onto the table. "Here's some of the King's coin which says he can do it, no problem."

Morgan looked at Wend, then at Joshua. "Yeah, if that's so, who is going to hold the target between his legs?"

Joshua shrugged his shoulders. "I will, of course. Show's you how much confidence I have in Eckert." He pounded the table so the coins jingled. "Here's your chance to get some of your money back!"

The Marylander who had held the wood between his legs walked up to the table and plunked a handful of coins down. "I'll take the bet. Nobody's as good as my brother, and he wouldn't think about doing that at seventy paces."

Now the waggoners from both states dropped coins onto the table, all the Virginia men betting against the Marylanders.

Joshua turned to Wend. "Come on, Wend. I know you got some cash with you. Lay it down. Here's our chance to make some real money!"

Wend was horrified. He grabbed Baird by the arm and dragged him off to where no one could hear them. "Joshua, you're soused. This is crazy. I've never tried anything like this. Those brothers have obviously been practicing the trick for a long time. The shooter knows from repetition exactly where to line up his sights. I'm going to be guessing. And the light is bad now. It would be hard enough at fifty paces, but at seventy I'm not going to be able to pick out all the details."

"Come on Wend, you regularly put balls in the center of a target at 150 paces. You took down those two Indians on the ridge at Bushy Run at near 200, and that was firing up hill. This should be nothin' special."

"Joshua, I can't even brace myself, according to their rules. Have you thought about what happens to your working parts if I'm just a little high?"

"Won't make much difference. I ain't getting much chance to use them lately, anyway. Lizzie Iverson is gone and even the Widow Downey wouldn't let me into her bed last time we was back there in Carlisle. So what does it matter?" He took another gulp from his mug.

"Joshua, the widow couldn't help you 'cause her house was overflowing with families and kids taking refuge from war parties. She'll be welcoming you with open arms when we get back east."

Baird laughed. "Hell, it ain't open arms I want from the widow! It's open legs I'm thinkin' about."

Wend shook his head. "You aren't making any sense. This won't work. Let's just tell everyone we thought better of it, and go down to our shed and a warm fire. We need sleep before we ride out tomorrow."

Joshua pulled away. "I'm tellin' you, we ain't backin' off. No sir, we ain't. Besides, the bet is made and look at all the money on that table. They'll laugh us out of here if we don't carry through. Give me your money and go get your rifle."

Wend was shivering all over as he handed over the coins he had on him and went to their campsite. By the time he returned with his rifle, powder horn, and shot pouch, Joshua was pacing off the distance, a wooden target in one hand and his mug in the other.

One of the Maryland men followed Joshua, checking the distance he was measuring. Soon they were both at he same spot. Baird handed the man his mug and put the target between his legs.

"All right, lad; let her rip!"

Wend gulped, and completed checking out his firearm. It was made from the finest piece of curly maple he had been able to find and crafted with his best skill. As he worked, he caught Morgan looking at the rifle with a critical eye, but had little time to reflect on his interest.

Wend settled himself into position. He turned so that his left side was directly facing Joshua, brought the rifle up, and aimed at the target. Then he found one small piece of luck: Baird's stand on the road was almost directly to the west of him, so the target was silhouetted in the last rays of the evening sun. Moreover, a faint bar of light shown between the top of the target and Joshua's crotch.

That satisfied him that he would be able to accurately make out the target. But as he sighted along the barrel, he could see the movement of the rifle in his hands. He must, somehow, make it steadier before he fired.

Then, as he hesitated, the Maryland brother who had been the shooter laughed out loud. "What's the hesitation, my fine lad? Too scared to shoot? Worried about what you're going to do to your partner's balls?"

Wend lowered the rifle, and looked at the man, but said nothing. He was feeling sweat breaking out on his hands, his shoulders, and all over his face. But he forced himself to concentrate, and then an idea came to him. He slid his left foot further toward the target. He moved his left hand back on the stock, far closer to the lock than normal, so that he had much more bend in his arm at the elbow than usual; in fact, it formed a sharp 'V'. Then he scrunched up his torso and cocked his upper body slightly backward until his upper arm and elbow rested on his side, just above the hip, forming a rudimentary brace for the rifle. Then he squinted along the sights. By God, he was steady! Wend pulled the sett trigger, then concentrated on placing his sight right below the shaft of light between Baird's crotch and the target, took a deep breath, and squeezed the firing trigger.

There were shouts from all the men except the Maryland brothers. Joshua whooped like an Indian, turned around and picked up the target from the ground. There was a well centered hole visible. Then he looked back at the gathered men and made a show of casually scratching his balls. The brothers from Maryland stood absolutely quiet, their mouths open.

Joshua walked back and joined the group of men standing around the table. Morgan took the target from him and held it up to the light. He looked over at Wend. "That was one hell of a shot, lad."

Morgan scooped up all the coins scattered on the table into one mound, and then carefully separated them into two equal piles. He motioned to Joshua to take one, and he split the other pile with his men. After completing that important business, he walked over to Wend. "That's a mighty fine looking rifle, lad. Can I take a look?"

Wend handed it to Morgan. The burly man examined the firearm closely, testing the lock and hefting the rifle in his two great, meaty hands. "This is one of the lightest I've ever felt. And one of the most elegant looking. Can you show me a ball?"

Wend reached into his pouch and handed Morgan a projectile.

The man held up the ball to get the fading light fairly on it. "It looks only about three quarters of the size of most rifle balls. Don't you have trouble bringing down large game?"

Wend shook his head and launched into his practiced explanation of the advantages of a smaller bore. He pointed out that the lighter ball flew with a flatter trajectory which gave better accuracy at long range, used less powder, and saved on the amount of lead. Morgan watched him closely as he spoke, nodding as he made his points. Wend finished out by saying that he could, of course, make a rifle of any bore the purchaser desired.

The big man asked, "Where are you working now?"

Wend told him about his shop in Sherman Valley. Morgan nodded, and looked as if he was about to say something, but he was interrupted as Joshua came up, counting the winnings from the bet. But it was the men who were with Baird who grabbed Wend's attention.

Joshua exclaimed, "Hey, Wend, look who showed up down here to visit with us common folk!" He turned and motioned to the man behind him. "Richard Grenough, no less. You met him back in Carlisle last summer in Colonel Bouquet's office."

Grenough stood beside Baird, an engaging smile on his face. He extended a hand to Wend. "I'm on my way to dinner with Captain Ourry, but I heard that my old friend Joshua was here at the fort, so I came down to pay my respects. As we walked up, I was amazed to see your demonstration of precise shooting, Mr. Eckert. Congratulations on the steadiest hand I've ever seen." He smiled and looked at Baird. "Especially since you managed to preserve Joshua's manhood in the process."

Wend responded, "I was very fortunate that the last of the sun's light helped me be sure of my target."

Grenough laughed. "Come on, Mr. Eckert, no false modesty, please. Few men could have done that in any kind of light." Then he remembered the man who stood beside him. "I'm forgetting my manners, gentlemen. This is my associate, Mr. Price Irwin. He's managing my operations here in the Bedford area."

Joshua nodded to Irwin, then spoke to Grenough. "I was surprised when Ourry told me you was settin' up a merchandise store here in Bedford, Richard. That's not your regular line."

"Just adapting to the war, Joshua. Trading with the Ohio tribes is finished, at least until the war is over. I've got to keep making money in the meanwhile, and, with all the contractors here to support Bouquet's next campaign, there's a good market for general goods. Besides, I think we're going to see a lot of growth here in Bedford—the frontier will shift westward after the war. So I'm setting up a store and warehouse here now and it will serve as my forward base when trading resumes."

Joshua laughed, "Well, you always was one to find money in any situation, Richard."

Wend had been stewing during the conversation. He felt the urge to shake Grenough's complacency. He looked at the trader. "Well, Mr. Grenough, there are at least some people who don't mind trading with the tribes during the war."

"Yes, and who would that be, Mr. Eckert?"

"Your old friends, Ross Kinnear and his partner, Flemming.'

Grenough's eyes flashed a momentary look of irritation; but then he controlled himself. "Oh, yes, I remember you and Joshua caught sight of them trading with some Delawares out on Sideling Hill back in the summer. But of course, you told me about that back in Bouquet's office in Carlisle last July."

Joshua put his mug down on the table. "Richard, truth is, we seen them again a lot later than that. No more than three weeks ago they was out on the western banks of the Allegheny."

Grenough's eyebrows arched, "On the far bank of the Allegheny River you say? How do you figure they got that far west without being sighted by the army along Forbes Road?"

Baird shrugged. "I thought about that. It's clear to me they packed their goods along trails from Aughwick to Kittanning, well north of the road, Richard. Ain't no army up there and precious few people of any kind. Then they came down the Allegheny by canoe to where we found them."

Donegal laughed, "But they'll 'na be seen anymore, Mr. Grenough."

Grenough stared at the highlander for a moment, then said, "A curious statement, sir. Just what do you mean by that?"

Donegal shook his head. "Those scoundrels was having a big time tradin' with the Indians. But it stopped permanent-like when our lad Wend here shot them dead right in the middle of their tradin'. Shot them both in the head at eighty yards from the top of a hill. Prettiest shots you ever saw."

Wend watched Grenough's face for his reaction. His control was admirable; there was only the smallest widening of his eyes as he comprehended that the two men, who Wend knew had been secretly part of his organization, were dead.

Grenough shook his head. "Well, then they paid the wages of sin. How did you happen to find them?"

Joshua answered, "Wend was leading a scouting party ahead of a company of the Black Watch. It was Wend, Donegal here, and his friend Corporal Kirkwood of the 42nd. He couldn't resist killin' the men who steered a Mingo war party to massacre his family back in '59."

Wend glanced at Irwin. He wasn't taking the news of the two traders' death with the same equanimity as Grenough; in fact, he had a visible look of dismay on his face.

Price asked, "Er, what happened to all the trade goods?"

Wend smiled. "Why, the Indians got them, of course. And kept their pelts in the bargain." He looked meaningfully at Grenough. "It was a very good deal for them." He thought a moment. Then he added, "By the way, Kinnear and Flemming seemed to have picked up a partner. There was a third white man working with them: A man with flaming red hair who I've never seen before."

Grenough looked sharply at Wend. "I suppose you shot him too?"

Wend shook his head. "No. By the time I got finished with the first two, all I had left to shoot with was a highlander's Brown Bess. The red-head was a hundred yards away. There was no chance of hitting him at that range with a musket. But I did scare him into a canoe; he was last seen paddling up the Allegheny toward Kittanning."

Joshua spoke up. "Thought I knew most of the traders in this part of the country—including the varmints who sell munitions to the tribes. But I never seen or heard of one with red hair like Wend here speaks of—you got any idea who this man was, Richard?"

Wend noticed that Irwin opened his mouth as if about to something. But Grenough discretely touched him on the arm and said, "No, Joshua, I've never seen or heard of a trader like that. They must have recently recruited him."

Grenough touched Irwin on the elbow. "Come on, Price, we're overdue at the mess." He nodded to Joshua and Wend. "Good seeing you both again, but we must meet with Ourry for dinner. Have a good trip back to Sherman Valley." And with that, the two of them were off toward the main stockade.

By now dusk had turned to virtual darkness. Baird looked around the tavern area, then up at the newly visible stars. He yawned and turned to Wend, "I think we probably had enough good times for tonight. Let's go down to our fire; we got to make an early start in the morning."

An hour later Joshua and Donegal, encouraged by the quantity of liquor consumed, were fast asleep in blankets beside the fire. Over by the Virginia wagons, Morgan's men were gathered around their bright fire, laughter periodically bursting from the group. Wend, working off the excitement of the evening's events, was not yet ready to sleep. He sat beside the fire, bundled in his overcoat against the cold, feeding the fire and watching the waters of the Juniata flow quietly a few yards from their camp.

As he worked through his thoughts, he heard footsteps and looked up to see Morgan approaching the fire, a mug in his hand.

The burly waggoner asked, "Mind if I join you for a moment?"

Wend nodded, and the waggoner sat down next to him. "That was pretty impressive shooting you done today, especially since it weren't too hard to figure that you wasn't much excited about the whole affair." He took a gulp. "But it came out good and put those Marylanders in their place. That's never a bad thing!"

The two of them laughed quietly. Then Morgan looked at Wend. "What are some likely fellows like you doing working with the army? Not many Americans I know would serve with them British if they could avoid it." He wrinkled up his face. "And what's worse, their officers are so arrogant you can't tell them what they don't know about fighting the Indians."

Wend felt himself on the defensive. "We've been working directly for Colonel Bouquet of the Royal Americans—he's a professional officer from Switzerland and a different proposition than British officers."

Morgan raised his eyebrows. "Isn't that the one who beat the savages at Bushy Run last August and broke the siege of Fort Pitt?

Wend nodded. "The very same." He motioned toward Baird's sleeping form. "Joshua's been working for him since '58 when they built Forbes Road, chased the French out of the Forks of the Ohio, and built Fort Pitt itself."

"So you and your friends was in that fight?"

"Yes. Joshua and I were signed on as scouts. Our friend Donegal was a corporal in the 77th Highlanders, who also fought at Bushy Run. The 77th is being disbanded and the men are on their way back to Scotland. He took his discharge at Fort Pitt and is going to stay in the colonies."

"I still don't understand why a man like you, with a good trade, decided to march with Bouquet's column. There was a lot of people in Virginia, Maryland, and Pennsylvania what was sure that Bouquet and his men were as good as dead when they left to try and relieve Pitt."

"Yes, but I had a personal reason to get out to the Ohio Country." He paused a moment to carefully select his words. "The girl I loved had been captured by the Mingo. I wanted to try to find her."

Sympathy flowed into Morgan's eyes. "I guess that's a right good reason. So was you able to find her?"

Wend looked at the waggoner. "Yes. Bouquet sent us on a mission, scouting for a company of the Black Watch, to present an ultimatum to the chiefs of the Ohio Country. And along the way we came upon the village where the girl—Abigail—was held."

Morgan stared at Wend with rapt attention. "So, I don't see no girl with you. What happened?"

Wend shook his shoulders. He wasn't about to go into great detail about Abigail's decision. "She had a child by the Mingo war captain who captured her." He paused and looked at Morgan. "And another on the way. She decided to stay with the Indians because she felt white people wouldn't understand her actions and would look down at the children's mixed blood."

Morgan stared at Wend for a long moment. "Yeah, I heard of cases like that, where women decided to live with the savages, even when they could easily return to the colonies." He screwed up his face. "Must have been pretty hard on you."

Wend looked at the ground in silence for long seconds, then shrugged his shoulders. "I'm becoming reconciled to her decision." He didn't want to talk about it and changed the subject. "But back to Bouquet—he's a thoughtful man. He has studied bush warfare, and particularly what went wrong at Braddock's fight. He's trained his men to take on the tribes on their own terms."

Morgan shrugged. "Well, if that's the case, he's different from any Crown officer I've known. And I've known too damn many already." He looked around at the fort. "Let me tell you a story: I was signed on to be a wagon driver with Braddock's army back in '55. We started out down at Fort Cumberland." He made a face of disgust. "Wasn't very long after we left there that I learned about British officers. Got into an argument with a young asshole lieutenant about how to handle wagons and horses. He didn't know what he was talking about, but he weren't anyway going to listen to reason. One thing led to another, and he was in my face, shouting at me. I gave him a push, just to get him away from my face. And in an instant the bastard had me up on charges." Morgan's face wrinkled with anger. "Had me before his colonel, he did, and they gave me a punishment of 500 lashes on my back, just to make an example."

Wend was astonished. "I thought that was enough to kill a man. My God, you were lucky to survive."

Now Morgan laughed. "Ha! I didn't just survive; I stayed awake through it all, which I'll wager not many men can claim. And I counted every stroke; it helped me keep my wits." He laughed harder. "And I got a secret, which you can bet I didn't tell the British. The man swinging the damned whip lost his proper count. He only gave me 499 strokes. So by God, I cheated them out of one! You could say I owe it to them." Morgan took another pull on his mug and grinned at Wend.

It occurred to Wend that Morgan was pulling his leg. "You're joking about the 500 lashes, aren't you?"

Morgan reared back. "You think I'm telling you a tall one, do you?" He stood up and turned around, his back to the fire. Then he pulled his shirt up above his shoulders.

Wend was immediately horrified and speechless. In the flickering fire light he could see a pattern of uncountable, thick, ugly scars, in a clear X shape across the man's back.

Morgan pulled his shirt back in place, then sat down again. "So now you know that I learned about British officers the hard way. And by God, I'll find a way to pay them back, some day. I don't know how, or when, but they ain't heard the last from me."

In the moments following Morgan's assertion, the two men sat in silence, interrupted only by Joshua's snoring on the other side of the fire. Finally Morgan looked up. "The main reason I came over was to finish what I was going to say before we got interrupted by that trader's arrival over at the tavern. I really admire that rifle of yours and the way you shot tonight shows you understand firearms as good as any man I know."

Wend shrugged his shoulders. "I started working as an apprentice to my father when I was seven. And I started serious target practice shortly after that."

Morgan continued, "Here's my meanin': We could use a young gunsmith like you down in the village I live in; it's called Berryville. The place is near Winchester, just west of the Shenandoah River. The town and the valley country around it are growing fast, what with folk moving down from Pennsylvania and other places up north. There's lots of good land thereabouts, in the big valley of Virginia. If you ever take a fancy to seek your fortune in new country, you could land in worse places. Come see me and I'll introduce you around, help you get set up in your trade, and find a decent homestead."

Wend looked at Morgan. "Well, thanks for the offer. I don't have any plans to move on now, but I will keep what you said in mind."

The big man nodded and smiled. He winked and pointed a finger at Wend. "Listen, lad, take it from this old waggoner: You never know when you are going to have to change your plans and pull up stakes. Believe me, I've had the experience."

They shook hands, and the burly waggoner strode back to his own campsite. A thought struck Wend as he watched him walk away. This man's life and physical appearance in many ways paralleled that of the bully Matt Bratton, yet his personality and attitude was remarkably different. Wend found himself wishing that he could find a way to have the two of them trade places.

CHAPTER TWO
Blood on the Snow

They got a late start from Bedford, largely because of Baird's copious whiskey indulgence of the previous night. And as they rode, it was evident that the veteran scout was still feeling considerable pain; he had a need to stop frequently and make short trips into the bush. So, as a result, the three men had reached no further than the crest of Sideling Hill by the time the sun was low on the western horizon.

Donegal looked out at the Great Cove, which lay far below them on the eastern side of the mountain. "Joshua, 'tis a bonnie sight ahead of us there. But I do na' fancy the idea of picking our way down the hill on this narrow path with these horses played out as they are."

Joshua shook his head. "I don't like the sky we been lookin' at all day. No sir. And it just feels like snow. If we get caught up here on the mountain, we'll sit here for days waitin' for the path to get clear. We should try to make the floor of the Cove by tonight."

Wend laughed. "If you hadn't been so hung over this morning, Joshua, we'd have gotten away a couple of hours earlier and moved faster. We would be down in the valley by now. The fact is, Donegal's right; we're all tired now—men and horses. One of these animals stumbles in the dusk on the way down the hill and we could have more trouble than if it snows. I say we take a chance—camp now and get away at first light in the morning."

Baird looked up at the sky, then around at the bare trees at the summit of the mountain. "Yeah, all right—we'll camp. And there's a good place close by to lay-over for the night." Then he looked over at Wend. "But you ain't gonna like it Eckert; you don' have no good memories of the place."

Wend puzzled for a moment and then understood. "You mean you're going to take us to that rock ledge where we hid out from the Delaware war party last summer?"

"Yup. Best place around here—close to the path and good shelter from the wind." And with that, he touched his heels to his horse and led off.

In just a few hundred yards further, Baird stopped and dismounted, motioning the others to do the same. They led their horses a short distance off the path and soon Wend saw the grouping of rocks and boulders which marked the ledge. They tied the horses to trees, unsaddled, and then, carrying their kits and supplies, made their way through the narrow opening in the rocks which led to the flat, stone surface of the outcropping. The great boulders acted as a shield against the gusty northwesterly wind which had been at their backs all day.

Donegal shrugged and stretched his arms and back. "Now this is a bonnie, snug place to spend the night. And sure enough, it feels good to be free of that pestering wind." He walked out to the edge of the ledge and looked down at the Great Cove which spread below, a mass of trees broken here and there by the fields and meadows of farms.

"Yes, we'll not have trouble keeping a sheltered fire," Baird nodded. "And the stone may be hard, but it ain't goin' to be near as damp as the plain ground."

Donegal looked at Wend. "So why do you ' na like a fine place like this to camp?"

Wend motioned back toward the stone wall which they had come through. "Look down at the base of that stone, Simon."

The highlander turned and looked back to where Eckert had pointed. "I see a wide slit along the bottom." He shrugged his shoulders. "So what's the point?"

"That slit is the opening to a deep pit, Simon. When Joshua and I had to hide from that war party, we crawled down into the pit. It was dank, dirty, and stank so much that we could hardly breath."

"That may be so, Wend. But if it saved your life, I still dunna' understand why you dislike the place so much."

"Donegal, it's full of snakes. Poisonous snakes."

The Scotsman's eyes opened wide and he shivered visibly. "Lord above, I can't stand those evil serpents. Now I'm understanding your hate of the place."

Wend looked at Donegal. "That's not the worst of it, Simon. While we were hiding, just as the Indians were crawling over the rocks looking for us, a snake crawled up my leg, right onto the bare spot above the top of the legging."

Donegal's mouth opened and he blessed himself. "Oh, Mary and Jesus! I'd have died from fright right there."

"Yeah, well I had to lay there frozen and quiet while the damn snake lay right on top of me. So *now* you know why I'm skittish about this place. But it ended all right—after the Indians were gone, Joshua was able to grab the creature and bash it's head against the rock of the side of the pit."

Joshua shook his head at the other two. "Time to stop all this talk about snakes. They ain't going to bother us tonight in this winter cold. They're all down at the bottom of the pit holed up keeping warm in their individual lairs. So let's get a fire started, the horses bedded down proper, fix supper, and get some sleep."

Later, after darkness settled in, and Baird was tending a pot of salt beef boiling over the crackling fire, Wend and Donegal stood near the edge of the ledge, looking out into the valley. "Look," Wend said as he pointed out into the cove, "I can see the lights from three farmsteads." He paused a moment. "Last time we were here, there was nothing but blackness—all the settlers in the cove were holed up in Fort Lyttleton while war parties ranged through their farmsteads."

Baird walked over from the fire. "At least for the winter, there won't be any war party raids, so the farmers have gone back to their homes. When we were at Bedford, Grenough told me that the militia company George Croghan recruited to man Lyttleton has been disbanded, and there's no garrison there now. It's only being used as a way-station by military convoys and travelers moving along Forbes Road." He thought for a moment. "After we get to the bottom of Sideling, we'll get off this back trail and travel along Forbes Road itself. That will allow us to move faster."

* * *

Near mid-day on the 14th of December the three travelers arrived at Wright's Ferry, which crossed the Susquehanna east of York. Once they reached the other side of the river, it would be several hours ride to Lancaster, where Wend would deliver Arnold Spengler's belongings to his parents. It was a cold, overcast, gray day which held the promise of snow. The men stood shivering, the damp wind cutting into them, as they waited for the ferry to make its way from the far river bank. Wend reflected that it would be a bone chilling trip across the river. But even more chilling to Wend was his dread of what the morrow would bring; not only would he have to talk with Arnold's mother and relive his friend's death, he would have to pass by his own family's old home. It would be the first time he had seen it since his entire family had been massacred by a Mingo war party four years earlier on Forbes Road.

They stood quietly at the landing, each alone with his own thoughts as they held the horses and pulled their coats around them for warmth.

Suddenly Donegal called out to the other two. "Hey, lads—riders coming—traveling fast!"

Wend looked to where the highlander pointed northward up the road which ran along the western bank of the Susquehanna and he could see three men pushing their horses at the gallop.

Joshua said, "They're ridin' like the devil hisself was on their tail—must want to be sure to get the ferry." He eyed the men for a moment, then took a step toward them and raised a hand to shade his eyes. "I'll be damned! Wend, take a sharp look at those three, and tell me what you see."

Wend squinted at the riders and was startled to realize that something was indeed familiar about them. Then shock came over him as he recognized who he was seeing. "Lord, Joshua—its Reverend Carnahan and Reverend Elder. And that's Franklin along with them."

"That's what I thought I saw. Now what the devil would they be doing here?"

It was indeed strange to see the three men at Wright's Ferry. Carnahan was the Presbyterian minister of Sherman Mill, more than forty miles to the north. He was also the husband of Baird's sister and the man who had sheltered Wend since his family had died. John Elder was the minister of Paxton, a town just north of Harris' Ferry, on the eastern side of the Susquehanna. Franklin was Abigail Gibson's former black slave, who had been captured in the same attack which had left Wend an orphan and Abigail the captive wife of a Mingo. Franklin had escaped from the Mingo village over a year ago and had been brought to Sherman Mill by Baird, where he now lived on the Carnahan's farm.

In a short minute the three men arrived at the landing and pulled up. Then Carnahan saw them. "Joshua, Wend! Am I glad to see you! We're going to need your help." All three dismounted.

Carnahan continued, "There's the devil to pay! Some of the Paxton militia are riding against the Conestoga Indians. They're out to destroy the whole village and everyone there. We're trying to warn the people before they arrive!"

Wend thought of his friend Charlie Sawak and the rest of the Conestogas, many of whom he had known since childhood. The village of the peaceful

Indian tribe was located near his old home in the countryside west of Lancaster. He shivered with a chill far colder than anything the weather could cause.

Joshua said, "Now how the hell did the Paxton men get an idea like that?"

John Elder put his hand on Joshua's shoulder. "This has been building since the summer. People have been spreading rumors that some of the Conestogas have been cooperating with war parties from the west. Back in September, a couple of traders went through Harris' and Paxton, spreading that word, swearing that they had seen Conestogas meeting with Delaware and Shawnee war parties. Lazarus Stewart has got a lot of the men stirred up about it, saying the Conestogas and every other Indian east of the Susquehanna should be eradicated." The minister stopped to catch his breath and marshal his words.

Baird exclaimed, "Good God, Reverend Elder, how could you let things get so far out of hand? Everyone knows Lazarus Stewart has an abiding, irrational hatred of all Indians. But he's a captain of your militia. Couldn't you stop him before things got this far?"

Wend thought about the irony of the moment: Elder was the very man who had organized the Paxton Militia—intended to protect settlers against Indian raids—which was now riding to attack the Conestoga tribe. He was often called "The Reverend *Colonel* Elder" in deference to his leadership of the settler's defense force.

Elder shook his head. "I thought I had calmed things and made everyone see how foolish that talk was. But just to be sure, I wrote a letter to the governor, saying it would be a good idea to move all the Conestogas east where they could be protected, until this damn war is over. That was in September, and they never answered me!" He paused and looked around at the three of them. "I rode over to visit with Paul at Sherman Mill and had no sooner got there then word came in that Lazarus and others were getting ready to ride. I should never have left Paxton!"

Paul Carnahan spoke up. "On this side of the river, Matt Bratton has been repeating the rumors about the Conestogas helping war parties and saying that the men of Sherman Valley and Carlisle should join the Paxton men. So the belief that the Conestogas are culpable has gained wide credence. After all the raids, people are looking for some way to strike out against Indians—any Indians." Carnahan shook his head in frustration. "We left as soon as we heard that Lazarus intended to attack the Conestoga people. We came down this side of the river since we had a shorter ride from Sherman Mill. And the Conestoga village is several miles this side of Lancaster. Maybe we can beat the Paxton men to the town. John thinks he'll be able to talk them out of any action, if he's there first."

As Carnahan spoke, the ferry made a grating noise as it pulled into the landing. After the westbound traffic—a single freight wagon with its six horse team—had been unloaded, the six men quickly led their horses aboard. They prevailed on the ferryman to depart immediately, and all of them champed at the slow progress the boat made across the wide stream.

Finally the boat touched the east bank and John Elder immediately swung up into his saddle. "It's several miles to the village. Let's ride as fast as the horses can manage!"

As they started the ride, the threat of snow from the overcast sky became reality. It started slowly, but picked up rapidly as they galloped eastward. Soon there was a significant accumulation, and they had to slow to ensure the horses could maintain their footing. Wend could feel the tentative nature of his mare's stride as she tried to carefully place her feet while not being able to see the ruts in the road. Several times she nearly stumbled as a hoof hit an uneven surface covered by the snow. Wend mentally cursed the storm, which reduced their visibility and impeded the ability to judge their progress. Nor could they see far enough ahead to detect any pillar of smoke, which would be the sign of an attack on the village.

It took them four hours to make the trip, for they had to dismount several times to rest the horses and clean the packed snow out from the cavities of the animal's horseshoes. There was little conversation but Wend could see the anxiety written all over the two minister's faces.

Then there was a shout from Joshua. "I saw a flicker of light up there, not far ahead!"

Wend shielded his eyes against the snowfall and stared in front of them. At first he saw nothing except the curtain of white. Then he suddenly caught a glimpse of the light Joshua had seen. But it wasn't the steadiness of a window light or a lantern. It was fire—a big fire—flickering through the storm!

Carnahan saw it at nearly the same time. "Something's on fire; burning brightly. God help us, it must be the village!"

The six men pushed their horses onward, urging the reluctant animals into a final burst of speed. Shortly, Wend realized that what they had seen was a house on fire, flames coming from both the roof and out through the windows.

John Elder held up his hand to stop them. "Let's dismount to approach on foot. Look to your priming."

Wend tied his horse to a tree, and pulled the cock back on his rifle. He heard the others doing the same. Cautiously, the six men advanced on the Conestoga village in a wide skirmish line, firelocks at the ready. Wend suddenly thought, '*My God, here we are, stealing up on a town with rifles ready in case of trouble from our own people! How have things come to this?*' Soon the men could see the rest of the town and the desolation which lay in every quarter. Several other buildings were burning. The town was made up mostly of frame buildings constructed of milled lumber, interspersed with a few log structures. Wend thought the place looked empty of inhabitants.

He had just formed that idea when he saw the first body. It was an old man, lying just on the other side of the burning house they had seen initially. Wend checked the man; he was long dead, his body cold, and had been scalped. Then he looked up and immediately he saw other bodies: men, women and at least one child, a little boy. He counted six of them, strewn through the center of the village and half buried by the snow. Franklin ran ahead, checking the other forms. He finished and called back to Elder. "Ain't none of these breathing, Reverend."

Wend walked along behind Franklin, fear rising in him that one of the bodies would be Charlie. He could see that all of them had been shot, some several times, and then mutilated with ax strokes. All had been scalped. He felt his stomach begin to turn, but was able to keep from retching. A sudden realization came to him: *Months of war had hardened him against sights of violent death.*

He saw that one of the bodies was that of a chubby young woman with a broad face and pug nose, maybe sixteen or seventeen. Her brown eyes stared at the sky. Her open mouth formed a near circle, showing stained teeth.

Donegal came up and stood beside him, looking at the girl's body. He said, "This was 'na just an attack. This was plain murder. They was after men, women, and children."

Wend looked up at the highlander. "Donegal, there are no more than twenty or twenty-five Conestoga Indians left. The tribe has been slowly dying since the early part of this century. This is their only remaining village." He paused a moment, then continued, "You see this girl? Well, my friend Charlie Sawak told me about her. Charlie and I have been friends since I was a young boy and we went to school together. The tribal elders wanted him to marry her. He and this girl were the only marriage-age people left in the tribe."

"You say there are 'na others?"

"That's it. If Charlie and this girl had married, their children could have carried on the tribal bloodline. But this girl's death means the end of the pure Conestoga heritage."

Wend stood up and saw that John Elder had seated himself on a log which lay in front of one of the houses, and had leaned his rifle on the log beside him. Carnahan sat next to him and Wend could see the anguish in both of their faces. Paul Carnahan had once told him why he had become a minister: In 1756, during the attack of Pennsylvania provincial troops on the Delaware tribal village of Kittanning, he had watched a militiaman in blood-lust shoot a woman in the head and split open her baby's skull with a hatchet. Although he had spent two years as a ranger officer and had participated in ruthless border warfare, the brutality of that particularly needless killing had made something snap in his mind and steered him toward life as a man of God. Now Wend looked into his eyes, and saw the same despair as when Carnahan had told him that story. He looked back at Elder, who now was holding his head in his hands. The two ministers looked like all the starch had gone out of them.

Suddenly a voice called out of the snowstorm. "All of you—put those rifles down and raise your hands!"

Joshua raised his rifle and turned toward the direction of the voice.

The voice shouted again. "I mean it, we'll fire! So ground those weapons now. I won't warn again!" A man stepped out from behind one of the houses, followed by others, all coming from different directions. Wend counted at least twelve of them, all armed with rifles or muskets.

Wend looked at Joshua; he slowly nodded and placed the butt of his rifle on the ground. Wend, Donegal, and Franklin followed suite.

"All right, I'm John Hay—Sheriff of Lancaster. I don't know who you scoundrels are, or what you thought you were doing, but you are under arrest. No one comes into my county and murders its citizens!"

He looked around at the carnage and the bodies. "Good God, you've killed the lot of them!"

Joshua spat and looked over at Elder and Carnahan. "For Christ sake, these bloody fools think we did this. Tell them the truth, Reverend Elder."

Then another man, thin and short, wearing spectacles, came out from behind the sheriff. He wore a long black coat and gray breeches, and carried no weapon. Wend immediately recognized his former schoolmaster, Mr. Dreher. He was about to say something to his old teacher when Dreher pointed a bony finger at Wend and spoke up.

31

"Wend Eckert, I recognize you! Of all people, what are you doing with this troop of murderers! My God, I expected better, much better of you. Your parents, bless their souls, would roll over in their graves if they saw you now with this Ulster trash!"

Wend set his face, then started to speak. "Master Dreher, I can explain...."

But Dreher cut him off. "I would have expected that wild, unruly boy who was your friend, that Arnold Spengler, to be involved in a crime like this. But you, Wend Eckert, one of my best students and son of a well respected family, why I'm shocked beyond adequate words. And besides, Charlie Sawak was one of your best friends—you were nearly inseparable. How could you turn on him and his family like this?"

Sheriff Hay waved a hand at the schoolmaster. "Quiet, Master Dreher. You can work out your feelings with young Eckert later." He turned back toward Elder. "If you men claim that you didn't do this, I need some explanations—and fast!"

Elder looked up at the sheriff. He spoke, and his voice showed a great weariness. "Sheriff, I'm Reverend John Elder, of Paxton. This is Reverend Carnahan of Sherman Mill. We rode down here to try to stop this madness. You think we'd be sitting around staring at this if we'd just finished killing all these people?"

The sheriff looked at the minister. "You're John Elder? I've heard that name. Ed Shippen, the magistrate, has mentioned you."

There was uncertainty in the sheriff's face, and he looked around at all the men again.

Wend held out his rifle and said, "Here, look at my rifle, and smell the bore. You can tell it hasn't been fired recently. He pulled out his hatchet from his belt. "You see any blood on this? Look at those bodies—they've been mutilated." He paused and looked at all the sheriff's men. "Go ahead—check all our guns and blades. You won't see any blood. And you won't find any fresh scalps on us or in the baggage on our horses."

The sheriff nodded. "We're going to do just that. He motioned to a man with a heavy beard, "Phillip, go check their baggage for scalps or any other evidence."

As the bearded man searched the horses, another inspected and sniffed the firelocks of the suspects.

Phillip came back from the horses, holding a bag. "Sheriff, look what's in here. Six scalps!"

The sheriff looked in the canvas sack.

Wend groaned to himself, then walked over and grabbed the bag from Hay's hands. He pulled out one of the scalps. "I said you wouldn't find any fresh scalps. Look at this; it's brown, from a white person, not a black-haired Indian scalp. And it's dry!"

Hay nodded and said, "I can see that it's old and dry. So why do you have it?"

Wend glared at the sheriff and at the other Lancaster men gathered around. "They're my family's scalps! My own family's, do you understand? They were all killed by Mingoes in 1759. During Bouquet's campaign, I took the scalps back from the Mingo village where they had hung for four years. He reached into the bag and pulled out a small, circular scalp. "You see that!" He waved the scalp at the sheriff's men. "That scalp is mine!" Wend reached up and pulled off his hair ribbon; his hair fell about his shoulders, making the missing part of his scalp plainly visible. Some of the men stared; others deferred their eyes after a brief look at the bare scars on the back of his head. "I lost that in the same massacre."

Hay was silent, and looked down at the ground for a long moment. Then he turned to one of the men with him. "Thomas Wright, do you think these are the men you saw riding through your ferry station this morning?"

The man stepped forward and looked around. "Sheriff, there was at least fifty men I saw, that came down the coast road. They arrived about midnight and camped around our village until early morning. But I don't recognize any of these men." He pointed at the overcoats Wend, Joshua, and Donegal wore. "And I didn't see anyone in gray coats like that."

Hay lowered his firelock, and after a few seconds thought, motioned for his men to do the same. "Well, Reverend Elder, give us your story: Who did this? Who were you trying to stop?"

"A band of men from my own town, sheriff; Paxton militia under Captain Lazarus Stewart." His voice was barely above a whisper; Wend thought he sounded incredibly tired and sad.

The sheriff looked around, still not sure what to do. Then suddenly an old man came out from behind one of the houses, looked around at the bodies, and then shuffled toward Hays. He was shaking from the cold or from fear, or more likely both. One of the sheriff's men called out, "Hey, that's old Captain John! He's an elder of the Conestogas."

Wend looked at the man, and recognized him from the days of his youth when he had sometimes visited the village in company with Charlie.

The sheriff walked up to the Indian, who stood looking around at the strangers. "John, what happened? Where is everyone else?"

The old man shuddered again, the whole of his upper body shivering. "They was a big band of men, sheriff. They set upon us three, four hours ago; it was just after the snow started. They came into the town from all directions, right out of the snowstorm, firing their rifles at everybody." The man paused and looked around again. "Some of us were lucky—we were able to run out into the fields or hide down by the bushes along the creek. The falling snow helped conceal us."

Captain John went to a gap in the buildings, and shouted into the woods around the creek. Shortly several more people, both adults and children, emerged. All were shaking; some hadn't had time to put on coats before making their escape. Wend called to Franklin and Donegal; the three ran through several of the buildings, collecting blankets. Then they covered the shivering villagers.

Sheriff Hay took a count. "I see 16 people, living and dead. Where are the others?"

Captain John said, "Out working for wages on neighboring farms or in Lancaster. They won't be back until later in the evening."

The refugees were looking at the bodies, staring at them in shock. One woman knelt beside the small boy's body, crying and wailing. She pulled him up out of the snow, and held him close to her. Reverend Carnahan went over and knelt to comfort her, whispering something Wend could not hear. Then Carnahan approached a small girl, four or five years old, standing over the body of a woman in her thirties, apparently her mother. Carnahan wrapped a blanket around the child and then took her into his arms and sat down with her on the log.

Then Wend recognized Charlie's parents, standing huddled together. He didn't know them well, but he had seen them several times during school days. He approached the couple and introduced himself. "I'm Wend Eckert, a friend of Charlie's from Master Dreher's school, years ago. Was he in the village when this happened?"

Charlie's father stared at Wend, as he searched his memory. "Eckert? Wend Eckert? I remember Charlie going to visit with you. You're family used to live just a couple of miles from here, toward Lancaster." Then he looked at Wend and shook his head "No, Charlie's not here. He's out with his cart, selling leather goods and brooms and other things we made. The trip began over a week ago. He should be back soon."

Wend breathed a sigh of relief. Then he turned back to Master Dreher, who stood a few feet away, still staring at the bodies. As a youth, Wend had harbored a great amount of admiration for the man's store of learning and his intelligent lectures to students. Dreher had been one of the adults he had looked up to and who had shaped him as a child. Now he looked at the narrow shouldered, bespectacled, sharp-faced man hunched over against the cold wind and felt profound disappointment. Anger flashed through Wend at Dreher's quick condemnation of him and his friends. He approached the schoolmaster and the man looked up from the bodies into Wends eyes.

Wend said, "Master Dreher, as a boy, I admired you, your knowledge and what I thought was your wisdom. And I believed you respected me as one of your best students. When I left school to start the trip to Fort Pitt with my family, you said you were proud of the way I had matured in the years at your school and how much I had learned. Yet today you were ready to accuse me of murder without even knowing the facts of the matter."

Dreher looked up at Wend, his face red in embarrassment. He sputtered, "Well-, well-, ah-, how could I be expected to think anything else when I come upon a massacre like this and see a group of armed ruffians standing around!"

"That's ridiculous, Master Dreher. You showed so little faith in me you couldn't even take time to ask some questions, to try to find the facts. For years I have held you in fond esteem, sir. But now—now it will be hard for me ever to think of you with respect." Wend thought for a moment. "And as for Arnold Spengler, that 'Wild, unruly boy' you spoke of, do you want to know what happened to him?"

"I know he ran off to the army. A tragedy—another aimless man wasting his days in some dismal barracks room."

"Well, you might want to know that he was a sergeant and died at Bushy Run. He died a hero in the service of the Crown, do you understand?"

Dreher's face wrinkled up. "Hero? That's a much over-used word. The fact is he lost his life as a nameless soldier filling a slot in line at a battle no one will remember a few months from now."

Wend wanted to slap the man across his smug face. But he controlled his fury. "Arnold went down leading his men in a desperate stand. They broke a fierce charge of Delaware and Shawnee Indians and saved the lives of the wounded and the women at Bushy Run. The officers and men of the Royal Americans know his name and what he did and won't forget. To the end of

35

my days, Master Dreher, I'll have more respect for him then I can now ever have for you."

Dreher scrunched up his shoulders and seemed to shrivel in the face of Wend's anger. He said no more, simply looking down into the snow at his feet.

In the wake of Wend's outburst, all the men stood around, their eyes avoiding the teacher's face.

It was Joshua who broke the silence. "If Wend here is through speechifying, we need to think about what we're going to do about these bodies and taking care of Captain John and his people."

Paul Carnahan looked around at the survivors. "Baird is right. We must get these people to shelter—this storm ain't going to let up. And this village is no place for them now."

Sheriff Hay looked around, at the bodies and the wreckage of the village. "That's the truth of it, Reverend. They can't stay here." He thought for a moment, then looked over at one of the men. "Schmidt, your farm is nearby. Go get a wagon hitched up and let's carry these people into Lancaster. They can stay together in the work house where we can get them food and they'll be warm and safe."

Schmidt and another man swung up into their saddles and disappeared into the storm. The sheriff motioned to his other men. "We can't leave these bodies lying around." He shook his head, stamped a foot, and shouted out into the wind, "This is a bloody disgrace! A damned outrage." Then he motioned to the others: "Help me get them into the shelter of one of the buildings which hasn't been completely destroyed. We'll come back and bury them after the storm is over." He turned to the elderly Conestoga. "We're going to take care of you and your people, Captain John. And I promise we're going to find and punish the men who did this!"

* * *

The citizens of Lancaster opened their hearts to the Conestoga tribe. After the word spread of the Indians' plight, people from all over the town—English, German, Swiss, and Ulster—brought food, blankets, clothing, bedding and furniture items necessary to make the survivors comfortable in the shelter of the work house. Town officials sent a dispatch to Governor John Penn in Philadelphia, communicating the story of the massacre and demanded protection from the colonial government for the Conestogas.

Paul Carnahan and John Elder remained with the tribe to care for both their physical and emotional requirements. Carnahan became particularly attached to Molly, the little girl who had been orphaned in the village massacre, spending much of the time talking and playing with her. The others also stayed to help, postponing their trip to Sherman Valley until Carnahan felt he had done as much as he could and was ready to return. In particular, they worked to cut and stack a supply of firewood to provide heat and cooking for the Conestogas.

It was Donegal who put words to the irony which the three former army scouts all felt as they worked. "Life is a funny matter, ain't it? A month ago we was killing Indians; now we're nursing them."

Charlie Sawak returned in the evening of the second day after the massacre.

Thomas Wright, who owned the ferry which served the road between Lancaster and York, was rounding up cattle from his meadow when he saw Charlie's cart come off the ferry and head up the wagon track toward Conestoga Town. He ran out and, as gently as possible, broke the news of the killings. Horrified, Charlie immediately slapped the reins on his horse's back and raced up the road to Lancaster. Wend and Franklin were tending the fireplace when the young Conestoga came storming into the work house, searching for his parents.

Wend watched as his friend's face turned from anxiety to relief as he saw his family sitting safe by the fire, quietly eating their evening meal. Charlie's mother jumped up and wrapped her arms around him, thankful that he was safe. There had been worry that, with the Paxton Rangers in open warfare against the Conestogas, he would be attacked on the road.

Hours later, Wend and Charlie walked over to Slough's Tavern, where Carnahan and the others were staying. They settled down at a table in the common room and Wend ordered supper for both of them since Charlie hadn't eaten all day. He also ordered a cup of whiskey for his friend, knowing he would need the stimulation.

While they waited for the food to arrive, Wend told Charlie the details about the attack, how they had come to be at the village immediately afterward, and how the town of Lancaster had been helping his people. It wasn't until after the meal that they began talking about why the Paxton men had come to attack the Conestogas.

Wend had had some time to think things over and to hear about events in the Cumberland and Sherman Valleys over the last few months. "Charlie, people are terribly afraid; there have been so many attacks; hundreds of people killed right here in Pennsylvania. And there has been so little success by the local militias in stopping the raids. They've intercepted a war party here and there, killed some warriors. But mostly the Indians hit a homestead or small village and get away clean. It's easy to see why so many people are frustrated."

Charlie was staring straight ahead, the muscles in his neck and face standing out. He answered in a voice which dripped sarcasm. "Yeah, I can see why they are frustrated. So they take it out on a village of people who are Christians, same as they are, just because we happen to look a little different. Yeah, that makes a lot of sense." He took a gulp of his whiskey. "Listen, we've had a treaty with the colony since the turn of the century. The tribe kept every part of that treaty. We willingly sold most of our land at cut rate prices to the whites. All we wanted was to live the same life as the people around us. And for that, the whites come and butcher old men, women and children."

Wend could say nothing in response.

Charlie slammed his fist down on the table, and looked directly at Wend for the first time since they had come to the tavern. "And they killed Sally Sheehays. The girl I was supposed to marry—the last girl with full Conestoga blood. So that's the end of the Conestogas. It may take years, but now my people will disappear."

Wend said, "Charlie, come on—be honest. You told me yourself that you had no love for Sally. You were going to marry her only out of a sense of duty because the elders were pressuring you to produce children to preserve the heritage of the Conestogas."

Sawak grimaced. "All of that is true; so what's the point?"

"But Charlie, you're still here. And I saw younger children among the survivors, and they have Conestoga blood. So no matter what happens, a remnant of the tribe will survive. There will be people who at least have some of the bloodline. It's not what you wanted, but it gives you some hope. And Charlie, they're going to need a man like you to make it happen, to be their leader. You're strong and know the ways of the white society."

"Fine. But there's still no Conestoga girl for me."

Wend smiled. "Charlie, what about that girl up in Harris' Ferry—the tavern maid. Her name was Rose Jenson; you really liked her."

"Yes, I've been seeing Rose for a year. She a wonderful, fun-filled girl. To tell the truth, I'm in love with her and would like to spend the rest of my life with her. But why bring that up? She's white and she's indentured. She won't be free for six years."

"But if you could marry her, you would produce children who were half Conestoga. And you could live with the rest of the tribe and rebuild Conestoga Town. It wouldn't be a perfect solution, but it would be a start, a way to preserve some of your heritage."

"And even if I thought that were feasible, you keep forgetting the little detail of her indenture. It couldn't happen for six years."

"Charlie, it could start right away if her indenture was bought out."

"Yeah, that would be perfect. It's a great idea." He looked askance at Wend. "Except for the tiny matter of the money to buy her out. He reached in his pocket, pulled out some coins, and dropped them on the table. "I don't think a few pennies would go very far."

Wend stared at the Conestoga. "Charlie, I have plenty of money. After the massacre of my family, I inherited the money my parents got from selling their land, house, and furniture here in Lancaster. It was in a barrel with a double bottom in the back of my tool wagon. The Mingo war party left it behind. I used some of it to set myself up in trade, and I've more than made up for that in profit from selling guns. That barrel is sitting in my room in Reverend Carnahan's house. Nobody knows it, but I probably have more actual cash than anyone else in Sherman Valley, even more than Tom Marsh, the miller, who, all things considered, is the wealthiest man in the valley."

Charlie was momentarily speechless. Then he shook his head. "I couldn't ask you for the money."

"Why not? We've been friends for fifteen years. And the amount to buy out the indenture wouldn't make much of a dent in my reserve. I'll recoup it in a year of sales, particularly with the demand for firelocks in this emergency."

Charlie considered for a moment. "No, Wend, the truth is, the Conestogas are at the end of the road. Many of the people back in the work house are already talking about moving away, trying to meld into the white world. They're afraid of going back to the village, for they'll be a target there. Besides, living in the village would be a daily reminder of the horror of that day and the ones who died. No, Wend, Conestoga Town is finished."

They sat quietly for a long time. Wend wanted to say more, to encourage Charlie in some way, but he couldn't think of anything that would make sense out of the matter. Then he thought about why he had come to Lancaster in the first place, and told Charlie about Arnold Spengler's death. "Charlie, I still have to go out and see Mrs. Spengler and take her Arnold's things. Why don't we go together in your cart tomorrow? We can also go over to Conestoga

Town and pick up your belongings and anything else which will help your people live at the work house."

Charlie considered for a moment and then looked at Wend with more interest than he had before. "Yes, I would like that. I spent lots of time over at Arnold's when we were young, and his mother and father were always kind. And to tell you the truth, I think I'll go crazy just sitting around the work house all day thinking about what has happened."

***

The next day the sun appeared, driving away the cloudy gloom which had blanketed Lancaster since the day of the Conestoga massacre. Wend and Charlie hitched up the cart and rolled out of the tavern yard an hour after full daylight. It was a cold but calm day; the sunlight felt good as they drove along the road toward the Indian village.

By noon they had finished their mission at Arnold's house. Wend told Arnold's mother about her son's service in the 60th and emphasized his role in keeping the final tribal attack away from the wounded in the flour bag fort. He told her about how Arnold's men had respected him and about the role he had played at Bouquet's headquarters. It warmed him to see the pride in her eyes, even as she cried over his death. Wilhelm, Arnold's father, sat quietly throughout, looking down at his hands which were clasped tightly together. But Wend thought he saw pride in his eyes also, particularly when he talked about Arnold's part in the battle. Then Wend gave Mrs. Spengler the bible and Arnold's belongings, and then the two of them took their leave.

Wend had been worried about how Charlie would react to visiting the Conestoga village, but his friend seemed to have found a way to keep his grief in check, for he displayed nothing but a stoic face as they scrounged through the buildings. They loaded useful items into the cart.

Somebody had come out from Lancaster and wrapped the bodies in blankets or canvas. They were all—five adults and a child—lined up on the floor inside a partially burned house, where they would stay until the ground softened enough for burial. Charlie walked along the row of corpses and for a moment Wend thought he would start unwrapping them to find Sally's body. But instead, he went to his knees, took his hat off, clasped his hands in front of his chest, and prayed silently for several minutes. He still showed little emotion, but Wend, standing respectfully behind, felt himself smothering tears and anger.

It was on the way back to Lancaster that Wend started telling Charlie his idea about how the massacre had been fomented.

"Grenough had a hand in it, Charlie. It's clear as a painting on the wall to me."

Charlie looked at Wend. "Richard Grenough? The big merchant? I know you hold him and his men guilty for the death of your family and the capture of that English girl Abigail, but how do you connect him to this?"

Wend thought for a moment, marshalling his arguments. "Last July, back in Carlisle, Grenough made a big point of telling Bouquet that he'd heard rumors about the Conestogas helping the western tribes. If he told Bouquet, you can bet he was telling other people the same story. And then Paul Carnahan told me, on the day of the massacre, that Matt Bratton had been going around claiming he knew the Conestogas were meeting with war party raiders and providing them with supplies and information. Charlie, we know that Bratton is a member of Grenough's ring. Finally, Reverend Elder said traders were at Harris' and Paxton saying the same thing and stirring up the people to attack the Conestogas." Wend looked at Charlie. "There's no doubt in my mind that those traders were some of Grenough's men."

"So what benefit does Grenough get from the killing of the Conestogas? How in the world does that help him?"

Wend looked at Charlie. "It gives him cover. Cover for himself, his men, and the entire supply operation. Think about it; as soon as the raids began, it became clear that the Indians were getting war supplies from somewhere in this area: Bouquet, Sheriff Dunning of Carlisle, everyone in the army knew the tribes were getting powder from some source. We even found a keg of powder from York at the Shawnee camp after the first raid on Sherman Valley—and York is Grenough's headquarters. After the war broke out, Joshua and I came across Kinnear and Fleming, the traders who set the Mingo war party on my family in 1759, actually providing it to the Delawares out at Sideling Hill. And back in July, I as much as called out Grenough in front of Bouquet, saying there had to be somebody with money running the whole operation. He made an effort to separate himself from Kinnear and Fleming, saying he hadn't worked with them or even seen them for years."

Wend reached out and touched Charlie's hand. "Charlie, you and I know that he's lying: We both saw Grenough and those two traders meeting at Larkin's Tavern in Carlisle last year."

Sawak nodded. "That's true, we saw them together. But that just proves they had a meeting, not that they were working together."

"In my mind, there's no doubt."

"All right. Let's assume they were working for him. I still don't understand why the killing of the Conestogas helps him."

Wend continued, "I figure that Grenough decided to capitalize on these rumors about the Conestogas. I'll wager that he and his men have been working for months to spread the rumors and convince settlers that the Conestogas were a major source of powder and lead to the war parties. That would keep people from speculating that he was the source. And beyond that, you know damn well it wouldn't take much encouragement for Lazarus Stewart to organize an attack on your people, if he could get enough men stirred up."

Charlie shook his head. "You've been pushing these accusations against Grenough for a year, Wend. I'll admit some of what you have been saying has come true. And you are starting to convince me. But I still say that you're never going to sell all this to anyone in authority, not with the war going on and people scared as hell. And not with all the friends Grenough has got in high places in the government." Charlie paused. "I've even heard his name being mentioned as a possible commissioner when time comes to negotiate peace with the tribes."

Wend gritted his teeth. He knew Charlie's words were true enough. Finally, he spoke the thoughts which had been gathering in his mind for months. "It may be true that the law won't deal with Grenough's band of thugs. That just means I may have to do it myself."

Charlie looked at Wend, and opened his mouth as if about to say something. But in the end he simply shook his head and tended his reins.

* * *

They arrived back in Lancaster in the late afternoon to find that the street in front of the workhouse was jammed with people.

Wend said, "Now what in the world is going on?"

Charlie shook his head and drove the cart up to the edge of the crowd.

Wend was surprised to see a woman standing on the outskirts of the crowd, crying with her hands to her eyes. Her husband stood comforting her with his arm around her waist. Wend felt a surge of anxiety.

The same feeling obviously came over Charlie, for he dropped the reins and bolted for the door of the work house, pushing through the people in the crowd. Wend followed. The sheriff and some of his men were standing around at the door, keeping the crowd at bay. Charlie tried to push his way through, but Hay caught him by the arm. "Son, you don't want to go in there."

Wend looked around, and saw Joshua, Franklin, and Donegal standing nearby. Donegal had a bandage around his head, and a woman was wiping streaks of blood off his face. Wend called to Joshua, "What happened? What's going on?"

Baird, who had been watching the woman treat Donegal, turned and saw Wend. "Lazarus Stewart and his friends came back. They rode right through town and up to the workhouse with their weapons at the ready. I was over in the tavern, and saw them ride up the street. There was near a hundred of them, Wend. And Matt Bratton was with them, riding right behind Lazarus." He pointed to the highlander. "Donegal was standing by the door, enjoying a pipe, and asked them what they wanted. Some big bastard jumped off his horse and smashed Donegal alongside the head with the flat of his hatchet and put him on the ground with his lights out."

Donegal was fighting mad. "I saw that man clearly before everything went dark, Wend. He's got a beefy red face and damn near perfectly white hair. If I ever come across him again, I swear I'll have his head off with my broadsword and not think twice about it. I did that to a Frenchie in the West Indies and I'll not hesitate with some lowland Ulster trash like him."

Charlie Sawak had heard enough. He wrenched himself out of the sheriff's hands and smashed his way past another man into the workhouse. Wend followed him through the door.

He soon realized he had walked into Hell itself. The interior of the building was a charnel house. All the Conestogas were dead. But not just dead, they had literally been chopped to pieces. Blood was pooled up on the floor and more spattered all over the walls, chairs, blankets, cooking utensils; everywhere Wend looked.

Wend saw what was left of the body of a male child in front of the fireplace. A bullet had hit him in the chest. But the killer had obviously felt that the shot was inadequate. A series of hatchet chops had turned his face into mush. The killer had then cut both the boy's hands off; they lay on the floor beside him.

Charlie's parents lay next to each other. His mother had been shot in the stomach and then nearly decapitated with an ax. Her head lay at right angles to her body, attached only by a shred of skin. Charlie's father had been literally hacked apart. Only his torso was whole. His arms, legs and head were strewn around the floor.

Wend looked around, and saw that the rest of the Indians had been disposed of in a similar manner.

Charlie was on his knees between his parents' bodies, his hands, clothing and face now covered with their blood. The blood on his face was streaked with tears. Wend could see indescribable hatred and fury in his eyes.

The sheriff had followed them into the workhouse. He stood by Wend, grim faced. "They were in here less than ten minutes. That's all it took to do this. Then they ran out, mounted their horses, and rode off. The bloody cowards! And they killed all of them." He pointed to Charlie. "He's the last one left, at least in town. There may be a few more living as workers on farms."

As the sheriff spoke, Charlie slowly rose to his feet and walked over to a body which Wend, with difficulty, recognized as belonging to Captain John. The man's severed hand was laying a couple of feet from the body, a piece of paper clutched in the dead fingers. Charlie bent over and gently pulled the paper from the hand's grasp. He looked down at the words, and a gasp escaped his lips.

Charlie strode over to the sheriff and brandished the paper. "Look at this and remember it. This is the treaty our chiefs signed in 1701: The promises we made to the white man. The promises we kept! And this is our reward! Look at it sheriff. Look at this room." He brandished the treaty again. "Peace treaty, Hell! We signed our own death warrant!"

Then Wend saw Paul Carnahan. He was sitting motionless on a chair near one corner, the limp body of little Molly in his arms. Wend could see the shock in his eyes, which were staring straight at the wall across the room. He walked over to the reverend and tried to take the child's body from his hands. But the minister clutched her more tightly. "Paul, she's dead. Let me take her."

Carnahan looked up at Wend, seeing him for the first time. "I know; she died in my hands. They didn't quite finish her off because she fell beneath another woman. I picked her up and she bled to death. The life just flowed out of her. Her eyes were pleading with me to do something, but I couldn't stop it, there were so many wounds."

And with those words, the Reverend Paul Carnahan, former captain of rangers, veteran of more than a dozen border skirmishes, the man who Wend had once watched unhesitatingly shoot four Shawnee warriors dead, broke down and bawled like a baby.

44

Wend, embarrassed at the sight, and choking back tears of his own, looked around. "Paul, where is Reverend Elder?"

"He left yesterday evening, Wend. He was going back to Paxton. He knew he had to do something to quiet the people up there. But he must have somehow missed the militia on their way down here."

Wend heard a shout and turned to see Charlie Sawak push past the sheriff and out of the work house door. He quickly followed, fearing that his friend was about to do something foolish. He caught up with Charlie at the cart, one foot up on the step to the seat. "Charlie, where are you going?"

The Conestoga took his foot down from the step, and stood beside the cart, his head down, hands on the side of the bed. "Wend, my tribe made the mistake of trying to live like white men. And look what it got them." He waved toward the workhouse. "Decline and extinction! So now I'm going back to my heritage: I'm going west to find a band of Mingoes or Iroquois who will accept me. Besides, if I stay around here, someone of Stewart's ilk is going to make a name for himself by killing me. They'll say that they were just finishing the job the Paxton men started." He turned around and looked at Wend. "Because of my travels selling the tribe's trade goods, many people on both sides of the Susquehanna know me as the face of the Conestogas. Make no mistake; I'm a marked man."

"Charlie, come with me to Sherman Mill. Reverend Carnahan will shelter you, just like he did for Franklin, and if you think about it, me. You can live there until this war is over and tempers cool. Then you can get on with your life." Wend thought for a moment. "You once told me that you wanted to settle down with some girl with whom you could really love and enjoy life. Well, eventually that can happen. Meanwhile, you can spend time with us getting your life back together."

Charlie put his hand on Wend's shoulder. "Wend, you've always been a good and true friend. And I know you are trying to do what you think is best for me. But I've had it with the English. I need to find my own life with people of the forest."

"For God's sake, you can't leave right now, Charlie. At least stay until they bury your parents and all the tribe. Surely you'll wait for that." Wend thought to himself that if he could get Charlie to wait a day or two, he would calm down and change his mind.

"No, Wend. I've done my mourning. I'm getting out of this blood-soaked place of death. There's nothing left here for me now."

Wend looked around. "All right, if you must go, let me help you. Come with me." He walked forward, grabbed the cart horse's halter, and led him toward Slough's Tavern. Charlie, almost trancelike, walked along behind. Wend looked over at the work house and called to Joshua, Franklin, and Donegal, who followed them.

When they were in the tavern courtyard, Wend stopped the cart. He turned to Donegal. "Go to your room and get the rifle I loaned you, the powder horn, molds, and all the lead you have." He turned to Franklin. "Please get my hunting shirt, leggings, and bag of gun supplies from my room."

Wend turned to Joshua. "Charlie's going west, to the Ohio Country, to live in the bush. He's going to have to get rid of this cart, probably somewhere west of Carlisle. Tell him about the best trails for him to use, and where to cross the Allegheny, while I get some food for him."

Wend ran into the tavern and pulled Slough, the proprietor, with him back to the kitchen. He dropped some coins into the man's hand, who immediately became amenable to Wend's requests for provisions. Working rapidly, they put everything suitable they could find into a sack. Wend carried it back out to the cart.

Donegal and Franklin had returned, and were holding the things Wend had requested. He grabbed the rifle from Donegal, and passed it to Charlie. "You're going to need a first rate firelock. And here are the supplies you need to keep it operating." He passed him the powder horn, charger, and molds that Donegal had in his hands. Then he reached into his supply bag and pulled out a small bag of flints and hardware and gave that to Charlie as well. Then he brought out two bottles of liquid. "Here's oil for the barrel and lock. And this bottle is for the wood of the stock. Don't forget to oil it on a regular basis, Charlie. That's what most Indians don't do; then the wood dries out and can crack." He turned to Franklin, and took the clothing from his hands. "You can't wear those city clothes out in the bush. Here's my hunting shirt and leggings." Wend thought for a moment, then reached into his belt and pulled out a pistol. "Keep this close at hand, Charlie. Don't let the powder get damp; change it out every few days."

Wend looked around to see if there was anything else to give Charlie. He pulled out the bag with the last of his coins. "Here, you need this. It's my army pay, which isn't much, but it may help you along the way."

Charlie looked at Wend and smiled for the first time since he had arrived back in Lancaster. "You sound like my mother, telling me how to take care of myself." His hand grasped Wend's shoulder. "Thanks, old friend. I will always remember you." Then he swung up into the cart and stowed the rifle and clothing behind him. He made a show of placing the pistol beside him and then he slapped the reins on the horse, and without saying another word, drove out of the courtyard and turned the cart westward on the street.

Wend walked out onto the street and watched the cart roll away into the distance. He suddenly thought: *I've lost everyone who was important to me in my youth: My family, Abigail, Mary Fraser, Arnold, and now Charlie.* A knot formed in his stomach and a profound loneliness swept over him.

* * *

The task of disposing of the Conestogas' bodies fell to Sheriff Hay and the jailor who ran the workhouse, a man named Felix Donnally. Donnally hired several day laborers who, fortifying themselves with ample doses of whiskey against the cold and disagreeable nature of their task, dug a large pit in the pauper section of the Mennonite Cemetery. A wagon took the collection of remains out to the cemetery. Wend watched as the body parts of people he had known and talked with and laughed with over the last few days, Charlie's parents, Captain John, little Molly, and the others—all jumbled together— were shoveled unceremoniously from the wagon bed into the grave with as much reverence as if they were trash or the remains of slaughtered beeves. Then, working quickly to get out of the January wind, the hired hands shoveled the chunks of frozen winter soil back into the hole.

Carnahan had thought that there would be some official commemoration service for the Conestogas. But despite all the hand wringing which had occurred after the attack on Conestoga Town and then in the aftermath of the workhouse slaughter, the town's religious leaders turned their back on the tribe when the time came to dedicate their grave. It was as if everyone wanted to sweep away the memory of the shameful act as soon as possible. Carnahan, fuming at the lack of concern, approached Thomas Barton, the minister of the main Anglican church in Lancaster, to request that he organize some sort of ceremony. But the minister declined, saying that although word of mouth had it that some of the Conestogas had adopted Christianity, they had never attended his church or to his knowledge any other, so he felt no duty or authority to officiate at their interment.

So, by default, Carnahan took on the job himself after the workers had closed the common grave. On that gray, cold morning two days after Charlie

Sawak had left Lancaster for the last time, the reverend spoke a simple prayer over the freshly turned dirt. In attendance were only the four other men from Sherman Valley, Sheriff Hay, jailor Donnally, and the day laborers waiting for their pay. Hay had passed word around town about the time of the service, but no other residents could spare the time to mourn for the Conestogas.

After the ceremony, Carnahan remained standing before the grave, lost in thought; a grim expression on his face. Joshua and Donegal went to get the horses. Wend's frustration and anger at the death of the tribe had been simmering below the surface for days. Now, moved to words by the gruesomeness of the mass grave, he stepped close to the reverend.

"Reverend, I've been thinking about something and I need to talk to you about it."

Carnahan turned to Wend. He looked like his mind was far distant. "What's that, Wend?"

"It's about Reverend Elder. His actions in this matter have bothered me."

Paul's eyes opened wide and bored into Wend. "I don't understand what you mean."

"Reverend, do you remember what Joshua asked Elder back at the ferry, just before the massacre at Conestoga Town? His words were, 'How could you let things get out of hand like this?'"

"Yes, I remember. And John distinctly said that he thought he had quelled the unrest before he came to see me."

"That's one of the things I'm wondering about. Why would he leave Paxton for a visit when he knew Lazarus Stewart and others were stirring things up? Why didn't he stick around to ensure that the lid stayed on tight?"

"Wend, he had been planning to visit me for a long time. It was his annual visit to look over the church as part of his role as the senior pastor in the area. We had set the date well in advance."

"Yes, Paul, but given the circumstances, making a routine visit to you could have easily been postponed."

"What are trying to say, Wend? For God's sake, are you accusing John Elder of being part of this conspiracy?"

"No. I don't think he had an active role. But I do think he sensed what was afoot and realized sentiment in Paxton was so strong that he couldn't prevent it from happening. And then he made sure that he was away so that no one in Philadelphia would blame him for allowing the Paxton Boys—his own militia—to carry out the attack."

Carnahan looked at Wend, but said nothing. But Wend could see irritation in the reverend's eyes.

Then Wend thought of another way of putting it. "Reverend, I think Elder was like Pontius Pilot in the Bible. He washed his hands of a matter he couldn't control."

Now Paul Carnahan found words. "For God's sake, Wend, I don't believe what you're saying."

But Wend now had the bit in his mouth and was determined to continue. "Well, there's more Paul. Think of this: Elder left just before the attack at the Lancaster Work House. He told you he was going to make sure that things were quiet in Paxton. But that second attack took place the next day. How did he miss a mass of armed men riding down the road from Paxton?"

Carnahan shook his head. "That is a good question. Maybe they passed him while he was stopping in a tavern for a meal. I just don't know."

Wend touched Paul on the arm, and spoke as quietly as he could. "But if Elder had still been at the work house, he might have been able to have stopped the murders. Would the Paxton militia have killed the Conestogas if their minister and commander had been standing in the door?"

Carnahan stared at Wend, obviously considering that idea. Finally he said, "No, Wend, you are right about that. His presence probably would have stopped the second massacre."

The reverend hesitated for a moment, then looked at Wend as if he was about to say something more. But just at that moment, Joshua arrived, leading their horses. He said, "I don't know what you two are cogitatin' on that is so serious, but it's time for us to be on our way." He handed them each the reins of their horses.

Without further conversation, the five men of Sherman Valley mounted their horses and started for home, heading northward toward Harris' Ferry.

CHAPTER THREE
The Fugitive Conestoga

The five of them pushed their horses hard to get to Harris' Ferry before nightfall. It was a quiet ride, for Carnahan was in a deep gloom and the others mostly kept their thoughts to themselves out of respect for him. They arrived at Harris' Ferry in the early evening, pulling up on the road about fifty yards from the landing as dusk settled in over the landscape. Their intent was to spend the night in one of the taverns which stood on the road near the landing and then take an early ferry the next day.

Baird exclaimed, "Damn, look at all the wagons and carts parked at the taverns here. I'll bet we'll have trouble getting a decent place to sleep. Not to mention, I ain't never found one of these ferry taverns what has edible food. Truth be said, makes you long for army rations."

Carnahan said, "You're right, Joshua. Why don't we ride up to Paxton and stay at the Phoenix. It's the best place around here and only a short ride to the north. And if we go to Paxton, I can go over and talk with Reverend Elder this evening."

Wend said, "That suits me. I placed one of my rifles on display for sale at the Phoenix just before the war started. Undoubtedly it's been sold and I need to collect my fee. Especially now that I gave all my army pay to Charlie."

The men turned their horses and started for the intersection where the road to Paxton led northward.

Then Wend had a thought. He pulled up his horse and shouted to the others, "Hey, you go on and I'll catch up. I have some business here which will only take a few minutes."

Baird wrinkled up his face. "What kind of business you got here, Wend?" He pondered for a moment, then smiled slyly and looked around at the other riders. "Say, I'll bet he knows some tavern maid here who he wants to talk up for a while. You know how girls like to drape themselves over our boy Wend!"

The others nodded and laughed.

Franklin smiled slyly. "Now Mr. Wend, don't you go gettin' too serious 'bout some lady over here. That Miss Elizabeth McClay over in Sherman Mill been just pining away for you! And she been tellin' ever' body what would listen that she goin' to give you a warm welcome you never forget. And that's the truth, particular after word got 'round that Miss Abigail weren't comin' back with you."

Wend shook his head. "All right, have your fun. The fact is I am stopping to see a girl."

Joshua laid back his head and hooted. "See, I told you! Wend ain't goin' to waste any time!"

Wend sat quietly until the laughing stopped, then he said in a low voice, "You can rein in your glee, Joshua. The girl I'm going to visit is a tavern maid here who Charlie was seeing. She's an English indenture named Rose. She needs to know that Charlie has escaped. She's probably heard only that the Conestogas were all killed."

Donegal shook his head. "Maybe it's better she don't know about Charlie. He's gone away to the Ohio Country. Truth be, she'll 'na ever see him again. Could be it's better she thinks he died with the rest of his tribe."

Wend looked at Donegal for a moment, thinking over what he had said. "No, Donegal, they were very close. It's better she knows the truth. I think it will comfort her that he got away."

Carnahan nodded. "I think Wend's right. The girl has a right to know." He motioned to the others. "Let's get moving. I want to get over to Reverend Elder's place before it gets too late."

As the others rode off, Wend dismounted from the mare and led her into the stableyard of the most rundown of the taverns.

Wend pushed through the door into the common room. The place was filled to overflowing with rough men and hazy with smoke. Patrons were eating, drinking, and relaxing with pipe in hand. Most were waggoners laying over for the night before taking the ferry across the Susquehanna or having just come off the ferry and pausing for the night before heading eastward. The tavern looked as ill-maintained as he remembered from the time he had stayed there a year ago, when he had visited with Charlie. His friend had been in Harris' to deliver a load of the Conestogas' trade goods to the warehouse of the merchant company Slough and Simon. That's when

Charlie had first met Rose Jensen and taken a liking to the young English tavern maid.

Wend looked around for the auburn-haired girl and couldn't see her amid the hubbub of the common room. He guessed she was in the kitchen or upstairs tending to the rooms. He walked up to the bar where the harried owner worked behind the counter, trying to keep up with demands from the thirsty crowd. The heavyset proprietor, sporting a stack of double chins, looked as slovenly and unkempt as Wend remembered from his prior visit. In fact, Wend swore that the man was wearing the same grease stained apron as during his previous visit—with the very same stains still visible.

He looked around for Rose again and saw only one server at work; a young boy.

Wend waved his hand to get attention and shouted above the hubbub to the proprietor, "Where's Rose; Rose Jensen?"

The harried man, busy filling three ale mugs, paused for only a second to glance at Wend then pointed at a piece of paper tacked to a support post by the end of the counter.

With difficulty due to the flickering candle light, Wend saw that it was a handbill. It had been initiated by a magistrate in Harris' Ferry that very day. It announced that an indentured tavern serving girl, going by the name of Rose Jensen, had run off from her master and was wanted under the law. She was described as 'An English Wench, Aged about 17 years, with Blue Eyes and Auburn Hair.' A reward of ten pounds was offered for information leading to her return.

Wend waited until the proprietor had finished filling the three ale glasses and the purchaser had taken them away. He pushed himself up to the counter and motioned to the inn keeper for attention.

"What can I get you, sir?"

Wend pointed at the handbill. "When did Rose run away? I met her some time ago and was just interested in seeing her again."

The proprietor shook his head. "Well, you're out of luck. She went missing just yesterday. She was late coming down to get ready for breakfast, and I went to her room to find she was gone, along with most of her things. And along the way, she helped herself to food from the larder." He paused, "The little bitch. I gave her a good home, treated her fair, and she's only worked off a year of her time."

Wend looked around at the shabby room. "Yes, I'm sure you have a marvelous place to live and work here."

The proprietor, missing Wend's irony, answered, "That's the damn truth. She's soon going to learn what she's missing." He grinned conspiratorially and pointed at Wend. "But I haven't a doubt the sheriff will have her back here soon enough. She ain't going to get far, not a young girl travelin' on her own. And with that red hair, she's goin to attract attention. Somebody's goin' to collect that ten pounds bounty."

Wend simply said, "Undoubtedly."

The fat man slapped his hand on the bar. "And when she gets back, you can bet I'm going to make sure she earns every penny of that extra ten pounds in a way that will make her forget takin' to the road again!"

Wend looked at the tavern keeper for a long moment, then said, "Yes, I'm sure you're just the man for that job."

* * *

The village of Paxton was only a short distance from Harris' Ferry. But after the hard-riding trip they had made from Lancaster, Wend could feel the weariness of the mare as he rode northward in the gathering night to Paxton, so he gave the animal her head and let her walk at her own pace. Meanwhile he thought about what he had learned at the tavern. Rose's disappearance, two days after Charlie left Lancaster, could be no coincidence. And that realization left a feeling of dread in Wend. For that meant that Charlie had come north instead of crossing the Susquehanna at Thomas Wright's Ferry, directly west of Lancaster. Crossing at Wright's would have been the safe move for Charlie because many of the residents of the little village, including Thomas Wright himself, were friends with the Conestoga people. But obviously Charlie had put his own life in jeopardy to come for Rose, traveling to the Harris'-Paxton area, the very hotspot of Conestoga hatred. Clearly Charlie had evaded encountering any Paxton Rangers on the trip northward and had somehow managed to convince Rose to go with him. But that meant he and the girl were on the run in the heart of enemy territory and had to find a way across the Susquehanna. Crossing at Harris' was out. The other logical option was to travel back to Wright's Ferry. But that would entail a journey over thirty miles of road where discovery would be highly likely. What would Charlie do?

Wend was still trying to puzzle out the answer when he guided the mare into the courtyard of the Phoenix.

As he entered the common room, he immediately noted that it was almost as crowded as the place in Harris' Ferry. But the difference was that Wend knew many of the men in the Phoenix. Baird, Donegal, and Franklin sat at a table near the staircase. In a far corner near the end of the counter stood Asher Clayton, captain of one of the two Paxton Militia companies, and some of his friends. Then Wend felt a touch of distaste as he saw the sharp, wolfish face of Lazarus Stewart at the other end of the bar. With him, talking and laughing, were several of his cronies; Wend recognized Mathew Smith and a couple of others who had come to Sherman Mill last spring to help patrol the valley after a Shawnee raid which had marked the beginning of the Indian uprising. Behind the bar was the tall, thin figure of Jared Caldwell, the owner of the Phoenix, whose cleanliness was in marked contrast to the proprietor of the Harris' Ferry tavern Wend had just left.

As Wend walked over to his friends' table, he shivered with the realization that some of the men in the room with him had participated in the attack on Conestoga Town and the butchery at the Lancaster work house. These were men he had been on patrol with in Sherman Valley last spring when the first attacks started. Indeed, some carried rifles he had made. That thought was heavy on his mind as he sat down with Joshua and the others.

Joshua smiled roguishly at the others. "Well, Eckert, did you get your sparking done with that girl down at Harris?"

Wend rolled his eyes, shook his head, and started to reply.

Before Wend could respond, Lazarus Stewart was standing by the table, ale mug in hand. The militia captain looked down with a sly smile on his face and addressed himself to Baird. "Well, Joshua, glad to see that you and young Eckert there are safely back from your little trip with the British."

Joshua simply nodded and said, "Hello, Lazarus, 'hear things been pretty busy around here since we left."

Stewart took a swig of his ale and responded, "That it has, Joshua, that it has." He paused a moment. "Been war party attacks on both sides of the river, all through the summer and fall. But we're finally getting things under control—hitting back against nests of the savages."

Wend looked up at Stewart and said, "Yes, Lazarus, including attacking peaceful, Christian Indians like the Conestogas."

Stewart pursed his lips and looked at Wend. "Well, Eckert, maybe if you and Joshua had stayed around here and had to fight all the tribal attacks, you'd know the truth about them so-called peaceful tribes."

Wend asked, "And just what is the truth Lazarus?"

"Them Conestogas—and the same goes for those Moravian Indians further over to the east—they been providing information to the hostiles which helped them avoid patrols and go right to unprotected villages and towns. Everybody knows that."

"And how did *everybody* come to know that, Stewart?" Wend asked.

"Traveling peddlers and some traders has seen members of the Conestogas associating with war parties, that's how. There was a pair of Indian traders what spied a Conestoga out on one of the islands in the Susquehanna, meeting with a war party. And a peddler saw the same man in a place where the war parties was spotted gathering for attacks."

Wend said, "So the Conestogas were slaughtered on flimsy information like that?"

"Well, nobody with any sense ever doubted that they were spies livin' right among us. But now the problem is almost taken care of!"

"Almost, Lazarus?" Baird looked askance at the militia captain. "The Conestogas have been wiped out, 'cept for one or two. What more remains to be done?" Wend looked up at Stewart expectantly.

"We know that at least one Conestoga got away. That friend of Eckert's—the one he had the gall to bring into this very tavern last year. Charlie Sawak, that's his name—and he's the worst of the lot. He traveled around both sides of the Susquehanna in that cart of his selling the tribe's goods. But he had plenty of opportunity to cooperate with war parties and give them information. Somebody needs to deal with him."

Wend looked sharply at Stewart. "How are you going to '*deal with him*', Lazarus? You going to go chasing all over the colony to find him?"

"We don't need no big search all over for him, Eckert. Your friend's been seen. A waggoner saw him driving that cart of his up the road from Lancaster day before yesterday. And Matt Bratton and a group of men found his campsite yesterday morning, just a few miles north of here on the riverside road."

Wend was momentarily stunned. "Matt Bratton caught him? What happened to Sawak?"

Stewart pursed his lips. "I said Matt found his campsite. They crept up on his fire, and saw nobody there. Then they was shot at from behind cover. So they hit the ground and started to crawl back to where they had left their horses." Stewart shook his head. "Then they heard another shot. When they got back to where they had left their mounts, they found that Sawak had wounded their horse holder and chased off their animals. They spent the rest of the day rounding them up and riding back here."

Donegal, who had been sitting silently, laughed out loud. "So one wee Conestoga on the run for his life manages to chase off the brave Paxton Rangers?" The highlander took a drink of his ale and smiled at the others at the table. "I've 'na doubt the 77ᵗʰ Highlanders could give you militia fellows a few lessons."

Steward slammed his fist down on the table. "We're going to fix the problem tomorrow. Come first light I'm taking a squad of militia and we're going to chase down Sawak. He won't get away this time."

Joshua squinted up through the smoke at Lazarus. "You're talkin' big, Stewart. But that's going to be a tough job. He's got a good many hours start on you. Where do you think he's headed?"

"I got it in my mind he's runin' for the Great Island; thirty miles north of here. That's where war parties been gathering and camping out between raids. I'll wager he's figuring on hiding out 'till he can link up with a bunch of them." Stewart swung his eyes around the table. "But that cart of his can only move so fast. It's sure enough we can overtake him on strong horses."

Stewart turned and started to walk back to the counter.

Wend called after him, "What happened to Matt Bratton and his friends? Where are they?"

The Paxton captain turned. He stared at Wend for a moment. "They went back across the river. Bratton said he had business in Carlisle and then he was going back to Sherman Valley." Stewart pointed upward. "But he left someone behind. One of your friends from Sherman Mill—name of Frank McKenzie—he was the horse holder who got shot. He's in a room upstairs."

There was a silence among the four men at the table as they considered what Stewart had said. Wend was the first to speak. "Joshua, back in Lancaster, you did tell Charlie to cross the river at Wright's Ferry, didn't you?"

Baird made a face and looked at the ceiling in disgust. "Of course. What else would I tell him; to come up here along the coast road and make himself a target for every Paxton militiaman who had a grudge against Indians? Besides, he knew that himself."

"No, I was just checking, Joshua; trying to figure out what he was thinking. Charlie knows the roads around here as well as anyone." Wend thought for a moment. "I'm going upstairs to see McKenzie and have a first hand talk about what happened."

Joshua asked, "Want me to go along?"

Wend shook his head. "No—it's best if I talk to him myself. He may be more open with someone closer to his age than you, Joshua."

"Dammit, Wend! You keep trying to tell me I'm an old man." Joshua smiled crookedly and winked at the other two men at the table.

Wend got McKenzie's room number from a tavern maid clearing away one of the tables and then climbed the stairs. He hesitated a moment before the door to gather his thoughts. Finally, he knocked once on the door and walked in without waiting for a response.

Frank lay in the bed. He looked up at Wend in surprise. "My God, Wend Eckert! What are you doing here?"

Wend stared at McKenzie, a youth of about his own age. It was obvious that he was suffering from his wound; he was pasty-faced and droplets of sweat were on his brow. Wend just stood silently, looking down at him for a long moment. Then he stepped to the bed and quickly put his hand on his brow. It was hot to the touch. Then he flipped the blanket off of McKenzie's body.

Frank's entire right leg was rapped in a crude, blood-soaked bandage. A large, round blood stain just below the knee showed where the ball had actually hit.

"Wend, for God's sake, what are you doing?"

"Looking at your wound." He paused for effect, then continued. "Tell you the truth, Frank, working with the army, I've seen a lot of wounds over the last six months. And I'm going to tell you straight-up: That's a bad hurt you've got. Has a doctor attended you?"

McKenzie bit his lip. "The tavern keeper brought in an old man; he's the local apothecary. They said he did some medical work. But he weren't no proper doctor, and he smelled of whiskey. Caldwell said he was the only medical person they got here in Paxton. But he probed around and got the ball out of the wound."

"Did he tell you whether the leg bone was broken?"

"I can move it a little, but it hurts like mad when I try to put any weight on it."

Wend pressed McKenzie's shin at several places, moving from the wound down to the ankle. The youth whimpered each time he put pressure on the bone.

"It's possible that the ball cracked your shin bone along its length, rather than across." Wend gave McKenzie a grim look. "Doc Monro, the surgeon of the 77th Highlanders told me about that kind of a fracture; it can actually be worse than a clean break."

The words had the desired effect; McKenzie looked down at the leg with fear in his eyes.

Wend asked, "So what are you going to do about treating that wound? If it doesn't get tended to proper—and soon—you'll lose that leg for sure." He paused for effect. "If it had happened in the army, the surgeon would have had it off by now. No time for niceties on the battlefield."

There was real fear in McKenzie's eyes. "You really think I'm going to lose it?"

"If it doesn't get attention soon and mortification sets in, you'll be lucky if that's all you lose. And you've already got a high fever." Wend hesitated for effect. "You were riding with Matt Bratton. And you work for his freight line as a wagon driver. What is he doing to help you?"

"He had to get over to Carlisle to meet someone; he and the two men who were with us had some business there. But he said he'd tell my Pa when he got back to Sherman Valley, so Pa could come get me with his wagon and take me to a Doc in Carlisle."

"That's wonderful, isn't it, Frank? You friend Matt has left you in a real fix while he goes off to 'take care of business'." Wend pulled the blanket back over the boy and sat down on the edge of the bed. "It may be over a week until your Pa gets here. At the very least, that leg of yours is going to be beyond help. And more likely he'll have made the trip just to carry your body back to Sherman Mill." Wend looked around the room. "Who is going to pay for your room and board while you lay here waiting for your Pa? And have you got money for that doctor's fee over in Carlisle?"

McKenzie's face crinkled up, and tears started to form in his eyes. "What am I going to do, Wend? I ain't got no money. And all this will more than clean out all my family's money." He paused a moment, and tears were streaming down his face now.

"Here's what you're going to do, Frank." Wend spoke softly. "You're going to tell me what happened yesterday—all the details of your chase of the Conestoga—and what happened when you and Bratton attacked him."

"Wend, I can't do that. Bratton and Lazarus Stewart told me to keep quiet about all this—all that happened in Lancaster and yesterday on the road north of here." He thought a second. "And I ain't got anything against you—you always been kind to me—but Stewart told me you was a friend of them Conestogas."

"Listen, Bratton and Stewart got you in trouble with the law, got you wounded, and now they're leaving you here to rot." Wend stared at the boy for a moment. "But I'll tell you why you should really tell me what I want to know: I've got money coming from Caldwell for the sale of a firelock. You come clean with me and I'll use it to cover your bill here at the tavern. I'll pay for Caldwell to make arrangements with a freight waggoner to get you over to Carlisle to see that English doctor, Highsmith. They say he's the best in the Cumberland Valley. You'll be on the road tomorrow and the doctor may be able to save your leg."

"You'll do all that for me? "

"I said so. Now start to talk, Frank. I want all the details."

McKenzie pursed his lips and considered for a moment. Then he started: "We was here at he tavern, just after everyone got back from Lancaster. . ."

Wend interrupted, "So you were there for the attack on the work house? I know that Bratton was there."

A look of fright came over the boy's face. "Yeah, I was there, Wend. But I din't even get into the work house or the yard. I just stood out on the street, like most of the men. It was all over in a few minutes. There ain't no blood on my hands."

Wend shook his head. "Frank, stop deluding yourself. You may not have killed anyone, but there's blood all over your hands if you were with that mob. And you'll never be able to wash it out. But that's not what I'm after. Tell me about what happened up here."

"Well, we had spent the night here in the tavern. And after breakfast, we was saddling our horses in the courtyard getting ready to ride back to Sherman Mill. That's when Stewart came rushing into the tavern with the news that that peddler of the Conestogas, name of Charlie Sawak, had escaped the attack and had been seen by a waggoner on the Lancaster road. The waggoner said he saw him and that cart of his, alongside the road at a creek, resting and watering his horse."

"So how did you and Bratton get involved in hunting Sawak?"

"Stewart saw that the four of us—Matt and me, and the two friends of his that had been with us all the time—were ready to move out. So he convinced Matt that we should go look for the Conestoga to save time." Frank thought a moment. "He said, 'Bratton, you four are well mounted and well armed—go take care of the last Conestoga'." And Matt just looked at him for a minute. Then he smiled and said, 'Leave it to us, Lazarus. We'll run him down and finish him'."

Wend nodded. "That makes sense. It would have taken Lazarus a couple of hours to round up some men and get started." He paused for a second, then asked, "Who were these two men with you?" Were they from Sherman Valley?"

"No, they're traders. They work as partners, trading with settlers and Indians out on the frontier. But they're out of work now, what with the war. The older one, and the boss, as far as I could see, was named Mathews. He's got hair that's gone silver white, even though he ain't an old man; he's in his thirties. They call him 'Gray'—Gray Mathews 'cause of the hair. And the other one is named Hugh Crowley."

Wend said, "How did you and Matt hook up with these two?"

"Well, they was already good friends of Matt's. We met them in Carlisle at Larkin's Tavern when we first came down from Sherman Mill. They was waiting there to join us. But Matt didn't explain much to me. In fact, they never told me much about themselves; they was sort of distant in the way they treated me. But they was always talking real friendly with Matt."

Wend said dryly, "Yes, I expect they were." *Undoubtedly they were part of Grenough's organization.* Then he prodded McKenzie. "So the four of you left to find Sawak?"

"Yeah. Everybody figured he was heading north along the coast road to get to the Great Island of the Susquehanna. There's been lots of word about war parties being seen up there, resting between attacks on settlements. In fact, Mathews said that last summer he and his partner had taken a pack train of goods up there, to sell to settlers in the area, and had seen Sawak and some other Conestogas camping out with what looked like a party of Delawares."

"So you took off along the coast road."

"Yeah, we traveled pretty fast, pushing the horses hard. We figured that Sawak had a good start. Matt had a theory that he probably had laid up along the road, hiding south of Harris' until he could steal through Harris' and Paxton in the night. So he maybe had four or five hours on us and that he wouldn't be wasting any time."

"That's logical enough. So where did you catch up with him?"

"We was surprised 'cause it was only about six or seven miles north of Paxton. We had been seeing some wheel tracks in the mud of the road, and figured that was him. Then, middle of the morning, Gray Mathews suddenly pointed toward the river. And there was smoke from a fire, down near the river bank. Just a little smoke, as if from a fire kept small as possible."

"All right, so how did you approach the camp?"

"It weren't hard. We could see tracks where that cart turned of the road and had pushed through the underbrush. Matt was smilin' real broad, and said, 'We're going to surprise that rascal. He didn't figure anyone would be onto him so soon.' Well, we dismounted and Matt had me hold all four horses. Then he and the traders checked their priming and crept toward the fire using bushes and trees to hide their movements. But when they got in sight of the fire, they was the ones surprised; there was nothing there except the fire; no cart, no horse, no blankets, nothing. They all came out of the bush and stood looking at the fire, wondering what was going on. Suddenly a shot rang out and it hit one of those traders in the hand. It just grazed him, but it was enough to make him drop his rifle. All three of them flattened to the ground and started to crawl back to the horses."

McKenzie stopped talking for a moment, collecting his thoughts. "That's when that Conestoga shot me. I was knocked right off my feet and lost hold of all the horses and those damned animals bolted."

Wend asked, "Did you see Charlie Sawak? Did he come out of hiding after you were hit?"

"No, I din't never see him. But I was mad at being shot and my rifle was by my hand. And I had seen the flash of a pan out in the bushes. So, soon as I hit the ground, I fired right at that spot. And by God, I hit him. I heard a shout of pain."

"All right, you hit the shooter. Did you hear any noise as he moved to get away?"

"Yeah, Wend—but that was later. After he shot again at the others."

Wend was surprised. "You say there was more gunfire?"

"Sure was, Wend. Matt and Gray and Hugh were creeping back to where I was and suddenly another shot was fired at them. It kicked up the dirt and clipped a bush right next to Matt. So they all froze. Just after that, I heard some movement in the bush and then it was quiet again. But in about a minute, I heard a whinny from a horse, just a bit north of my position, and then the noise of cart wheels crashing through the brush. It went out to the road, and headed north, makin' fast time. I could hear the hooves beating loud on the wagon track."

Wend said, "All right, I have the picture. After Charlie had gotten clear in his cart, your three friends came back to you."

"That's right. Matt looked at my leg, but couldn't do much to tend it 'cause all our kit was on the horses. All he could do was use his belt to make a tourniquet above my knee to slow the bleeding. Then all three of them went to round up the animals while I just laid there." He pursed his lips and looked up at Wend. "My leg was still bleeding some and hurt like Hell, and it was more than an hour for they had collected the mounts. Maybe longer, cause I passed out for a while. Then Matt bandaged my leg and they helped me up on my horse. We headed back here, and I can tell you ridin' on that animal with this leg and the ball still in it was the most painful thing I ever done. I near passed out a couple of times."

Wend got up from the bed, and paced around the room, going over the story in his mind. Then he turned to Frank. "Is there anything else you can tell me, particularly about the fight itself?"

McKenzie bit his lip. "Well, there is something I ain't quite figured out. That Indian shot me, and I know I hit him right afterward. May not have been that serious, but I know he was hit from the cry he made. But then it was only a minute or so later that he shot at Matt for the second time. I didn't hear no noise of him moving to get into a good position to shoot at the other three, where they was crawling back from the fire, but the sound of that shot was not from where he shot me. If it were, I would have seen the flash in his pan or his muzzle flame. So somehow he moved a goodly distance toward those other three without me bein' aware of how he got there."

Wend went to the window and looked out into the courtyard, mainly to hide his face and the broad smile he couldn't contain. He asked McKenzie, "Frank, did it ever occur to you that there might have been two of them?"

"Two of them? But everybody said there was only one of the Conestogas who escaped. And that waggoner down on the Lancaster Road said he only saw the one Conestoga with the cart."

"Yeah, that's probably correct. Just a thought on my part. Now, can you think of anything else you saw or heard during the fight?"

Frank McKenzie wrinkled up his face in thought. There was silence for over a minute. Then he looked up at Wend. "You know, there is something I ain't thought of 'till now that you made me go over the fight. But I guess it's been in the back of my mind, just laying there. This is the thing: When my ball hit that Indian, the sound he made was sort of funny. It weren't like you would expect."

Wend was all ears. "What do you mean; it wasn't what you would expect?"

"It was very high pitched, not deep like you would 'spect a man to make. Almost like a woman's shriek." He shook his head, "Now ain't that funny? Maybe gettin' hit surprised him so much that he made that girly sound."

* * *

After leaving McKenzie's room, Wend stood at the top of the landing, turning what the wounded youth had told him over in his mind. The big question was: Why had Charlie and Rose been only a few miles north of Harris' Ferry and Paxton when Bratton and his men caught up with them? Then it came to him: Charlie had had to wait until the tavern had closed for the night to approach Rose, probably sneaking into her room through the back door of the tavern and waiting for her there. She wouldn't have been finished until after midnight. Then it had taken time to explain his plan and convince her to come with him. Even an adventurous girl like Rose would hesitate to go with her lover to live in the wilds among people she thought of as savages. And then she would have taken some time to get her possessions together and, as the tavern proprietor had said, sneak into the kitchen and steal a supply of provisions. So the two fugitives might not have left until just before dawn. That indeed would have put them only a few miles north of Harris' by mid-morning.

It was also clear that Charlie had expected to be followed and had purposefully set up an ambush. Wend wondered if Charlie had actually caught sight of the pursuers while on the road before he set up the ambush, or had perhaps built the fire for a diversion to delay anyone trailing the cart. *Well,* Wend thought, *I'll never know the answer to that one.*

Then he thought over the details of the fight that McKenzie had described. There was no doubt that Charlie had stationed Rose near where the cart and horse had been hidden—to stand guard over it and keep her away from where he knew the attack would come. Then he had placed himself in a position to shoot at anyone who approached the decoy campfire. Obviously, Frank had been shot by Rose, probably using a pistol from a short distance. That's why he had been able to see the flash of the pan. Then Charlie, using the rifle that Wend had given him, fired the two shots at Matt and his compatriots. Wend wondered to himself if Charlie had intended to fire only to scare the men or he was just not a very good shot. But at any rate, the ambush ruse had worked and had ended the pursuit. But they had not gotten away cleanly: Rose was wounded, and Wend wondered how seriously. If she was hurt badly, it could prevent their entire escape plan. Suddenly it came to Wend: *I've got to try to find out how things turned out and help them if I can.*

When Wend joined his friends at the table, he found that Reverend Carnahan had returned after visiting with John Elder. Wend gave them all a quick summary of Frank's condition and what he had said about the fight with Charlie, omitting saying anything about Rose.

Then, after a few minutes discussion, Joshua stretched and said, "Let's get a quick supper and get to bed. We got a long ride tomorrow to get to Carlisle." He smiled slyly and looked around at his friends. "Can't deny I'm looking forward to tomorrow night with the Widow Downey. Been near eight months since I spent any time with her."

Carnahan looked around the table, a twinkling in his eyes. "I'm sure Joshua wants to make sure all his parts still work, after all that time sleeping alone."

There was laughter all around. Afterward, Wend broke the silence. "I won't be riding with you to Carlisle tomorrow."

Joshua looked at him sharply. "You in such a hurry to get back to Sherman Mill that you're goin' to take the road along the west bank of the river and then the trail up through Sherman Valley? That's pretty chancy this time of year, particular if we get a big snow."

Carnahan stared at Wend for a moment, his hand on his chin in the manner he always did when he was thinking things through. Finally he said, "No, Joshua. I think Wend is planning to stay on this side of the river for a while." He looked around the table. "I'd guess Wend is thinking about finding out what happened to Charlie Sawak."

Wend nodded slowly. "The reverend's got it right. I'm riding north to check out the site of the ambush and then try to track where Charlie went from there. From what he told me in Lancaster, he isn't going to go up to the Great Island nor does he have any idea of joining a war party. He just wants to get across the river and make his way to the Ohio Country, to join a Mingo band. The Mingoes are of Iroquois heritage, just like the Conestogas." Wend looked around at his friends. "And Frank believes that he hit Charlie in that skirmish; he may be holed up somewhere, too badly wounded to go any further. I won't be able to rest until I'm confident he made it across the river."

There was a silence around the table. Carnahan still had his hand up to his chin. Baird pursed his lips and crossed his arms.

The reverend spoke first. "Wend, going up there alone could be dangerous. You could run into a war party. That isn't likely, this time of year, but it's possible. But I'm more worried about what Lazarus Stewart would do if he came across you alone. He's gotten increasingly hot-headed and irrational over the last few months and he's already down on you 'cause you're close to the Conestogas and Charlie is your personal friend."

Donegal laughed. "Course, it didn't help any that our friend Wend here baited Lazarus a wee bit earlier this evening."

Carnahan looked over at Baird. "I say let's go with him. He could use the help of experienced trackers and a few extra rifles."

Joshua stared at the reverend for a long moment, then took on a look of resignation. "Yeah, yeah, Paul. I see where this is going." He wrinkled up his face and shrugged his shoulder. "What's another night or so away from the Widow after all this time?"

* * *

The five men left Paxton in the morning dusk, heading northward on the road which paralleled the river. The village was shrouded with sheets of fog rising from the nearby Susquehanna and Wend got an eerie feeling as they passed among the houses and shops. Waggoners hitching up their rigs and farmers performing morning chores around their barns were shadowy, ghostly figures as the men from Sherman Valley rode out.

Wend looked around at his companions, grateful for their company. He reflected that there could not be a better prepared group for the job at hand. All were well mounted and armed to the teeth. Each carried a long rifle— Wend had borrowed Frank McKenzie's firelock to arm Donegal in place of the rifle which had been given to Charlie—and all but Franklin carried at least one pistol. Everyone had a hatchet and a good knife. Donegal had taken his broadsword out of their baggage and carried it slung over his shoulder. But Wend knew that the real strength of the group was in the experience and bush smarts which resided in the men. Baird and Carnahan had nearly thirty years of frontier hunting and warfare between them. The reverend had been the captain of pathfinders who had guided Colonel John Armstrong's force of over 300 men to Kittanning for the punitive attack on the big Delaware town in 1756. Franklin had more than three years of daily tracking and hunting experience from his time as a captive of Wolf Claw's Mingo band. Donegal had spent his youth as gamekeeper on a large estate in Scotland and had just spent seven months of intense scouting for the army. And Wend himself, the youngest man in the party, had been hunting and scouting since the age of seven.

In less than two hours they found the place where Charlie had ambushed Bratton's party. It was easy to see where the cart had turned off from the wagon track toward the river. There were clear tracks in the ground; bushes and tall grass had been pushed aside. Wend, sitting his horse at the place where the cart left the road also saw the answer to how Charlie had known he was being followed; the turn-off point was just beyond a sizeable ridge, and

65

from the crest it was possible to look back over the road for more than a mile. Clearly, Charlie had seen his pursuers and decided to lay a trap for them.

The five men dismounted at the edge of the turnoff and tied their horses to trees next to the road.

Then Carnahan led them on a detailed investigation of the ambush site. Or rather, he led Baird and Franklin, while Wend and Donegal stood back to stay out of the way and watch three skilled trackers at work. Carnahan and Baird—trappers, hunters, and rangers together for more than a decade— communicated almost wordlessly; a finger pointed at a bush or the ground, a hand motion highlighting an area of interest, a shared nod of the head as they both looked at a place in the grass, a tap on the shoulder by one to attract the attention of the other. Franklin moved by himself, scouring the ground with intense concentration, sometimes calling attention of the other two to something he had found. Wend watched with admiration at the men's skills as they started at the site of the fire, then examined the entire area, carefully working back toward the road. Finally, after looking over all places where action had occurred, the three ended up at the spot where Frank McKenzie had seen the flash of the gun which had fired at him. The three men stood at the assailant's hiding place, staring down at the ground.

After a brief moment looking at the area, Carnahan glanced at Baird and asked, "Any doubt in your mind?"

Joshua pursed his lips and shook his head. "Not a bit, Paul." He looked around at the whole group. "There was two of them working together. We been seein' two sets of tracks—and one set is a mite smaller than the other. No, there ain't no doubt in my mind." He turned and looked right at Wend. "Your friend Charlie had a woman with him—an' she was the one who shot Frank McKenzie, probably with a pistol."

Paul Carnahan grounded his rifle in front of himself. He cocked his head and looked sharply at Wend. "Joshua, I'd wager you aren't telling Wend anything he doesn't already know. He's known since last night why Charlie came up here instead of crossing at Wright's Ferry and he knows who the girl is with the Conestoga."

Baird's head snapped around to look at Wend where he stood a few feet away, close to where Frank McKenzie had held the horses. "You know'd all this time there was two of them? Why you been holding out on your friends?"

Before Wend could form his answer, Carnahan spoke up. "Yes, Joshua. He held out on us. Look at his face—its got that stony look he always puts on when he doesn't want to show what's going on inside his head. After having him in my home for near five years, I'd never mistake what that face means." The reverend looked around at the entire group with a sly smile on his face. "But I'm also sure Wend had a good reason for not telling his friends what he knew." He nodded toward Wend. "And he's going to explain that to us right now."

Wend smiled. "Reverend, I'm sorry for keeping you and everybody else in the dark." He looked around at the group. "The truth is, the girl with Charlie is Rose Jensen, the indentured tavern maid who he has been seeing for the last year. Back in Lancaster, he told me he was in love with her. Anyway, when I went to the tavern in Harris' last night, I found out she was missing since the morning before, and that her master had put a price of ten pounds on her head. I knew right away she had gone with Charlie. But I didn't say anything about it last night because I didn't want us to be overheard talking about it by anyone in the tavern. I was afraid that someone would go after her for the reward. Also, I didn't want people connecting Charlie with her: If they did that, we could be accused of aiding a runaway slave simply because we went to help Charlie." He paused for a moment. "I was planning to tell you as early as possible, once we were out on our own. But in looking over the ground here, you have confirmed what seemed logical to me after I talked with McKenzie: Charlie used the girl to help him, and she's the one who shot Frank."

Carnahan spoke up. "But there's also something else that's important, isn't there Wend?"

Wend nodded. "Yes, Reverend. Rose was the one shot by McKenzie. And we don't know how serious she's been hurt. If it's bad, it's could hinder them in getting away. Charlie might even try to find her medical attention, no matter how much that would hinder their chances to escape."

Donegal commented, "This Rose seems to be spunky lass, at least for an English girl."

Wend said, "You're right. She's very adventurous: She wasn't indentured by some court in England for petty crime or debt. Rose arranged an indenture herself so she could get her passage paid to the colony. She figured she had a better chance to make something of herself over here than becoming a servant in England."

Joshua laughed, then said, "Spunky or not, all this investigation is keeping me away from Alice Downey. I'm looking to have a little adventure of my own in her bedroom. So we need to get moving." He turned to Wend. "You still figure that Sawak plans to cross the river and head west, or has that crafty little mind of yours figured out that he's going to do something else now?"

Wend shook his head. "No, I'm certain that as long as Rose was able to move, Charlie will try to cross the river." He considered a moment. "In fact, this fight took place two days ago. He's probably crossed already if they were able. The only problem is where. He would have to find a place to make it reasonably easy, what with Rose along. That's the problem for us—finding evidence of the place they crossed. And of course, there's still the possibility that they're holed up somewhere, tending to Rose's wound. We have no choice but to examine all the likely places along the river bank from here northward, to see if they have crossed yet."

Donegal said, "Lord, I don't envy them. Wading through a great, wide river like this in January. Sure'n it's shallow, but it's damn near freezin'. And I saw patches of ice along the bank and chunks floatin' out in the middle."

Carnahan answered, "Indeed, it would not be pleasant. But Joshua and I crossed this river in winter once ourselves. It was well to he north of here. That was a long time ago, though, when we were young. Even so, my body didn't seem to thaw out for days afterward. I wouldn't want to do it now."

Joshua snickered, "There's a lot of things what we wouldn't do no more, cause we got smarter over the years. But truth is, this river can be crossed, and I agree with Wend, mad as I am with him for keepin' me in the dark about Charlie and his wench. Fact is, they're probably on the other side and headed west. So let's go find the place and be sure about it, so we can go back to the ferry and get on the road to Carlisle."

Wend looked at the others. "I'll say again, why don't you all return to Harris' and continue home. I'll search for Charlie by myself. I'm grateful for the help you've been already."

Joshua exclaimed, "Shit, Eckert. I ain't said anything about quitin'. We're in this now; we'll keep at it till we find out what happened to your friend and his gal." He looked around at the others, a grin on his face. "Besides, I want to be able to taunt Bratton about how he and all his men let one scared Conestoga get the better of him."

Carnahan smiled, then added, "Don't worry, Wend. Joshua just likes to gripe. It makes him feel better."

Baird nodded. "Be'in all that as it may, there ain't no need for us to search every damn foot of this river bank for miles to the north. Let's do this the smart way. There be a couple of good places to ford within ten miles of here; I got one particular in mind. If our friend Charlie has done as much travlin' around here as every one says, he'd know about it and make a beeline for there. So let's save ourselves a lot of time and check that out first."

* * *

They rode northward, watching the road carefully for vehicle tracks, and for any sign of a rig turning off the track toward the river. The sun was a couple of hours past noon when Joshua reined in his horse and looked down toward the Susquehanna.

He pointed at the river. "The fordin' place I'm thinkin' about is just down there. But we should have seen sign of the cart turnin' off by now, if he was going to use this spot to cross."

Carnahan sat his horse for moment, then looked over at Joshua. "Sawak has been pretty cagy so far about everything he's done. That ambush was a pretty smart move. So it strikes me that he would have found a way to cover up his approach to the river in case someone else took up the pursuit after Bratton and his boys got back to Paxton with their bad news."

Still on horseback, they picked their way down toward the river, not dismounting until they were with fifty yards of the bank. Joshua led them on foot out to the edge of the water. He motioned out toward the river. "You see why this is a good place to ford, 'specially in the winter?"

Wend looked out on the river, and immediately understood what Joshua meant. The stream was as wide as ever, nearly a mile, but was spotted with a multitude of islands, most just small groups of inhospitable rocks projecting upward out of the water. But several were fairly substantial, with trees and large bushes covering them.

Joshua continued, "With them bigger islands, you could take your ford-ing in stages, stopping on dry land to warm up along the way. If you were able to take the time, there are a couple of islands where you could stay overnight and have a fire to thaw you out proper like."

While Joshua had been talking, Franklin had been exploring the area. Suddenly he shouted from a spot upriver, but slightly away from the bank. "Mr. Joshua, I found something. Come here and take a look at this!"

The other four men hurried to the sound of his voice. And there, among a cluster of high bushes, were the broken-up remains of a cart. The wheels lay together, to one side of the debris. Wend noticed right away that the horse har-ness and much of the wood was missing. He tried to think of what it meant.

It was Reverend Carnahan who had the answer on his lips while the oth-ers were still thinking things over. "They used one side of the cart as a raft to get all their provisions and other stuff over." He looked around at the wreck-age. "There's nothing of any use left here."

Meanwhile, Joshua and Franklin had gone down to the water's edge. "Reverend," Franklin called, "Here be the place they went in!"

They all hurried over to the river bank. Soon Joshua was standing almost in the water, looking back up at the bank, pointing to various places. "Lots of footprints and hoof prints. And here's where the raft was pulled into the water." Joshua laughed. "That Conestoga is damned clever: He figured a way to rig it so the horse could pull the raft across. Probably had all their things lashed to the raft, so they won't loose them if it got upset by ice or hitting a rock."

Donegal had a puzzled look on his face. "I can't see how that raft would work." He pointed out into the river. "With all this current it wouldn't tow well behind the horse. 'Na, the current would be working to pull it downstream. It would be dragging the horse downstream and they would 'na be able to control it."

Wend realized Donegal was correct. But then he thought about it a minute and an idea jumped into his mind. "You're right, Simon. But they must have found some way of holding the rear of the raft up into the current. Maybe they connected a strap of the harness to the rear and one of them held onto it to keep the raft directly behind the horse."

Carnahan looked across the river. "Whatever way they did it, it couldn't have been easy. And I'm sure they stopped several times along the way, on the islands. I wouldn't be surprised if they did camp overnight on one of those big islands out there." He looked around at the others. "But one thing's got to be true if they got across all right: That girl is not too badly wounded. She had to walk across and she had to help with the raft. There's no other way they could have made it." The reverend bit his lip and thought a moment. "I'd guess that the girl led the horse and Sawak was behind controlling the raft."

They were all contemplating the reverend's words when the sound of horse hooves became audible. Then they heard shouts, first out on the road and then approaching their position.

Joshua shouted, "Whoever that is, could be trouble. Quick like, get the horses down here, and look to your firelocks!"

They all moved rapidly and were standing in a group just up from the bank, rifles or pistols in hand, when the voices became louder and Lazarus Stewart and his mounted squad of Paxton militia came into sight. The horsemen pulled up, Stewart in the lead surveying the men and the area in front of him. Wend quickly counted seven men besides the militia captain.

Stewart looked over at the wreck of Charlie Sawak's cart, then at the weapons in the hands of the men. After taking all that in, a sneer slowly spread over his face. But he nodded to Carnahan and touched his hat in a nominal show of respect. "Afternoon, Reverend. Hadn't expected to see you in these parts."

Paul Carnahan acknowledged Stewart with a nod. "Nor had we expected to see, you, Lazarus. Word I had was you were on your way to the Great Island."

"Indeed we were. We was on the trail of that renegade Charlie Sawak. But we got a few miles north of here and realized we weren't seein' anymore traces of cart wheel tracks. Nothin' but hooves from riders. So we got to thinkin' that maybe that sneaky Conestoga had gone into hidin' or had decided to ford the river. So we doubled back, searchin' for any sign of him leaving the road that we hadn't picked up before. And then we saw where your horses turned off into the bush and followed your trail down here."

Carnahan waved toward the wreckage of the cart. "Looks to me like the Conestoga has crossed the river. Probably yesterday afternoon. He's likely half way to Aughwick already and there's no catching him. So it seems your self-appointed mission is over, Lazarus."

"That it does, Reverend: A sad development. And now that he's got away, I got one question which is really bothering me. What are all you Sherman Valley men doin' up here? This doesn't look like the road to Sherman Mill." He smiled slyly. "Unless of course, you was plannin' to ford the river here yourself. But I wouldn't think that likely, with a nice, dry ferry available just down the road at Harris'."

There was a round of giggles and outright laughter from Stewart's men.

Stewart swung his glance around at the five of them as they stood in on the ground in front of him. "You know, the word is out in Paxton about how you all were down in Lancaster, providing comfort to those back-stabbing Conestogas. It don't take much to think maybe you all are in cahoots with Sawak. I don't like to say it, Reverend, but maybe you came up here to protect him and help him get across. And that puts you square against us and the people of Paxton. I'd hate to think that was the case—you not being grateful after all the time we've spent in Sherman Valley to help protect you against war parties."

Carnahan stared silently at Stewart. Wend looked over at the reverend, and saw a fierce expression on his face that he had never seen before, not once in the years he had lived with the man. Clearly he was suppressing a rage which threatened to overwhelm his control. Then the reverend began to open his mouth, forming an answer to Stewart.

But Wend, nursing anger of his own, beat him to it. "The fact is, Stewart, there's no reason we shouldn't have been helping Charlie. He's done nothing wrong. No magistrate has charges on him. And the Conestogas are supposed to be under the protection of the colonial government, by provisions of a treaty. You and your men are the ones who are doing something outside the law."

"Outside the law? You're out of your damn mind, Eckert. This Conestoga deserves to be dealt with just like the rest of his village. Like I told you last night, he's been seen talkin' with war parties. He's an enemy of every peaceful settler on both sides of the Susquehanna."

"You say that, Stewart, based on rumors from some nameless traders. You don't have any real evidence."

Stewart smiled broadly. "Nameless traders? No real evidence? Well, Eckert, meet Mr. Reilly. Mr. Shane Reilly, to be exact. He's not only a merchant and trader, but he'll tell you right now that he's personally seen your friend Sawak cavorting with Delaware and Shawnees." Lazarus waved a hand in the direction of a man behind him.

Wend looked at the man and his heart skipped a beat. Sitting his horse just behind Lazarus was a man in a green jacket and a floppy hat. And the hat covered flaming red hair of a color Wend had last seen at an illegal trading camp beside the Allegheny River, just six weeks ago. He had only seen that man for a few seconds, and that at a distance of more than eighty yards. But he instinctively felt certain that he was looking at the trader who had fled his shots in a canoe and who was a member of Richard Grenough's outlaw trading ring.

Reilly smiled down at Wend. "That's right. I'm a trader, doing business with both Indians and settlers on the border, or at least I was until this uprising broke out. But that's all over for now; I've been turned into a peddler to the settlers back here along the Susquehanna. But last summer, I was traveling up by the Great Island and I spied this Sawak fellow with a bunch of Delawares. I hid quiet-like in the bush and they never knew I was there. They came right by me, and crossed over to the island, setting up camp and starting a fire. They thought they were all alone, but I was able to spy on them for quite a while. And the Conestoga Sawak was thick as thieves with them, I can tell you that!" He looked around at the Paxton men. "I saw him taking gunpowder kegs out of that cart of his and giving it to the Delawares."

Stewart smirked at Wend. "So, Eckert, we know your good friend has been dealin' out information which hostile warriors used to plan their descent on the settlements and attack innocent white people. And giving them provisions and war supplies. There ain't no doubt in my mind he's guilty." He looked around at all the watchers. "And now you are just as guilty of protecting him in his attempt to get away. You care more about this double-dealing Conestoga than you do about your own people! Now that he's gotten away, I'll wager he'll be back in the spring with a war party to help attack the settlements!"

Wend felt rage sweep over him. "Stewart, you're making wild assertions about Charlie and about me. And you've been using your office in the militia to commit the murder of innocent people just because of the hatred you bear for all Indians. Come down off that horse and say those things to my face and I'll give you some of the same kind of treatment you doled out at Conestoga Town and the Lancaster workhouse!"

Lazarus tilted his head back and laughed out loud at Wend. "You're right, Eckert. It's about time you and I had it out." Stewart handed his rifle to Reilly and quickly swung down off his horse.

But as soon as he saw Stewart start to descend, Wend took a quick step forward and pulled his pistol from his belt. Stewart had just reached the ground and was turning toward him when Wend whipped the iron barrel of the pistol right across the captain's mouth with every bit of strength in his arm.

Stewart crumpled to his knees, stunned by the blow. Blood oozed from his mouth. Wend raised his pistol, ready strike again if Lazarus tried to get up and lash out at him. Then he reached down, pulled the man's pistol from his belt and tossed it into the bushes.

Lazarus shook his head, then reached up and wiped some of the blood off his lips. He turned and spit out a tooth. Then he said through clenched teeth, "You underhanded bastard, that weren't fair. You knew you couldn't take me in a fair fight."

Wend took a step back and lowered his pistol. "Lazarus, you're right. You'd probably whip me in a brawl. But I spent the last seven months marching with real soldiers and fighting real warriors in battle. The first thing I learned was that there isn't any such thing as a fair fight in war or anywhere else. There's just winning and losing. And what I just did is deal out a little of what you gave the Conestogas."

Wend took another step backward. He looked around and was thankful to see that his friends had casually raised their rifles so that they covered the closely bunched squad of militiamen. But it wasn't really necessary, for Stewart's men were just sitting still on their mounts, looking down at their leader with expressions of shock, but not making any moves to support him.

And Donegal had pulled out his broadsword and stepped close to Stewart, clearly ready to use the blade if the militiaman made any move on Wend.

Stewart slowly reached up, grabbed the stirrup of his saddle and used it to help pull himself to his feet. Wend could see that blood was smeared on his face and had spattered all over his linen hunting shirt.

Lazarus picked up his hat, spat again, then mounted his horse. From the saddle he looked down at Wend. "You attacked me, Eckert. That's assault under the law. When we get back to Paxton, I'm going to the magistrate. You're going to be a wanted man by the end of today. Mark my words; I'm going to make sure that you get arrested when you go back through the village. And far as I know, you're still a corporal in the militia. A corporal who struck his superior officer, a captain. Since the militia has been made official by the colonial assembly, you just committed insubordination. So you're going to be up on military charges as well."

Then Carnahan spoke out in a loud voice. "Not so fast, Stewart. Before you go around making charges down in Paxton, you better go see Reverend Elder. I spent some time with him yesterday evening. And he had just got a letter direct from the governor of the colony. Governor John Penn himself. I wasn't going to say anything about it, I figured to let Elder tell you in private. But here's the long and the short of it: The governor is mortified about what happened to the Conestogas. And he plans to take action about it. Fact is, he has already started. He's relieved John Elder of his role as colonel of the Paxton militia because he let things get out of hand. And he's stripped you of your captaincy. You aren't to have anything more to do with the militia. Asher Clayton has been promoted to major and is to be in charge of all the Paxton militia."

Stewart's face wrinkled up in disbelief. "That's crazy. I don't believe you."

"Like I said, Lazarus, go talk to John Elder—then you'll believe me." Carnahan looked around at all the men. "And I can tell you something else. When we get back to Sherman Mill, I'm going to do everything I can to pull the Sherman Valley company out of the Paxton militia. We'll stand on our own feet from here on."

Stewart and his men sat their horses in silence, digesting the information. Then Carnahan spoke out again. "And Lazarus, instead of making charges against young Eckert here, you better spend your time figuring out how you are going to answer questions about your part in the raids down in Lancaster. So I suggest you and your men ride back to Paxton and tend to your own business."

One of the militia men said quietly, "Come on, Lazarus, let's get back to town and find out what's going on. I'll tell you I don't want no trouble with the colonial government." All of the mounted men except for Stewart and Reilly turned their horses and headed back toward the road.

Stewart gritted his teeth and stared at Reverend Carnahan for a minute, then shifted his gaze to Wend. But in the end he said no more and followed in the wake of his men.

Reilly turned his mount to follow Stewart. But Wend ran over beside the red-headed man's horse. He reached up and grabbed hold of the bridal.

"Hey, what are you doing?"

Wend smiled up at the man. "We've done some business before, Reilly, haven't we?"

Reilly looked down at Wend. "What do you mean, Eckert? I ain't never seen you before. Let me go!"

"Not before I refresh your memory." Wend looked up into the man's eyes. "We did a piece of business out on the Allegheny, back in November. Business with lead balls at a distance of about a hundred yards. And the last I saw you, you were paddling up the river in a canoe, fast as you could."

Reilly's eyes opened wide, nearly bugging out of his face as the memory of that day surged through him. And Wend saw something else in his eyes: Abject fear.

"You're crazy, Eckert. I've never seen you before. And I ain't been out to the Ohio Country since before the uprising started."

Wend felt gratification and smiled up at the trader as broadly as he could manage. "That's bullshit, Reilly; I'm promising you that we're going to finish that business, sooner rather than later. Just remember what happened to Kinnear and Flemming, and keep looking over your shoulder, Reilly." Then he released his hold on the bridle and smacked the horse's flank as hard as he could. The animal trotted off after the others.

Wend turned and walked back toward his friends.

Joshua stood with his rifle grounded in front of him, smiling mischievously. "Hey Wend, if all the fun is over now, can we get started back to Harris? Pushing the pace, we might just make the last ferry this evening and I can be enjoying Alice Downey's charms tomorrow night!"

Simon Donegal looked at Joshua. "Speaking of women, does that widow of yours have any female friends who might want to share their charms with a handsome highland gentleman?"

Baird winked at Carnahan, and replied, "Handsome highland gentleman? Do you know any, Donegal?"

When they finished laughing, the five men turned to their horses to lead the animals down to the edge of the river to water them for the trip back to Harris' Ferry.

Carnahan put his hand on Wend's arm, pulled him aside, and said quietly so only the two could hear, "I thought you'd want to know this: Last night when I talked to Reverend Elder, I asked him your questions about his actions in regard to trying to prevent the Paxton Boys from attacking the Conestoga—why he left the village when things were so unsettled and why he missed them on the road between Lancaster and Harris' Ferry."

Wend asked, "So what was his explanation?"

"To tell you the truth, Wend, he couldn't give me a rational response; he simply mumbled a few words and then changed the subject. I didn't pursue it beyond that. But it is clear that he didn't want to answer the questions." Paul hesitated a moment, then continued, "That's when I decided that we must pull our militia company out of the Paxton organization. Sherman Valley must shed itself of any taint of being associated with the Paxton Boys."

Wend thought a moment. "Obviously the Governor had similar questions; that's why he removed Elder from control of the militia."

Paul Carnahan looked at Wend for a moment, sorrow in his eyes; then he simply nodded and led his horse to the river.

As Wend stood beside the mare at the river's edge, holding her reins and stroking her neck as she took her fill, he looked out across the rocky, treacherous Susquehanna to the far bank and the western territory beyond. Charlie and Rose were out there somewhere under the gray, overcast sky, pushing hard for the Ohio Country. Wend shivered in the winter chill and was suddenly filled with a thrill of admiration for his friend. He thought, *Charlie, you devil! You did it! Against all odds, you've made a clean escape, saved the tribal bloodline, and snatched away your girl, all at the same time. In their own heaven, the spirits of the long line of Conestoga elders and chiefs are looking down and smiling at you with pride.*

CHAPTER FOUR

Carlisle

"For God's sake, Joshua, it's been near seven months since you marched away with Bouquet and his little army! Now you turn up here unannounced with four other men?"

The Widow Downey was having her fun with Baird. She stood in her doorway with one hand on the door frame and the other in her hip. Her legs were spread akimbo, her hips cocked to one side, giving her an undeniably provocative profile as she confronted her man. "Seven months it's been! Most of the soldiers and waggoners from the expedition were back here in October. But I didn't even get a letter or a word passed from some friend of yours, not the whole time. You realize that it's coming on the second week in January now?"

Baird was standing on the doorstep of Alice's house, his blanket roll and saddlebags slung over one shoulder and his rifle in his other hand. Wend and the others sat their horses at the edge of the dirt street, enjoying the confrontation in the growing gloom of evening. They had crossed the Susquehanna at Harris' Ferry on the first boat that morning and pushed their mounts to cover the twenty miles to Carlisle by dusk.

The widow looked past Baird, an ironic smile on her face, and sent Wend a quick wink. Then she turned and addressed Baird again. "Now, you scoundrel, I'll wager you have the gall expect me to put up the five of you with all your gear." She stamped her foot in mock anger. "How do you know I'm not full up with boarders already? Don't you know that a woman has to earn a living?"

Reverend Carnahan spoke up. "Excuse me, my good lady: Not the five of us—Franklin here and I are going down to Washburn's Tavern."

Meanwhile, Donegal, on his horse alongside Wend, leaned over and whispered, "The lass does have a bonnie set of tits, doesn't she? And you can see the legs are long and shapely, even under that skirt."

Wend smiled and nodded to the highlander.

Joshua hunched his shoulders and cocked his head slightly as he weathered the widow's verbal volley. "Come on, Alice. You know'd I'd have been back long ago if there was any way."

He paused to marshal his thoughts, then continued, "I was in the hospital for weeks, healin' from an arrow in my hip, and then Bouquet sent us on a mission to the Ohio Country that didn't end until almost December. I came back as soon as I could!"

"You were wounded?" A hint of concern crossed the widow's face, but then she quickly hid it with a return to the countenance of mock anger which she had been displaying.

"That's the Lord's truth, Alice: I took a Shawnee arrow in my hip at Bushy Run. I'll show you the scar tonight."

"Oh, you will, will you?" The widow shook her head, "I can hardly wait." Then she looked inquisitively up at Donegal. "Who is this man with you wearing the bonnet—did you capture one of those wild highlanders?"

Joshua smiled and nodded. "That's the truth of it, Alice; but we've tamed him and taught him his manners. We're trying him out today without his leash to see if he behaves."

Donegal ignored Baird's jibe. "Ma'am, I'm Simon Donegal, late corporal of His Majesty's 77th Highlanders. Now, of course, I am a person of property with land granted by His Majesty himself in light of my distinguished service." He took the bonnet off and nodded to the widow. "It's a pleasure to meet a fine, bonnie woman like yourself, ma'am."

The widow smiled and nodded her appreciation of Donegal's complement. Then she looked back at Joshua. "Maybe you could take lessons from this highland gentleman. I'll wager he wouldn't have let his woman languish without even a letter for all that time."

Donegal nodded, and gave the widow another visual inspection. "That's the truth of it."

Joshua just shook his head and started to plead, "Alice, for God's sake, please…"

But the widow, having milked Joshua's discomfort to her satisfaction, now relented before Baird could finish. "All right, the three of you: It turns out that I do have room for you. Joshua, you know very well where to put your kit. Wend, you and Mr. Donegal will share the front room at the top of the stairs." Then she thought for a moment and a wry smile came over her face. "And I damn well want you all scrubbed clean before you start lounging around my downstairs rooms or crawl into one of my beds."

* * *

After depositing their gear at the widow's, Wend and Donegal led the horses down to the stable at Washburn's Tavern. A stable boy, whom Wend knew from previous visits, helped them bed down and feed the animals. The mare, always spirited, was excited by the many other horses present in the stable and, despite the day's long trip, pranced as Wend led her into the stable and guided her into a stall. Then she tossed her head and leaned across the partition and whinnied at a tall bay stallion in the next stall.

Wend stroked her neck, and said, "Come on girl, stop showing off and eat your oats." The mare nuzzled him and then concentrated on her feed.

With the horses secured, the two men walked across the tavern's courtyard and pushed through the door of the main building into the common room for a drink. Wend wanted to greet George Washburn, the proprietor, who had been a friend of his father and whom he had first met in 1759, just before his family had been killed. The room was well lit by candles and a large fire crackled in the hearth. Wend was a little surprised at the paucity of patrons at the dinner hour. He led Donegal up to the counter and waved to the proprietor, who had just come out of the kitchen. Washburn waved and hurried down to where the two men stood.

"Hello, Wend. I see you finally made it back. And indeed, as good as new." He smiled briefly. "I was talking just a few weeks ago with Captain Robertson of the 77th Highlanders, who told me about your service with Bouquet's expedition. Seems you've done well, lad."

Wend said, "Thanks for the kind words, George." Then he introduced the burley proprietor to Donegal and ordered ale for both of them.

Then Wend pointed to a pair of pegs on the wall, which were just above a plaque with brass lettering which proclaimed, *Wend Eckert, Gunsmith.* "George, it's been seven months since we marched out with Bouquet, and now it is way past time for me to get back to my trade."

The tavern keeper nodded vigorously. "That it is—I'll be able to sell a firelock from you as soon as you can get one down here. Everybody expects more war party raids as soon as the snow thaws in April or May."

Donegal pointed up at the pegs and plaque on the wall and asked, "So, does Mr. Washburn here sell guns for you?"

"Yes, George does and so do several other tavern keepers here in Carlisle, Paxton, and in other places in the Cumberland Valley. They display my rifles and take a small commission for every sale. I'd never make enough money just building guns for the people of Sherman Valley itself."

Washburn laughed. "You'd be surprised at how appealing one of his firelocks, the wood oiled and gleaming, the barrel and the brass all shined up, can look to a man who has had a few drinks. It almost has the allure of a woman—it arouses his desires and a man finds it easy to convince himself that he must have a new rifle." The tavern keeper beamed at Wend. "And the truth is, there's no better name in gunsmithing on either side of the Susquehanna than Eckert. Johann Eckert started the tradition and his son, here, has done nothing but enhance it."

Wend waved his hand around the nearly empty common room. "I've never seen the place so empty at the dinner hour like this, George."

Washburn shrugged his shoulder. "Oh, no doubt it will fill up shortly. Most everybody's gone down to the meeting at the square."

Donegal asked, "What meeting would that be?"

Washburn looked between Donegal and Wend, a puzzled look on his face. "I guess you two haven't heard—you've just rode into town." He motioned at Wend. "Your friend Matt Bratton and some friends of his are here recruiting for men to ride with the Paxton Rangers to attack the Moravian Indians, just like they did to the Conestogas in Lancaster, and then march on Philadelphia."

Wend asked, "March on Philadelphia, what's the purpose of that?"

"I don't know much about it, but what I gather is, the Ulster people want to petition for the colony to spend more to defend the settlement area, and they want more say in the government." Washburn shrugged his shoulders. "I confess that I haven't paid much attention, but that's what I've been able to pick up just from talk here in the tavern."

Wend downed his ale. "Come on, Donegal. Let's go down to the square and see what this is all about."

"Now, lad, must we? I'm ready for another ale, after all the riding we been doing. Let's stay here where it's warm and snug."

Wend pulled on his coat. "Suit yourself, Simon. But I'm going to the square; I want to see who is talking at this meeting besides Bratton, and how well it is attended." He nodded to Washburn and headed for the door.

Donegal rolled his eyes. "All right, all right, wait a second. I'm coming, but you'll have to buy me a bit of rum or whiskey later to shake the chill we're sure to get."

As they walked to the door, Washburn shouted after them, "Wend, you make haste to get a rifle down to me as soon as you can—I'm getting inquiries all the time! I tell you, I can sell it at a premium!"

* * *

"Dammit, Wend! That's 'na other than the man who smashed me in the head at the workhouse in Lancaster. He's one of the mob what chopped up the Conestogas!" Donegal stood in rage looking up at the man who had mounted a flatbed wagon parked near the Carlisle square. Around them was a substantial crowd of perhaps 100 raucous men and young boys. Although the evening light was fading, many in the crowd had brought torches and two more had been stuck in the ground next to the wagon to illuminate the improvised stage. The audience was held in rapt attention by the speaker and frequently shouted encouragement or clapped loudly after he made each point. Beside the wagon stood Matt Bratton and another man who Wend had never seen before.

Wend looked up at the speaker, who had taken off his hat. He was startled to see that the man had totally white hair. Immediately he realized that he was undoubtedly looking at the trader Frank McKenzie had identified as Gray Mathews. That meant that the one who stood beside Bratton was Hugh Crowley. Wend thought: *So this is the important business that led to Bratton hurrying to Carlisle and leaving McKenzie to his own devices—stirring up a mob of men to ride with the Paxton Rangers.*

And as Wend listened, it was clear that Gray Mathews was making a convincing job of it. The man was accusing the Moravian Indians of the same treachery that had been attributed to the Conestogas by Stewart and Reilly on the other side of the Susquehanna. He spoke of Moravians meeting with war parties, evidence that the Moravians had spied for the hostiles, and even of having seen them traveling with war parties to lead them to villages or farmsteads that were unprotected. Then, having worked the crowd up, he shifted to talk of the forthcoming march on the Moravians and Philadelphia.

"It's time we strike back. And we need to do it now! You can bet the Ohio Country tribes are getting organized for war parties in the spring. If we destroy the Moravians, we'll at least eliminate one source of their support! A lot of good men, just like yourselves, are joining us. For your sake, for your family, and for your property, you must join this march!"

There was a round of cheers and a few shouts of agreement. Someone called from the back of the crowd, "You got it right, Mathews!"

Mathews waved a hand in the direction of the shouters, then continued his spiel. "And after we take care of the Moravians we're going to ride on Philadelphia itself. We'll confront those fat Quakers and English who sit there secure in their big city without a thought what it's like to live out here on the border. They ain't under fear of the war parties. They don't got to worry about their wives and children getting' killed or carried off. They ain't ever seen a field of their wheat, ready for harvest, going up in smoke! They don't have to give no thought to savages burnin' down their property that they built with their sweat and their own two hands!"

A voice was raised from the crowd. Wend couldn't see who was speaking. "So you ride into Philadelphia. And just what are you going to do when you get there? Start shooting? Break into the assembly hall and spank all those Quakers on their behinds?"

There was a wave of laughter through the crowd.

Mathews looked in the direction of the voice, an expression of exasperation on his face. "We got that all thought out. We'll present the governor and the assembly with a list of our demands. If there are a thousand of us, like we plan, all those smug city men will have to listen. They'll have to vote money to raise troops to defend the border like back in '56. And they'll have to help us get all these so-called peaceful Indians out of the settled part of the colony. And they'll be forced to give us more voice in the assembly so they can't just forget about us out here." He paused and smiled as he looked out on the crowd. "They won't have much choice but pay attention to us when they're looking at the barrels of a thousand loaded firelocks!"

There was a chorus of cheers and voices agreeing with Mathews. A young man near Wend called out, "When do we march?"

Mathews pointed at the man. "That's a good question you asked. And here's the answer: Ten days from now! The beginning of the last week in January." He paused a moment. "All of you gather your kit and your firelock. Make sure you got all the powder and lead you can get your hands on and as many days provisions as you can carry. Don't ride anything but a strong horse. We'll be travelin' fast and covering a lot of ground!"

Matt Bratton spoke up from his place beside the wagon. "Listen sharp! We need a good turn-out from over here on the western side of the Susquehanna. The Paxton Men are counting on us to support them and finish what has been started. Let's show them that the men of Cumberland Valley have stout hearts!"

Mathews spoke again from the wagon. "Talk to your friends. Convince them to come with us. And meet us, ready to travel, at dawn ten days from now at Ezra Callaway's pasture, right at the eastern side of town, on the road to Harris' Ferry!" He pointed to the eastward. "We'll ride to Harris' and join up with the Paxton Men there. Then we'll ride down to Lancaster an' meet up with the men coming from Shippensburg and York and the Conococheague country. After that, the whole lot of us, a thousand strong, will head for the Moravian villages and Philadelphia itself!"

There was a murmur of agreement around the crowd, and Wend heard a few calls of "I'm with you!" Then Mathews climbed down from the wagon and the gathered men began to disperse.

Donegal started to walk up toward where Bratton, Mathews, and Crowley stood talking with some of the onlookers. Wend grabbed the highlander's arm. "Where are you going, Simon?"

"Why, lad, I'm going to give that bastard Mathews some of what he gave me over in Lancaster. Just like I promised. After I get done, his head will be hurtin' so much he'll wish I had just taken it off with my broadsword and saved him all the pain." He patted his hip, where the sheath containing his dagger rode. "Come to think of it, I might just do that with this wee knife and make it hurt the asshole even more as I slice at his neck."

Wend grabbed Donegal's arm and held him back. "Simon, this isn't the time for getting even."

"And why not? There's that gray-headed bastard standin' right in front of me!"

Wend smiled at his friend and spoke in a calm voice intended to soothe the Scotsman. "Look at all the men around here. They'll pull you off Mathews as soon as you get started." Then he pointed at a man standing off to the side, his arms folded across his chest, quietly watching the crowd disperse. "But the main reason, Simon, that you don't want to attack Mathews now is because of that man right over there."

"And what has that gentleman have to do with anything?"

Wend winked at Donegal. "That gentleman happens to be John Dunning, High Sheriff of Cumberland County."

Donegal made a face. "That's the sheriff of the whole county?"

"Yes, and his jail is just off the square. You rearrange Mathews face or put a hole in him and that's where you'll be spending a lot of days. Dunning will take a man up to the magistrate in a heartbeat."

Donegal wrinkled up his face. "That's 'na very understanding: Locking up a man for merely settling a personal score."

Wend patted Donegal on the shoulder. "And he won't be giving you any hot rum in the evenings while your sitting in one of his cells."

Donegal smiled and asked, "No hot rum?" He shook his head. "The man's an absolute barbarian." Then the highlander pointed in the direction of the sheriff and said, "Don't look now, but he's coming toward us."

Dunning waved to Wend. "Eckert, I heard that you and Baird had just got back from Fort Pitt." He extended a hand to Wend. "Glad to see you again." Then he looked over at Donegal. "Your friend here looks suspiciously like one of Bouquet's highlanders."

Wend said, "You're right, Sheriff. This is Simon Donegal, just mustered out of the 77th Highlanders. He'll be staying with us up in Sherman Mill for a while."

Dunning nodded. "Oh yes. I guess you took your discharge here in the colony. As a matter of fact, we had the remnants of the 77th come through here a few weeks ago on their way east. I had ale with Captain Robertson down in Washburn's." He smiled. "His men were certainly ready to have a good time when they got here; this was the first real town they had seen in six months and the first place they had to spend their pay from the campaign." He laughed out loud. "Several of them spent their first night here in my jail instead of down at the encampment. I particularly remember a drummer— name of McKirdy—who broke up a tavern down on the west side over some girl. A huge sergeant, named McCulloch, came down and bailed them all out. I went easy with all of them, and dropped charges, seeing where they had been all this time and how they fought at Bushy Run."

Wend and Simon looked at each other and broke into spontaneous grins.

Donegal said, "Donald McKirdy is a great one for having a good, loud time of it when he's feelin' his liquor and there are women about." He put his hand on Wend's shoulder. "Eckert here knows all about McKirdy. Happens that he had to fight him over a girl out at Fort Ligonier just before the battle with the tribes at Bushy Run."

Dunning gave Wend a surprised look. "I never heard of you doin' much fightin' or being one for the women, Eckert. Fact is, you always been known as going out of your way to avoid brawls."

Wend laughed, "You pick up a lot of new habits when you spend time with the army." Then he changed the subject. "Are you here to watch the meeting?"

"That I was, Eckert. Colonel Armstrong has been commissioned back into the Pennsylvania Regiment by the Governor to run the militia west of the Susquehanna, and I've been helpin' him. He wants to send a warning letter about all this unrest back to Philadelphia, so he asked me to watch this assembly and see if these people are really serious."

Wend asked, "Do you really think they'll march on the Moravians and Philadelphia?"

Dunning shrugged his shoulders. "Hard to tell. I think some of them will. But I got a feelin' that a lot of them, for all the big talk, won't show up when it comes time to ride out." He thought a moment. "But it won't be the fault of your friend Matt Bratton and the men with him. They've been goin' from tavern to tavern, workin' hard to recruit every man they can."

Donegal looked over at where Bratton and his comrades still stood talking. "We was over in Lancaster when those Paxton Men hit the Conestogas and then we went to Harris' Ferry and Paxton on the way here. I'll not lie to you Sheriff; them Paxton people are dead serious about killin' the Moravians and takin' on the Quakers in Philadelphia. If the people here are as upset, I'd 'na be surprised if more men than you expected decided to join that march."

Dunning stood deep in thought for a moment. "You may be right, Scotsman. I am going to keep a very sharp watch on all this." Then he looked at Wend. "Say, I heard that you and Baird and Reverend Carnahan were over there helping the Conestogas. Is that true?"

Wend nodded. "Yes, we were. I used to live near Conestoga Town, and one of my best friends was Charlie Sawak, who used to come through here selling craft goods all the time."

"Yes, I know about Sawak. I've seen him and his cart here in town often enough." Dunning paused, considering his words. "You want to watch out for yourself, Wend. There are people, particularly like Bratton, who weren't too happy with you for marching off with the British instead of staying to help defend Sherman Valley with the militia. And now word's got around that you were cozy with the Conestogas. That has made other people suspicious of you 'cause you're a Dutchman from Lancaster."

Wend felt a flash of anger. "Sheriff, I've been living with the Ulster-Scots for near five years. I feel like I was born to it. I even talk like the Ulster now. When are people here going to accept me as one of them?"

"Calm down, lad. There are plenty of people who admire you and your work: Men who were with Bouquet talk about how well you scouted for him and that you were in the thick of the battle. And everyone in Cumberland

and Sherman Valley knows there ain't no better rifles to be had than yours. I'm hopin' all this unrest will die down soon, particularly if we don't have too many Indian attacks next summer." He looked around and saw that the crowd of men had dispersed and that Bratton and his friends had also walked off. "Well, I got to get along to see Colonel Armstrong and let him know what went on here tonight."

Wend said, "Good evening, Sheriff. Donegal here and I are on our way to Larkin's Tavern for supper and a few drinks."

Dunning grinned broadly at them. "Larkin's, you say? Now that's a rowdy place! Well, have a good time, but make sure that you don't have reason to see me on business later tonight!" He laughed, and strode off along Market Street toward Armstrong's house.

* * *

Larkin's Tavern, located across the street and a few doors down from the Widow Downey's house, was a food and drink tavern. It served tradesmen during the day and was a popular rendezvous at night for the younger set in Carlisle. It featured cheaper fare than larger taverns like Washburn's. Wend and Donegal pushed through the door into the smoky, well-lighted common room and took seats at a table near the counter which ran alongside the right side of the room. There was lively music played by a fiddler and several couples danced front of the fireplace.

Tom Larkin waved a greeting to Wend and came out from behind the counter to join them at their table. Wend introduced Donegal to the proprietor.

"I been wondering when you and Baird would be getting back." He laughed. "Them highlanders in the Black Watch and the 77th had a lot to say about what you and he did at the battle. And I heard about what happened to Arnold Spengler. It's a damn shame—he was a good man." He shook his head. "That man sure spent a lot of time here when he was in Carlisle with Colonel Bouquet's staff."

Wend reflected, "Arnold brought me the first time I was ever here. I was only 15, and my family was on the way to Fort Pitt. I remember, Tom, thinking that I had never seen any place like this in Lancaster."

Larkin threw back his head and laughed. "I remember it well! It was an odd pair you two made: Spengler in his uniform and you in those black and gray Dutchman's clothes we don't often see around here. I nearly sent you home, thinkin' you were too young to be here with our night-time crowd. I only let you stay 'cause you was big for your age."

Wend nodded. "That was the night I first saw Matt Bratton. He and Arnold's friend John McCall got into a fight over Mollie Reed. And then he knocked around me and Arnold for trying to stop him from beating on John when he was down and unconscious." Wend thought for a moment, then continued, "Well, that was five years ago and things have changed a lot since then."

Larkin smiled, and then leaned over toward Wend and Donegal. "Time has passed, but some things haven't changed much. Bratton is still seeing Molly when he visits the town."

Wend nodded, "Well, I've seen him romancing young girls here and in other places. But I'm surprised he's still involved with Molly. I thought that a likely looking girl like her would be married by now."

"Who says she isn't?" Larkin smiled knowingly. "She's been married for these three years now, but that ain't stoppin' Bratton or her for that matter. She's married to a peddler, name of Cartwright. She's Molly Reed Cartwright now, but her man's on the road all over the county many days a month. Our Molly ain't got no children and gets easily bored. Word is that Bratton's been seen going into her house at night when she's alone."

Donegal winked at the other two. "Maybe a lusty lass like that would like to try her luck with a handsome highlander who's been deprived of a woman's comfort for many months."

Wend shook his head. "Come on Donegal. With your luck, word would get out and you'd be running from both Molly's husband and Bratton at the same time."

Larkin nodded. "Well, Donegal, you may get your chance with her at that. Bein' married hasn't stopped Molly from coming 'round here now and again when she's feeling 'specially lonely." Then the tavern keeper gave the Scotsman a sly wink. "Of course, if you're in a real hurry to be with a woman after all that time in the Ohio Country, you could go on down to Mrs. McNulty's house at the west end and see one of her girls. Providing, of course, that you got enough of the King's coin to satisfy her tariff."

Donegal smiled. "Now that's an idea. I've spent more than one night playing with bawdy women. But I think that maybe I'll just sit here for a while and see if any of the young ladies in here take to my good looks and friendly ways."

Larkin said, "Well, we do get some girls looking for fun in here. That's always helped my business." As he was speaking, a whiff of cold air swept through the room and Larkin looked over at the door and then glanced at Wend. "Well, speak of the devil, here's your friendly neighbor from Sherman Mill."

Wend looked up and saw that Matt Bratton stood just inside the door, unbuttoning his coat and glancing around the common room. Then his eyes stopped at their table and a look of recognition spread across his face. Bratton smiled slyly and walked over to stand above the three men.

"Well, if it isn't Wend Eckert, the Dutchman; fhe Dutchman of Sherman Valley." Bratton's voice was full of disdain. "I been hearing a lot about you, Dutchman—on both sides of the Susquehanna."

Wend look up at the towering, burly waggoner. "You call me 'Dutchman', Bratton. And that's true. I was born of German stock. But I've been living for five years among you Ulster in Sherman Mill as part of Carnahan's family. So I consider myself Ulster-Scot by up-bringing. That makes me German by birth and Ulster by adoption. And mark this well—I'm equally proud of both of those strains. I wish you'd remember that."

Bratton opened his mouth to speak, but Donegal interrupted. "And I say he's a highlander by the test of battle. Ask any man in the 77th Highlanders; he earned the title at Bushy Run. So think of him as a German by birth, Ulster by adoption and highlander by war. I call that quite a heritage."

Bratton scowled at Donegal for a moment, then looked back at Wend. "Yeah, I heard you made a name for yourself with the army, sure enough." He snickered. "Of course, while you was off scouting for Colonel Bouquet, you deserted your neighbors in Sherman Valley who could have used your help when we was gettin' raided by war parties last summer. Not to mention you are the only one in the valley who knows how to repair firelocks." He took his broad brimmed hat off and leaned over Wend. "And it's all over Paxton how you came straight from Fort Pitt to protect them scheming Conestogas. Not that it helped them much; good men took care of those back-stabbing Indians proper-like and finished them off." He slapped the hat against his leg. "But you showed your true colors—you think more of them Conestogas than you do of your own people."

Wend controlled his anger and looked right into Bratton's eyes. "I wasn't alone helping the Conestogas. Reverend Carnahan and Reverend Elder and Joshua were all there, too. It was the humane thing to do. And the truth is, the Conestogas did nothing to deserve what that mob did to them."

"I'll not banter words with you, Eckert. I don't hold nothin' against Carnahan and Elder; they're men of the Lord, their business is charity. But you and Joshua should have just kept out of it."

Donegal had been sitting quietly listening to Bratton. Now he spoke up again. "Say, Wend—is this the waggoner Matthew Bratton you and Joshua told me about out at Bedford?"

Wend nodded. "The very man, Simon."

Donegal leaned back in his chair and smiled broadly at the burley man. "Say there, Mr. Bratton. My name's Donegal; Simon Donegal, late of the 77th Highlanders. I just want you to know that I was there, too—helping those poor Indians." He picked up his army bonnet from the table and ostentatiously dusted it off with one hand. "And I'm 'na a man of the Lord. Fact is, I spent the last seven years fightin' on the border for His Majesty the King. I fought Cherokees and Shawnees and Delawares and all them tribes who live around the lakes. After all that time, I learned to recognize the difference between warriors lookin to raid settlements and Christian Indians trying to live peaceful like as farmers."

Bratton shrugged his shoulders. "What of it? What's your point?"

"Just this, Bratton: Maybe someday, when you got a little time on your hands, I'll teach you how to tell the difference, so you'll learn how *not* to go out and massacre innocent people."

Bratton glared at the grinning highlander. "I can't wait to hear what you have to say, Scotsman. But I'll warn you, I might just have a little teachin' of my own for you at the same time." He turned back to Wend. "But all this don't make no difference now. Them Conestogas have been wiped out. And we're about to deal out the same justice to those Indians being sheltered by the Moravian ministers."

Wend smiled. "Your information is a little incomplete, Matt. There's at least one Conestoga you didn't manage to get: Charlie Sawak got clean away. Of course, I hear he managed to surprise you and some of your friends before he took his leave."

"Yeah, Dutchman. He hid out and took some shots at us. And he put a ball in Frank McKenzie's leg. But Lazarus Stewart went after him with a squad of men as he headed for the Great Island. I've no doubt they've run him down and finished him by now."

"You're wrong again, Matt. Joshua, Carnahan, Franklin, Donegal here, and I rode up the eastern side of the Susquehanna the day after he ambushed you. We tracked Charlie and found out what happened after you left to come here to Carlisle. Sawak didn't go to the Great Island; he outsmarted Stewart and forded the river. He's on his way to the Ohio Country right now."

For once in his life, Bratton stood quietly at a loss for words. Then he shrugged his shoulders and said, "Well, that's your story. One way or another, our business with the Conestogas is finished."

Wend said, "Yes, but you left some other business unfinished in Paxton, didn't you Matt?"

"Unfinished business? What do you mean by that, Eckert?"

"You left Frank McKenzie with a gunshot leg, alone in a tavern room with no doctor to treat him but some old drunk apothecary. McKenzie works for you and rode with you out of loyalty. That's a fine mess to leave behind while you go off to recruit men for this march on the Moravians."

"Frank will be fine, besides I'll let his Pa know about him when I get back to Sherman Mill in a few days. His old man will take his wagon and go get him."

Wend stared at Bratton. "You knew damn well that he'd lose that leg if you left him untreated for ten days."

Bratton shrugged his shoulders. "So would you expect me to do about it? McKenzie knew he was taking a chance when he rode with us."

"You could have gotten him to a real doctor—down to Lancaster or over here to Carlisle."

Bratton frowned. "What's done is done. Like I said, his family can take care of him. I can't change things now."

Wend stared directly into Bratton's eyes. "That's right, you can't. But you needn't worry about Frank. I've already done what you should have. I arranged for him to be carried over here in a freight wagon. And he's at Doc Highsmith's place right now. It's days late, but he's getting proper care now and if he's lucky he may keep that leg. But no thanks to you, the man who is his boss and who he used to admire. But I expect he's learned a lot about where to place his trust."

Bratton wrinkled up his face. "Now why would you do something like that? Frank ain't no special friend of yours."

Wend smiled broadly. "Because despite what you said about me, I do care about my neighbors in Sherman Valley. Even gullible boys who follow you without knowing what they're getting into."

The big waggoner shook his head. "I ain't got no more time for standing around talkin'." He abruptly walked over to the counter and shouted to the server for ale.

90

Donegal took a sip of his own ale and looked at Wend and Larkin. "Quite the cordial lad, isn't he? I'm beginin' to think life is going to be very interesting up in Sherman Valley."

*　*　*

The next morning, shortly after breakfast, Wend put on the city clothes which he had kept stored at the widow's house during the military campaign and walked eastward along Market Street, the main road through Carlisle. The brown coat and breeches, along with the cream waistcoat—all of which had been made for him by Patricia Carnahan—felt snug and constraining after the loose work clothing and hunting shirt he had warn for so many months. Some distance after passing the square, he came to the apothecary shop which was also the office of physician Charles Highsmith. The shop had large windows in the front so that the morning sunlight brightly illuminated the room and the shelves which lined the walls, holding their shiny glass bottles and ceramic jars.

Wend walked in to find the good doctor himself seated at a desk, bent over some papers, a rapidly moving quill in his hand. He was a lean man well beyond middle age, with thinning hair which was beginning to turn gray. A pair of Doctor Franklin's spectacles rested on his nose. As Wend approached, he could see the physician was involved in some calculations. He looked up from his desk and said, "I shall be with you in just a moment, sir; let me finish my sum before I lose track of all the numbers."

Wend waited quietly as the man murmured under his breath. Then, with long, delicate fingers, he dipped the quill in an inkwell and drew a line under a column of figures and quickly wrote a total underneath. He nodded to himself and then looked up at Eckert.

"Sorry to put you off, young man, but I'm getting together my monthly order of medical supplies from the dealer in Philadelphia. It needs to get into this afternoon's post." He pushed the spectacles up on his forehead and swept an appraising glance over his visitor. "What can I do for you? I must say, you don't look like you need my services."

"I'm here to enquire about Frank McKenzie, who should have arrived here late the day before yesterday in a Conestoga freight wagon. I wanted to find out how he is doing, and where he is staying."

"May I ask what your interest is? Are you a relative?"

"I'm Wend Eckert, a friend from Sherman Valley who also happens to be the one who paid for him to be carried here from Paxton and who will be paying you for his treatment."

The doctor's face brightened. "Ah, well, in that case, you are in just the place where you need to be. Young McKenzie is in one of my back rooms, very comfortably resting in bed."

"Were you able to save his leg, Doctor?"

"He arrived here just in time, Mr. Eckert. I may say that while he will always have a visible scar, a pronounced limp, and some aching of the bone in the cold and damp of winter, he should fully recover and regain at least some use of that leg."

Wend smiled. "I'm glad to hear that, Doctor. I'm sure he will owe his recovery to your good offices."

Highsmith beamed. "It is always gratifying when one is able, through his knowledge and service, to provide a boon to others. Of course, it was also helpful that Mr. McKenzie is otherwise a very healthy young man."

Wend nodded and said, "Indeed, Doctor. Now I'd like to go in and talk privately with Mr. McKenzie for just a few moments. Perhaps while we are talking, you could prepare your bill of particulars for me, and I'll attend to that before I leave."

A look of anticipation and happiness spread across the doctor's face, and he quickly showed Wend through a door in the back of the shop, through a hallway, and finally into a small room. Frank lay in a narrow bed with a view of the back yard and stable.

When they were alone, Wend said, "Frank, the doctor says you are going to be able to go home in a few days. I'm riding to Sherman Mill today and I'll get the word to your Pa as soon as I get back. So he'll be here to pick you up soon."

McKenzie pulled himself to a sitting position against the back of the bed. "Wend, you sure kept your word. I'll always be indebted to you."

"I'm just happy you will be all right, Frank. But right now I need some more information from you."

"But Wend, I already told you everything you wanted to know, over in Paxton. There ain't no more to tell."

"Frank, you spent over a week with Bratton and his two friends—Mathews and Crowley. They had to do plenty of talking between themselves while you were with them. Search your brain and try to remember the conversations. I want to know if there was anything you overheard while they were talking that puzzled you."

McKenzie wrinkled up his face. "Well, they were always talking about the Paxton Rangers going after the Moravian villages. Sort of planning on where they would get more men or what they would do after they finished off the Indians. They talked about how they would scare the people in Philadelphia." He shrugged. "Other than that, it was just jokin' and talkin' round the fire at night. We didn't say much during the day 'cause we was ridin' hard."

Wend stared out the back window. In the doctor's yard, a chubby woman, whom he assumed was the lady of the house, was spreading chicken feed on the ground. Several hens and a rooster scrambled to peck at the feed. As he watched, he thought of a question to spur McKenzie's memory.

"Frank, you told me they seemed like old friends with Matt; that they were waiting for you and Bratton here at Larkin's Tavern when you came down from Sherman Mill." He turned back toward the bed and asked, "Did they ever say anything about working together on some other venture beside this Paxton business?"

The boy's eyebrows furrowed and he looked into the distance. Then his eyes seemed to come into focus. "You know, Wend, now I do remember something. A couple of times, when I wasn't right with them, but could hear parts of their talk, one or another of them said something about what they just called 'the next job' or sometimes 'the next trip'. It was like they were going to do something together, but didn't want to explain about it to me." He shrugged his shoulders. "That's all. I guess it don't mean much, but that's all I heard."

Wend thought a moment. "You sure they weren't talking about this march on the Moravians?"

"No Wend. The talked about that right in front of me all the time. I just got the impression this 'next trip' was separate and they didn't think it was any of my business."

Wend crossed his arms and looked out the window again. Based on Frank's words, he was sure now that Mathews and Crowley were part of Grenough's illegal trading ring, just like Matt Bratton. Wend's investigations had already uncovered evidence that Bratton had the job of transporting gunpowder, lead, and other war supplies from Grenough's warehouses at York and Shippensburg through the settled parts of the border country in his large Conestoga wagon. The wagon would attract little attention in areas where there were good roads and lots of other wagons traveling. Then, somewhere in a covert location, he would rendezvous with traders like Mathews and Crowley, where the goods would be transferred to pack horses to be taken along back country trails to meet with war parties. Clearly, the talk of a "next trip" referred to an upcoming trading operation, probably early in the spring to supply the first wave of war parties coming from the Ohio Country.

Wend thought about the pledge he had made over his father's grave to uncover and destroy Grenough's operation. It was time to begin acting on that pledge and exact vengeance on the man, and his underlings, who had caused the death of his family. But where to start? Then it occurred to him: *I need to go to the source—and that had to be Grenough's warehouses.* That meant he had to find a reason to travel to York and Shippensburg and confirm that they were the headquarters of a vast outlaw conspiracy.

Wend bid farewell to McKenzie, again assuring him that he would get word of his condition to his father, and went back to the apothecary shop to pay the doctor's bill. Then, with much on his mind, he hurried back to Alice Downey's house to pack his belongings for the trip home to Sherman Mill.

Part II

Riders in the Winter

February – March 1764

CHAPTER FIVE

Winter in Sherman Mill

"I tell you this whole thing is indecent! Indecent, do you hear me? My own sister is putting me on display in front of everybody in the house." Joshua Baird was standing in the middle of the Carnahan's great room, stripped down to his long underwear. Patricia Baird Carnahan was kneeling behind her brother, a hand on each of his hips, examining the effect of his arrow wound. Reverend Carnahan stood leaning against the doorway, a twinkle in his eye and a pipe in his hand. Wend and Donegal sat in chairs beside the hearth, watching the show with amusement at Baird's discomfort.

Wend couldn't resist saying, "Not everyone, Joshua—the two Donaldson children are out in the barn playing."

Patricia tapped her brother on his side and responded, "Nonsense, Brother. There's no indecency here. I've seen you stark naked or washing in a wooden tub more times than I can count. And don't tell me every one of these men ain't seen you the same way often enough out on the trail." She continued her inspection and then said, "I can feel a difference between your left side and your right, Joshua. The left hip has been distorted by the arrow. Or maybe it got messed up when the surgeon took out the head. I'll wager he wasn't working under the best of conditions."

"Listen, Doc Monroe is a good surgeon. I don't doubt he fixed me up right."

Patricia shook her head. "Don't matter how good a Doc he is; sometimes there's a limit to what can be done. The truth is, you got permanent damage there, Joshua."

Baird sighed. "Come on Patricia, it's just taking a long time to heal. Come spring, things will be fine again. I'll just take my ease over the winter here. You'll see."

"Raise your right leg, Joshua."

Baird easily raised it high.

"Now do the same with the left."

He was able to lift the leg only about half as high and the attempt caused signs of strain to come over his face.

Patricia tapped her brother's left hip and shook her head. "You're dreaming, Joshua Baird. You remember on the day you left to go with Bouquet I told you that the Lord would take care of a scoundrel like you in his own way and time? Well, this is his way of telling you it's time to settle down. You aren't going to be walking the trails for the army or going on long hunts any more; this leg won't support it." She paused, thinking for a moment. "I'll bet you can't even run very well now. You'd be easy pickings either for a warrior or a mother bear defending her cubs." She stood up and looked him over. "So now you got to think about how you're going to get along living like the rest of us."

With Patricia standing next to him, no one could have missed that she was Baird's sister. She had his lean, rangy body and was actually taller than him by at least an inch. Her brown hair was an exact color match for his, and she had the same narrow, chiseled face.

Joshua started to put on his clothes, grabbing his breaches from the floor and pulling them over his legs. "You're all against me. Ever since we left Fort Pitt, Wend here has been treatin' me like an old man, tryin' to put me into a rocking chair. Now my own sister makes me out to be some cripple who can only hobble around the farmstead." He grabbed his shirt and wiggled into the sleeves. "I tell you this now: When the snow melts in the spring, I'll be ridin' out to join Bouquet for the next campaign, fit as a fiddle." He looked around the room, ignoring his sister's eyes and the smiles of the other men. "Right now, I'm going down to McCartie's Tavern to get some proper medicine to warm my bones against this infernal damp and cold."

* * *

Wend left with Baird but instead of heading for the tavern he walked to his workshop which was across from the Carnahan's house. The Carnahan farmstead was situated on a rise above the village of Sherman Mill. It was almost a hamlet in its own right, laid out on both sides of the wagon track which ran up a long steep hill from the village proper and continued westward to service several other farms. The Carnahan's sturdy, two-level log house stood on the north side of the road. Next to the house towards Sherman Mill was the building which served as the village's church and school, where Paul Carnahan functioned both as minister and schoolmaster. On the other side of the house was a small log cabin which was the home of Franklin and his Mingo wife, Ayika, who had come with the black man from his days as a captive. Just to the west of the farm buildings rose a long hog-backed ridge which paralleled the wagon road. On the south side of the road, directly across from the house, were a stable for the horses, a barn, and several sheds for wagons and other equipment. Wend's workshop was in a small shed near the stable. He and Carnahan had expanded the shed shortly after his arrival in the village in 1759. One major addition to the building had been an open lean-to shelter which provided cover for Wend's rifling machine, used to cut the spiral grooves in gun barrels.

Wend stopped and leaned against one of the support posts for the lean-to roof and watched Baird as he walked down the hill toward the village. Just at the bottom of the hill on the right, or south side of the road, lay the gristmill of Thomas Marsh. Next to it was the pond formed by damming up Sherman Creek. Clustered around the mill were the proprietor's house and several outbuildings, including his stable. Almost directly across the wagon road from the mill was McCartie's Tavern, also with its own stable and out-buildings. The other commercial buildings of the little village stretched out along the road beyond McCartie's. These included the combination black-smith shop and livery stable run by Matt Bratton's father and a general store. The remainder of the buildings were small log cabins of day workers who found employment at the farms throughout the valley of Sherman Creek. Just beyond Marsh's millpond was the ford where the road which connected Sherman Mill with Carlisle crossed the creek and met the wagon track which ran through the hamlet.

In surveying the village, with its rough buildings, Wend felt a warm senti-ment flow through him for the town and its people. Despite the animosity of Matt Bratton and his cronies, Wend had to admit to himself that most of the people of the village and the valley had accepted him in the five years since Joshua had brought him to the Carnahan's house. He was particularly close to the merchants of the town and their families. And, as the only gunsmith in the valley, he had occasion to deal with virtually every family who resided in the area at one time or another.

After watching Baird disappear into the tavern, Wend entered his shop and resumed the clean-up work which had occupied him since his return two days previously. In the wake of his seven month absence, the place was deep in dust and he had been systematically scrubbing the shop, the workbenches, and furniture. He had checked out his treadle-operated lathe and the rifling machine to make sure they were in working order. He wasn't surprised to find that his normally well-ordered parts bins had been disturbed; obviously people had pawed through them, looking for hardware to fix firelock discrepancies. So, after getting the room and work areas clean, he concentrated on inventorying his supplies and putting the bins back in order. As he worked, he thought about how to restart his business. Of course, as word spread that he was back, people would start bringing their firelocks for repair and service. But Wend's real source of income was the sale of guns and he realized that his first priority was to quickly build some rifles for display at taverns. Luckily, he had an adequate inventory of barrels, lock parts, and brass to get started.

Wend was inspecting his collection of curly maple and walnut wood, looking for the most likely pieces for rifle stocks, when he heard the sound of a wagon pulling up at the Carnahan's, followed by feminine voices greeting each other. Then, just a couple of minutes later, he heard the patter of light steps approaching. He turned to see the shapely figure of Elizabeth McClay fill the shop's doorway. The girl hesitated momentarily in the door, silhouetted by the light.

She smiled at him and said, "Mother and I were on our way down to the general store. She wanted to stop and visit with Patricia for a while." Then she ran to him, throwing her arms around his shoulders and giving him an enthusiastic hug. "Oh, Wend! I was so worried about you!"

She contrived to press her entire body against him. He could not help noticing that she had filled out considerably in the time since he had left in the spring and she now seemed to have a much more mature set of breasts. As she hugged Wend, it occurred to him that that the trip of the two McClay women to the store was merely an excuse for Elizabeth to visit with Wend. It was an open secret in the Carnahan house that both the mother and daughter had their sights set on him as Elizabeth's husband. Then Wend suddenly recalled that while he was gone, she had turned sixteen. He thought: *Now that she's clearly of marriageable age, they're undoubtedly going to press their campaign.*

Elizabeth managed to brush her lips against his cheek, and then continued to hold him tight, saying, "We heard all about that battle near Fort Pitt, Wend. So many men were killed! At first we didn't know whether you were alive or dead. I was *so* worried." She looked up at him and flashed her eyelashes. "And then we heard that you not only survived, but were such a hero in the middle of it all. I'm so proud of you, Wend."

Wend said, "I just did what was necessary. Lots of men did that." Then he gently broke away from the girl and placed a chair for her beside his desk. Wend reconciled himself to treating the girl with hospitality.

Elizabeth seated herself in the chair and made a show of fussily rearranging her gown and petticoats. As she did so, one of her legs peeked out from under the petticoat, visible long enough that Wend couldn't miss seeing the curve of her calf. After allowing the display to go on for a long moment she pulled the skirts back over her leg.

Wend pulled his glance away from the girl's leg, and, to start a conversation, asked, "Did you have many attacks by raiding parties last summer?"

Ellen nodded. "Oh yes, Wend, it was *so* scary. Worse than I remember from back during the French War in '56, when I was a little girl. We had several attacks—mostly down in the center of the valley to the east of here, right off the New Path." She paused a moment to gather her thoughts. "They burned down a farmstead just past the Junkins' place in the first raid. We all ran to Robinson's Fort and then the same war party hit another place further east. We saw the smoke."

Wend asked, "Was the militia able to catch them?"

"Paul Milliken led ten men out on a search, but didn't find any Indians. They'd apparently made their escape after looting the farms they had hit. Then we waited another day at the fort, but didn't see any more sign of the war party, so everyone went home." She paused, then said, "Sheriff Dunning heard about the raid and sent some armed men up from Carlisle to help out. That made us feel more secure for a while. But in just a few days, another war party attacked and the Carlisle men went after them. They walked right into an ambush. Several of them were killed or wounded. The Indians got away with their loot, but that was the last attack we had." Elizabeth looked up at the ceiling. "We lost maybe five or six people here in the valley, not counting the sheriff's men who were killed."

Then she smiled brightly at Wend, and asked, "Now that you're done with the army, are you going to join with Lazarus Stewart and Matt Bratton and the other men they are gathering to ride on those Moravian Indians and Philadelphia?"

Wend stared at the girl for a moment. "No, Elizabeth. I've got to get my trade going again." He looked sharply at her. "And even if that weren't necessary, I wouldn't ride with those men."

A puzzled look came over her face. "But Wend, we've heard so much about what the Conestogas and Moravians have done to help the war parties."

"How did you get your information about that?"

"Why, Matt's been telling us. And he even brought some traders friends of his up here, who told a gathering down at McCartie's about all the things the so-called friendly Indians have done. The traders saw them meeting with the hostiles and helping them plan their raids."

Wend said, "Let me guess: Did one of those traders have silver gray hair?"

"Why, yes—yes he did. He spoke very convincingly, having seen it all for himself."

"Yes, I'm sure he did."

The girl nodded, then said with enthusiasm, "I hope they clean those Moravians out, just like they did with the Conestogas!"

"Good lord, Elizabeth! I can't let you go on believing what you've just said." Then he continued, more vehemently than he intended, "Neither the Conestogas nor the Moravians were of danger to anyone. I grew up next to the Conestoga village and was friends with many of their people. I'm telling you plainly that they just wanted to live peacefully and the attack on them was plain murder." He thought for a moment. "And the Moravians live so far east, near Philadelphia, that they simply aren't in a position to help the war parties who raid the settlements."

Elizabeth seemed startled at Wend's reaction and instinctively answered in a defensive tone, "Well, Matt's been saying different for several months now. And no one, 'cept you, has contradicted him."

Then she looked at Wend and saw the distress and anger on his face at the mention of the Christian Indians and calculated that she had struck the wrong chord with him. She quickly changed direction to get out of dangerous waters. "Well, anyway, they also plan to confront the colonial assembly and the governor. Those Philadelphia people haven't done anything to help us out here in the settlements during this emergency. The Paxton men want to force them to give us more representation and raise provincial troops to help protect the settlements."

Wend shook his head. "Everybody knows that the colonial government has done little to aid the western settlements. Of course we're all upset about that. But I'll have nothing to do with a plan to threaten the use of force to gain attention; it's a recipe for more bloodshed. I've seen enough of that in the last seven months."

Elizabeth sat looking at him, not knowing how to take his words.

Wend decided to pump the girl for information. "Do you think that a lot of men will be riding with Bratton to join the Paxton Rangers?"

Elizabeth pursed her lips. "Well, I don't know, but my Pa says he thinks that only a few of the younger men will go. The older men can't leave their farms, their livestock, and businesses."

"So—have you heard about any who are going?"

"Well, it seems like just Matt's friends and a few others. Ezra McCord, Joe Finley, and a couple of others." She thought for a moment. "I guess that Frank McKenzie will go with Matt, since he works for him running that cargo wagon between here and Carlisle."

"Elizabeth, Frank won't be going anywhere soon. He's got a bullet hole in his right leg, put there by a Conestoga that he and Matt were trying to kill after he escaped from Lancaster. Frank's in a room down at Doc Highsmith's place in Carlisle right now and even when he gets back he'll take a long time to recover." Then, in a few words he told her how Bratton had abandoned the young man in Paxton with a wound which threatened to cost him his leg or his life.

Her face registered shock and she sat speechless. Then, as the import of Wend's words impacted her, she asked quietly, "He could have died?"

Wend nodded. He was about to change the subject when there was a call from Sarah McClay for her daughter to join her at the wagon.

Elizabeth rose from the chair and Wend stood up. Elizabeth put her hand on his arm and whispered in an intimate fashion, "Well, Wend, you must know that I am so glad that you are back in the valley." Then her face lit up. "Won't you sit with me at church on Sunday? I'd really love that; it would save me from having to tend my little brother."

Wend resigned himself to politeness. "Why of course, Elizabeth, I'd be happy to join you. I'll wait at the door to meet you."

The girl flushed with pleasure. "Oh, wonderful! I'll see you Sunday!" Then she was gone in a rustle of skirts and Wend was alone again in his workshop.

Wend sat considering his feelings about Elizabeth. She was indeed maturing physically in an attractive way. She had luxuriant brown hair, a thin face with high cheekbones, petite nose, and attractive mouth. He had already felt the affect of her breasts and viewed the long legs which she had taken care to display. Wend had never been able to arouse any romantic interest for her; but now he realized that his disdain might have stemmed from the very aggressiveness of the girl's pursuit of him. Or perhaps that his obsession with recovering Abigail Gibson from captivity had blinded him to the attractiveness of other women.

Then he caught himself and thought: *Had blinded him to the attractiveness of all other women except Mary Fraser.* Mary Fraser was the orphan daughter of the 77th Highlanders. In 1759, as a child of age twelve, she and her mother, Lizzie Iverson, had patched him up and then nursed him for days. That had been after the highlanders of Captain Robertson's company had found him near death on Forbes Road following the massacre of his family and the capture of Abigail. Then, as he had lived among the Ulster-Scots of Sherman Valley, he had forgotten about her until the outbreak of the Indian uprising in the spring of 1763. After joining Colonel Bouquet's expedition as a scout in order to find Abigail, he had again encountered the girl, now sixteen and serving as a nurse for the highlanders' doctor.

Mary had matured into a beautiful, auburn haired, waifish woman who had been orphaned in 1762 when Lizzie and her stepfather, Sergeant Iverson, had died of yellow fever in the British Army's West Indies campaign. Despite his quest to recover Abigail, he and the young highland girl had fallen in love, presenting Wend with an unresolvable conflict as the campaign progressed. But fate had intervened, for Mary had been severely wounded in her side while treating injured men at Bushy Run. For weeks she had seemed on the road to recovery, but in October, just as Wend had been ordered to leave on a mission into the Ohio Country for Colonel Bouquet, her health had rapidly deteriorated, her wound infected. Surgeon Monroe of the highlanders had told Wend that her life was out of his hands and that she had mere days to live. Wend had tried to stay with her, to be at her bedside to the end, but Mary had tearfully told him that she knew death was near and that he must go on the mission where he might be able to find Abigail. With heavy heart he had left to serve as the scout for a company of Black Watch soldiers tasked with delivering a diplomatic ultimatum to the Ohio Country chiefs. When he returned to Fort Pitt in late November, the 77th had left for the east and transport back to Scotland for disbandment. There was no one left at the fort to tell him of the details of Mary's death.

Now, in the wake of Elizabeth's visit, Wend inevitably compared the two girls in his mind. Both were of the same age and undeniably alluring in a physical way. Both were intelligent and hard working. Both had an amiable disposition and an ability to make men comfortable in their presence. But that was where the similarities ended. Mary Fraser had, under a sweet disposition, a core of steel forged by years of strenuous life as a camp follower and the experiences of battle. She had watched many men die under her care. And there was something else: Through all of that, Mary had maintained a fierce determination to achieve her own goals and avoid what seemed to be her inevitable fate—army wife and life as a camp follower. To that end, she had spent hours under the tutelage of the regimental chaplain, learning to read, write, and make calculations. Her objective had been to become the teacher or governess for the children of a wealthy family. In furtherance of that, she had declined the inevitable barrage of marriage offers from young corporals and sergeants. A pang hit Wend's heart as he realized that the only man she had been willing to sacrifice her own goals for was him. On the other hand, Elizabeth had never shown Wend any goal in her life except marriage to a desirable man and the production of a large family. Moreover, as he had just witnessed in their conversation, she seemed to have no fixed convictions; instead she bent like a willow tree in whatever direction the wind blew. Elizabeth's whole manner seemed to be contrived and much less mature than the highland girl. He remembered Mary's independent spirit and realized this girl had none of her fearless spunk.

But then Wend remembered something else. It had occurred on the evening of the November day when he had found Abigail and she had told him that despite the love she still felt for him, she would stay with the Mingo band. That night, Captain Thomas Stirling of the Black Watch had called Wend to his campfire in an attempt to buck up his flagging spirits and force him to think about his future. He had pointed out that Wend must face up to his disappointment and get on with his life. And part of that was finding a good, practical girl to start a family of his own. It now struck Wend that, despite the fact that Elizabeth had never appealed to him, most men would consider her one of the most eligible girls in Sherman Valley. Moreover, she had indeed changed in the last few months from a giggly girl to a woman who most men would consider more than passing attractive. And given her pursuit of him, he had merely to say the word and he could, in short order, be a married man with a comfortable home.

Wend walked out the door to the lean-to where he could look down at the village. He saw the McClay wagon parked in front of the general store. As he watched, Elizabeth emerged from the store carrying a basket of supplies which she deposited in the wagon bed. The girl glanced up at Wend's shop for an instant, then turned and hurried back into the store. He thought she probably hadn't seen him watching her. But it now occurred to him that, having just reached the advanced age of twenty, he might have to take Stirling's words to heart and reconsider his feelings about young Miss McClay.

* * *

Wend had just gotten back to work when his best friend in Sherman Mill entered the shop and stood at the door staring at the gunsmith. Wend smiled and said, "Ah, there you are: I wondered when you would be showing up."

The visitor did nothing to acknowledge Wend's presence or his words; instead he walked in with the air of one who feels he owns the world and then made a circular tour of the room, stopping to studiously inspect various objects. Finally, he reared back on his hind legs and jumped up to the surface of Wend's workbench. Moving on silent paws, he walked to a spot just to the left of where Wend stood before the bench and plopped his body down with his rear end pointed directly at the gunsmith. He waved his tail back and forth in Wend's direction several times, then tucked it alongside his body, and pointedly stared directly away from him.

"Yeah, Cat, I know you're angry at me for leaving you alone these seven months." Wend reached out and stroked the animal's gray fur from just behind his ears down to the point where his tail began. The cat angrily mewed once, rose to his feet, and moved a few feet away to where Wend could not reach him. Then he plopped himself down again.

Wend had been adopted by The Cat, one of many who hung out around the farmyard, just after he had set up the shop in 1759. At that time, the animal had just been beyond kittenhood and Wend liked to think that they had matured together. It had been a year after their first meeting that he had started talking to The Cat, a habit which helped dispel the loneliness of working long hours in the shop without human companionship. Of course, Wend carefully kept the fact that he talked to a cat as his deepest secret.

"Well, Cat, go ahead and punish me. But tomorrow I'll bring you your morning milk, just like before, and I'll make a wager that the day after that you will have decided that I've been punished enough. So take your anger out on me now and enjoy it."

Wend went back to this work of cleaning up a piece of curly maple which would form the stock of a rifle. As he stood there performing the routine work, a portion of his mind returned to the problem of finding out about Grenough's warehouse operations, an idea which he had first taken up in Carlisle. Then a thought came to him: He should plan to travel there during the time that the Paxton men and their supporters were riding on Philadelphia. They would be gone for an extended period and he realized that many, if not all, of Grenough's outlaw ring would be riding with the mob to help keep them stirred up. Suddenly, another idea came to mind—there was a good chance that Grenough himself would go to Philadelphia at the same time. But he wouldn't be riding with the protestors; he would go independently to observe events from nearby. That way, he could secretly provide instructions to his men as they worked to keep the Paxton men agitated. And at the same time he would be rubbing shoulders with the governor and other important men at the capital, playing a double game. In fact, Wend was sure the men in the government would call on him for advice because of his first-hand knowledge of the settlements and sentiments of the border settlers. *Grenough would be in a position to steer events from both sides!*

Wend thought about traveling to the southern part of the Cumberland Valley. It was not a long trip: He could be in Shippensburg in two days if he had clear weather. A more important question was thinking up a plausible excuse for leaving Sherman Mill so soon after returning from the west. After his long absence, everyone would expect him to be hunkered down in his shop building firelocks. Then he remembered the contents of the letter which had been waiting for him in the Carnahan's house when he arrived in the village. It was from Mr. Henry Froelich of Shippensburg. Froelich was, like Wend, a gunsmith of German heritage. He was actually about the age Wend's own father would have been if he had survived and Froelich had known Johann Eckert by reputation. Wend had met him at a shooting match in Sherman Mill, where the older man had come to satisfy his vice of wagering. The letter had been dated several months before, in July, when Wend had been scouting for Bouquet on the march westward to Fort Pitt. It had been gossipy, clearly intended to simply maintain their relationship rather than address any specific business. But in passing, Froelich had mentioned something which now interested Wend very much. It seemed that someone had started an iron furnace and forge near Shippensburg. And that could provide the excuse he needed for his trip. Wend could say that he wanted to visit the forge to see if it was capable of making blank barrels of suitable quality for gunmaking. Wend normally obtained his barrels from the well established Kurtz Forge, located near Lancaster. Their products had the reputation of being the best in Pennsylvania. But Wend could say that he wanted to see if the new forge could produce barrels of reasonable quality which would be cheaper than the Kurtz barrels because of the shorter shipping distance.

Wend thought about the time frame: He knew that the rendezvous date for the Cumberland Valley contingent of protestors was now only a week away. It was clear that they would be gone for ten days at the minimum. So he determined that he would leave Sherman Mill in about ten days—that would give him time to finish his first new rifle and he would have enough time to visit Shippensburg and York and return to Sherman Valley before the protestors returned.

* * *

Wend drove his wagon westward along the track which ran from Sherman Mill. Beside him sat Ellen McCartie, the younger daughter of the tavern keeper Donovan McCartie. They day was chilly but filled with the light of a bright January sun. After passing the Carnahan farmstead, the hogback ridge rose above them on the right, its trees and shrubs winter brown except where an occasional patch of evergreens stood. The track ran along the base of the ridge out to the Donaldson farm, then swung around the western end of the hill to terminate at the McClay's place, which was sited on the north side. The team was happy to be in harness, having been lightly used since the fall harvesting had been completed.

Wend slapped the reins on the backs of the horses—Joe and Lucy—to pick up the pace, and then turned to Ellen. "During the summer, Franklin alternated my team with his for the farm work, so they wouldn't get lazy in the pasture all summer while I was away. But they haven't had much to do since the end of November."

Ellen adjusted the gray bonnet around her brown hair and pulled the matching cloak more tightly around her shoulders. Then she screwed up her angular face as she considered his words and looked over the horses. A smile came over her; it didn't just affect the mouth, but spread all over her countenance, transforming her face. She said, "They're a powerful pair, Wend. You can see their strength as they move."

"Yes, it's a pleasure to drive them and they have good endurance. But I must find ways to use them more frequently over the winter, to keep them in shape. Anyway, my black mare needs a long period in the pasture to rest her from the trip back from Fort Pitt."

She nodded, and they were quiet for a while. Then she said, "I appreciate you doing this for me, Wend. You're always been such a good friend. I've wanted to visit Johnny's grave, but I didn't want to go alone."

Wend looked at the girl, and saw a shadow pass over her face and her lips tighten into a small frown. Thinking to cheer her up, he asked, "Has anyone been able to find out what will happen to the Donaldson farm?" The Donaldson family had been killed in the first Indian raid of the insurrection, which had occurred the previous May. Her boyfriend, Johnny Donaldson, who was also Wend's best friend in the valley, had died defending the house. Only the two youngest children had survived because they had been sent running to hide in bushes beside a small creek when the attack started.

Ellen answered, "The reverend sent a letter down to the sheriff at Shippensburg, enquiring about the Donaldson's relatives who were supposed to live in that area. After several weeks, he got a letter back saying that there had been a family named Donaldson living on a farm to the south of the town, but they had moved on years before." She thought for a moment. "So now it looks like the Donaldson's place is going to be sold; they had some debts, and the county is going to auction the place off to pay the creditors and the taxes."

Wend said, "That's a shame. It was a nice place, with good, well cleared land. And they had a goodly amount of acreage still to be cleared."

"Well, the word around here is that Tom Marsh is thinking to buy it. Lord knows, he makes enough money from the mill. He may break it up into two or three separate farm plots; there's enough land for that many." She considered a minute and Wend saw that she was biting her lip as if deciding whether to tell him something. Finally she looked over at Wend and said, "Hank Marsh was telling me that he's thinking of taking the piece of land where the Donaldson's homestead was for himself to go into farming. He's not interested in being a miller like his Pa."

There was quiet again as Wend digested that information. He was surprised at what Ellen had said, for Hank had always seemed a conscientious understudy in his father's mill. He wondered how Thomas would take the news, for he had often talked about Hank taking over the business.

Then a new subject came to his mind. He looked at Ellen. "Well, I guess even the most terrible events sometimes have some good aspects. At least Patricia Carnahan finally has the young children she always wanted." Wend had been surprised when he returned to find that the Donaldson kids were still living at the Carnahan's house. But with no known relatives, it now seemed that they would become a permanent part of the reverend's household. He smiled at the girl beside him. "She dotes on those two in true mother hen fashion. Charles and little Margaret have become the center of her life. And she smiles more than I've ever seen as she goes about her chores."

Ellen laughed. "Aren't you jealous? She always considered you her son."

109

Wend shook his head. "No, not in the least. But it was funny: The night we got back, after she had put the children to bed, I made a joke about that—telling her I was envious of all the attention she paid to them. Then she came up to me and put an arm around my shoulders and whispered, "Don't worry, Wend, you'll always be my first born, even if I didn't really carry you. I felt enough pain seeing how bad you were wounded to have actually given birth. And you were so helpless after you got here it was like caring for a baby until you gained strength."

There was another period of silence as they rode on; then a question came to his mind.

Wend casually asked Ellen about what Bratton had been up to, hoping that she would provide some information on his activities during the summer.

"The truth is, Wend, he hasn't been here that much. He said he's been helping to get supplies to Fort Bedford and Fort Lyttleton with his wagon." She thought for a moment. "And when he isn't out freighting, he's been with the Paxton Rangers, helping patrol against the Indians to the north of Harris' and Paxton."

Wend felt anger toward Bratton and thought: Bratton was sure-enough freighting—for Grenough. And his items got to Bedford all right—carried by Indian war parties after they traded with Kinnear and Flemming. And when he wasn't freighting, he was spreading vile rumors about the Conestogas for Grenough. Then he thought to ask Ellen about his plans toward Peggy. "Have Matt and your sister set a date for their wedding yet?"

A look of frustration came over Ellen. "No, he keeps saying he needs to earn more money. But he's been working on this freighting contract for over a year now and he was supposed to be making a lot of money." She shook her head. "To tell the truth, I've got plenty of doubt about Matt Bratton's intentions. In fact, I've said that to Peggy several times and she just gets mad at me." Ellen crossed her arms in front of herself and looked defiantly at Wend. "I think he's just playing her along. Peggy is supposed to be smart and worldly; but she seems so blind about Bratton."

Wend answered, "Perhaps she does sense the same thing that you do, Ellen. But she just can't come to admit it to herself." Then he thought: *Peggy has always considered herself the most desirable girl in the valley and has been proud to be with the leader of the young set. It would be hard for her to concede that she had allowed herself to be led on and deceived by Bratton.*

Shortly they arrived at the remains of what had once been considered the model farmstead of the valley. But now the barn was just a pile of blackened wood. Only the charred rear wall of the house stood. Ironically, all the small sheds and outbuildings remained standing, as did the fencing for the pasture and fields. Wend realized that the place could easily be put back in operation by raising a good barn and house. Then he pulled the wagon up to a string of four crosses which stood on small hillock near the far end of the pasture and helped Ellen down from the wagon.

The girl went up to the cross at Johnny's grave and knelt in prayer. Wend joined her for a long minute and then helped her to her feet when she had finished.

She looked over at him and said, "At first, I was angry because you and Franklin rushed to make coffins for all the Donaldsons and closed them up with so many nails that it was impossible to open them for the funeral. Then, later, when my grief subsided, I realized you had sealed them because you didn't want me to see how badly Johnny was burned. Now, I'm grateful that you did it."

"What you would have seen wasn't the Johnny we knew. Better to remember him as he was in life."

She nodded. Then she smiled and said, "You can give me the ring now."

Wend opened the collar of his shirt and took a crude brass ring on a cord from around his neck. Johnny had fashioned it and given it to Ellen as a token of their love. Then, on the day that Wend had left to join Bouquet's expedition, she had loaned it to him to take into battle, as sort of a form of vengeance for Johnny's death.

She took the ring in her hands and looked over at Wend. "I guess you were puzzled about why I wouldn't let you give me the ring back until we came up here."

"A little; but I was glad to bring you here for whatever the reason."

Ellen hesitated a moment, then said. "At first I thought to keep the ring in my memento box forever. Or even wear it on my finger. But then it occurred to me that it would be better if I put it on his cross like a badge of his valor. And you carried it for him in the battle which vanquished the Indians who did this to him, so in a way you did obtain vengeance for him."

Wend grinned. "I think that would be very appropriate. And I want to tell you something. The ring played a great role in helping me keep my courage during the battle. After the first day, Colonel Bouquet sent me out into the night to scout a portion of the land for an action he planned on the next day. As I was crawling back to the British lines, a warrior attacked me in the darkness. It was terrifying, but I managed to cut his throat with my knife and

111

get back to the lines. He literally died in my arms. It was the first time I had killed someone in hand to hand fighting."

"Lord, Wend, that must have been terrifying."

"It didn't affect me at first. I guess I was numb. But later that night, as I was trying to get some sleep before the fighting resumed, the events of the day—and particularly the fight with the warrior—kept running through my head. I became terrified that my turn with death would come the next day if we lost. I fanaticized about warriors running after me and then catching me. I imagined over and over again what it would feel like to have my own throat cut and have the blood welling up in my mouth, drowning me. Then, I reached down and felt the ring. And it reminded me of the courage that Johnny had shown defending his house, even though he knew it was hopeless and that he must die in the end. It steeled my nerve; I vowed that if he could show that kind of bravery in the face of overwhelming odds, so could I. The thought calmed me and I was able fall asleep."

Wend walked over to the wagon and fished through the box of tools and supplies which he kept underneath the bench seat. Soon he found what he was looking for, a u-shaped nail. He also grabbed the hammer from the box and returned to Johnny's cross. He took the ring from Ellen, and quickly used the nail to affix it to the cross right at the juncture of the vertical and horizontal pieces. Together they stood back and looked at the result.

Ellen looked up at Wend. "Thank you, Wend. You are the best friend a girl could have." She stood looking at the cross for a while, and Wend could see that something was going through her mind. Finally she looked at him again, and said, "Wend, there was another reason I asked you to come out her with me. I wanted to ask your opinion on something important."

"From the expression on your face, if must be really serious. What's bothering you?'

"I was wondering if it was too soon after Johnny's death to start seeing someone else."

Wend smiled to himself. "Well, it's been eight months since the attack here. Do you have anybody in mind?"

"Hank Marsh has been paying attention to me. Coming to see me all the time. I've been putting him off, but the truth is, I like him a lot." She wrinkled up her face. "But I feel terribly disloyal to Johnny when I'm with him."

It was all Wend could do to keep from breaking into a broad smile. He had just won an argument with Ellen's sister. But instead he made a stern face and said in a severe manner, "And well you should. In fact, why aren't you wearing black and staying in your room, deep in mourning, when you're not at work in the tavern?" Then he forced himself to glower at her.

She looked at him in surprise and an expression of confusion came over her face. She started to reply, but Wend cut her off by putting his arm on her shoulder.

"Ellen, that's a joke. Look, you're only sixteen. After eight months, it's time for you to move on. After all, intense as it was, your romance with Johnny only lasted for a few months. The fact is, I'm really happy that you have someone new in your life."

"Oh, Wend, do you really mean it?"

"Of course, and I know Hank is a solid fellow. He'll soon be eighteen and any girl could do a lot worse." He thought a moment and then smiled slyly at her. "And now I know why you were talking about him on the way up here."

She blushed. "I do think he's smart and quite handsome." Then she put her arm on Wend's, and said, "But I need a real favor from you."

"You can always depend on me for help, Ellen. But what do you need?"

"I'm hoping you could find a good time to talk to Hank's father and tell him that he wants to be a farmer, not a miller. Hank hates being cooped up in the mill all day long and being covered in grist dust. He wants the outside life of being a farmer, raising animals, and watching crops grow. But he doesn't know how to tell Tom about his feelings. It will be such a disappointment to his father who is counting on Hank to start managing the grist mill while he works to expand by building a sawmill." She paused to gather her thoughts. "I know Mr. Marsh will take your words seriously, Wend. All the merchants treat you as an equal, even though you're so much younger. They've seen how you've built up your business and now they respect you even more because of what you did in the war."

Wend turned to Ellen and put his hands on her shoulders. "Like I said, I'll do anything I can for you. But there's one important condition."

"What's that, Wend?"

"I'll talk to Tom Marsh only after Hank does it himself. Hank must have the courage to explain, man to man, his feelings to his father. If he can't do that, he isn't as much of a man as I think he is, and— listen carefully Ellen— he isn't the man you want in your life." He paused to let the words sink in and then continued, "When you can tell me he's done that, I'll go to Tom and give Hank all the support I can."

Ellen nodded. "That's fair, Wend. I'll talk to Hank about what you said." She stretched upward and gave him a sisterly peck on the cheek. "I don't know what I'd do without a friend like you."

Wend took her arm, walked her back to the wagon, and helped her up onto the bench seat. They drove away from the wrecked farmstead in silence; the only sound was the hooves of the heavy draft horses pounding on the cold, hard-packed winter ground.

Some distance down the track, Ellen looked over at Wend. "What about you, Wend? We all know why you went with the army to the Ohio Country. You were trying to find and rescue that English girl from Philadelphia. Joshua was down in the tavern the other day and he told me and Peggy how you found her, but that she wouldn't come back with you because she had children by that Mingo chief." She paused, then asked, "So now, are you going to think seriously about marrying some girl from Sherman Valley? There are lots of girls who will set their cap for you now that the word is going around that you are available." She smiled mischievously at Wend. "Course, they know they're going to have to fight past Elizabeth McClay for your attention."

Wend said, "Yeah, it is time for me to start a family. But it's hard for me to think about that while I'm trying to get my business going again."

"It isn't you who has to think about it. The girls will find a way to get your attention. I was out drawing well water and saw Elizabeth running into your shop the other day."

"Well, Elizabeth is a nice girl."

"Yes, and she's been staking out her claim to you to anyone who will listen. But that doesn't carry any weight with me, 'cause I know the girl who really loves you and is going to end up marrying you. The girl I'm thinking of has had her eyes on you since you first came to the valley five years ago."

Wend turned to stare at Ellen. She sat looking ahead with a self-satisfied smile on her face. He asked incredulously, "Do you care to share your knowledge with me?"

"I'm not telling you any more than that. But in my mind, it's a sure thing. Wend Eckert, you're real smart about a lot of things, but understanding the way women show their love ain't one of them. Mark my words, it may take a while, but you'll end up with the girl I'm thinking about."

* * *

Wend was better than his word to Ellen. The afternoon following their visit to the derelict Donaldson farm, he took a break from work in his shop and wandered down to the mill, ostensibly to call on Tom Marsh after seven months of absence, but in reality to start to condition him to his son's ambitions. The mill proprietor held the status of unofficial mayor of the settlement. That was largely due to the fact that village had sprung up around the mill and Marsh was the wealthiest man in the valley. Also on that basis, he had been elected captain of the valley's militia company.

Wend entered the mill to find that its machinery had been disassembled. Mechanical parts were carefully laid out around the floor while being cleaned or repaired as necessary. The miller knelt over a set of gears, pointing out something to his younger son, Edward, who had just turned thirteen and was busily engaged cleaning the gear. Hank was working on the millstones themselves.

Thomas Marsh turned to see who was entering his mill and then smiled broadly when he saw it was Wend. "Ah, the prodigal son of Sherman Valley returns!"

Wend shook the proffered hand and commented, "I don't believe I've ever seen you doing so much work on the mill at one time."

Marsh took a cloth from his pocket and wiped his hands. "We normally do extensive maintenance in January. He pointed over to where Hank was working. "We have two sets of grinding mill stones and can disengage one set at a time to work on the other. That's our normal procedure. But this year, with the farm crops so low due to the war party raids, I decided to perform a complete overhaul of all the equipment."

Wend asked, "What's Hank doing over there?"

Marsh led Wend over to the millstones. Hank smiled up at Wend, but continued working.

"He's dressing the stones." He pointed at one stone which was still mounted in its normal place. "That's the bottom, or bedstone. It's always stationary. We can work on cleaning it up and dressing the furrows right in place." He turned and motioned to another stone, which was lying on the floor. "That's the top, or running stone. It's the one which rotates. We had to detach that from its mounting—the rind—and then use a block and tackle to hoist it, turn it face up, and then lower it to the floor." Marsh pointed to a small wooden derrick which Wend saw could be relocated as necessary to hoist the running stone of either set of millstones. "That's the most important part of the overhaul we're doing. We have to make sure that each furrow has a clean, sharp edge to properly grind the grist and efficiently channel it outwardly as the stone rotates."

Wend said, "Well Tom, I've always been interested in milling. As a mechanic like you, these machines fascinate me."

Marsh nodded. "Wend, there's no doubt that our crafts—milling and gunsmithing—are the two most complex out here on the border. Each of us needs many different skills to serve our customers." He reached into his pocket and retrieved his pipe and a tobacco pouch. "Hey, let's go into my office where it's quiet and we can sit down for a talk."

After they sat down and Marsh had lit his pipe, he pointed to a paper with rows of figures which lay on his desk. "Like I said, our business is off a little bit because of the effects of the war. But I've got enough capital saved away to get started on a project I've had in mind for a long time. These are my calculations about building and running a sawmill. I'm going to erect it right across the creek, and it can use the same mill pond as the gristmill. And I'm going to buy the old Donaldson place. It has 150 acres that hasn't been cleared—that will supply me with good logs for years of production."

Wend considered Marsh's words for a moment. "Are you sure there will be enough demand for milled lumber? Most people use the least amount possible. They either make rough planks themselves or get lumber hauled in from Carlisle. But that's very rare and it is expensive."

"That's the point Wend!" Marsh tapped his hand on the desk. "If I cut and saw the wood here, it will be a whole sight cheaper for people in the valley. I've proved it to myself, working nights on these calculations. And the best part is, I can get that Donaldson land for a song, just paying a little over the value of the back taxes."

"Yeah, Tom, but I'm still not sure who's going to buy the wood. Most people here in the valley are quite comfortable with logs for most of their building."

"I'm betting that once the war is over, we'll get more people moving here. And the ones that are here will start looking to make improvements in their farmsteads. They'll want to make better quality doors, window frames, and shutters for their houses. Women are going to want more shelves and cabinets. Families with dirt floors in their cabins will want to lay planks. So I think people will be ready to buy milled wood, if I can keep the price down." He wagged his finger at Wend in enthusiasm. "And look at all the settling that's being done down to the south of the mountain, between here and Carlisle. That will be another market for my lumber, soon enough."

Wend considered what Marsh said, and nodded. "You know, Tom, it may work out."

"I know it will. And I'm anxious to get started." He leaned forward and whispered, "That's why I'm letting Hank do most of the work on overhauling the gristmill. He's going to be eighteen soon enough. And you know he's smart as a whip and keeps his mind on his work. I figure to make him manager of the gristmill so that I can concentrate on getting the sawmill built and running." Marsh pointed in the direction of the mill's machinery room. "I'm even going to let Hank do the remounting and alignment of the millstones when he finishes dressing them. That's the hardest and most critical job of the entire overhaul. You got to get them mounted exactly parallel to each other and properly set up the adjustment mechanism so the stones can be kept the right distance apart for each type of grain. If you get it wrong, they'll scrape against each other and can spark. If that happens, it can ignite the floating dust from the grist. Many a mill has been burnt down from millstone sparks. But Hank's helped me with the alignment several times. I know he can do it correctly. And then he'll have the right experience to take over the mill."

Wend answered, "You know, now that you mention it, I do remember my father telling me that grist floating in the air can be even more explosive than gunpowder." Then he nodded, and said, "I think you have a solid plan, Tom. And there's no doubt Hank has his head on straight."

"Yes, he does. And what's more, he's ready to settle down. He doesn't know it, but I've been watching him sparking Ellen McCartie." He laughed heartily. "Nothing like a comfortable woman to make a man think about starting a family and making himself secure in his trade."

"Ellen's a good girl and her experience at the tavern will make her a good wife."

"Yes, she's wiry and a good worker. She'll carry babies well." He smiled slyly. "It will be a good match and once they're mated and sleeping in the same bed, Hank can concentrate his mind on keeping the mill in good shape and profitable."

Wend looked at the pleasure in Marsh's eyes at the prospect of having his son working at his side over the years. The miller believed it to be a sure thing. Wend thought to himself: *Marsh is justified in thinking that Hank will follow in his footsteps. Most tradesmen expect that their oldest son would do so. My father would have been shocked if I hadn't taken a strong interest in gunsmithing.* But then he thought about his friend Arnold Spengler. He had hated the prospect of spending his life following the trade of coopering. When he told that to his father, it had sparked a heated argument. Finally, Arnold had run off and joined the Royal Americans; he and his father never spoke to each other again. In that case, the situation had been made worse because the elder Spengler had no other son to take up his trade. Wend thought, *At least Tom has another son to fall back on if Hank does take up farming.* But then he looked at the pleasure in the miller's face as he contemplated his plans for the mill and realized how difficult it was going to be for him to get used to the idea of his first son leaving the business.

But Wend was determined to prepare the ground. He asked very casually, as if it were just a passing thought, "How would your plans work out if, for some reason, Hank weren't able to take over the mill's management?"

Marsh's face wrinkled up in surprise. "Why, it would make things almost impossible. I'd have to manage both mills myself, at least until Edward got to be seventeen or eighteen." He shrugged his shoulders. "In fact, I might have to reconsider building the saw mill." The miller bit his lips and shook his head. "But Wend, that's not going to happen. Why would Hank ever consider leaving the milling profession? He likes the work and he's in line for a great situation."

* * *

"Welcome back, lad! I was wondering when you'd come down for a drink here in the tavern." Donovan McCartie, sporting his trademark clean and sparkling white apron, reached over his counter to shake Wend's hand. He waved to a table where Joshua and Donegal relaxed before the hearth. "Those two there, they been down every day since the lot of you got back."

"Well, I've been busy up in my shop, Donovan. I've got to get some fire-locks built for sale."

"Damn right, Wend." The tavernkeeper waved at the empty pegs on his wall behind the counter. "It won't feel right until I've got one of your rifles for sale up there." He waved a finger at Wend. "And this spring, we'll have some fine shooting matches. McCartie rubbed his hands together. "My business has been way down over the last year because of the uprising. But I'm hoping we'll make some good money when the warm weather comes and we can start the matches again. They'll draw people from all over the valley and up from Carlisle."

Wend reflected that the shooting contests sponsored by the merchants of Sherman Mill had become like a local fair. They were day long events held in the spring and fall in the cleared area behind the tavern. The merchants set up display tables around McCartie's place and did a lot of business. Then in the evening there was music and dancing.

He said, "I hope you're right, Donovan. But it depends on a lot of things. If the tribes can raid east again like last summer, there'll be hard times. I talked to Colonel Bouquet about that before we left Fort Pitt. He thinks some of the chiefs are ready for peace, but others are determined to keep up the fight. If the colonial governments raise the provincial troops they've promised and round up enough supplies and wagons so his campaign into the Ohio Country can start early in the spring, the chiefs will have to keep their warriors close to their villages. But if there are delays getting the expedition together they'll be free to resume the attacks here in the settlements. We'll just have to see what develops in May and June."

McCartie was considering that thought when Wend sensed someone near him and looked over to see Peggy McCartie standing on his left.

The raven-haired girl put her tray down on the counter. "Father, I need ale for that peddler over in the corner." Then she looked over at Wend, and said, "So, Wend Eckert, you've finally come to the tavern." She smiled slyly, and asked, "Well, are you going to go with Bouquet on his next campaign, or, now that the English girl you were mooning after has told you she preferred sleeping with her Indian lover, are you going to stay with us here in the valley?"

Wend looked into the girl's blue-gray eyes and saw sparks of the same anger she had displayed toward him the last time they had talked. That had been two nights before Joshua and he departed to join Bouquet's march on Fort Pitt and the very night that Franklin's Mingo wife, Ayika, had given birth to her first child. Peggy had flared up, accusing him of deserting the people of the valley at the very moment when they were threatened by Indian attacks.

Wend said to Peggy, "Yes, I've resolved the situation with Abigail Gibson. I'll be staying here to pick up my trade and to carry out my responsibilities in the militia to defend the valley."

She tossed her head and pushed a strand of hair back under the round, white cap which was pinned in place. Then she reached down and brushed off her white apron and blue work gown. "Well, at least you can admit I was right about what I said by the fire that night after Ayika had her baby boy. I told you that you were wasting your time and that Philadelphia girl wouldn't come back with you."

"Correction: You were *partially* right, Peggy—you said I wouldn't ever find her, that I would get myself killed, and that I would lose the rest of my hair. I remember what you said very well." He smiled at the girl. "It turns out that I did find her, it's just that she wouldn't come back because she thinks her Indian children wouldn't be accepted here in the settlements. But obviously you were dead wrong about my fate: Here I stand very much alive, and, as you can see, I have just as much of my hair as when I left." Then an amusing thought struck him as he remembered that he had the rear section of his own scalp in a bag up at the house. He grinned at her as broadly as he could manage. "Actually, I came back with more of my hair than when I left."

Peggy cocked her head and shot him a look of puzzlement. Then she shrugged her shoulders and said, "Well, I was mostly right. Anyway, now that you're back, I suppose you'll take up with that Elizabeth McClay. *She* certainly thinks so."

He said in a teasing voice, "Well, she has grown up to be a pretty young girl, hasn't she?"

Peggy frowned and shrugged her shoulders. "There are some who say that."

Wend continued, "On the other hand, your sister tells me that other girls in the valley think I might be a pretty good catch. I never considered that before. But maybe I'll have to pay attention to them now."

She stared at him for a long moment. "You've come back thinking a lot of yourself, haven't you, Wend Eckert?"

Wend grinned. "Not any more than I did when I rode out. I was just repeating what I've been told. But then, war does change a person. And I'll be the first to admit that I've learned a lot over the past seven months. Particularly how to speak a little more assertively on my own behalf."

Peggy laughed. "You won't get no argument on that from me."

Then he thought of something else. "By the way, I hope you'll admit that I was right about Ellen."

Peggy's face wrinkled up. "What do you mean by that?"

"Don't you remember? We had a little talk in Robinson's Fort on the day that Johnny Donaldson was killed. You were worried that Ellen was so plain that she wouldn't ever find another suitor and would end up spending her life as a spinster. I said that boys liked her warm smile and her pleasant manner and that you might be surprised at how fast other boys came courting. Well, it seems that Hank Marsh is sparking her." He raised his eyebrows at her. "So at least you'll have to give me credit for getting that right."

Peggy pursed her lips and there was a spark of irritation in her eyes. "I don't need to give you credit; you seem be doing a good job of claiming it on your own behalf."

Wend was seized by a devilish impulse. He grinned and asked, "By the way, have you and Matt Bratton set the date for the wedding yet?"

She gave him a steely look. Then, instead of responding, she abruptly put the mug of ale her father had given her onto the tray and quickly made her way back to the peddler's table. He watched for a moment as she stood making small talk and giggling at jokes made by the peddler, a man in his thirties. Wend recognized him; he regularly made trips up to Sherman Mill to sell goods to the general store.

Wend scanned the common room and saw many of the men surreptitiously eyeing Peggy as she played the coquette. There was no doubt that the girl, with her beauty and vivacious personality, was the tavern's most valuable asset, pulling men in from all over the valley after a hard day's work. Moreover, she obviously gloried in the attention, like an actor on the stage. But after five years as her neighbor in Sherman Mill, he also knew that she was intelligent, practical, and carried more than her share of the tavern's daily workload.

Then Wend looked back at Peggy as she dallied with the peddler, and remembered that he had reason to believe that the girl had a darker side. One night a year before, when he and Charlie Sawak had met in Harris' Ferry, Charlie had repeated a rumor to him. They had been talking of the charms of various tavern maids the Conestoga had spent time with in his travels through the Cumberland Valley. Then Charlie had said, "Actually, we should be talking about Sherman Mill. There is some girl up there in the tavern who is a legend among waggoners, peddlers and other traveling men. Supposedly she has a face so beautiful it will make your heart stop, long black hair, and legs so long she could squeeze you to death with them and you would go to your Maker with a smile on your face." Charlie had grinned slyly, and continued, "And what's more, she's a willing wench who will share her affections for a few coins or the pick of a peddler's merchandise."

A shocked Wend had realized that he could only be referring to Peggy and wondered why a girl like her, who was betrothed to Matt Bratton, a man with a prosperous business, would play the tart for money or barter. At first, he had wondered if the rumors were started by men frustrated in their attempts to enjoy the girl's favors. Then he had remembered a comment Peggy had once made to him, in fervent terms, about not wanting to be stuck in a boring place like Sherman Mill all her life. It had occurred to Wend that perhaps she had made up her mind not to depend solely on Matt Bratton for her passage out of the valley and was prostituting herself as a way to accumulate her own funds. Indeed, that would be consistent with what he knew was her frustration with Bratton's refusal to set a date for their marriage. So perhaps the two were playing a double game with each other.

Then Wend's thoughts were interrupted by a loud laugh from the peddler and he watched as Peggy giggled, then reached down and put her hand on the man's arm. The two looked at each other silently for a moment, smiles on both of their faces. Suddenly Wend had a thought: *After the tavern closed, would Peggy be entertaining the peddler in his room or perhaps on a pile of hay in a corner of the stable?*

CHAPTER SIX
Race in the Moonlight

Wend had pulled his wagon up to the front of the shop and was loading it for the trip to the southern part of the Cumberland Valley. Matt Bratton and his followers had left Sherman Mill two days before to join the march on the Moravian Indians and Philadelphia. As far as anyone knew, Wend was traveling to Shippensburg to check out the new furnace. He planned to leave early the next morning.

Elizabeth's guess had been correct. Although there had been much discussion at the tavern about teaching the Penns and the Quakers a thing or two, in the end it was only four young men who rode out of Sherman Mill to join the Paxton men. The group consisted of only Bratton and his immediate cronies. Part of the reason for that had been an earnest—and at times fiery—sermon by Reverend Carnahan in the church service on the Sunday before the protestors were to leave. He had started by reminding the congregation of his long service as a ranger during the French and Indian War. He pointed out that he had fought against rampaging warriors intent on raiding the settlements and frontier farmsteads. Then he provided the congregation with a graphic, vivid description of the massacres at Conestoga and Lancaster, making the point that they were, in fact, the most vicious attacks he had ever witnessed. He told them how the little girl, Molly, had bled to death in his arms. Wend, sitting with Elizabeth McClay near the back of the church, was able to observe that his words had great impact; the listeners were hearing the real story of the Conestogas for the first time. He saw shock on men's faces and actual tears on some of the women. He glanced at Elizabeth, and noted moisture in her eyes. Then, having drawn the attention of all members of the congregation, Carnahan decried the actions of the Paxton men at Conestoga Town and Lancaster for acting on the basis of rumors and hearsay. Keeping in mind that people of his congregation knew many of the men involved, he portrayed the majority of the Paxton attackers as honest men misguided by a few zealots. The reverend followed the story of the killings with an appeal for peaceful action to change the attitude of the government, not a mob action which could lead to bloodshed.

Just at the height of the reverend's sermon, Matt Bratton rose from his seat, and, after glaring momentarily at Carnahan, stocked out of the church. His action may have been stirred by simple anger or perhaps he meant it as a protest to arouse the men he believed were ready to ride with him. But no one followed and the action in fact isolated the waggoner, for it seemed to prove the point Carnahan had made about the zealotry of the Paxton leaders. A sober group of parishioners left the church that morning and any who had been inclined to follow Bratton changed their minds.

Now, a few days later, Wend looked down at the village. In the afternoon sun, the buildings were beginning to cast long shadows. He saw young Edward Marsh out on the millpond dam, adjusting the slats to increase the flow of water and realized that, for the first time since he had arrived back in Sherman Mill, the water wheel was turning. He guessed that the overhaul of the mill was complete and the Marshes were testing the machinery. His guess was confirmed by the appearance of dust wafting from the windows and other openings of the building.

Wend went back into his shop to get the rifle he had just finished. He planned to take it with him and put it on display at Washburn's Tavern down in Carlisle, where it would appear before the largest number of potential customers. He hoped for a quick sale which would start to bring in cash. After carefully wrapping the rifle in a canvas case, he also picked up a bag of tools and gun supplies and carried everything out to the wagon. He looked down at the village again, and saw that the flow of dust from the mill had gotten quite heavy. Meanwhile, the front door of the tavern opened and Ellen came out with a pair of buckets in her hands. Wend watched as she walked over to the well in the middle of the courtyard, and started to draw water.

In that moment, a burst of debris shot out of the mill, flying all over the road and into the courtyard of the tavern. Shards of wood clattered against the walls of the tavern itself. Instantaneously, a sheet of flame followed the debris and then quickly dissipated. Finally, a sharp bang reverberated through the village. Wend could feel it where he stood frozen in shock beside the wagon.

He came back to his senses almost immediately and, without thinking about it, took a few steps down the hill toward the mill. He knew that Tom Marsh and Hank must have been inside the building, operating the machinery. His first thought was to check their condition. But then he saw the flicker of flame through a window. He stopped and ran back to his shop and picked up two buckets he kept there, then turned and rushed down the hill. As he left the shop, he found that the entire Carnahan household was out staring at the mill. He shouted as he ran, "Quick, bring buckets for a fire brigade!"

It took only a few moments for him to descend the hill and reach the mill. To his relief, he found Tom sitting on the ground beside the building. Wend called out, "Tom are you all right?"

But the miller seemed stunned. He just stared at Wend, slowly moving his head from side to side. Wend tried again. "Tom, listen to me. Where is Hank? Was he in the mill?"

The miller still said nothing, but simply pointed at the mill.

Wend dropped his buckets, rushed passed the sitting man, and reached the door. He looked into the milling room, and saw flames licking at some of the wooden parts of the machinery. The place was filling with smoke. But the fire had not yet caught on the walls, flooring, or other parts of the structure. As his eyes scanned the room, he saw that the windows, which were made up not of glass, but rather of adjustable wooden slats for ventilation, had been blown out. He realized that the slat material had been the source of the wooden shards which had blown across the road.

Then he saw Hank. The boy lay in the corner of the room, right up against the wall. He rushed to the prostrate figure and shook him. He was immediately gratified to see his eyes open. As he looked at his face, he noticed that the right side was red from the effect of the blast. He grabbed Hank under the armpits and started dragging him toward the door. As he moved, Donegal burst through the door.

"You need some help, Wend?"

"No, I'll get Hank out. You organize a bucket line!" Wend glanced at the fire and realized it was localized in just a few areas. "Do it fast. If we work quick, we can save the mill!"

Donegal turned on his heel and was quickly out the door. But he had no sooner left than Edward Marsh burst through, carrying two buckets of water. He quickly ran to the largest concentration of flames, which was licking along the wooden linkage rods that controlled the system for switching between the two sets of millstones. He put one of the buckets down, and using both hands, deftly threw the water right on the base of the flames. Then he did the same with the second bucket. As Wend reached the door with Hank, he glanced back and could see that Edward's actions had all but extinguished the linkage fire. But other small fires around the room remained to be dealt with.

Then behind him he heard Carnahan shout, "Watch out!" and the reverend brushed past him, carrying another two buckets. Donegal was right behind with more. The two men used their water judiciously and, as Wend dragged Hank out the door, he could see that all but a few remnants of the fire had been cut down.

Wend put Hank down on the ground beside his father, but even as he did so, the boy was starting to move his hands and legs on his own. Then Wend suddenly became aware of loud voices and a woman screaming hysterically on the other side of the road. He looked toward the sound and saw a group of people gathered around the tavern's well. The woman screaming was Susan McCartie, Donovan's wife.

A cold hand grabbed Wend's heart. He ran across the wagon track to the crowd by the well and pushed in beside Donovan. Ellen, face down, lay motionless beside the well. A pool of blood was on the ground below her torso and more oozed out of her mouth. Then Wend saw the cause of it all: A large splinter of wood projected from her back. Susan was on her knees by her unconscious daughter, crying, "My baby; my baby! Oh, God, my baby girl!" Gathered around, besides Donovan, were Bratton's father, Asa, his wife Lenora, Patricia Carnahan, and Phillip and Carolyn Carr, who owned the store. All of them seemed in shock at Ellen's condition and unable to react.

At first, Wend thought the girl was dead. But then he saw slight motion in her chest. He fell to his knees opposite from Susan and put his ear down beside Ellen's face. He could hear shallow breathing and saw her eyelids flicker. Suddenly, hoped surged through him that the girl had a chance to live. An idea sprang to his mind. He screamed at the top of his voice, "Donegal! Donegal, get over here!"

The adults stared at him, but before anyone could ask him what he intended, Donegal arrived and pushed his way to Ellen's side. He shook his head. "My God! Oh, the poor lass!"

Wend looked up at him. "Simon, what do you think? Take a look at the wound."

Donegal ran his hand lightly around the place where the splinter projected from the girl's back. Then he gently lifted Ellen's head slightly and scooped up a sample of the blood from her mouth and examined it closely. He looked over at Wend. "There's 'na any bubbles of air in the blood. I dunna think' it hit her lung. If that be true, she's got a chance of living." Then he shook his head. "But she'd need a real doctor to save her, and there ain't none near here, that's for sure."

Asa Bratton looked down at Donegal. "What does some ignorant highlander know about medicine? You're giving the mother false hope. Let's be honest; she'll be dead before sunset. I say all we can do is make her comfortable for her last hours."

At the blacksmith's words, Susan wailed again and covered her face with her hands.

Donegal reared back and his temper flashed. "After seven years of war, I know a damn sight more about wounds than some lowland scum like you. Keep your mouth shut, blacksmith. Or I'll get up and shut it for you."

Donovan, tears streaming down his face, said, "I fear Bratton's right. That's a fearful wound."

Wend put his hand on Donegal's shoulder and looked around at the others. "For God's sake, be quiet the lot of you! We don't have time to settle old scores between highlanders and Ulster people right now." He glared at all the people gathered around. "Now listen: I think Donegal's right. He's seen lots of wounds. And I saw men survive a lot of terrible injuries at Bushy Run. The fact is, this is similar to a bayonet wound. I watched Surgeon Munro save a man with a wound like this."

Donegal nodded. "I've seen it done myself. And I saw men saved who had musket ball wounds in the same place."

Wend had been thinking fast. He stood up. "The only chance is to get her down to Carlisle. And we must leave as soon as possible."

Bratton shook his head. "How are you going to get her there safely? I'm saying she'll die if you try to move her. That wood shard will shift and cut her more. She'll bleed to death."

Wend said, "Maybe you're right, Mr. Bratton. But we have to try and here's my plan: I say we put her in my wagon, which is ready for travel up there by the shop. We put something thick enough to cushion her on the floor of the wagon. Then I'll drive through the night to get her to Doc Highsmith down in Carlisle. He's the best around here."

Suddenly the strong voice of Peggy McCartie rang out. "Wend's right. It's her only chance. I'll get a feather mattress from one of our rooms and we can use that to cushion her." She thought some more. "And we'll stuff pillows along the sides to brace her from rolling around as the wagon bounces."

Wend nodded. "That's a great thought, Peggy; go get the mattress and we'll get the wagon hitched up and down to here."

Then Wend looked up and saw Hank Marsh push his way through the crowd. One side of his face was bright red from the effect of the blast, but he appeared otherwise uninjured. The boy cried out, "Ellen! Oh my God, what have I done? I've killed her!"

Wend could see that Hank was distraught and blaming himself for the accident. "She's not dead, Hank. But she is seriously wounded." He realized that he had to do something to keep Hank busy. Then an idea came to mind and the beauty of it was that it would actually help. He looked around and saw Franklin was standing behind the crowd. "Franklin, you and Hank go up to our stable. Get my mare saddled; she's the strongest horse in the village." He thought a moment to properly phrase his next words. "Hank, you've got to ride over the mountain and down to Carlisle as fast as you can. Warn Doc Highsmith that we're bringing Ellen to him and explain to him about her condition. And you have to do one other thing along the way. When you get over the mountain, stop at that new store and stable which was just built last year. It's called Haroldson's Store. They trade in horses and teams. Beg them to have a four horse team ready for us in the early morning, because I'm going to need fresh horses by the time we get over the mountain." Wend stood up and put his hand on Hanks shoulder. "Were you listening? Can you remember all that?"

For a moment Wend thought the boy was too shocked by Ellen's condition to make sense of what he had said. But then he looked up and nodded. "I'll get it done, Wend. And they'll have relief teams ready for you at Haroldson's if I have to beat it into them."

"Good lad! Now get the mare saddled and ride out of here! We'll see you in Carlisle!"

Wend turned to Franklin. "After you get the mare saddled, harness my team and get them hitched to the wagon. Then drive it down here."

As Hank and Franklin ran up the hill, Wend turned to Asa Bratton. "Mr. Bratton, I need one of Matt's Conestoga teams harnessed and ready to act as the lead team in front of mine. I'll need four strong horses to get over the mountain as fast as possible."

"So you're doing the driving? You're taking a lot on yourself, Eckert."

"Listen, Mr. Bratton: I've gone over the mountain on business many times. I know the road well."

"Have you ever done it with a four horse team? Do you even know how to handle four horses?"

"I've handled four horse teams on Forbes Road, Mr. Bratton. I'll guarantee that's rougher than the road over North Mountain. My father taught me how to double up when we had to get our wagons over the steepest part of the mountains. I tell you I can handle a double team."

Bratton pursed his lips. Then he said, "I don't feel free to let you use Matt's property. What happens if you hurt the team? What if you break one of their legs or permanently lame one in your mad haste?"

Donovan McCartie strode over to the blacksmith. "For God's sake, Asa! Your son is marrying my daughter. We're soon going to be related by marriage. Now are you going to stand here and quibble when my other daughter's life is hanging by a thread? Damn it man, we've got to try this!" He stamped his foot. "And I trust young Eckert here to take a wagon over the mountain more than anyone in the village except your son."

Asa Bratton suddenly realized that the people clustered around Ellen were all staring at him with rising impatience. Abruptly, he turned on his heel and strode toward his stable. Then he called back over his shoulder, "I'll have my strongest team ready in twenty minutes!"

Wend knelt back down by Ellen and motioned to Patricia Carnahan. "Help me raise her up for a second, Patricia. I need to check out her front." Together they gently raised Ellen's right side and Wend found what he had feared. He looked grimly up at the faces of the people gathered around. "The tip of the splinter has gone all the way through. It is projecting through her skin just above her right breast." He shook his head. "I'll have to nurse the wagon as much as I can."

Just then Peggy came running out of the tavern dragging a feather mattress. She laid it down beside Ellen, then turned and ran back in to get pillows and blankets.

Wend motioned to Donegal. "Help me get her onto the mattress." Together they eased her body onto the softness of the down. Ellen groaned faintly as they moved her. But Wend was encouraged by that, for she was at least responding to the motion of her body. He looked around at the men above him, which now included Carnahan and Baird. "When we load her into the wagon, we'll all work together and use the mattress like a litter. We'll lift the mattress and her at the same time and slide it right into the wagon bed."

While they waited for the wagon to arrive, Wend got up and walked over to see how Tom Marsh was faring. He found him on his feet and staring through the door into the wrecked machinery room of the mill.

The miller looked at Wend. He spoke slowly, as if in a trance. "My son did something wrong. He misaligned one of the millstone pairs. We tested the first one and everything worked right. We ran it a good long time with no problem. Then we shifted to the other set and the runner stone seemed to be spinning correctly. Then we poured in the grist. Hank adjusted the runner down to what should have been the proper setting, but it hit the bedstone and sparked. They were making hard contact. And it blew right after that." He shook his head, then said again, more softly, "Hank must have done something wrong. And I trusted him."

Wend put his hand on Marsh's shoulders. "Tom, it's too early to try to figure out exactly what happened or to try to blame someone. You can figure out exactly what went wrong after everyone has recovered from the shock of today."

"No, Wend. You don't understand. We'll have to rebuild the mill. My plans for expanding will have to be put off." He shook his head. "No, I shouldn't have trusted Hank. He made a big mistake."

Wend realized that the miller was still disoriented and not thinking rationally. He was about to say more to try to console him when he heard the sound of hooves and Hank came galloping down the hill astride the mare. He pulled up briefly and looked with concern at his father and then at Wend. But he said nothing, simply making a brief wave. He guided the mare to the creek and let her pick her way through the stones of the ford. Then he again brought her to the gallop and was gone done the road to Carlisle.

Wend looked back up the hill and saw Franklin was coming with the wagon, the iron-rimmed wheels grating on the hard ground as he drove the team down the hill. Wend ran back to Ellen's side, and they quickly loaded the girl and mattress into the wagon bed. As they were doing that, Asa Bratton appeared leading a team of heavy wagon horses. Working together, Wend and he quickly hitched them to the tongue of the wagon. It was an easy job, for the front end of the tongue had long ago been modified with an eye-ring to accept the double-tree of a second team.

When Wend got back to the wagon, he found Peggy up in the bed, stuffing pillows around Ellen. Then she took blankets her mother was holding and covered the girl. She put a stern look on her face and looked at Susan. "Mother, I'm going with Wend. I'll take care of Ellen during the trip and help make arrangements with the Doctor."

Susan McCartie looked confused. "Oh no, I've got to go with my daughter. I need to nurse her."

But Peggy was adamant. "Mother, you're too upset. Look, you're shaking and you can hardly stop crying. And I'm younger and stronger. I'm going, and that's the end of it."

Susan broke out in tears again. "But I must go! I must be with my baby. We'll both go to take care of her!"

Wend looked at Peggy and then at Susan. "Mrs. McCartie, I need to keep the wagon as light as possible. It will jostle Ellen less and we need to make the best time we can."

Donovan nodded at Wend and then spoke to his wife. "Now Susan, it's better to let the young people take care of this. Besides, we have guests at the tavern. We'll stay here and work to take care of them. It will keep our minds off of poor Ellen and we can't help her anyway." He walked over, put his arms around his wife, and nodded to Wend. "You had better get going."

Franklin climbed down from the wagon seat. "Mr. Wend, I put a jug of water and your pistols in the wagon there. And here's your overcoat. You'll need that up on the mountain."

Peggy settled herself in the wagon bed next to Ellen. She looked up to Wend. "I packed a small bag for myself. I'm ready."

Wend nodded and took up the reins. He looked down at Franklin and said, "Go up to the front team and lead us through the ford; keep us clear of the stones. I'd hate to have one of the horses injured right at the beginning."

Franklin nodded and ran up to the leader, carefully helping the team pick their way through the rocky bottom of the shallow crossing. Then they were safely on the other side and Wend slapped the reins down on the backs of both teams to start them southward. He glanced back and saw virtually all of Sherman Mill's residents standing together in silence, watching them leave.

* * *

Wend could feel the power of the four horse team as they pulled the lightly loaded wagon along the Carlisle Road toward North Mountain. He brought them up to a trot and then actually had to hold them back, for in their freshness they wanted to move fast. As he looked over the two sets of animals, he thought he could sense competition among them. Joe, the lead horse of his own team, had snorted several times and pawed the ground when Bratton's team had been added to the rig. Wend was sure that he resented being hitched behind a set of unfamiliar horses. Horses were herd animals; Joe's herd was made up of the working teams and riding horses in the Carnahan stable. Now he was being forced to work with animals from another herd, and, beyond that, he was breathing their dust. Wend also thought that the Bratton team would know they had something to prove to animals from another stable. He thought: *All to the good, I want these animals determined to put out everything they have, for they're going to need it tonight.*

As he drove, holding the reins to the two teams in his hands, he had to suppress a surge of self-doubt in himself. For, despite his assertions to Asa Bratton, Wend knew that his actual experience handling four-horse rigs was minimal. He had done it only at the very beginning of the Eckert family journey along Forbes Road, five years ago, and then only when they had temporarily doubled up their teams to get wagons over steep ridges in stages. He realized that he was unversed in the complexities of controlling multiple teams. Moreover, much of the driving would be in the darkness which would soon fall over them. He would have to keep his wits about him and think ahead carefully about every aspect of his driving.

Then, as he was deep in thought, Peggy spoke up from her seat in the wagon bed next to Ellen. Her voice was tinged with anxiety. "For God's sake, Wend, can't we go faster here on the flat, smooth part of the road? We should cover as much ground as we can before the light fades!"

"I'd like to, Peggy. But I must save the horses' strength for the steep parts of the mountain. We can't wear them out down here on the flats." He glanced back at the girl. "These horses are bred for power, not speed. And it's power we'll need as we climb the ridges of North Mountain."

Within two hours they were in the foothills and then the evening dusk was on them by the time the horses were straining on the actual grades of the mountain. Wend found a reasonably flat stretch of the road, halted the team, and climbed down from the wagon. Peggy looked at him curiously.

Wend stepped to the side of the wagon next to where she sat. "How is Ellen doing?"

"Just the same. I'm not seeing any new bleeding, and her breathing seems to have settled down. A while ago she groaned a little bit." She looked up at the darkening sky. "Why have we stopped?"

"Partially to rest the horses a bit." Wend also looked up at the sky. "There's one piece of luck. We're going to have a nearly full moon, and the sky has been clear all day. I hope that holds and we'll have decent visibility of the road." Then he pointed at the tool box under the seat. "Reach up there and look in the box. Get out the candle lantern, the flint-lock mechanism, and the powder horn and hand them down to me."

While Peggy searched the tool box, Wend gathered several handfuls of dead twigs for kindling material. Then he arranged the kindling at the side of the road the shape to make a small fire..

Peggy came to the side of the wagon with the requested items in her hands and saw Wend's preparations for a fire. A frown came over her face. "For God's sake, Wend, why are you making a fire? Do you think you're going to brew tea? We're in a hurry!"

Wend saw the concern and incipient anger in her face. He said to her, "Parts of the road have been washed out by the heavy winter rains. We had to pick our way around deep ruts and gullies when we rode up from Carlisle on horseback last week."

Wend stopped talking while he deposited a small amount of gunpowder under the kindling. Then he triggered the flintlock and was able to get the gunpowder under the twigs to flare up on the second attempt. There was a *whoosh*, and the kindling flamed brightly. He worked quickly to light the candle wick before the fire faltered.

Then he told Peggy, "There are sections of the road where one of us may have to walk ahead and light the way if we are to avoid banging into the ruts or sliding sidewise in a washout." He held the lantern up to make sure it was fairly lighted, then handed it to her. "We'll also want light to see how Ellen is faring. In the meantime, you keep the lantern secure and lighted. There're fresh candles in the tool box when you need them."

Peggy looked down at Wend and now there was doubt and fear in her eyes. "Are you sure we can do this, Wend? Perhaps Asa Bratton was right and this is too hard; maybe we're going to kill her."

Wend kicked out the tiny fire and then said, "We'll make it, Peggy. Remember, I'm as fond of Ellen as you are. And if she's going to die, I think she'd rather go in the midst of a fight instead of in a deathbed with everyone standing around wringing their hands over her."

He remounted the bench, released the brake, and slapped the reins over the horses' backs. They made their way upward as the darkness intensified and began what would turn out to be the longest night of Wend Eckert's life. It lasted longer even than the night between the first and second day's fighting at Bushy Run, longer than the night the previous November when he and the mare had fought to survive a snowstorm which had overtaken them on the way to Harris' Ferry.

The road climbed the mountain in a series of switchbacks which made the distance much longer than if they had somehow been able to drive

133

straight over ridges. The wagon track itself had originally been cut to a width of twelve feet to allow two meeting wagons to pass each other. But over the years, the underbrush and tree limbs had encroached on the cleared area so that in places the track was barely eight feet wide. As they rolled upward, branches often brushed against the sides of the wagon. Twice Wend got down with the lantern and Peggy climbed up to take the reins while he led the horses through rough areas where winter storms had gullied out the road. And despite Wend's best efforts, the wagon was severely jolted several times as he worked the rig over large ruts and exposed tree roots. There were also a couple of places where he had to ease the wagon through small, spring-fed creeks which crossed the road. Wend mentally thanked God that at least they had had a sustained period of dry weather, for he feared what the journey would have been like in mud or even light ice and snow.

Wend looked at the moon and estimated that it was around midnight when they finished the last switchback on the north side of the mountain and entered the gap through the very crest. He turned around on the seat. "Peggy, look behind us."

She looked up from her sister and did as he said. "I see a couple of lights; very faint."

"Those are from Sherman Mill, Peggy. Probably from the tavern, the only place likely to be lighted this late."

She sucked in her breath. "I'd probably be closing up the place right now if I were back there." Then she paused a moment. "Poor Ma and Pa: They're probably sick with worry right now."

They traveled a very short distance and soon were at the southern side of the gap. Wend stopped the horses. "We'll rest the horses here for a while. Come on up here Peggy and look at the valley ahead."

She climbed up onto the seat. The moon was still shining bright, and there was a patch of lights in the distance.

Peggy pointed out ahead. "Are those the lights of Carlisle? There are so many of them!"

Wend laughed and stretched his shoulders and arms, relieved at the break from handling the reins. "There's a tavern on nearly every block in Carlisle. That's mostly what we're seeing this time of night."

"It's beautiful up here in the night." Peggy pursed her lips. "I feel guilty saying that, what with Ellen laying near death back there, but I never thought I'd see anything like this. It's almost like we were birds up in the night air."

134

Wend answered, "Yes, it is. I remember coming back from Fort Pitt with Joshua and Donegal. We camped one night on the crest of Sideling Hill. We could see the lights of the farms. That was also pretty." Then he thought of something. He stood up and looked toward the bottom of the mountain.

Peggy asked, "What are you looking for?"

"I'm trying to see if there is a light where Haroldson's Store should lay." Then he pointed. "There—I see the flicker of a faint light! Tree branches are waving in front of it." He set his chin. "I pray that's the store and they're waiting with a fresh team for us!"

"How far away is that, Wend?"

"In straight distance, no more than three miles. But we got as many switchbacks ahead of us as there were on the north side. So it could be double that distance we have to travel."

Peggy shivered and pulled her cloak more tightly around her shoulders. "It's beautiful, but it's cold up here. Let's get moving again."

"Yes, but I think the worst of the trip is over. It's all downhill from here— let's push on and get to Haroldson's place." Wend waited for her to climb back down to the wagon bed, then touched the reins to the horses, and they started the trip down the south side of the mountain.

It was less than twenty minutes later that they met with disaster and Wend knew it was his fault.

They ran down the initial leg of the first switchback. The wagon and the horses picked up speed as they descended. Wend kept his foot on the brake lever, pushing it frequently to slow them at the steepest parts. He was confident that he had the team well under control. But the first switchback turn came up faster than he expected and turned out to be sharper and steeper than he remembered. The result was that they almost overshot the curve, and Wend jerked the reins to get the team back into the middle of the road. They made the turn—but just barely—and tree branches whipped over them and beat against the side of the wagon.

Peggy was startled and fearful. "What's happening, Wend?"

"We overshot that turn by a little bit. But it's all right—I've got it under control." Wend felt the tension flow out of his body and congratulated himself on avoiding a potentially disastrous situation. And just as he was thinking that, they ran into the real disaster.

A great gully loomed before them, running right across the road. It was too late to pull up or hit the brake. The horses navigated it well, but the wagon slammed down horrifically. And at the same Wend heard a loud noise, like the sharp crack of a rifle firing. He instinctively knew something was wrong with the wagon.

He pulled up as soon as they were back on good road beyond the gully.

Peggy asked, with rising anxiety in her voice, "Why are we stopping? What's wrong?"

"I think we broke something, Peggy."

Wend climbed down from the seat. "Hand me the lantern."

Peggy complied and he walked around the wagon, soon finding what he feared as he inspected the left front wheel. "We've broken a spoke of the front wheel on this side. It's badly split from near the hub outward."

She jumped down from the bed and ran around the wagon to stand beside him, looking down at the spoke. As she stared at the damage, she began to shiver and Wend heard her teeth chatter.

Peggy asked, "Can't we just run it the way it is, if we're careful?"

"It's weakened greatly. The whole wheel will fail on the next heavy bump. No, we can't go any further with it this way."

Wend could sense the girl beginning to panic. She said, "We'll have to ride the horses. Put Ellen up in front of me and I'll hold her carefully."

"No, that's no use, Peggy. That splinter would shift as she moved against you and kill her."

"Then build a litter. Cut saplings and we'll use the blankets to support her. We can find a way to carry her between two of the horses."

"That would take too long, even if we had enough rope to lash something together. Then we'd have to figure out how to safely attach the litter between two of the horses." He shook his head. "No, if she's going to get to Carlisle alive, it's got to be in the wagon."

Peggy was near panic. "But you said we can't run on that wheel anymore. We don't have a spare." Her voice was a sob in the night. "For God's sake, what are we going to do? We must do something!"

Wend looked at the girl. She played the coquette in the common room of the tavern. But he had always respected her for the firm control she had displayed in times of excitement or stress. Now, for the first time, he witnessed her losing her grip. To her credit, it was with worry over her sister.

In a spontaneous reaction, he put his arm around her shoulders. He spoke as calmly as he could manage. "Peggy, now listen: I'm going to fix the spoke. Then we'll be on our way."

"How are you going to fix it? You're no wheelwright! You don't have the tools, and anyway, what can you do here in the dark?"

"I know a way. It will be temporary, but it should hold up if we drive carefully." He took his arm from around her, and climbed back up onto the wagon seat. "Peggy, hold the lantern up so the light is on the wheel. I'm going to move the rig forward until the broken spoke is directly upright above the hub. Do you understand what I mean?"

"Yes, I'll tell you when it's there."

He eased the horses forward until Peggy signaled him. Then he set the brake and climbed down again. He wordlessly took the lantern from Peggy's hand and searched along the side of the road until he found several large stones. He placed these in front of the forward wheels to keep the wagon absolutely still in case the horses moved. Then he climbed into the bed and searched through the tool box. Shortly he handed a spool of small diameter cord and a wooden carpenter's clamp down to Peggy.

As he climbed down, Peggy asked, "How is this stuff going to help fix the spoke?"

He put the lantern down on the ground, moving it around until it cast the most light on the wheel and the spoke. "We're going to fish the spoke."

"You're going to do *what*?"

"It's something my grandfather learned on the ship coming over from Germany. It's a way sailors use to fix split masts or spars on a ship, when they can't stop to replace them. They use line to wrap around the split to hold it together and keep it from breaking further. Grandfather worked out a way to use the system to fix cracked and broken spokes and he taught my father."

Peggy shook her head in doubt. "Have you ever done this before?"

"I helped my Pa do it once, but never did it by myself." He looked at the girl and said, "Now listen: It takes two people working together to do it right. You're going to have to help me all along the way." He thought for a moment. "But unless something goes bad wrong, we should be on our way in an hour or two."

Wend dropped to his knees and handed Peggy the clamp. "Look—do you see that the split starts about six inches above the hub and the end of the split part is separated by more than an inch out near the rim?"

"Yes, yes, I see what you mean."

"All right, I'm going to press it together at the end of the split part as hard as I can with my hands. You need to get right down beside me and get the clamp over both parts of the split about half way between the hub and the rim."

Peggy nodded. "I understand."

"Once you've got the clamps around the spoke, you'll have to twist the screws to tighten it. We've got to get the split closed up as much as possible before we start winding the cord."

Wend squeezed the ends of the split toward each other with every bit of strength in his wrists and fingers. He was able to get it nearly closed up. And he said a little prayer of thanks, for he had feared that it might break at the bottom of the split when he applied pressure at the top. "Go ahead with the clamp."

Peggy moved in close beside him and worked the clamp arms around the spoke. "Is this where you want it?"

"Exactly, Peggy. Now start to twist the screws and tighten it against the wood. Alternate between the two screws to keep the clamps parallel. Mind you, they'll get harder to turn as it tightens down." He looked at her face, its features highlighted by the flickering light of the lantern. "Get it as tight as you possibly can."

Peggy started to work. Soon Wend could feel the closing of the clamp taking pressure off his hands and he pressed the ends even harder. She continued turning the screws and the split closed more tightly.

"Wend, I can't do it any tighter. The toggles on the screws are cutting into my fingers."

Wend released his hands from the split, now held closed by the clamp. "I'll take over now." He began twisting on the screws, and was able to squeeze the clamp arms a little tighter. "You did real good, Peggy."

They stood up, looking down at the spoke. He felt Peggy shivering beside him in the bitter cold and wind at the top of the mountain. He unbuttoned his heavy wool over-coat and took it off. "Here, take your cloak off and put this on. We're going to be here for a while and we can't have you freezing. I'll be doing most of the work, so I need to be free to move."

Peggy looked up at him, her mouth and jaw set. He thought for a moment that she was going to refuse, but then she quickly took off her cloak and Wend helped her wriggle into the coat.

It was too big for her, going down to the ground. She rolled up the ends of the sleeves so that she could use her hands.

The girl shivered again as the warmth of the coat spread through her body, but then she said, "Thanks Wend, that's much better. I didn't know how long I was going to be able to stand that cold."

Wend knelt down again and picked up the spool of cord. "Get down here with me, Peggy. We're going to have to work as a team from now on until it's finished." He took the end of the cord and tied it off at the place where the spoke joined the hub. Then he took the spool and pushed it around the spoke, making the first wrap of the cord, and pulled it as tight as he could manage. Then he held the cord and kept tension on the wrap. He handed the spool to Peggy. "You'll do the wrapping of the cord around the spoke. After each wrap you make, I'll seize the cord and pull it tight. We have to keep the wrapping as tight against the wood as possible, but without breaking the cord."

Peggy nodded. "I see what you're doing."

Wend continued. "And the coils also must be tight against each other." He took his knife from the sheath on his hip. "I'll use the butt of this to tamp them down against each other every time you make a loop."

And so, working together, they made twenty wraps of the cord. Then Wend told Peggy to stop winding. "Now we come to a ticklish part, Peggy. Every so often we have to tie it off. If we don't, we could lose everything we've done if it breaks or we somehow lose the tension. So every twenty wraps we'll just dip the line under itself, pull it tight, then start looping it again. It's kind of like a sewing knot. Then problem is keeping the tension on the line as we do it."

Peggy grasped the idea immediately. "I know what to do. I'll dip the line. You just make sure you hold everything tight until I've tied the knot." She did it with deft fingers. And they were soon ready to do the next twenty turns.

They repeated the procedure until they had wrapped the spoke nearly up to the clamp. Then Wend had Peggy hold the tension on the cord while he loosened the clamp, slid it upward six or eight inches, and then re-tightened it.

Working together, they continued until the spoke was tightly rapped all the way up to the very rim. He finished by tying it off with a double knot Then, wearily, they both stood up and looked down at what they had accomplished, neither saying anything for long moments.

Wend looked over at Peggy. The flickering lantern light illuminated the features of her face, highlighting the high cheekbones, large round eyes, well formed mouth and lips, and the strong chin. Some of her raven colored hair had escaped the bondage of her hairpins and cap and was blowing in the wind, giving her a disheveled appearance. A thick lock lay across her forehead and eyes. In the oversized coat with rolled sleeves, she looked like a little girl. Wend had always been immune to the affect that her beauty seemed to have on all the other men in the valley. But suddenly, right in the midst of the gusty wind and chill on the mountain, he found himself aroused and seized by a desire to wrap her in his arms. Peggy looked up from the wheel and into his eyes, and for a few seconds they stood gazing at each other in silence.

Then Peggy spoke and her words broke the spell which had momentarily overcome Wend. "The wrapping has pulled the parts of the spoke together even more tightly. Do you think it will hold?"

Wend shook his head. "I don't know Peggy. All we can do is travel on as carefully as possible and hope we don't hit any more really big wash outs." He picked up remaining cord and the clamp and put them back into the tool box. He looked up at the moon. "Best I can figure, we've lost a couple of hours. I'd guess it's around two in the morning. Climb back into the wagon, and we'll get started." Wend picked up Peggy's cloak and wrapped it around his shoulders.

It turned out that they did hit several more rough spots, but Wend was now extraordinarily tense and alert. He drove with his eyes focused as far ahead as he could manage, keeping the horses reined in carefully on the downslopes and the turns in the switchbacks. Doing so, he was able to nurse them over the bad sections. An hour and a half saw them into the foothills below the mountain and a half hour after that they were pulling up at Haroldson's. Wend saw a small light shining through the front windows of the store and another from an upstairs window. Just as Wend was dismounting from the wagon, the front door swung open and the proprietor came down the steps, lantern in hand, and hurried over to them.

He was tall, lean man, with a stubbly beard covering his face. "I've got a matched four horse team ready for you, hitched and standing in the paddock on the other side of the stable."

Wend said, "I can't tell you how much we appreciate this. I'll have them back to you as soon as possible."

Haroldson stepped over to the wagon bed and looked down at Ellen and then up into Peggy's eyes. "Think nothing of it. But you're hours late; I thought something must have happened to you. I'd almost made up my mind to unharness the horses and go to bed." Then Haroldson stopped in his tracks and stared at Wend. A broad smile came over his face and his eyes twinkled. "Say, is that what all the men are wearing in Sherman Mill these days?"

Wend glanced down, wondering what the storekeeper was talking about. Then he remembered that he was still wearing Peggy's cape with its obvious feminine appearance. He looked up at Haroldson and smiled back. "Actually, it's just the thing for running a night wagon over the mountain."

* * *

The sun was coming up as they carefully forded Conodoguinet Creek and began passing the first outlying buildings of Carlisle. With the increased visibility of morning dusk and now driving a well trained and matched team, Wend had set a fast pace over the relatively smooth road between Haroldson's and the town. Just as the sun was clear of the horizon, they turned onto Market Street and headed eastward for Doctor Highsmith's place. When they pulled up in front of the apothecary shop, Hank Marsh immediately burst out through the door. The right side of his face was covered with a white bandage. He was followed, with more deliberation, by the doctor.

Hank cried out, "How is she?"

Peggy brushed the strands of her black hair away from her face "She's still breathing and I can feel her heart beating. She doesn't seem to be losing blood since we left Sherman Mill. That's all that I know."

Highsmith put on a pair of spectacles and looked into the wagon bed. "Please uncover the patient."

Peggy pulled the blanket away from Ellen, exposing the splinter sticking out of her back. If the doctor was shocked, he didn't show any sign of it. Instead, he simply asked, "Is the point all the way though her?"

Peggy nodded.

Highsmith clucked his tongue and then reached up and gently moved the splinter. Ellen groaned softly. He nodded to himself. "At least she is responsive. All right, let's get her into the shop. I have a room made up with a bed ready for her." He looked over the mattress and pillows. "We can move her right on the mattress—that would be best, disturbing her as little as possible."

The doctor looked over at Wend. "Mr. Eckert, you certainly bring me some interesting cases. If you keep this up, I may have to start paying you a commission."

Wend, tense and exhausted, felt a flash of anger. "Doctor, that's a cavalier attitude you are taking. I resent that remark, made over a woman near death."

Highsmith smiled at Wend. "Now, now, Mr. Eckert. I am sincerely sorry: It was just a little medical humor which burst out without any thought." He looked at the three of them. "Let's get her inside and I'll look her over in detail."

They carried Ellen into the shop, with the doctor's plump wife holding the door open for them, and carefully deposited her in a bed within the first room down the hall.

Wend looked over at Highsmith. Still testy, he asked, "Have you ever taken care of a patient in this kind of condition?"

Peggy joined in. "Yes, I have the same concern. Forgive me for asking, but do you have any experience with a wound this serious? We're dealing with my sister's life."

Highsmith looked around at Peggy, Wend, and Hank, who were all staring at him. He smiled as if at a joke only he understood. Then he said, "Permit me to briefly discuss my resume. Before coming to the colonies and taking up my practice here in Carlisle, I was the surgeon of His Majesty's Frigate Minerva, 32 guns, for several years during the late war. I have dealt with wounds from muskets, bayonets, cutlasses, roundshot, grapeshot, chainshot, and whatever else our esteemed enemies the French could throw at us. Most of the injuries from those instruments of destruction led me to amputate the affected limb. But now, I ask you to search your minds very carefully and reflect on what the main result of a heavy roundshot hitting a wooden ship's hull or spars happens to be?"

He looked at the three young people as they began to understand what the doctor was implying.

"As I expect you have now calculated, the inevitable result of roundshot hitting a ship is massive clouds of flying splinters. My dear lady and gentlemen, I can assure you that I have extracted splinters of all sizes from virtually every part of the human anatomy." He looked directly at Wend. "Mr. Eckert, I can, in all modesty, say that you have, quite by chance, delivered your young lady friend here to the one man in all of Pennsylvania most experienced with treating *precisely* the kind of wound which we have in front of us."

In chagrin, Wend looked at the smiling doctor. "I regret having questioned your ability and experience, sir."

"Nonsense, lad. I dare say it was a fair question. However, we are now squandering valuable time. I propose that you and Mr. Marsh here retire to my sitting room, while my wife, the patient's sister, and I get to work."

* * *

Wend, sprawled on a cushioned chair in the Highsmith's sitting room, was pulled out of his deep sleep by a persistent tapping on his shoulder. He opened his eyes to find Peggy bent over him, her face only a few inches from his own. He rubbed the sleep from his eyes and shook himself to full consciousness.

Peggy said, "The doctor has finished with Ellen. I was there all the time while he worked. He got the splinter out and probed through the wound to make sure it was clean. Luckily, the splinter was pretty smooth along its edges so that there weren't many small fragments to break off in her flesh. Then he was able to sew it up without too much more bleeding. But she's very weak. The doctor says we got her here just in time." She smiled thinly. "The next few hours will tell the story, but the doctor thinks she will make it if mortification doesn't set in."

"They always say that—about mortification, I mean." He thought a moment. "Is she awake yet?"

"No, and Highsmith has no idea when she'll regain consciousness. He says it's best for her to sleep for the present, anyway."

Wend sat up and saw bright sunlight. He realized he was very hungry. "What time is it?"

"It's just before noon. By the way, I asked Hank to take the wagon and horses down to the stable at Washburn's Tavern, since you said you had business to do there."

"Yes, I use his stable when I'm in town." He stood up. "Why don't you get ready and I'll take you to the best tavern in town for lunch. You certainly earned it last night and this morning."

A half hour later Wend and Peggy arrived at the front steps of the Walking Horse Tavern.

Peggy looked up at the sign. "I've heard a lot about this place. It is the finest and most expensive place in Carlisle, Wend. This is where all the best people dine." She put her hand to her hair and then looked down at her dress and petticoats. "These are my work clothes; I can't go in there like this."

"Nonsense—sure you can. And they'll welcome us with open arms. I promise." He took her arm and hustled her up the steps before she could protest. "Besides, I'm also dressed in my shop clothes. So we're a matched pair."

She looked at him in puzzlement. "How can you be so sure they won't throw us out?"

"Not to worry." He took her arm and before she could say anything else led her up the stairs and through the entrance. In a few instants they stood in the receiving area of the brightly lit common room. All the tables were set with white tablecloths, flower vases, and eating utensils. About half the tables were occupied with lunch patrons.

A server came up to them. Before he could speak, Wend peremptorily said, "I'd like to speak to Mr. McCallin, please."

The serving man looked puzzled, but went to find the proprietor. Presently, a short, stout man dressed in a white shirt, black waistcoat and breaches, came out of the kitchen and approached them. Suddenly the man stopped abruptly, his eyes widening as he saw Wend.

Wend smiled broadly, stepped forward and grabbed the proprietor's hand. "Hello, Mr. McCallin. I'm delighted to see you again. You do recognize me, don't you?"

The little proprietor gulped. "Of course, sir. The memory of your last visit is etched permanently in my mind. You are Mr. Eckert of Sherman Valley and you were in here just before Colonel Bouquet's expedition departed in July. What can I do for you now?"

"I thought you'd remember my visit, sir." He motioned to Peggy. "We're here for lunch. And we'd like your best window table." Wend pointed to an empty table in the front corner of the tavern. "That one looks perfect."

"Of course, sir. Here—I would be delighted to escort you." He led the way and seated Peggy with a flourish. "A server will be here immediately, Mr. Eckert."

Peggy stared at Wend with astonishment in her eyes. "He treated you like royalty. My father always told me this was a stuffy place that would treat ordinary persons with disdain."

Wend laughed. "Your father was right. But McCallin treats me with respect because the only other time I was in here I threatened him with bodily harm and then paid three times what his meal was worth."

Peggy shook her head and sighed. "Wend, stop talking in riddles."

Wend smiled. "Its true! The last time I came in here was July. I was escorting a young camp follower of the 77th Highlanders. Her name was Mary Fraser. I had just bumped into her on the street outside after not seeing her for four years. She and her mother meant a lot to me—they spent many days nursing me right after the massacre of my family back in 1759. When we came in to get some tea and pastries, McCallin tried to throw us out because he thought we were trash who couldn't afford to eat here." Wend shook his head. "The truth is, I don't blame him. I was getting ready to guide a column of troops to Fort Bedford and was dressed in my hunting shirt and leggings. She was wearing a hand-me down, patched dress with muddy shoes." He laughed. "Peggy, army women have a hard life and often are dressed in cast-off rags." He motioned to their work clothes. "We look elegant by comparison. Anyway, McCallin pulled me aside and very haughtily asked if we could afford to eat in his place. There was no way I was going to let McCallin

144

embarrass the girl who helped save my life. Moreover, I wanted her to have the experience, at least once in her life, of eating in an elegant tavern. So I grabbed his arm—very roughly, I might add—dragged him to the counter, and threw down enough coins to buy half the food in the place. Luckily, I had just got cash for a rifle sale from Washburn." Wend grinned ironically with the memory. "You should have seen his eyes light up! Then I told him I would thrash him if he didn't give the girl his best service."

Peggy looked over to the counter where McCallin was admonishing one of his servers about something. She laughed and said, "I'd love to have seen that. And that was quite thoughtful of you. I'm sure that girl will remember your kindness all her life. Where is she now?"

Wend looked out the window for a moment. "She's still at Fort Pitt. Actually, Peggy, she and I fell deeply in love as the expedition marched westward."

Peggy's face wrinkled up. "Wait a minute, Wend. What about that English girl you were searching for? That was your whole purpose for marching with the army. You mean that, after four years of ignoring all the girls in Sherman Valley, you were distracted by a camp follower?" She threw her head back and laughed out loud. "Ha! She must be some girl!"

Wend stared quietly at Peggy for a long moment. Then he said, "She was indeed a lovely young girl, as pretty in her own way as Abigail. All the young bucks of the 77th were in love with her." He hesitated, then said, "In fact, I had to fight one soldier who had the impression that she belonged to him."

Peggy slapped her hand down on the table. "This is getting even better! You mean that you, Wend Eckert—of all people—got into a fight over a girl's affections? I can hardly believe that! So why didn't you bring her back with you after that English woman told you she wanted to stay with the Mingoes?"

Wend took a deep breath and locked his eyes with hers. "Mary died from a mortified wound she got at Bushy Run. I was away in the Ohio Country when she passed away. She's buried in an unmarked grave at the Fort Pitt cemetery."

The mirth which had been on Peggy's face faded. She was momentarily speechless; then she reached across the table to touch Wend's hand. "Forgive me, Wend. I'm sorry for making fun of her. It must have been devastating for you to lose two girls you loved within a few days."

They sat there quietly looking at each other for several long seconds, Peggy's hand lingering on Wend's.

He was about to answer when he felt a hand on his shoulder. He looked up to see Sheriff Dunning standing beside him. With the sheriff was John

Armstrong. McCallin was there too, obviously leading his two distinguished customers to a table.

Dunning said, "Hello, Eckert! Good to see you again. I must admit I'm a little surprised that you are back in Carlisle so soon." Then he looked at Peggy. "And Miss McCartie, it is always a pleasure to see you. Please extend my greetings to your father and mother."

Peggy smiled at the High Sheriff. "It's nice to see you again, sir. It's been a long time since you've been up to Sherman Mill."

Dunning turned to Armstrong and made introductions. Wend stood up. "It's a pleasure to meet you, Colonel. I've heard a lot about you. My father, Johann Eckert, was the contract armorer in your battalion during General Forbes campaign against Fort Duquesne in 1758."

"Ah, yes. Of course I remember him clearly." A look of puzzlement came over Armstrong's face. "But I was led to believe that he and his entire family died in 1759 during a war party ambush near Sideling Hill."

Dunning said, "The Pennsylvania Gazette's article was in error. Young Eckert here was the sole survivor, John." He wagged his finger at Armstrong. "You'll be interested to know that after the massacre, he was taken in by Paul Carnahan and his wife, up in Sherman Mill."

"The devil you say, Sheriff! Now there's a coincidence." He turned to Wend. "How is my old friend Reverend Carnahan? I greatly respect him for his service during our expedition against the Delaware at Kittanning! He made a fine soldier and I've always been mystified why he chose the way of the collar after the raid."

Wend responded, "He's doing well. And I'll always be grateful for the kindness that he and his wife have shown me over the years."

Dunning spoke up. "You know, John, we've been talking about this Paxton Boy situation. You might be interested to know that Carnahan and Eckert here were trying to help the Conestogas at the Lancaster Work House when the second attack occurred. They witnessed it all, or at least the aftermath."

Wend nodded. "I had a very good friend among the Conestoga. His name is Charlie Sawak; he and I went to school together when I lived in Lancaster."

Armstrong raised an eyebrow and looked at Wend as if he were apprais-ing him in new light. "You were friends with Sawak? The one who escaped?" He pursed his lips and shook his head. "I confess that I find it hard to get a good handle on this Conestoga situation. I had always believed them to be peaceful farmers. But since the uprising began, there have been many stories about them helping the war parties. Most people find the tales convincing, particularly given how murderously effective the war party attacks have been. I don't know what to believe myself, but they do say where you have a lot of smoke there must be some sort of a fire. I have to tell you that there is strong feeling that the Conestoga tribe got what they deserved. And this fellow Sawak is at the center of many of those stories about Conestogas consorting with the enemy."

"Whatever you've heard, Colonel, I'll give my word that Charlie was simply a peddler. I'm certain that the stories about him and any other Conestogas helping the hostile Indians are groundless gossip."

There was silence as Dunning and Armstrong exchanged glances. Then Armstrong said in a firm voice, "Well, Eckert, that puts you in opposition to some very influential men who argue differently; men such as our good friend Richard Grenough. I've always found his counsel to be very accurate and spot on the mark."

Wend sighed to himself and said, "Yes, I'm rapidly learning how many people trust Mr. Grenough."

Armstrong shook his head again. "On the other hand, I personally don't condone what was done to the Conestogas. Nor do I support the march of this Paxton militia on the Moravian villages."

Wend asked, "Isn't there some way to stop an attack on the Moravians?"

Armstrong's brow furrowed. "Actually, Eckert, my contacts tell me that that the governor is working out something to protect them." He paused and looked momentarily at Dunning, then back to Wend. "But I have to tell you that, even given my cordial relationship with the governor, I am sympathetic to the petition that the Paxton men want to deliver to the assembly. The government *can* and *should* do more to protect the settlement area. In fact, as I was just telling the sheriff a moment ago, I've decided to leave early tomorrow for Philadelphia. Riding hard, I can be there before the protestors. I want to use any influence which I might possess to preclude violence and to support the sentiment of their petition."

There was silence for a moment, and Wend took the opportunity to ask a question. "Colonel, how many men from around here rode to join the Paxton Men?"

Dunning spoke up. "I've been watching that, Eckert. 'Twas more than 150 men I saw ride out from the Carlisle area. And I got reports from Shippensburg and York that there was an equal number from those two towns put together. And more from the Conococheague country and the area around Chambers' Fort. I'd not be surprised but what 400 men from this side of the river joined those Paxton Boys."

Armstrong nodded. "I talked with Grenough. He thought there would be about that many. That was just before he left for Philadelphia himself—he's going to offer his services to the governor in this time of crisis." Armstrong grimaced. "And I think his wise advice will be needed in the negotiations with the protestors."

After exchanging a few more comments and pleasantries, the two men left for their table. Wend mulled through what he had heard. His guess that Grenough would travel to Philadelphia to influence events had been correct. And, after listening to Armstrong's words, he realized two things: First, Armstrong was as much under Grenough's influence as other important men in the colony. Second, it was becoming clear that despite official expressions of horror, there would be little enthusiasm for punishing the men who had murdered the Conestogas.

Wend realized that his personal mission to destroy Grenough and his organization was more important than ever, for he could look to no one in the colony's government for help. And as critical as the trip to save Ellen had been, it had put him at least three days behind his schedule. He must act swiftly to get down to Shippensburg and York before Grenough and his men returned.

Suddenly his thoughts were interrupted by Peggy. "My God, Wend. You look lost in thought and you have such a fierce expression in your eyes: It's scary."

Wend brought himself back to the business at hand and smiled. "Sorry Peggy, I was just thinking about some things I have to do. Well, shall we make our choice for lunch?"

CHAPTER SEVEN
The Warehouse in Shippensburg

Wend sat on the wagon's seat, the reins loose in his hands, letting Joe, the lead horse, set the pace as they rolled along the Great Wagon Road down through the Cumberland Valley. The road originated in Philadelphia, ran through Lancaster, curved northward to Harris' Ferry, and thence west to Carlisle. From there it turned south and led through Pennsylvania's widest valley until it crossed into Maryland about ten miles south of Fort Loudoun. Ultimately it stretched through the southern colonies all the way to Georgia. It was, in short, the artery which formed the basis for land commerce and communication through the middle and southern colonies. Visible on the road ahead of him Wend could see four Conestoga freight wagons headed southward, and he had met more than ten heading northward since he had left Carlisle that morning. An hour before, a postal rider had whisked by him on a strong horse, waving as he rushed on his way to the south.

Wend was comfortable on this stretch of the road, for he had traveled it several times in the last five years. First had been with his family in 1759, on the initial stage of their abortive trip to Fort Pitt. Then, after the massacre, he had come back over it enroute to Carlisle, riding on top of an army cargo wagon while Mary Fraser and her mother had cared for his wounds. Last July, he had ridden with Colonel Bouquet's expedition to relieve Fort Pitt in the early days of the Indian uprising. So now, on a cold but sunny January day, he was well aware that they were about two hours from their destination of Shippensburg and he was satisfied that they would arrive in the town before nightfall.

The trip southward had given Wend time to review the events of the last few days and make plans for his investigation of Grenough's establishment. After he and Peggy had left the Walking Horse Tavern, he had escorted her back to the doctor's and then gone to Washburn's. There he hitched the borrowed team to his wagon and drove it down to a wheelwright who had his shop at the western end of town. It was there that he made an intriguing discovery.

As he walked into the shop, he found the proprietor and his apprentices busy at work on a Conestoga freight wagon of the largest size. Wend was shocked to recognize that it was Matt Bratton's and that major modifications were being performed. The rear end was up on a heavy jack and both wheels had been removed. Two apprentices were at work on the rear axel. Wend's interest was immediately aroused. After greeting the proprietor, he casually asked about the amount of work done on the wagon.

The wheelwright shook his head. "Lord knows, it's a big job; not like any I've done before. The owner wanted new axels and wheels installed on both front and rear. Not only that, he specified much heavier, stronger construction than normal. Here, you can see we've finished the front end." He put his hand on the top of one of the tires. "Look at the thickness of those spokes and rims. Now we're doing the same to the rear set."

Wend stared at the wagon, his interest sharpened. "Why do you suppose he wanted that done? These freight wagons are heavily built to start with."

"You're right about that. It's all custom work; I asked him why he wants such strong wheels and axels and he just said he had to do some heavy duty hauling over rough roads. And for the money he laid on the table, I wasn't asking any more questions than that."

Wend made arrangements to have his own wheel fixed; the proprietor said he would put one of his apprentices on the job and could get it done by the next afternoon. Wend unhitched his wagon and led the team back toward Washburn's stable. As he walked up Market Street he went over the implications of what he had found out. There could be no mystery about the modifications Bratton was having made to his wagon. Clearly, it was preparation for the upcoming "Next trip" that Frank McKenzie had overheard Bratton and his trader friends discussing. Obviously, on previous trips, Bratton had had breakdowns on the extraordinarily rough roads which were the norm beyond the Conococheague country. Moreover, Bratton must be making ready to carry a heavier than normal load. If that were the case, it was likely that the traders were setting up to supply many war parties with the goods they needed for an extended campaign.

Wend returned to the doctor's to inquire about Ellen. Highsmith told him that Ellen had briefly regained consciousness. She had looked up at her sister, smiled, tried to say something, and then gone back to sleep. Wend and Hank Marsh visited together at her bedside about an hour later. Ellen was in deep sleep but Wend could see that she had a much healthier color on her face.

As the two men looked down at her, Peggy said, "Doc Highsmith says she's out of danger. He thinks she's going to make a full recovery."

After discussing the situation, they decided that Hank should take Wend's mare and ride for Sherman Mill immediately. Pushing it hard, he could be back just after nightfall. The McCartie's would be desperate for news of their daughter. He could also tell them that the doctor wanted to keep Ellen for several days and that Peggy would stay to help nurse her.

Wend had driven his wagon back to Sherman Mill the morning after repairs were completed.

Mindful that the emergency trip to Carlisle had used up three days, he knew he must hurry to get to Grenough's warehouse locations before the trader and his men returned. Accordingly, he spent only one night at the Carnahan's, packing clothing and money for the trip, and then had departed the very next morning. His haste had surprised everyone in the Carnahan household.

Baird had looked askance at him, clearly suspicious. He had smiled slyly and asked, "You're sure hot to get down to Shippensburg; what have you got goin' on down there? Some other girl we ain't heard about yet?"

Wend had simply repeated his story about visiting the new forge and insisted that he wanted to travel while good weather persisted. But he knew that Baird was still suspicious and Paul Carnahan, who had heard the conversation, put his hand up to his chin, which was a sure sign that he was thinking things over. But nobody had said any more and Wend had departed with the dawn of the next morning.

* * *

Hilda Froelich, wife of the gunsmith, was busy cleaning up the dinner table as Wend and Henry put their coats on and made ready to visit a local tavern for after-dinner drinks. Wend had suggested that they visit a tavern because he wanted to talk with Froelich away from his wife and two teenage children. Immediately after arriving, Wend had discovered that the matronly Hilda had two obvious attributes. The first was a disconcertingly large set of breasts, which preceded her in her movements like the advance guard of an army. The second was a very sharp tongue which she never hesitated to exercise.

At the moment she was using it on Henry. "I know why you want to go out to that tavern. Don't try to fool me, Henry! You're going to play cards again. You do it every night that you can think of an excuse to get away. I despair to think how much of our hard-earned money you've wasted at cards and those endless wagers at sporting events."

Froelich rolled his eyes. "Now my sweet, it's nothing like that. Mr. Eckert has never been in Shippensburg before and I promised to show him a good tavern for his lodging."

"Yes, and I'm sure you'll steer him to the Widow Piper's Tavern, down at the square. Everyone knows that place has a game of cards going on every night in the back room. And you'll be there 'till all hours."

"Now my dearest, nothing could be further from the truth. I'll be right back after I get Mr. Eckert settled in his room. And he wants to talk to me a little bit about the new forge out to the west of town. It won't take long at all."

"I don't see why Mr. Eckert can't stay here. There's an extra bed in Charlie's room. Its got a fine down mattress." She turned to Wend. "Why don't you reconsider, Mr. Eckert? It would be so much more convenient for you. And I don't understand why you two can't talk right here." She looked at him pointedly. "Unless this is a conspiracy between the two of you and you're planning to play cards also."

Wend smiled and said, "I don't play games of chance at a table, Frau Froelich. I'm staying overnight at a tavern because I want to get about my business very early in the morning and I don't want to cause you any inconvenience. But I do appreciate being able to stable my team in your barn."

Then Wend thanked Hilda for a fine dinner and the men escaped out into the crisp night air. The two strode silently along the small town's main street. Wend stole a glance at the gunsmith, and he could see Froelich, now free from the effect of Hilda's verbal bombardment, relax as they walked.

Presently Froelich broke the silence. "The truth is, Wend, I *am* taking you to the Widow Piper's. It is the best tavern in town. They've got clean sheets and decent food."

Wend smiled. "Beyond being the place with the hottest card game in the back room?"

"Indeed. Of course my dear wife is correct. But naturally I couldn't admit that to her. Besides, I won't be playing tonight. I will hurry back home and therefore confound her."

They soon arrived at the tavern, which was a large stone building with a two story main section and a one story wing on one side. It appeared to be one of the most substantial buildings in the town.

After obtaining his room, Wend joined Froelich at a table for a drink. The tavern common room was nearly empty. But Wend could intermittently hear laughter and other loud voices through the door to the back room. He asked: Where is the widow? The only manager I've seen is a man. Does he run the tavern for her?"

Froelich laughed. "The Widow has long since gone on to her rewards. But she started this tavern almost thirty years ago, when Shippensburg was just a few houses and farms. Fact is, the magistrate used to hold court in here and all the business of the town was conducted right in this room for many years. So even after the current proprietor bought the place, he kept the name."

Wend turned to Froelich. "Let's get down to business. How long will it take to get out to this new forge tomorrow?"

Froelich pursed his lips. "It's built into the side of a hill less than a half-hour's wagon ride west of town. But I don't know why you want to visit that place. They've just got started. Mostly what they're making is some bloom iron. It's good for pots and perhaps simple tools. I heard that they just finished building a blast furnace, but they're still a long way from really good wrought iron, let alone the quality of metal and the skill necessary to make firelock barrels."

"I have no doubt you're right," Wend smiled, "But the truth is that I'm using the trip to the forge to hide the real purpose of my visit to Shippensburg."

Froelich froze with his ale mug halfway between the table and his mouth. "Hide the real purpose of your visit? What do you mean, lad?"

Wend looked around. No patrons were within earshot of their table. Then, for extra secrecy, he spoke in German. He told Froelich the whole story about Grenough and his conspiracy, describing in detail all the evidence and guesses he had about how the organization operated. He went into the story of his family's massacre and particularly the role of Grenough's traders in leading the Mingo war party to the wagon train on Forbes Road. Then he reminded Froelich how tight Grenough was with the colony's hierarchy and pointed out that at that very moment, Grenough was advising the governor and other officials on dealing with the Paxton men.

When Wend stopped talking, Henry Froelich, still speaking in German, said, "I find your evidence intriguing, although much of it is indirect. And Mr. Grenough's complicity, if true as you say, would be devastating."

Then he asked, "Why are you telling me all this? And what has this to do with your visit?"

"Because, Henry, I intend to take direct action against Grenough and his men. I can't tell the authorities about Grenough because they would just scoff at me. But I need more information and confirmation of what I suspect about his warehouse operations before I take drastic action. The fact is, I believe Grenough has massive amounts of war supplies stored in his warehouses here and in York." He paused and looked over at the bespectacled gunsmith. "Henry, that's where you come in; I need your help getting a look inside Grenough's warehouse here in Shippensburg."

Froelich looked puzzled. "How can I help you with that? I've seen the building, but I don't know anymore about it than its location."

"It's very simple. I intend to break into Grenough's warehouse tomorrow night. Your part will be very simple: I just want you to act as a lookout in case someone comes along who might discover me and alert the sheriff."

"I see." Froelich stared at Wend with an impassive face.

Wend looked at the little man and could get no sense of his feelings. Fear spread through him that the gunmaker would turn him down. He suddenly wondered what had made him think that a middle aged, married man with a family, secure in his trade, would jeopardize everything to help him in a dangerous quest.

Froelich asked, "So let me get this straight: You want me to stand by outside while you cut the warehouse locks, enter the building illegally, and then rifle through the goods in there so you can confirm a suspicion that Grenough is stockpiling illegal trading supplies? An act for which I could be arrested as an accomplice in thievery? Am I correct in that assumption?"

Wend nodded. 'That's right, sir. But now that you express it that way, it does sound very sordid. I'm sorry for asking you to get involved in something which could be of such hazard to yourself and your family. I'll find a way to do it on my own."

Froelich sat up straight and smiled broadly. "Nonsense, lad. Of course I'll help you!" He threw back his head and laughed out loud. "Had you going, there, didn't I?"

Wend was confused. "Yes, I admit you did."

"Look, Wend. We both know how boring it can be to sit in a shop all day turning the crank on a rifling machine or shaping a gun stock. Why do you think I gamble? I need a little excitement in my life. That's why, despite the displeasure it causes my sweet Hilda, I spend time gambling or wagering on sporting events like that shooting contest in Sherman Mill where we first met." He leaned across the table and spoke conspiratorially, "Frankly, you're little foray into Mr. Grenough's domain sounds far more exciting than even winning a big wager." He slapped his hand down on the table. "So count me in on your little nocturnal venture!"

* * *

"So here is where we slow burn the wood to make the charcoal." Mr. Wilhelm Hesse, manager of the Shippensburg Furnace and Forge, was, with very evident pride, showing Wend and Froelich around the iron making establishment. He was a balding man in his late forties who was beginning to put on weight around his middle. The two gunmakers stood beside Hesse as he waved his hand at a large field of sod-covered mounds from which wisps of smoke were wafting upward in the still air. "We place the wood in a pattern which will allow air to circulate, then cover it with earth and sod, leaving a hole at the top. We light it from the top and the fire travels downward, partially burning the wood as it goes; the residue is charcoal. The charcoal, of course, gives us a hotter and more even fire in the iron furnaces."

Wend asked, "How do you get your wood here? Do you employ laborers?"

"We may do that eventually. Right now, we're contracting with farmers who cut the wood and transport it here in their own wagons at times when work in their fields is slow. It provides cash for them and spares us the expense of maintaining a force of laborers and waggoners for that purpose."

Froelich looked around. "That takes care of your fuel." He pointed to a mound of dark gravel-like stone material which was located on top of the low hill which was located along the edge of the industrial area. "I see a supply of ore for the furnaces. But where's the quarry? I would think you would build the works next to your source."

Hesse nodded. "That's a good observation, Mr. Froelich. Ideally, we would have done that. Our quarry is about a quarter of a mile away. But there's no creek there. So, since we need flowing water to power our forced air furnaces, we had no choice but to build the ironworks here near that creek you can see over there and ship in the ore by wagon."

"That must take some significant manpower," Wend said.

"Yes, for that we employ a team of men who dig the ore and transport it to the works here. That's one of the bigger expenses we have."

Hesse led them toward a row of what Wend thought looked like large ovens. Each was of the same design and was a little taller than a man. "These are our bloom furnaces. They produce the lowest grade of iron we make, which is used principally for things like cooking pots, simple tools and stove tops." He stopped at one of the furnaces which was not in use and bent over to point in through an open access. "We shovel a measured supply of ore and a bit of limestone in the center, mixed up. Then we surround the ore with charcoal and light it." He pointed to accesses pipes around the furnace. "Air is sucked in through these pipes to provide for combustion. The ore melts into a red hot, thick mass which we call the 'bloom.' Then, once the fire is out, we pull the bloom out with a rake. It cools a little bit in the air, and then a black-smith hammers it into a square ingot for storage. Later it can be reheated in a forge and hammered into whatever shape is desired."

Wend and Froelich took turns looking into the bloom furnace.

Then Hesse said, "Come along and I'll show you our first blast furnace; we just put it into operation."

He led them to a large stone structure erected close to the creek. Wend saw that it was a pyramid shape, but with a flat top. The rear of the edifice was dug into the side of the hill and a wooden platform extended from the hill to the top of the furnace.

Hesse motioned upward. "This is the blast furnace, or as we refer to it, the 'stack'. It's about thirty five feet high." Then he pointed to the creek, where a dam had been built to form a pond. A wooden sluice had been con-structed to carry the water to a large wheel. "You can see that we've made the millpond big enough to provide for a steady flow of water to the wheel; we need to keep it constantly turning while the furnace is under blast."

They followed the ironmaster underneath a shelter roof mounted on posts. "Here is the linkage and gearing which converts the circular motion of the wheel to an up and down action to operate the bellows."

Wend watched the machinery—which reminded him of the wooden gearing in Marsh's Mill—in operation. It moved a pair of huge wood and leather bellows—they must each have been nearly twenty-five feet long—up and down in tandem. There was a groaning sound on the downward part of the cycle and then a "*whooshing*" sound as the bellows expelled air. He noted that an iron pipe connected the discharge end of each bellows to an opening in the furnace.

The ironmaster saw him examining one of the pipes and said, "We call that pipe the 'tuyere', Mr. Eckert; it runs directly into the very bottom of the stack. With the force of the air from the bellows, we get the combustion temperature inside up to nearly 3000 degrees; that's several times the temperature in the bloom furnaces and sufficient to fully melt the ore."

They stepped outside of the machinery shelter and Hesse pointed up to the top of the stack. Wend could see two men standing on the wooden platform which ran out to the top. One of them held a shovel.

Froelich said, "I assume those men are loading the furnace?"

Hesse nodded. "Yes. The man with the shovel is one of two 'fillers' on the upper level who actually shovel the ingredients into the top of the furnace. The other man you see is the supervisor who runs operations of the stack; he's called the 'founder'."

As they watched, a third man rolled a loaded handcart out along the platform; the man with the shovel began loading the contents into the furnace as the founder peered down into the opening.

Hesse said, "The founder's job is crucial; he is in charge of making sure that the correct mix of materials—ore, the limestone flux, and charcoal—gets loaded into the furnace and are layered properly. Obviously, that's essential to producing good quality iron."

Hesse motioned Wend and Froelich to walk around to the front of the furnace. Then he led them under another shelter roof. "Gentlemen, we're in the 'mold house'. This is where the iron ingots are formed. He pointed to a narrow opening at the base of the stack. "That's the mouth of the furnace. It is plugged with a mass of hard-packed clay: Then the heat of the fire inside rapidly transforms it to brittle ceramic material. When the ore is fully melted, the founder and his assistant, called the 'moulder', use this pole," he pointed to a long iron rod leaning up against the front of the furnace, "to smash the plug so that the liquid can flow out into the molds. We call that process 'tapping' the furnace."

The ironmaster waved his hand to a deep bed of sand which had been dug into the ground outside the wall of the furnace. A long, narrow channel had been cut in the sand to carry the flow of molten metal from the mouth of the furnace. Several oblong-shaped holes dug into the sand were connected to the central channel so that the metal would flow into them. Hesse looked at his two guests and smiled. "That central channel is called the 'sow' and the oblong molds on the side are called the 'pigs'. Very appropriate, don't you think? Pigs suckling at the sow's teats! Anyway, that's how we get the name 'pig iron'. That's the highest quality metal that we make."

Wend inspected the molding system and saw a separate channel which led off from the sow close to the mouth of the furnace, well before the pig molds. It led to a round-shaped mold. He asked, "What's that for—its shaped differently from the other molds?"

Hesse smiled. "Very observant, Mr. Eckert. That's for what we call the 'slag'. As the molten iron pools up at the bottom of the stack, impurities from the ore, the lime, and the charcoal float to the surface. They're lighter than the metal. Then, after we've tapped the furnace, the moulder stands near the mouth watching the flow of the liquid iron. When he sees the impurities start to appear, he uses his shovel to quickly dam up the sow channel and divert all the slag into the round mold."

Then he turned to Wend and said, "When you arrived, you said you were interested in gun barrels. Well, we're in the early days of making pig iron: It will take time and experience to make sure that our product is of good enough quality and that our men have the skill to forge it into barrels. So I personally think it will be a couple of years until we're ready to put out a finished wrought iron product of that caliber."

Froelich said, "Actually, the word around town was that you weren't going to build your first blast furnace for at least another year. I mean, it is an expensive proposition. What prompted you to move ahead so early?"

Wend waved his hand around the establishment. Besides the production area, a small village with houses for workers, a store, blacksmith shop, stable, and warehouse had been built. "Yes, all this takes a lot of men to operate and you seem to be very well financed. One business person to another, how did you get the cash together?"

Hesse laughed. "Look, I'm the manager and run the operation here on the site. But this forge is owned by a syndicate of about twenty men, most from Philadelphia and other towns in the eastern part of the colony. They each invested a share of the capital needed. I put in my own share, a rather small one. In reality, what I brought to the syndicate is my experience. I was trained from the bottom up in several ironworks, including both the Colebrookdale Furnace and the Cornwall Furnace."

Wend looked at Hesse with newfound respect. He knew that the Colebrookdale Furnace, sited to the northwest of Philadelphia, was the oldest in Pennsylvania, having been started by Thomas Rutter in 1716. And the Cornwall Furnace, located near Lebanon, directly east of Harris' Ferry, was also long established and well regarded for its product.

Meanwhile, Hesse continued, "I report back to a guiding committee made up of the major investors, who make the most significant decisions.

But the investors know that they have to be ready for several years of losses before we begin to show a profit."

He turned to Froelich. "In answer to your question, Mr. Froelich, the reasons we moved ahead of schedule to a blast furnace are twofold: First, we got word that a syndicate led by a certain Mr. William Bennet is in the preliminary stages of building a blast furnace north of York on Codorus Creek. We expect him to be in operation by next year. Our investors decided that we needed to make sure we could be competitive with him. Second, we unexpectedly received a large, lucrative order that will continue over a couple of years. That gave us the market assurance to spend the money necessary to move into the pig iron process."

Wend asked, "What kind of a contract would provide that kind of assurance?"

Hesse shrugged. "Here, I'll show you." He led them to another open shelter which covered workbenches adjacent to a blacksmith's forge. Hesse nodded to three heavily muscled blacksmiths who were at work under the shelter. "We're making a series of implements for our customer. The first is a large number of hatchet heads. The customer provides us with steel blades which he bought from a source in England." He picked up a thin, shiny piece of steel. "This is the cutting edge of the hatchet head. It's our job to make the rest of the head from wrought iron and then forge the two pieces together. That's what these fellows are doing."

One of the blacksmiths held up a finished head with the steel edge attached. Hesse said, "It's a very flexible design: If you put a short handle on it, it will be a hand hatchet. But it's large enough that, with a longer handle, it will make a usable axe. The iron head gives it good heft and the steel will hold a sharp edge. All and all, a very functional tool for any farmer or a settler of any kind."

Wend queried the manager. "Can you say who this is for?"

"I don't see why not. It's for Charles Grenough. You might have heard of him; he made his money as a frontier trader, but now he's moving to merchandising for settlers. He says he's opening general stores in Bedford, Cumberland, and several other places along Forbes Road from here to Pittsburgh. He wants these and other tools we're going to produce to help stock those new stores. In fact, we're up against a strict deadline. Mr. Grenough says he wants a supply of these hatchet-axe heads, and knife blades which we're also making, by early April at the latest."

Wend and Henry Froelich turned simultaneously to look at each other. Both realized that their visit to the forge had just ceased to be a mere cover for Wend's trip to Shippensburg.

Wend smiled broadly at Hesse. "Yes, you know, now that you mention the name, I do seem to recall having heard of Mr. Grenough before."

* * *

Grenough's warehouse was located on a sizable parcel of land in the western end of town. Numerous houses and shops of tradesmen were located around the long, narrow building which was constructed largely of logs. It had several large double doors along the side, sized so that a freight wagon could be pulled in to load or unload goods. Behind the warehouse was a large stable and a pasture with crudely constructed split rail fencing.

In the afternoon, Wend and Henry Froelich rolled by the warehouse on their way back from the ironworks and were able to scout out the layout. Wend was happy to note that there was no movement around the warehouse itself; he could see that the doors were shut and secured with chains and padlocks. However, there was some activity around the stables. A large herd of horses grazed in the pasture and he saw a boy throwing hay with a pitchfork within the stable itself. He noticed a smaller building built onto the side of the barn which looked like a workshop. Under a lean-to roof attached to the shop another man was making repairs to a pack-horse saddle and Wend could see many others stacked up alongside.

Much later, just after midnight, Wend and Froelich left the gunmaker's stable in Wend's wagon. They drove along King Street under a moon which was waning, but still cast enough light to be helpful. Shippensburg was a town of only a few hundred and they saw only one other person, a rather inebriated tavern patron, walking unsteadily on his way home. The paucity of encounters raised hope in Wend that they would be able to complete their nocturnal mission in complete secrecy.

Wend would rather have walked down to Grenough's property, for the wagon and horses made a goodly amount of noise. But he knew he was going to need tools to break into the storehouse and the only way to make sure he had what he required was to bring the wagon with its toolbox. And he was comforted by the fact that he had seen no caretaker's house on the Grenough property. So he thought it unlikely that there would be a watchman around.

As they drove, Wend looked over at his companion. "What did you tell your wife when you left home earlier tonight?"

"The usual—she thinks I'm down at the Widow Piper's in that card game. I could feel her anger follow me as I went out the door."

Wend said, "I'm sorry to cause you this problem. But I need to confirm my suspicions and tonight should provide part of the answer."

"Not to worry. She finds some reason to be mad at me every evening. Let's concentrate on the night's business."

They drove past Grenough's property very slowly, looking for any sign of human activity. But the entire area was silent and still. The surrounding houses were just as dark and quiet. Wend turned the wagon around and then, with as little noise as possible, took the short alleyway which led up to the warehouse. Each side of the building had three equally spaced sets of double doors which matched a set on the other side. Thus with corresponding doors opened on either side, a wagon could be pulled straight through the warehouse. Wend drove the wagon along the side of the building away from the stable and workshop. If the stable boy was sleeping in the barn or the workshop, he would not be able to see the interlopers at work. Then he stopped the wagon at the last set of doors, the farthest away from the main road.

Both men jumped down from the wagon. "Keep your eyes on the main street, Henry, while I take a look at how they have these doors secured. And hide in those bushes on the far side of the wagon. Then, if anyone comes upon us, you can stay hidden and they'll only catch me."

As they had earlier determined, the doors were secured by a lock and chain. The chain was looped through two matching U-shaped bolts which were imbedded in the edge of each door and the ends of the chain were connected by a large padlock. He immediately understood that the easiest, most likely way to gain access would be to remove one of the U-bolts, thus dispensing with the need to break or file through the chain or hasp of the lock. He prayed that the bolts were simply driven into the thick wood of the doors rather than secured by nuts on the interior side.

Returning to the wagon, Wend took a J-shaped, long handled iron pry-bar and short handled sledge hammer from the tool chest. He wedged the pry-bar under one U-bolt and applied all the pressure he could. There was no movement. Cursing to himself, he shifted the pry-bar to the bolt in the other door and pushed with all his strength. He was gratified to feel a slight wiggle in the bolt. Wend leaned against the bar and felt more movement of the bolt. He pushed several more times, but it was soon clear that getting it out would require the sledge. He wedged the pry-bar in a way to get the most leverage, then struck the end sharply with the hammer. The clanging noise reverberated so loudly that he feared it was heard throughout the little town. He looked around, almost expecting to see lights come on in nearby houses.

Froelich called in a quiet voice, "My God, Wend, that's loud. It'll wake the sheriff! His house is only five doors down the main street."

Wend whispered back, "Now you tell me about the sheriff! You might of thought of that when we were planning this job."

"Wend, this is my first time as a thief. I can't be expected to think of everything."

Wend froze and waited for long minutes in the darkness. But no lights showed around him. He carefully swung the hammer again. This time he was encouraged to feel significant movement of the bolt. He waited another long minute and struck the pry-bar again. More movement. He repeated the process three more times, and with the last hammer blow, the U-bolt popped out of the wood and dropped to the ground. Wend carefully placed his tools back in the wagon, then returned to the warehouse and swung open the doors all the way back against the side of the building.

He called softly to Froelich: "If you see someone coming, throw a rock into the warehouse. That way you won't have to shout, but I'll still get the warning." Then he climbed onto the wagon seat and drove the rig right into the warehouse.

The inside was a sea of blackness. But even in their inexperience, he and Froelich had anticipated that particular problem. He reached into the wagon bed and removed a piece of canvas loosely draped over an object under the seat. It was a brass stable lantern containing a burning candle; dim but usable light shown through the pattern of holes punctured in the casing. Wend picked up the lantern and opened the access door on the side to increase the amount of illumination. Then he held it high and could see stacks of goods stretching from one end of the warehouse to the other. Virtually the only open floor space was for the wagon access between the three sets of doors. Wend moved deeper into the warehouse and began his search.

* * *

After what seemed like an eternity, Wend carefully backed the team out of the warehouse bay. As he climbed down from the wagon seat, he heard a soft call from Froelich. "My God, that took nearly an hour. I nearly froze out here in the cold. What did you find?"

"Stay where you are, Mr. Froelich, and keep watching. I'll call you when I'm finished with the door."

Wend shut the doors, then slid the U-bolt over a link of the chain, and inserted it back into the door in the original holes. Then he tapped it several times with the sledge. He stepped back and looked at his handiwork. At least to a casual observer, it appeared as if the chain and lock had never been disturbed.

"Come on, Henry, let's get out of here."

Froelich emerged from his cover and climbed up to the wagon seat, shivering visibly. Wend slapped the reins on the backs of the team, and they headed back toward King Street.

"So what did you find in there?"

"Let's get out on the main street first. I'm worried about somebody seeing us near the warehouse. Once we're out on King Street, we'll have plenty of time to talk it over."

They soon reached the end of the side road and Wend stopped at the intersection with King Street to look around.

Froelich smiled and looked over at Wend. "Well, at least I got a little excite. . ."

Wend put his hand on Froelich's shoulder. He whispered urgently, "Shhh! Somebody's coming!"

A mounted man emerged from the darkness, his horse at the walk. Wend could see that he was dressed in a long linen hunting shirt with a blanket coat over it. He wore leggings and a floppy hat pulled down to just above his eyes. Across the pommel of his saddle he balanced a long rifle.

Wend realized that the man would see them and note that they were pulling out from behind Grenough's warehouse. He would undoubtedly be suspicious of what they were doing, and, at the very least, remember their presence if someone started asking questions later.

Suddenly an idea came to Wend. He turned to Froelich. "Make like you're drunk and passed out. Lean up against me! Do it now." Froehlich's eyes opened wide for a moment, but he caught on almost immediately and slumped against Wend, his eyes shut tight.

Wend pulled the wagon out on to King Street and headed eastward toward the rider. They were just passing him when the man pulled up his horse and called out, "Hey, you there, stop a minute!"

Wend halted the wagon beside the horseman and looked over at him. Suddenly he realized that the rider looked familiar.

The man said, 'Hey, don't I know you?" Then he glanced over the wagon. "Yeah, you're Joshua Baird's friend. You was with him scouting for Bouquet last summer." He paused to think a minute. "You're young Eckert, the Dutchman!"

Wend looked closely at the man and recognized him after a few seconds. It was Daniel Carmichael, a hunter and scout who was a good friend of Baird and often worked for Colonel Bouquet. Suddenly, Wend remembered that Bouquet had mentioned that Carmichael lived in Shippensburg. He said, "Hello, Dan. Good to see you again. Last time we talked was out at Fort Ligonier in August, just before you left to carry messages back east for the colonel."

"That's a fact. Just before the battle." He smiled, then wagged his finger at Wend. "Say, I been talkin' to soldiers who was at Bushy Run. They all said you did some powerful long range shooting there. Yeah, I heard you took down a couple of warriors standing up on that high ridge near Andrew Byerly's place. Supposed to have been at 220 yards or so."

"I figured it at a little short of that, Dan. Maybe 175 or thereabouts."

Carmichael laughed. "Well, these stories do grow over time. But anyway, everybody says it was damn good shooting. I heard about it from these Black Watch lads who are mannin' the forts over the winter." He paused, then said, "That's why I'm riding in so late tonight. I'm carrying dispatches up from Fort Loudoun to Carlisle. Got a late start from Loudoun and thought I'd stop by and see my old lady overnight before I rode on tomorrow. Can't fault a man for that, can you?"

Wend laughed. "Not a bit, Daniel."

Carmichael glanced over at Froelich. "Hey, ain't that old Henry Froelich, the gunmaker?" He squinted and stared at the sleeping man. "What's wrong with him?"

Wend laughed and shook his head. "Yeah, that's Henry, sure enough. Fact is, that's why I'm out here tonight. I came down here to Shippensburg to check out the new forge and I'm staying at his house. He was friends with my father. Anyway, he went out to play cards at the tavern, and didn't come back when he said he would. So Hilda, his wife, rousted me up from a deep sleep and sent me out to fetch him back."

"Ha! That sounds just like Hilda. That lady is some piece of work. I tell you, I'd be down at the tavern every night if I was married to that woman, and that's no lie. Fact is, I never been able to understand how old Henry there handles livin' in the same house with her." He stared at the gunmaker for a moment. Froelich chose that moment to make a loud snoring noise. Carmichael laughed again. "But I never seen him passed out drunk before, much as I would have expected it, all things considered."

Wend said, "Well, it's certain that his wife does have a sharp tongue and knows how to use it. But I've never been married and not really in any position to judge how a man and woman get along under the same roof. Anyway, I got down to the tavern and they said Henry had played cards for hours, guzzling whiskey the whole time. Then he walked out, drunk as a skunk. Only thing he had said was he was going home. Since I hadn't seen him on my way from the house, I figured he must have headed in the wrong direction when he left the tavern. So I searched down here on the west side, and sure enough I found him asleep sitting with his back against that warehouse back there."

"Yeah, that's the big trader Grenough's place. Funny Froelich came down here, exactly the wrong direction. But you just can't tell where a walking drunk is going to end up."

Wend nodded in agreement. "You're right about that, Daniel. But I better get him home."

Carmichael laughed. "Yeah, you do that. And give my regards to that old asshole Joshua when you get back to Sherman Mill. Tell him we need to get together and toss back a few, just like the old days." Then he kicked his horse's flanks with his moccasin clad feet and was off into the night.

Wend roused the team, and they rolled eastward along the main street. "It's all right now, Henry; you can sit up."

Froelich moved away from Wend and looked around. "That was quick thinking, Wend. I'm sure Daniel is not suspicious in the least."

Wend smiled at the gunsmith. "Well, you did a masterful job of acting. That little snore was very convincing."

Froelich pursed his lips. Then he said, "But Wend, did you have to agree so readily with him about my Hilda? I know she sounds shrewish sometimes, but when we're alone, she really can be a sweet, caring woman."

Wend controlled his urge to laugh. "Henry, I'm sure you are right. But I just went with the flow of the conversation."

Froelich was quiet for a moment, then asked, "So what *did* you find in the warehouse?"

Wend shook his head in bitter disappointment. "*Nothing!* Absolutely nothing that a legitimate trader or a store owner shouldn't have in his warehouse. Iron and copper pots; reams of material for clothing; some tanned hides. Many coils of rope. Kegs of nails. Empty bottles and jugs. Mostly stuff that would fit in with supplying Grenough's new store out in Bedford or providing inventory for traveling peddlers."

"No gunpowder or lead?'

"Three small kegs of gunpowder and a small supply of lead. A perfectly justifiable amount that any merchant would have in stock." Wend gritted his teeth, then continued, "No trade muskets or firearms of any kind, nor any blades suitable for making into fighting knives."

"Are you sure you didn't miss something? Maybe in innocent looking kegs or crates?"

"No, I looked carefully. I even broke open some crates and then re-sealed them. The fact is, Grenough has nothing illegitimate in there. Our little expedition has been a waste."

Froelich looked over at Wend. "Maybe your suspicions about Grenough are wrong? After all, it's hard to deny that he has a record of being very loyal and helpful to the governor."

"No, Henry, there's too much evidence and actual skullduggery which I know to be true. I'm certain that Grenough is operating illegally. Remember those hatchets out at the forge? I have no doubt they're intended for use by warriors, not settlers. But this night has taught me one thing: Grenough is far more crafty than I thought."

CHAPTER EIGHT
Seat of Conspiracy

With the sun low in the sky, Wend pulled off the road and into the courtyard of a tavern which he knew was about a mile to the west of Grenough's estate on the outskirts of York. The tavern's sign was a red-colored crowing cock, and lettered below the picture was the name, The Proud Rooster Tavern. As Wend climbed stiffly down from the wagon seat, a stable boy came out to help and together they unhitched the team, removed the horses' harness, and got Joe and Lucy settled in clean stalls.

Wend asked the boy, "Do you have a saddle horse for hire that I could use? I need to visit a friend who lives not too far from here."

"Got just the item for you, sir. Sort of old and docile, but he'll get you there and back long as it's not too far from here."

Wend answered, "That will be fine. Saddle him up and I'll be leaving right after I get some supper."

Wend entered the common room and was grateful to find that it was clean and had a comfortable aura. He went to the counter and arranged for a room, then retreated to a table by the hearth to absorb some warmth after the chill of the long day on the wagon seat. Wend sat there deep in thought, planning his activities for the night. He realized that he was way behind his schedule and that Grenough's men could return from the eastern part of the colony at any time. *Pray to God that they're not already back.* While he would have liked to have rested in the tavern overnight and spent the next day scouting out Grenough's estate and mercantile buildings, he was certain that he didn't have that luxury. So he must take the chance of stealing onto the trader's place and breaking into his storehouse that very night. He had just started planning his actions when he realized someone was standing above him.

A young serving maid had approached the table and assumed a coquettish posture—hand on her hip and head cocked—that would have done credit to Peggy McCartie in one of her most provocative moments. She had reddish brown hair, a round face with pug nose, and lips which Wend thought could have had a pouty look when at rest, but which presently formed a broad smile.

"Hello, I'm Colleen. But most people just call me Colly." She smiled even more broadly and changed her pose so that she had both of her hands on her hips. "Mister, that's a mighty grim, steely look you got all over your face there. Like you was working through all the problems of the world and had to get it all done before some demon came and got hold of you. What can I get you that will make you relax a little?"

Wend smiled up at the girl. "Well, I suppose I was pretty deep in thought. I've got some tough work ahead of me."

She laughed. "Whatever it is, it will go better with hot buttered rum. Why don't I get you one?"

"Yes, do that. And get me a plate of whatever your best meal is for tonight."

Two hours later, in full darkness, Wend left the tavern on his hired mount and headed eastward toward the Grenough property. The horse had turned out to be little more than a decrepit old nag and not at all happy about leaving his stall on a cold night. Wend reflected that if he had to make a fast exit following the night's activities he would be in real trouble.

Wend had filled a canvas bag with the tools he thought he might need and now carried the bag suspended from his shoulder by a strap. In his belt he carried two pistols. Before leaving he had changed to the darkest clothing he had.

Wend arrived at Grenough's estate in about twenty minutes. In the distance to the east he could see the faint glow of lights from York. He pulled up his horse and observed the manor from the wagon road. There was just enough light from the moon and stars for him to see the location of several buildings. The merchant's house was a substantial edifice situated about 100 yards to the south of the wagon road. It consisted of a two-story, central section built of stone, flanked on either side by one-story additions constructed of milled lumber. Two chimneys rose from the stone section and each of the extensions had its own chimney. Wend observed a light shining from a second story window and another from a window in the right side extension. He assumed that Grenough's wife or other members of his family were in residence. There were several outbuildings directly behind the house and Wend was surprised to see that the largest of these also had a flickering light emanating from a window. He wondered if that was the servants' quarters. Then he picked out the stable, located down a lane from the house. A large fenced pasture was nearby. Beyond that he saw a hulking building similar in shape to the warehouse he had visited in Shippensburg and he assumed that to be his objective for the night. He quickly noted that the warehouse was not more than fifty or seventy-five yards from the edge of a stand of woods which extended right up to the wagon track. He thought, *I can use the woods to cover my approach to the warehouse and quickly cover the remaining open distance in the darkness.*

Wend turned the horse around and walked him westward along the road, carefully inspecting the edge of the woods. He found a suitable hiding place for the animal about 150 yards to the west of the estate's cleared area and tied him in the woods about twenty yards off the road.

It took him less than a half hour to pick his way through the woods to the edge of Grenough's cleared land. Actually, he first came to a small, treeless cove which seemed to have been cut into the woods along the border of the cleared area. He was thankful for that, for it would be a good landmark for him to re-enter the woods on his way out. He walked along the edge of the cove until he came to the main part of the cleared meadow and saw the warehouse directly ahead of him.

Wend spent a long time standing frozen at the tree line, observing the warehouse and the rest of the estate. His background as a hunter and scout for the army had infused him with caution and the value of patience. He had a visceral fear of going into any open area until he was sure of exactly what lay before him. Now he stood watching to make sure no servant or other person was moving about in the night and that he understood completely the lay of the land and structures.

Once he had convinced himself that no one was moving, he slowly and silently crept to the warehouse, moving carefully to prevent the contents of his tool bag from clinking as he walked. He reached the corner of the warehouse on the side away from Grenough's house and crouched down to inspect the building closely. As he had sensed from the road, it was indeed essentially a twin of the Shippensburg structure, with three double doors per side. But then he looked up from his position and saw the shape of a window just a few feet from the corner. He stood up to inspect it and quickly realized it might offer more rapid access than the doors. It was in fact the type which swung open sidewise like double doors instead of sliding up and down. He pulled on the window and found that it was locked but that he could move it slightly.

He felt the latch in the center and immediately became convinced that he could easily break it.

Wend reached into his bag and pulled out a chisel and the short handled sledge hammer. As part of his preparation for the night's work, he had rapped the head of the hammer in rags to prevent the loud clanging noise he had experienced in Shippensburg. He smiled to himself: *Clearly, practical experience was as important to thievery as it was to any other trade.*

He put the chisel against the window latch and hit it once with the hammer. It cut right through the flimsy latch. Wend reached up and swung the window open. Exhilarated at the ease of gaining access, he quickly pulled himself up through the opening. He landed in the darkness on the flat surface of a piece of furniture covered with papers. Wend realized that he was on a desk and that he had entered an office.

Enough moonlight filtered into the office window so that he could see through an open door into the warehouse proper. Wend stepped through the door and bent down to the dirt floor. Reaching into his tool bag, he pulled out a bundle of dry kindling material he had gathered earlier in the day. After loosening it up to facilitate combustion, he again reached into his bag for the flintlock sparking device and a candle. It took him several tries, but in about five minutes he had the small fire going and the candle lit.

In the flickering light Wend went back into the office and saw that it contained only the desk, a cabinet, and chair. Papers had been stacked up on the desk, but he had knocked them all over the floor when he entered. Holding the candle high, Wend walked into the main area of the warehouse. He was infused with a sense of anticipation and even triumph. Now he was confident that he would finally find the contraband items which were the objective of his search.

An hour later Wend sat down on a crate near the center of the storehouse, crestfallen and shaking with frustration. For he was as confounded as he had been at Shippensburg. He had counted heavily on finding in York the guns, powder, lead, and knife blades that he was sure Grenough was providing to the hostile tribes. And all he had seen was the same mercantile stores which had been at the other location. He broke out into a cold sweat and momentarily felt a wave of doubt sweep over him. Was it possible that he had been wrong all along and that somehow Grenough was in fact just an honest merchant? But then his mind rapidly paraded all the evidence he had to the contrary and realized that the real answer was that the trader had hidden his store of illicit supplies somewhere else, in a secret cache. He berated himself for his own stupidity: Grenough was clearly smart enough to keep the incriminating items out of his known warehouses and Wend knew he should have figured that out. He spent a few moments mentally castigating himself.

Finally he shook himself into action. It was time to get out of the warehouse. He walked back toward the little office and kicked dirt over the tiny area of blackened earth where he had made the fire. Then he had a thought. Entering the office, he reached down and gathered up all the papers which had been knocked to the floor and stacked them on the desk. Holding the flickering candle in one hand, he quickly scanned the information in the papers, hoping that they might give him the name of another location or some other clue to Grenough's secret store of goods. But they were all simply routine invoices and delivery receipts and the only addresses he could find were for York and Shippensburg.

After a few minutes, he extinguished the candle, crawled out through the window, and swung it shut behind him. There was, of course, no way to properly secure it, for his chisel had destroyed the latch. At any rate, the break-in would be discovered as soon as Grenough or his clerk entered the office, for they would see the disturbed papers and soon find evidence of the fire. He shrugged and headed back for the woods.

Wend walked toward the tree line in the general direction of the little cove which was his landmark. He moved hunched over, but not really trying hard to conceal himself, for he was now confident that no one was around. His mind was working hard, trying to figure out some way to learn where Grenough had his war supplies hidden. It could be anywhere—he simply had no idea and no way of finding out. He looked up and realized that he had walked into the cove near its center, not the edge where he had come out. He turned northward to get to the cover of the woods.

That was when the ground under him literally gave way and he fell at least eight feet, landing on hard packed dirt. The fall momentarily knocked the wind out of him, and, as he lay there, pine boughs fell over and around him.

Wend reached out, pushing the pine branches off of him. He got to his knees and started to feel around himself in the absolute darkness. He was in some sort of pit and the pine branches had been used to hide it. He panicked, fearing that he was trapped. Then on one side he felt a log, and above it another, and another above that. He continued upward, finding more, and realized that they formed a rough stairway. The rising panic he had been feeling subsided, for he now knew he wasn't trapped and could get out of the pit. He went back down to the bottom and felt around the side of the pit away from the stairway. He immediately felt the shape of a door and the wooden planking of a wall. The door was chained and padlocked in a fashion similar to the doors at Shippensburg. Wend felt his tool bag, reaching for the pry-bar.

Then suddenly he heard a sound in the distance. *My God, voices!*

At first the voices were unintelligible. Then someone said clearly, "He was heading that way. Toward the underground storeroom!"

Wend felt rising panic. He must get out of the pit immediately! He turned and climbed to the top of the stairs, pushed aside several pine boughs, and looked out into the night. He saw two shadowy figures coming in his direction. Immediately he crawled out of the pit, and still down on all fours, scuttled along toward the tree line as close to the ground as he could manage. He was there in a few seconds and hid under a bush, lying perfectly still and breathing as slowly as he could manage. But he couldn't stop his heart from beating like a drum. He had no idea if he had been seen.

A skeptical sounding voice called out in the darkness. "Reilly, for God's sake, you just saw a deer. There are always plenty of them out grazing around here during the night. I've seen them many times. Come on, we've ridden a long way today and it didn't help any that we got held up waiting for the boat at Wright's Ferry. Let's get some sleep."

"Price, if I saw a deer, then this one's figured out a way to start walking on his hind legs. I tell you it was a man who came out from behind the warehouse, crouched down low and headed this way."

In a few seconds more Wend saw two figures arrive, visible only because of the dim starlight. The two men stopped near the pit. Then one of them approached it, and reached down to feel around the pine boughs which covered it.

"Deer, hell! Someone's pulled away some of the pine branches." The man disappeared down the stairway. Shortly he called up, "Price, there are pine branches and needles all over the ground down here."

The man above answered in a startled voice, "The devil you say! What about the lock, Reilly? Has anyone broken in there?"

Wend could clearly hear the rattling of the chain. "No, Price, the powder and other stuff hasn't been touched, far as I can tell."

"Good, but now somebody knows about this stash. And even if they didn't get inside, it won't take much for them to figure what kind of stores are down there. Don't take no genius, and that's a fact, to guess it's powder."

Reilly called up from the pit. "Price, if someone was nosing around in the night like this, we got to figure that they're suspicious about Grenough's trading operation. No common thief would be scouting out this place."

"That's no lie. Well, Grenough's due in here tomorrow. No doubt in my mind he's going to be upset. If it were up to me, we'd get Bratton down here with his wagon and haul all this stuff to that new place out near Shippensburg that the boss has Mathews and Crawley building. Anyway, we was planning to store all those new axe heads and knife blades there; if we move this lot there now, it will all be stashed in one place when we're ready for the first trip west in the spring."

Reilly emerged from the pit. "Makes sense to me, Irwin. But you may have trouble convincing Grenough. You know how he likes to keep things spread out and hidden all over the country. I heard him say often enough he wants to keep it all separate so no one can discover the whole lot."

Irwin said, "Yeah, I hear what you're saying. But let me talk to him tomorrow and see what he says after finding out what happened tonight. This is the first time we ever had somebody snooping at our operation."

Reilly answered, "That's true enough. And we better go check the locks on the warehouse. I'll wager we'll find signs of a break-in."

"Damn right, Shane. We'll get a lantern and take a look."

Wend watched as the two men spent some time spreading the pine branches over the opening, then walked off back toward the warehouse. He remained still in his hiding place for a long time, his heart-beat slowly returning to normal.

* * *

Wend spurred the ancient nag back to The Proud Rooster at the fastest pace the animal could maintain. Meanwhile, he kept his ears cocked for the sound of pursuing hooves. Once, imagining that he heard something, he pulled up to listen. But he could hear no noise except those made by his own horse. Finally, after a ride of a very long fifteen minutes, he dismounted in the court-yard with the horse breathing heavily.

The stable boy looked at the animal and exclaimed, "Mister, I ain't never seen this old boy break a lather before. You must have been riding like you was chased by the devil hisself!"

"In a way, you're right," Wend replied. He reached into his pocket and flipped the boy a coin. "If anybody asks, you saw no one arrive from the direction of York tonight. Do we understand each other?"

The boy looked down at the coin. "I understand well, sir. And I'll give them the answer you want even if they offer to pay more than this." He paused, smiled, and then said, "But if they do offer more, I'll be looking you up in the tavern to match their amount."

Wend grinned at the stable boy. "Lad, you are going to do well in the world of commerce."

A few minutes later the tavern maid Colly had delivered hot rum to Wend back at his table by the hearth. He was surprised to realize that, despite all the activity of the evening, it was still just a little before eleven. Wend took a sip of his rum and felt the tension finally start to flow out of his body. He thought of the danger he had been in, but reflected that had finally all been worth it, simply to hear the words of Reilly and Price Irvin. Their conversation, had for once and all, eliminated any doubts about the extent of Grenough's operations, the identity of the men involved, and particularly the involvement of Matt Bratton. Now he could return to Sherman Mill and think out a path to retribution. With the warmth of the hearth and the rum taking their effects, Wend sensed a feeling of comfort and satisfaction flow over him. He also felt the first stages of drowsiness and resolved to take to his bed as soon as he finished his rum.

All thought of which was instantly dispelled when the common room door was thrown open and Price Irwin strode in briskly, followed by the hulking figure of the red-headed Shane Reilly. Both had pistols in their belts. Wend's lay in the chair on the other side of the table where he had put them along under his coat.

Irwin stopped just inside the door, slowly moving his eyes around the common room. Then he saw Wend. First he looked puzzled, but then recognition slowly spread over his face. He turned to Reilly, who had also now spotted Wend. The two of them whispered for a moment, then Irwin walked directly to Wend's table. At the same time, Reilly walked over to the counter which positioned him to Wend's right. There he could watch what transpired and cover his cohort if necessary.

Price stopped right at the edge of the table, and stood towering above Wend. For his part, Wend steeled himself to sink back in the chair and assume the appearance of maximum casualness. He forced a broad smile on his face as he looked up at the man.

"Well, what have we here?" Price asked. Aren't you Wend Eckert, the gunsmith who I met out at Bedford about a month ago? The man who shoots wood chips out from between people's legs?"

Wend nodded. "The very same. And as I recall, you're Grenough's manager; Price Irwin, I believe it is?" He lifted his rum and took a sip while Irwin stared down at him. "What brings you here? I should think there would be a lot of work starting up that new store Grenough was talking about."

"I'm here on company business. But the real question is, what are you doing in York? I thought you worked out of Sherman Valley."

"I do indeed. I also happen to be down here on business. Not that what I'm doing is any of *your* business. But since you seem so interested, I've been checking out furnaces and forges to see if any of the ones on this side of the river can make gun barrels good enough for me to use. It's expensive to get them shipped in from the Kurtz forge over in Lancaster."

"Listen, Eckert, we've come from Grenough's place down the road. Just arrived there from Philadelphia tonight. Somebody broke into his warehouse and we saw the scoundrel running off into the woods. We're just looking around to see if any likely person had stopped here."

Wend played dumb. "Grenough's place? Is that around here? I haven't spent any time in York before. But I'm sorry to hear that you had some trouble out there." Then he tried to shift the conversation. "You were in Philadelphia? I don't suppose you were riding with those Paxton Boys?"

"Yes, we damn well were. We was over 600 strong. And I can tell you, we put a scare in the governor and all those precious Quakers in the city."

Wend asked, "And I suppose you wiped out all those Moravian Indians, just like the Conestogas?"

Irwin stared at Wend for a long moment. "We didn't get the chance: The governor had magistrates collect up the whole lot and then he got the army to escort them to New York. There was some company of highlanders in Philadelphia, and they did the job. Hadn't been for them, we'd have finished off those savages."

Suddenly another voice interrupted. "I guess you're pretty happy about that, Eckert. Specially since you spent so much time helping your Conestoga friend Charlie Sawak get away. Hadn't been for the army, we'd have wiped out the lot of those Moravians, just like happened at Lancaster."

Wend looked up to see that Reilly had quietly walked over from the bar and now also stood next to the table, one hand on the butt of the pistol in his belt. In fact, he was hovering above the chair where the two pistols lay; Wend would have no way of getting to them if trouble erupted.

"Well, if it isn't my old friend Shane Reilly. You keep turning up in the most unlikely places—the Ohio Country, the Susquehanna, and now here. You certainly are a busy fellow." Wend looked over at Irwin. "So you know this fellow, Price? I guess that means he works for Grenough?"

Irwin looked startled at Wend's words. He had just realized that Wend had exposed the fact that Reilly wasn't just an independent trader. Clearly, they hadn't expected to meet someone who could connect the red-head to both illicit trading in Ohio and to Grenough. "That doesn't matter, Eckert. What I'm here to do is find who was sneakin' around Grenough's place. So, just to make me feel better, how about tellin' me where you been tonight?"

"Why, right here all the time, of course. I spent some time in my room after dinner, resting after my day's journey. Then just a few minutes ago, I came down to get some rum before retiring. What would I want out at Grenough's estate?"

Irwin suddenly broke into a sly grin. Slowly, with great care, he reached down and pulled something from Wend's collar. "Excuse me, Eckert. But you seem to have this little pine twig under your collar." He raised a short piece of pine with needles attached. "Are they keepin' pine trees up in the guest rooms these days?"

Reilly broke in. "Maybe we should all go outside peaceable like and discuss this in the courtyard. We seem to be distracting all the guests here." He grinned at Wend. "And like you said back on the Susquehanna, we do have some personal business to finish."

Wend realized that Irwin was now certain that he had been the intruder. But he said, "I have nothing to hide. The only person who can force me out of this tavern tonight is the sheriff. If you think you have evidence against me, go see him."

Price was about to say more when a new, feminine voice interrupted things.

"Mr. Eckert didn't go anywhere tonight. The truth is, he was with me. Out back of the tavern, in the pine grove. That's where he got that little sprig." Colly had walked over to the table, her tray in one hand and the other hand on her hip.

Irwin looked down at the girl. "With you out back? Doing what?"

Colly tossed her head back and looked at Irwin with a coy smile. "Do I have to spell it out for you, mister?" She laughed, then said, "But if you insist, naturally we was just having a friendly conversation." She winked knowingly at Irwin. "What else would we be doing? He was just leaning up against a tree the whole time, and some loose needles and sprigs dropped down on him. I brushed him off before we came in, but I must have missed that little sprig."

Price cocked his head. "Eckert, you said you was in your room. That doesn't square with what the girl is saying."

Wend, surprised at the girl's intervention, played along. "I was just trying to keep her out of trouble with the proprietor."

Colly turned toward the bar and waved her hand at the other serving girl. "Edith, tell him what you know."

Edith, a tall, raw boned, horse-faced, brown haired girl, shook her head. "I'll tell you that's the truth of it. She was gone for the better part of an hour with that man. Left me to handle all the work. And it ain't the first time she's done that to me. I always got to cover for her when she has one of her little escapades with the guests."

Meanwhile, the proprietor had come out of the kitchen and had noted the tension. He looked around and saw that there was a silence throughout the room as the other guests had turned and were staring at the proceedings. He walked over to Wend's table. "Gentlemen, I'll brook no disturbance here tonight. So why don't you two sit down at a table or leave. Mr. Eckert's a guest with a room and I'll not have you upsetting him or the other guests in this place."

Irwin looked around and realized that the common room was filled with witnesses if he tried something. He looked back down at Wend. "It appears the girl is able to vouch for you, Eckert. But just remember this: I don't know what you are up to, but here's fair warning—don't let me catch you nosing around Mr. Grenough's property." He motioned to Reilly, and then turned and left the tavern.

Reilly lingered a moment. "Like you said at the Susquehanna, Eckert, there will be a time to settle all of this. And I'm beginning to look forward to it. And I'll tell you now—when I take care of business, it's finished perma- nent-like. If you know what's good for you, you'll stay in Sherman Valley." Then he followed Irwin out the door.

Wend jumped up from his seat, grabbed one of his pistols, and strode quickly to a window. He watched as the pair mounted their horses and rode eastward at the trot. Then he went back to his table, sat down, and took a quick gulp of his rum. Wend found that his hand was shaking and he spilled some of the rum on the table.

He had almost calmed himself when Colly came back over to his table from the bar. She smiled at him, produced a rag and wiped up the spilled liquor. Then she sat down at the table and leaned close to him. "Was that true about you being a friend of Charlie Sawak?"

"My home in Lancaster was near Conestoga Town. Charlie and I went to school together and have been friends for as long as I can remember."

"Everybody's been saying that all the Conestogas are dead, but that red-haired man was talkin' like Charlie escaped. And he said you helped him." She looked into Wend's eyes. "Is all that true?"

Wend nodded. "He was with me, away from the work house, when the other Conestogas were murdered. So he survived and I gave him some clothes, a rifle, and provisions. Then he took off in his cart. Some of the Paxton militia chased him, but he got away across the Susquehanna. He plans to go live with the Mingoes in the Ohio Country."

Joy spread across the girl's face and lighted up her eyes. "The Lord be praised! Charlie and I have been seeing each other for more than a year. He used to come off the ferry over at Wright's and drive right by here in his cart on his way to Shippensburg and then up through the valley. He'd always stay overnight in the stable and spend time with me. He's a handsome man who I could never resist. We laughed all the time and he had the most gentle manner with a girl. We spent many happy hours together."

Wend mentally thanked God that he hadn't told Colly about Rose. He asked, "Was that why you helped me with those men?"

"Of course. I wanted to hear what you had to say. And if you had helped him, like that red-haired one said, I felt like I owed you." She thought a minute. "If Charlie is out in the Ohio Country, I guess I'll never see him again. But at least now I know he ain't dead."

He smiled at the girl. "Yes, it's good that he was able to get away. By the way, my first name is Wend; Wend Eckert. For what ever reason you helped, I'm the one who has a debt to you. If I can ever help you, you must let me know."

"You helped me by just by telling me Charlie is alive." She stood up, then laughed and said, "But since you said that, I'll figure out how you can pay me back. Truth is, men around here who know me understand I don't come cheap."

* * *

Wend finished his drink and then carried his coat, pistols, and bag of tools up to his room. He was in bed by midnight, his pistols and hunting knife carefully placed on a chair by the bed, in case Grenough's men had any ideas. But he thought they probably wouldn't try any lethal moves without their boss' approval and Grenough wouldn't be around until sometime in the morrow, probably late in the day. By that time, Wend planned to be miles away. He settled into the sheets and waited for sleep to overcome him. But he was still tense from the excitement of the evening and slept only fitfully.

He had no idea how much time had passed when he heard a quiet noise in the hall outside his door. Wend came awake rapidly, his heart pumping. Had he miscalculated about Irwin and Reilly? He reached over, grabbed one of his pistols, cocked the hammer, and slid it under the covers. But he remained lying in the bed, feigning sleep. As he watched, there was a click of the latch and the door slowly swung open; then a ghostly figure stole into his room. After standing by the door for a moment, the intruder swung it shut and padded on silent feet toward the bed. Wend fingered the trigger on the pistol with his right hand and moved his left into position to fling off the bedcovers. But in another second he relaxed. He realized that the approaching figure was that of Colly. She was dressed in a linen sleeping shift and had let her dark hair auburn down over her shoulders.

Wordlessly the girl stopped by the bedstead and unbuttoned her shift. It dropped off her shoulders to the floor. Then she lifted the covers and slid in with Wend. He could smell the woman scent of her and then the faint aroma of the kitchen in her hair as she pulled herself close to him.

She reached out to touch him and instead put her hand on the coldness of the pistol.

"Lord above, do you always sleep with a firelock?" The whites of her eyes and her teeth were clearly visible as she giggled. "Are you some sort of highwayman being chased by the sheriff? Or did you really steal something from those men tonight?" She paused a moment and then continued, "Johnny, the stableboy, told me you paid him a lot of money to keep quiet about the lathered up horse you brought back from your little trip tonight."

Wend reached over her and laid the pistol back on the chair. "No, I'm a gunsmith from up in Sherman Valley. Just here on business—like I said."

He could see her pucker up her face. Then she said, a tone of disappointment in her voice, "That's too bad. It would have been much more exciting to think that I was in bed with an outlaw who had done something nasty to those two toughs. With that stone face of yours and grim set of your mouth, you look like the kind of hard man who could do damage to anyone who crossed him."

"I've had other girls tell me they couldn't read my face. But you're the first who told me I looked like a hard case." Wend wondered, *Good God: Has seven months of campaigning with the army changed and toughened my countenance that much?*

Then he looked over at Colly. "However, young lady, the pertinent question is what are you doing here in my bed?"

"Shouldn't that be obvious? You told me that you would do anything that you could to repay me for helping you last night. You *did* mean that, didn't you?"

"Of course."

Colly didn't answer immediately. Instead she pressed her body close against Wend and wrapped her left arm around his neck and shoulders so that her breasts lay against his chest. Then suddenly she reached out with her right hand and grasped his cock, her fingers wrapping tightly around it. She said in a businesslike voice, "Well, I've come to start collecting my payment right now, Mister Wend Eckert. And from what I can feel, what you've got there is big enough to satisfy your debt if you know how to use it."

* * *

After the frenzy of their lovemaking, Colly lay against Wend with her head on his chest. Presently she asked him to tell her the story of Charlie's escape in the aftermath of the Conestoga massacre. Wend gave her a carefully edited version, eliminating any hint of Rose's existence. He told her about how Charlie had evaded discovery as he worked his way up the road from Lancaster to Harris' Ferry and had been able to sneak through Paxton Village. She laughed with pleasure at how Charlie had ambushed Bratton's group and how he had crossed the Susquehanna under the very noses of Lazarus Stewart's militia patrol.

But then she asked the logical question which Wend had been carefully avoiding in his narrative.

"Why do you suppose Charlie went up the eastern side of the Susquehanna? He could have crossed at Wright's Ferry, where they were friendly to him. Then he could have come straight here where I could have helped him hide overnight and given him more supplies. That's a real puzzlement to me."

Wend shook his head. "I have no idea. It's a puzzle to me also. Maybe Charlie figured that so many people knew him in the Cumberland Valley that it might be better just to go northward on the other side of the river, then cross the

Susquehanna opposite Sherman Valley, where he could head straight west on the New Path through Aughwick." As he said it, Wend knew the lie sounded lame, but there was no other logical explanation without telling Colly about Rose.

After he finished, there was a moment of quiet between them and then Colly suddenly rose up on one elbow and smacked Wend on his cheek. Surprised, Wend asked indignantly, "Hey! What was that about?"

Colly said, "My Ma followed her heart and married a man who turned out to be a no-account n'er-do-well. One day he left her alone with two girls to bring up on her own. That's how I ended up indentured to this place. But one thing Ma didn't do was raise any stupid daughters. It's clear you ain't tellin' me the whole story about Charlie. I've finished five years of an indenture here and one thing I've learned about is men and how they behave. I'm damn sure a handsome rake like Charlie had girls all over his routes. So I'm guessin' that the reason Charlie went up to Paxton is 'cause he had some girl there he wanted to see. Now, how about telling me the truth?"

Chagrined, Wend rubbed his cheek. "Her name was Rose. She was an indenture from England, serving her time in a run-down tavern at Harris'. Charlie had been seeing her for over a year and was really in love with her. So he convinced her to escape from her indenture and go with him to live with the Mingoes. She's a brave girl and helped him ambush Bratton and his men." He paused a moment and then said, "Now you know the whole story. I just didn't want to hurt you by telling you he had another girl."

"I ain't hardly insulted. I liked spending time with Charlie and I'd surely have helped him get away. But he ain't the only man in my life. And there's no way I'd go live in some Indian village with any man." She thought for a moment. "So, all things considered, Charlie made the right decision."

Wend thought for a moment, then asked Colly, "Did Charley visit you at all since the beginning of May last year, that is, since the start of the tribal uprising?"

"Sure—several times. Why do you ask?"

"Well, Charlie is at the center of a lot of the stories that were used to justify attacking the Conestogas. They say he was seen consorting with hostile Indians. The one you hear most often is that he was seen at the camp of a war party up at the Great Island of the Susquehanna, north of Paxton." He paused to choose his words carefully. "Did he ever mention anything about having talked with Indians from the Ohio Country?"

"Yes, Charlie was real worried about what white people was saying. The fact is, Charlie did run into Indians up on Great Island. But it wasn't like he

Robert J. Shade

was trying to meet them; they was the last people he wanted to see. It happened when he was on his way up to settlements above Shamokin and Fort Augusta to sell stuff. He knew a good place to camp on the island and he decided to spend the night there. He had just finished startin' his fire and was feedin' his horse when he was suddenly surrounded by a party of Delawares."

"So what happened?"

"Charlie was scared. But he invited them to his fire. They was hungry and made him feed them, saying they was carrying a limited amount of food. The Delawares lived off provisions gathered up in raids on farms and they hadn't hit any place in a couple of days. Matter of fact, the war party ate up everything he had." She laughed, and said, "They was really pissed off that Charlie wasn't carrying any liquor. A pair of them rifled through his cart, looking for whiskey or ale, and laughed at him for not having any with him." She paused to think about her story. "Then they started to bait him, making fun of him and the whole Conestoga tribe. Sayin' the Conestogas was traitors to the Indian nations and the Master of the World himself, cause they had takin' to living like white men and worshiped the white God."

Wend asked, "Was that all that went on—the war party making Charlie feed them?"

"No. Charlie told me that after they had eaten, they started demanding that he tell them things that would help them in their raiding; things like where the militia was patrolling; what was the size of the garrison at Fort Augusta; which towns had started a militia; and which ones had built their own forts for protection."

Wend was now listening intensely; this was the nub of the question. "So how did Charlie handle that?"

"He told me he didn't give them nothing that would help their raiding. He just said there were lots of militia companies all over the place and practically every town had built some sort of blockhouse or stockade. He realized that they didn't know that he traveled all over the area, so he could get away pleading ignorance of those types of things."

"Did the Delawares believe him?"

"They must have, because finally they all settled in for the night. Charlie said he didn't sleep a bit. He was scared 'cause he wasn't sure how the Delawares would deal with him in the morning. But when dawn came, the war party just packed up and went on their way."

"That relieves me very much, Colly. I have a lot of faith in Charlie, but hearing what he told you makes me more sure that all these stories are false." Then he recalled another question which had occurred to him after listening to Irwin and Reilly talk at Grenough's place. "Have you ever had a waggoner in the tavern called Matt Bratton? He's a big, hulking man with brown hair from Sherman Valley who likes to talk up women."

"Yeah, how did you know? He's been here. A couple of times." Colly Giggled. "First time, he tried to get me to go to bed with him." She looked up at Wend. "But I didn't fancy him. He was too full of himself. So I pushed him off and that made him real mad. He started calling me a tart and other names. It was like he couldn't believe I would turn him down."

Wend nodded. "That definitely sounds like Bratton. Do you remember when he was here?"

"Now let me see." The girl thought for a moment. "Seems the first time was last year in the early spring. Must have been first part of May." She stopped and thought for a moment. "And the second time was a little later in the summer."

Wend stopped to think about that. Certainly the visit in May would correspond to picking up a load of goods which would have supplied the first wave of war party attacks in late May and June.

Colly interrupted Wend's train of thought. "Hey, why are you asking so many questions? You know what I think? I think you *are* up to something, like maybe you are a thief after all. Those men who were chasing you tonight were from Grenough's place. And Bratton told me he was here hauling goods for Grenough." She looked up at Wend. "I say you lied to me about just being here on gunsmith business, just like you lied to me about Charlie. You're snooping on Grenough in some way. Are you planning to rob his warehouse?" She rose up on her elbow again and raised her other hand. "You better level with me now, or I'll slap you again and it won't be gentle like last time!"

Wend looked at the girl, thinking from the tone of her voice that she was really angry. But he saw her smiling and heard a quiet giggle. He decided to tell her more of the story. "All right, I did come here specifically to investigate Grenough's warehouse. Traders who secretly worked for him organized the massacre of my family by a Mingo war party five years ago. The girl I loved was captured in the same raid and ended up as the hostage wife of a Mingo war captain. The reason they did that was because I had accidently become aware that they were trading war goods with the Indians." He paused a moment. "Last December, when I was working as a scout for the army, I caught the two traders who were involved and shot them dead."

Colly stared into Wend's eyes. Then she said slowly, "Yes. Now I believe you. But if the men who got your family killed are now dead, why are you after Grenough?"

"Because they weren't acting on their own. Grenough was running the whole scheme and he is still trading with the Indians."

"So you're out to stop him?"

"Yes, but there's more to it. The fact is, Grenough is behind all these stories about Charlie and the Conestogas helping the war parties last year. Some of his men rode with the Paxton Militia when they killed the Conestogas. That red-haired man who was in here tonight was with the men who tried to stop Charlie and Rose from getting across the Susquehanna. They would have murdered Charlie if they had caught him. Those two men also helped encourage and organize the men who rode to protest in Philadelphia. Grenough's doing it all to distract people from getting suspicious about his trading operations."

"And you're trying to stop Grenough and get revenge for your family and Charlie!" She smiled broadly. "That's even better than you being a highwayman. I knew all along I was right about you being a hard man on a secret job!"

Wend laughed. "I'm glad if that makes you happy. But there's something you can do to help me, if you will."

"I all ready helped you by lying to Grenough's men. What more do you want me to do?"

"It's easy, Colly. Just send me a letter by post to let me know if you see Bratton down here again. I have a feeling they may be moving some of their goods to another location and they'll use his wagon when they do."

"Well, I'd like to help, after what you did for Charlie. But truth is, I never learned to write, beyond signing my name." She screwed up her face in thought for a second, then it brightened and she smiled. "I know—Edith can write some. She'll write it for me and I know she'll be quiet."

Wend nodded, "I'd really appreciate that." Then he ran his fingers through her long hair. "Now I guess we better get some sleep. It's been a long day for me and I know you have to get up early."

She giggled again. "Yes, you better get some sleep. 'Cause I'm going to wake you up just before I go down to work and I'm going to make you pay me some more. You're going to pay me in advance for sending that letter."

Wend groaned. "My God, Colly, after all the payments, as you call them, that I just made, I'm not sure I'll be able to do it then."

Colly laughed slyly. "Don't even think about that. Every girl who has any experience knows that first thing in the morning is the strongest and hardest any man is going to be. So I'll expect to be paid very well indeed."

CHAPTER NINE
The Good Colonel

Wend drove his wagon into the courtyard of Washburn's Tavern a little before noon. He had been on the road from York for a day and a half, and planned to rest the horses for an hour or two before traveling on to Sherman Mill. Wend jumped down from the wagon and gave the stable boy instructions for the horses. Then he walked briskly into the tavern's common room, more than ready for a good meal.

Washburn was behind the counter in his usual ebullient mood. "Ah! Eckert, I'm damned glad to see you! Look up there on the wall."

Wend looked up at the empty pegs above his name plate. "So you've already sold that last rifle I brought down? That was fast."

"Damn right, Wend. Fact is, I had a couple of gentlemen actually bidding on it. They loved the brass embellishments." He went over to his cash box and counted out some money. "There's your payment, less my commission, of course."

Wend smiled. "George, I'm sure the fast sale owed a great deal to your powers of persuasion."

"Well, my good wife says I do have a smooth tongue, and she should know!"

"George, I have no doubt your wife is right. You always sell my firelocks rapidly. I'm usually thankful for that, but this time you've put me in a hard place. I'm trying to rebuild my business after all the months with the army and I still haven't had time to get rifles on display at two other taverns." Wend laughed. "But since you move them so fast, I'll have another one down here as soon as I can."

Washburn slapped his hand down on the counter. "I always say, money talks, and by God, if you keep a rifle up on my wall, you'll keep the money coming in, lad."

Wend looked around the common room, just in time to see a corporal of the Royal Americans enter and walk through the room to a door which led to meeting rooms in the back. He turned to Washburn. "Is Bouquet here?"

"Yes, he just rode in with his staff and escort yesterday. He's on his way from Pitt to Philadelphia. He's using my back rooms for his offices, like he usually does, for the next couple of days."

Wend said, "Well that's a surprise. I may just pay him a call."

Washburn nodded. "I know he'll be glad to see you. It's no secret he takes a special interest in you since the massacre."

Wend walked back and pushed through the door into the room which served as Bouquet's outer office. The corporal he had seen now sat at a small writing table, copying out a letter. Next to him a young lieutenant was ensconced at a larger table, going over some papers. Wend noted that the officer was dressed in a very elegantly tailored uniform of fine material and had more frilly lace on the collar and cuffs of his shirt than he had ever seen. He also wore a fine, white powdered wig, which most officers of the 60th avoided wearing out in the settlements. Even more curious, he seemed to have some sort of rouge on his face, like a woman.

Wend felt rising excitement at the prospect of seeing Bouquet again. He stepped up to the lieutenant, nodded slightly in token of salute to him, and said, "Good morning, sir. I'm Wend Eckert. Here to pay a call on Colonel Bouquet, if he's available, sir."

The officer slowly looked up from his papers. He took a long time moving his eyes over Wend, who felt like he was undergoing inspection on the parade ground. A look of disdain swept over the lieutenant's face.

"I'm Lieutenant Welford, the adjutant. May I ask what business you have with the colonel? He is quite busy trying to get through a great amount of dispatches and mail we received when we arrived last night. And he does have several *very important* appointments coming up this afternoon." The lieutenant looked over Wend again. "Not to mention, if I may, sir, that you might take greater care in your appearance before presenting yourself for a call on the Colonel of the Royal American Regiment."

Wend had been in his normal traveling clothes; a shirt, waistcoat, and breeches under the gray army overcoat he had obtained from garrison stores at Fort Pitt. He had left the overcoat in the common room. Now he looked down at himself; though worn, his clothes were as clean as might be expected and they were well mended. He instantly felt anger rising at this dandy's criticism.

"Ah, Mr. Eckert, perhaps if you came back late this afternoon, and, shall we say, had time to change to more appropriate attire, I could fit you in for a few minutes with Colonel Bouquet."

Wend put on his steely face and said in a very low voice. "Well, Mr. Welford, I was dressed a sight more roughly than this and covered in an Indian warrior's blood when I sat beside the colonel's campfire and gave him the lay of the land at Bushy Run. And as for later this afternoon, I'll be driving my team up on the slopes of North Mountain, well on my way to Sherman Mill."

Welford screwed up his face. "I'm afraid to say that I am completely unfamiliar with the name of a place called Sherman Mill or why I should be concerned with the urgency of you traveling there."

Wend advanced closer to the desk so that it forced Welford to take a half-step backward. As he did so, he caught a whiff of scent: He thought, *My God, this man is wearing perfume!* "Look, Mr. Walford or Welford, or whatever your name is, why don't you just knock on the colonel's door and mention that I'm here, and see how he reacts?"

"I have absolutely no intention of bothering the colonel for some rough, and I might say, very rude, mechanic. Now come back this afternoon as we discussed, or simply depart, sir."

Wend suddenly remembered his conversation with the waggoner Daniel Morgan at Fort Bedford—how he had been lashed for talking back to a young lieutenant. Welford certainly fit Morgan's description of arrogant British officers unwilling to listen to anyone below their own social class. Wend felt frustration; he had always been treated with polite respect by Bouquet's officers and those of the highland regiments he had marched alongside.

Suppressing his growing anger, Wend spun on his heel to leave, but before he could get to the door, Bouquet's own door opened and the colonel stepped into the room. He was in his waistcoat and wearing spectacles. He held a piece of paper in his right hand. Bouquet started to speak, "Say, Mr. Welford, we must deal with this matter . . ." Then he saw Wend and a smile broke out over his face. "By God, it's young Eckert! Lad, I'm glad to see you!"

Wend looked at Welford, raised his eyebrows, and threw him a broad grin. Then he turned back to Bouquet. "Good morning, Colonel. I heard you were in town and thought I'd pay you a brief call. I know you're busy, so I won't take much of your time."

"Nonsense, Wend. I'm delighted to see you. Let me get my coat and we'll take an early lunch together out in Washburn's common room. I do like his fare."

They walked out together, the dandy lieutenant staring at them in puzzlement as they left.

* * *

While they were waiting for their food, Wend asked Bouquet, "Sir, when did your new adjutant begin his assignment? I don't recognize him from Fort Pitt."

The colonel laughed, "Mr. Welford is new to the regiment. *Very new.* He met me at Fort Bedford, on his way out to Fort Pitt from England. His family has connections, if you know what I mean. He is joining us from the 1st Foot Guards in London. In view of the fact that his service has exclusively been in London, I thought it propitious to take him under my wing as adjutant and send his predecessor back to company duties." Bouquet smiled and leaned forward to speak more confidentially. "How shall I say this? I believe the skills he learned in the society of the capital will make him useful to me in Philadelphia and New York, whereas, at present, he would be ill-suited to leading a half-company on patrol along the Allegheny."

Wend nodded. "With respect, sir, I agree he doesn't seem to understand conditions here on the border."

Bouquet grinned mischievously. "Wend, let me advise you a little bit about army culture. Young, upcoming lieutenants of position and wealth don't voluntarily sell their commission in an ancient, prestigious regiment like the Foot Guards to buy a lieutenancy in the Royal Americans and the 'privilege' of serving in remote outposts of the colonies. In short, I smell a whiff of scandal in Mr. Welford's background. Undoubtedly something to do with a woman, drink, or gambling." Bouquet grinned and winked at Wend. "Or some combination of the three."

Wend smiled. "I think I understand."

"Yes, indeed. I dare say, eventually we'll sniff it out in the long days at Pitt. The close society of an officers' mess always does that in the end." Bouquet took a drink of his ale. "Once we've done that and Lieutenant Welford has shed some of his London arrogance, we may be able to make a proper campaigner out of him."

"I'm sure you will, sir," Wend replied.

Bouquet's face assumed a thoughtful look and he hesitated a moment before speaking again. "The truth is, we're soon going to have to deal with a lot more officers like Mr. Welford here in the colonies."

"What do you mean, sir?"

"I mean there's going to be more British army stationed here than the colonists have ever seen before in peacetime. I've just received a plan for what the government calls 'The American Establishment'." He paused to gather his thoughts. "Wend, before the French war broke out in 1754, the only regular troops here were a few independent companies assigned to man forts and patrol the borders. Now there will be a significant number of—they're talking of as many as fifteen—regular battalions maintained here in the colonies."

Wend was surprised. He asked, "Why is that necessary?"

"Well, the government wants to have troops in place in case of any adventurism by the French or Spanish, who of course still have considerable holdings in the south. And this uprising of the Ohio Country tribes has alerted London to the unpredictable nature of Indian relations and the potential for hostilities at any time."

Wend nodded. "I can understand all that."

Bouquet continued. "I've been very satisfied working with these highland troops—the 42nd and the 77th. They're a rough lot, but just the sort we need in the wilderness. But I'm not sure about regular troops from England itself. As we saw in the late war, soldiers recruited from the streets of London or towns throughout England need special training to accommodate themselves to bush warfare."

Wend asked, "Like the training you've given the Royal Americans?"

Bouquet nodded. "That's right, Wend. But I fear that the officers of the mainstream army are already forgetting the lessons we learned in the late war about fighting here in the American wilderness. For example, we have orders to abolish the light company in every battalion and reassign those troops to the line companies."

Wend was shocked. "But Colonel, those are the very troops which proved most useful in fighting the tribes!"

"Yes, but the powers that be seem to think they're unnecessary. Our new commander here in America, General Gage, was a pioneer in developing light infantry and techniques for fighting in the bush. He learned his lesson as an officer in the Braddock debacle. I don't understand how he can allow this to happen, unless he is being overruled by the army command."

"At least there will be your own regiment, the 60th, which has been trained to fight on the frontier."

"Yes, that's true, Wend. But economy is he watchword throughout the army now. We've been directed to reduce the regiment from four battalions down to only two, which means that we'll be spread out very thinly." Bouquet screwed up his face for a moment, then said, "In fact, parliament is so worried about paying for the army that they're considering new taxes here in the colonies."

"New taxes, Colonel?"

"Yes. It is the custom in Britain that each area pays for the troops which are garrisoned there. In Great Britain itself, there are the English, Scottish, Irish, and Welch 'Establishments', as they call them. Each region pays taxes to maintain the army regiments based in their territory." Bouquet shrugged. "I just received a letter from an acquaintance in London who says that the regiments based in the colonies will be designated the 'American Establishment' and that the parliament is considering the kind of taxes to assess on residents here. He mentioned several options, the most likely being what they call a 'Stamp Tax'. Apparently such a tax is already assessed in the home islands to pay for the army. It means that a stamp would have to be bought from tax collectors and placed on virtually any document which was drafted." The colonel took a sip of his ale. "There is also mention of something called the Sugar Act, which would replace the existing Molasses Act. As I understand things, it would consist of duties on molasses and certain other imported goods. And enforcement would be made more rigorous than has been the practice here in the colonies."

Wend thought over what the colonel said. "As you describe it, sir, it sounds logical. Clearly the army has to be financed somehow. But we here in America aren't used to paying much in taxes beyond assessments on land which are paid to the colony."

"I understand what you are saying. But just maintaining troops in garrison costs money and conducting field operations like this upcoming campaign against the Ohio Country tribes will be even more expensive."

Wend nodded and decided to change the subject. He asked, "Colonel, speaking of campaigns, how are preparations for the march into the Ohio Country coming?"

"Damned slow, I'm afraid. Now that winter has come and the tribes aren't raiding settlements, all the colonial governments are dragging their feet in making preparations. They're trying to convince themselves that the Indians won't attack again next spring. And the only regular troops I'll have will be the 500 men of the Black Watch. So we need at least a couple of provincial battalions and some border militia acting as rangers to round out my force. The expedition must be imposing enough to cow the Indian sachems into deciding that it is in their interest to sue for peace instead of resisting our advance." He shook his head. "That's why I'm bound eastward now. I'm going to Philadelphia to talk with the governor. Then it will be on to New York to talk with General Gage about details of the campaign. I hope he can shake up the governors of Virginia and Maryland."

"Indeed, Colonel. What about Pennsylvania? Is the government going to support you at all, or are they going to try and sit this out?"

"A very perceptive question, my young friend. As usual, they are trying to do as little as possible, using their religious scruples as an excuse. Of course, I've no doubt that *expense* is the underlying reason. Regardless, we're trying to get them to form a battalion of provincials for the expedition. Unfortunately, all they will say is that they may—I repeat, they *may*—form one for defense of the border settlements only. It could not be used for offensive operations in any way." Bouquet grimaced and slapped his hand down on the table, making the utensils and china rattle. "They never realize, or more likely refuse to admit, that the only real way to protect the settlements is through offensive action. Garrisons in frontier forts provide but the illusion of security: All they're really able to do is go out and clean up the mess after raiding parties attack."

That brought up another question in Wend's mind. "Do you think we'll see war parties raiding here in the Cumberland Valley this summer?"

"I would say, yes, unfortunately. My informants among the tribes tell me that the chiefs seem about evenly split on how to proceed in the spring. Many have taken to heart the ultimatum we sent out on Stirling's diplomatic mission last fall; they are inclined to meet with us on the Muskingham River to talk peace. But it seems a very significant number are planning to continue the war and send raiding parties eastward when the weather permits."

Wend said. "So we'll be in for another long summer."

"That's why we must get this campaign underway. The sooner we start, the sooner those raiding parties will be pulled back to the Ohio Country." Bouquet stared thoughtfully for a moment. "The biggest incalculable I have is something we've talked about before, out at Fort Pitt: How well supplied are the tribes with powder and lead?"

Wend had been looking for an opening to talk about that very subject. "Colonel, do you remember when we found that site where outlaw traders were meeting with the Indians on the Allegheny River?"

"Yes, of course Wend. Last November. You shot Kinnear and Flemming. How could I forget that?"

"Do you remember that there was a third man? A red-headed man who escaped?"

"Yes, I remember you mentioning that during a meeting at Pitt. What of it?"

"Well, I've seen that man again and learned his name."

"The devil you say! Tell me about it."

"His name is Reilly. Shane Reilly to be exact. I first saw him riding with some of the Paxton Militia. He was helping them pursue a Conestoga Indian who escaped from the massacre in Lancaster."

Bouquet cocked his head and looked sharply at Wend. "Why would he be doing that?"

"I think his purpose was to hide the fact that he was actually an outlaw trader. He claimed that he had been put out of business as a legitimate trader by the uprising."

"Well, if he actually was the man you saw out on the Allegheny last November, your supposition may be right."

"There's no doubt in my mind, Colonel. Then I saw him again, near York. I was down there to look into new forges as a source for gun barrels."

"You say he was in York?"

"Yes, sir. And let me remind you, that keg of powder we found with that Shawnee war party which raided Sherman Valley last spring came from York. So I'm convinced that that town, or the area around it, is the source of the war supplies which are getting to the Indians."

Wend had the momentary impulse to confront Bouquet with the entire results of his investigations. And accuse Grenough of being the mastermind and let the cards fall where they might. But he bit his tongue and an instant later he was glad he had done so.

Bouquet's face wrinkled up in thought. "That's very interesting information. I'll tell Sheriff Dunning about this man Reilly. He can try to find him and at least ask him some questions." He thought again and then his face brightened. "And I'll mention his name to Richard Grenough. He knows something about most of the men engaged in trading."

Wend answered, "Yes, I'm sure that Grenough will be able to tell you something about him." He had to work hard to keep the irony out of his voice. But he thought to himself: *Mentioning Reilly was a mistake. If the colo-*

nel actually talks about him with Grenough, the merchant will be alerted to what I know and confirm in his mind that I'm moving against him.

"I'm looking forward to having Richard along with me as Indian Commissioner on this new campaign." Bouquet beamed. "Beyond his broad knowledge of all the Indian politics, he's a damned good companion out on the road. He always keeps the mess laughing with his store of amusing tales and back country wit." Then the colonel thought of something. "In fact, I just got a note from Grenough when we arrived here last evening. He said that he was in Philadelphia, trying to help contain this damned Ulster-Scot insurrection. Of course, he's the very man to do it."

Listening to Bouquet, Wend despaired. He knew that he would have to have much more convincing evidence before he could confront the colonel with Grenough's culpability.

Then the colonel was talking again. "Say, Wend, speaking of the campaign, can I count on you to come along as a scout this spring? I'm looking forward to your help."

Wend chose his words carefully. "I can't promise anything, sir. Truthfully, I've got to repair the damage that seven months with the army did to my business."

Bouquet's face wrinkled up into a crafty smile. "Well, this might change your mind. We've written a draft treaty to present to the chiefs. One of the provisions should interest you personally. It specifies that all white hostages held by the tribes must be turned over to the army for return to their families. That would, of course, include the dazzling Miss Gibson."

Wend thought for a moment; the matter was tempting. But then he broke out into a smile which was only a little forced. "It won't work, Colonel. For a couple of reasons: First, you know what the Indians are going to do. They'll hide many of the hostages—particularly women who have children by warriors—and deny they know anything about them. Second, Abigail will want to stay. I'm convinced of that by what she said to me last year. She's afraid of how her half-cast children will be treated by the whites. And she's become committed to doctoring the people of the villages in her area." He shook his head. "No, I'm not going to put myself through all the pain of seeing her again for just a short time. As you told me at Fort Pitt, I've got to get on with my life."

"Well, at least I tried, Wend." Bouquet took another drink of his ale. "Anyway, when you get back to Sherman Mill, tell Joshua I'll send a message when it's time for him to join the expedition."

"I'm afraid there's also bad news about Joshua, Colonel."

Bouquet looked up quickly and stared at Wend. "Bad news? What bad news?"

"It's that arrow wound of his. It's healed on the outside, but it looks like he's got a permanent limp. He's loath to admit it to himself, but I don't think he can work as a scout anymore, at least on foot. And that's essential in many situations."

"Damn! That's truly bad news. Joshua has been with me since the campaign of General Forbes in 1758. No one knows more about the terrain of the back country and the leaders of the tribes and villages out there beyond the Allegheny River." Bouquet set his mouth and chin firmly. "All right, even if he can't walk, can he ride? He can be an aide on my staff. I need his knowledge and advice more than I need a scout. I can get Carmichael from Shippensburg to do the scouting and we might convince Byerly from Bushy Run Station to come along with the expedition."

Wend said, "I think he can operate that way. But I'll just tell him you expect him to be down here when the expedition starts to gather. You can talk to him about his role when he gets here. But thinking about going west again will put a smile on his face."

CHAPTER TEN

Winter Decisions

Wend's intended short stop in Carlisle had been lengthened by his meal with Bouquet. After saying goodbye to Bouquet, Wend considered staying overnight at the Widow Downy's house. But then he calculated that it would be well worth the hassle of crossing North Mountain in the evening gloom to avoid extending his trip another day. He wanted to get back to Sherman Mill before people began wondering what had happened to make his trip take so long. Moreover, the thought of sleeping in his own bed that night felt very attractive. With all that in mind, he departed late in the day even though he knew it would mean getting into Sherman Mill well after dark.

Wend pushed himself and the team as they made their way over North Mountain. After a chilling ride they came down off the last switchback on the mountain in the dim light of a moon partially obscured by clouds. Looking at the night sky, Wend estimated that it was near ten o'clock and they had maybe three miles to go before reaching Sherman Mill. He figured that they could make it in just outside of an hour.

In a few minutes they came to a small, nameless creek which flowed down from a spring on the mountain. He eased the team through the ford, barely moving as the horses picked their way across the stream bed. And then suddenly Lucy, the off horse, whinnied in surprise and pain and stopped midstream. He could see her trying to move her left rear hoof, and realized that it had caught in a gap between rocks in the creek bed. Then suddenly she kicked the leg free, raising it out of the water several times. Wend jumped down from the wagon seat and waded into the creek, shivering in the shock of the cold winter water. He reached down and felt the hoof and leg, but could feel no obvious damage. He moved to Lucy's head and stroked her neck and mane. "Are you all right, girl?"

Lucy simply tossed her head. Wend went over to Joe and grabbed his bridle. He slowly led the team and wagon up the creek bank to the wagon track. Then he went back, got the reins from where he had left them on the seat, and, walking on the left side of the wagon in the style of a freight waggoner, slapped the reins on the horses to start them moving. He carefully watched Lucy's leg as she tried to pull her weight. But after a few steps he stopped the team for it was obvious that she was favoring the leg. Clearly she could not pull the wagon any further.

Wend thought briefly of unhitching the team and spending the night in camp beside the road. But he quickly discarded that idea. There was no reason to believe that Lucy would be in any better shape in the morning and, in fact, her leg would almost certainly stiffen during a night in the cold. He determined to push on to Sherman Mill. But he knew he had to take the burden off of Lucy. So he unhitched the animal from the wagon tongue and tied her to the back of the wagon.

Thankful for even the dim moonlight, he worked, often by touch, to modify the wagon rig to enable one horse to pull the vehicle. Normally, each horse was connected, by harness straps and trace chains on each side of the horse, to a "singletree", which was a wooden drawbar about three feet wide behind the animal. Each horse's singletree was in turn attached, by a link in its center, to the doubletree. The doubletree was a wooden spar that was connected across the wagon tongue by a large bolt which allowed it to pivot. So under normal conditions, the animals pulled on their single trees, which in turn pulled on their side of the doubletree, which in turn moved the wagon. The purpose of the system was to allow the rig to take into account the different strides and variations of the horses' movement while providing a steady pull on the wagon. But now, with Lucy out of the rig, it would be out of balance: When Joe started to pull, the doubletree would rotate forward on his side and the other end would smack against the wagon. Wend detached Lucy's single tree and dropped it into the wagon. Then he fished through his storage box and pulled out a length of sturdy rope. He tied one end to the outside end of Lucy's side of the doubletree, and then ran it forward to the eye-ring on the front of the tongue. The tight rope would keep the doubletree perpendicular to the tongue when Joe began pulling.

When everything was ready, Wend went up to Joe and, taking hold of his bridle, began leading him on their way.

As they started out he encouraged Joe. "Come on, old boy. We've a way to go and you've got to do the heavy work. I know it's hard for you without

Lucy on the other side of the tongue to share the load." He reached up and rubbed Joe's ears and then his mane. "But we'll go slow, and stop to rest along the way. I'll be right here beside you, walking to keep the wagon light. But I know you can do it and at the end you'll sleep in your own stall tonight with good hay and oats to eat."

Joe understood what he had to do. There was no whinnying, no balking in protest. The powerful lead horse plodded stolidly along the track in a display of unwavering strength and determination. Wend's admiration for the animal grew as they made their way along the track.

It took over three hours for them to cover the remaining distance to Sherman Mill. Finally, in the dim moonlight, Wend could make out the shapes of buildings in the sleeping village. Even the lights in the tavern were out. He eased Joe and the wagon across the ford and then turned in the direction of the hill up to the Carnahan farmstead.

Then he was startled by a loud bang which pierced the silence. It emanated from the tavern stable. Wend looked over to see that a door had slammed open and hit against the side of the building. He stopped to see what was going on. Suddenly a shadowy form stepped out of the door. In the moonlight, Wend could make out Peggy McCartie; the girl was in the same dark cloak that she had worn the night they had taken Ellen to Carlisle, but it was open in front and he could make out a white sleeping gown underneath. Her disheveled hair was down around her shoulders.

She stopped abruptly, turned around, and looked back at someone in the stable. "I'm telling you, this is the last time I'm doing it for a scarf." She wagged her finger like a mother admonishing a child. "And don't try to get my services for some other piece of clothing you've got in your wagon. Next time you come up here, if you want me to satisfy you, you better have some of the King's coin for me! I mean it, David, I want money. I'm not going to entertain you for anything less."

The object of her words stepped out through the door. Wend recognized a peddler who made frequent trips to Sherman Mill. As Wend watched, the man worked to finish pulling up and hooking his breeches. "Now, come on, Peggy. How many times have we been together? You've always been happy with some of my goods before. I got to keep the cash to feed that wife of mine and her little brats."

Peggy laughed. "Well, then, you'll just have to be satisfied with what you get from her, because you won't be getting any more from me."

Then Peggy spun around and took a step toward the tavern. But as she turned she caught sight of Wend and his wagon, less than fifteen yards away. She froze for an instant, the whiteness of her face illuminated by the moon, her mouth wide open in astonishment. Then she picked up her skirts and ran on quiet feet toward the rear exit of the tavern, disappearing in a few moments.

The peddler paid no attention to Wend, but instead, muttering to himself, turned and walked to the privy located behind the tavern.

Wend tugged on Joe's bridle to get him moving again and soon they had climbed the grade to the Carnahan place. Wend went into the house, lit a candle lantern from the coals of the hearth, and brought it to the barn so he could see what he was doing. Then he rapidly stripped the harness from the two horses and led them into their stalls. When he took the limping Lucy into her stall beside Joe, it was endearing to watch the lead horse reach his head over the partition and nuzzle his team mate, as if consoling her. Wend drew oats from the bin and gave a generous helping to both of the horses.

It was then that The Cat, curious at all the noise and activity at this odd time of night, slunk into the barn and sat on his haunches as he watched Wend give Joe and then Lucy a quick currying.

Wend said, "Good early morning, sir. Sorry to interrupt your hunting. It's just us coming in late; I hope you found some good prey tonight."

The Cat responded with a yawn and proceeded to begin grooming himself. Wend took that as an affirmative answer; he had long ago learned that the animal celebrated a successful hunt with a thorough grooming.

As he worked on the horses, Wend thought about what he had seen down at McCartie's stable. It removed any remaining doubt in his mind about whether Peggy was prostituting herself. But the fact that she was demanding hard money from her customer also confirmed his suspicion that she was hedging her bets in her relationship with Matt Bratton. In June, before leaving to scout for Bouquet, he had observed her growing impatience with the waggoner's refusal to set a date for their marriage. Now he was sure that she was putting together a nest egg so that she could leave the valley on her own if Bratton eventually reneged on their marriage. Sooner or later she would confront Bratton about his intentions. Wend smiled to himself: *That would undoubtedly be a stormy day for the waggoner.*

* * *

Ellen was in a chair beside the fireplace in the sitting room of the McCartie's living quarters behind the common room. Even in the warmth of the hearth, she was bundled up in a quilt against the February chill. But her face now had a normal color and Wend was gratified by that and the other evidence of her recovery and regained strength.

It was the afternoon after Wend had returned to Sherman Mill. After sleeping for an extra few hours, he had hurried down to the tavern to check on Ellen's well-being. But it had taken only a few minutes of talking with her to see that her mind was in turmoil. He had finally come out and asked what was troubling her.

The girl blurted it all out. "Oh Wend, I don't know what to do. Thomas Marsh has forbidden Hank to court me."

Wend was shocked. He remembered his conversation with Marsh before the mill explosion; then the miller had been happy about the prospect of Hank and Ellen becoming a couple. "Are you sure about that, Ellen? When I talked to him before the accident, he was glad to see you two together."

"Yes, of course I'm sure! You've been gone most of the time since the explosion. Mr. Marsh has gotten angry and sullen. He's hardly talking to anyone. What's worse, he is blaming Hank for the problem in the mill. And he's blaming me, too, Wend. He says that Hank had his mind on romance instead of concentrating on the details of the work necessary to get the mill's machinery back together correctly."

Wend reflected for a few seconds. "I think he'll get over it. Maybe when they've finished repairing the mill and things are back to normal, he'll start to see things in a better light."

Ellen shook her head. "You just don't understand! It's even worse than that, Wend. When Hank got back here from Carlisle, he and his father got into a terrible row over why the mill exploded. In the midst of the argument, Hank told Tom about wanting to leave the milling business and become a farmer. He said he didn't care if he didn't spend another day in the mill."

Wend thought about Tom's mindset when he had hinted at Hank not wanting to follow in his father's footsteps. "Oh my God, Ellen, that's the worst thing Hank could have said right in that moment. Tom was so convinced that no young man in his right mind could resist the idea of taking over his mill. When Hank said that, he put a knife right into Tom's heart."

Ellen looked at Wend, accusation evident in her eyes. "For God's sake, Wend. Hank just did what you said he should. He told his father that he didn't want to be a miller. You said he had to be enough of a man to do that."

"Yes, I said that. But Ellen, timing is everything. If he had done it in a quiet moment of conversation, when he could have explained his feelings and motivation, that would have been one thing. But blurting it out in the heat of an argument was the worst thing he could have done!" Wend raised his hand in frustration. "That would have just further aggravated Tom. Don't you understand, Ellen? In matters like this, a man must learn when to hold his tongue."

"All I know is that I love Hank and he wants to spend his life with me, Wend. I lost Johnny Donaldson to a Shawnee war party and now it looks like I may lose Hank because of a stupid family argument." Tears formed in her eyes. "Please, Wend. You always see things so clearly and you have a gift for persuading people. You've got to help me."

Wend looked over at the girl. He saw a mixture of desperation and hope in her eyes that he found irresistible. Reluctantly he said, "All right, Ellen. I'll try to think of some way to approach Tom Marsh. But you'll have to give me some time and be patient."

* * *

Wend bent over the stove in the corner of his workshop, stoking up the fire. Then he threw in some additional firewood. With the stove throwing renewed heat, he settled himself at his workbench and resumed the carving he was doing on the stock of a new rifle. But a few minutes later he was distracted by the sound of loud grunting outside his shop. Then he heard his name being called.

"Wend, come on out. It's Frank McKenzie and I need to see you!'

He went to the door, curious at why Frank hadn't just come into the shop. His question was soon answered. Frank was standing just outside the lean-to which covered his rifling machine. In his right hand was his hat and in his left hand was the end of a rope. The other end of the rope was tied around the neck of a massive hog which was the source of the grunting Wend had heard.

"I've seen people lead dogs around on a leash like that," Wend commented, "But that's the first time I've seen it done with a pig."

"My Pa told me to bring it to you. We ain't got no money, so he's yours for getting me to Doc Highsmith and paying for him to treat me. This is the biggest hog we got. Pa said for me to tell you he wished he could give you more, but right now we ain't got any cash and we need the rest of our hogs and cattle to get through the winter."

"You already paid me a lot through the information you gave." Wend patted McKenzie on the shoulder. "But just tell your Pa that this squares the deal as far as I'm concerned." He looked over the hog. "Let's get this fellow over to the sty and introduce him to his new friends."

A few minutes later, the hog safely ensconced in his new prison, the two young men leaned on the fence side by side and watched as the other residents of the pen investigated their new companion.

Wend asked, "How are you doing now that you are home?"

"I'm all right now, 'cept that the Doc says I'll always have some stiffness in my leg. It's sure my days as a freight waggoner are over."

"So, I guess you'll be working around the farm from here on out?"

"That's the truth. But I still got to figure out what I'm going to do, long term." Frank shrugged his shoulders. "I ain't goin' to be able to take over Pa's farm. I got two older brothers, and the eldest is already due to get the farm one day. There ain't no argument over that in the family. So the other two of us got to find our own land or make up our mind to do something else for a living." He shrugged his shoulders. "That's why I was running freight for Bratton in the first place. I was trying to get a start on my own business."

Wend asked, "Have you thought where you'll go if you take up farming? There's still some land here in the valley, but it is getting more costly than it used to be."

"Yeah, and I ain't got no money to speak of. I only put a little aside from my job with Bratton. And you know that I used most of that to buy a rifle from you and that colt I got last year from Paul Millikan." He looked into the distance. "I ain't going to make any money working fields for my Pa, that's for sure."

Then Wend thought of something. "I heard that Tom Marsh is going to buy the Donaldson place for the tax arrears."

Frank nodded. "That story's been going around for the better part of six months. But that don't help me any."

"Well, I've been told, Frank, that he's going to split it up into at least three parcels. They'd all be large enough to make good farms."

"That still don't do me any good, Wend. He ain't gonna sell those parcels cheap."

"No, but Marsh told me something else: He's planning to build a sawmill. He's been set back some because of the explosion. But I don't doubt sooner or later he'll get to it." He looked at the young man. "He's going to need a source for logs and he told me that he planned to use the timber that comes from clearing that Donaldson land. And before the Donaldsons were killed in that Shawnee raid, Johnny told me they had more than 150 acres of land that was still in timber."

McKenzie screwed up his face. "So how does that help me? Aren't you listening? I ain't got any money."

"Frank, maybe you could make a deal with Marsh. He's going to need someone to cut those logs and get them to the mill. Maybe he would sell a parcel in exchange for your labor in cutting and transporting the timber. Otherwise, he'd have to pay someone to do it." Wend's business mind worked for a minute. "And after he gets through repairing the gristmill and building a sawmill, Marsh isn't going to have much cash left."

The light was coming on in Frank McKenzie's eyes. "So maybe it would be worth it to trade land he got cheap for labor to get the first batches of logs to his mill? You're right, Wend, there might be a deal there."

"Yes, but you have to be patient. Just keep the idea in your mind while you work at your father's farm and keep watching what Marsh is up to."

"Wend, this proves what everybody says—that you are always thinking way ahead." He laughed. "Course, no one can see what's going on behind that stone face of yours. But thanks for giving me this idea!"

Wend took Frank's arm. "Remember, nothing's going to happen real fast. You have to bide your time, keep your ear to the ground, show that you are free from Bratton's influence, and above all, that you are a good worker. I'll guarantee that Marsh won't consider any deal like we talked about unless you got the reputation for being serious and trustworthy."

"I understand what you are saying. But I'm a step ahead of you on the part about Bratton and his gang. All of them got back from the east a couple of days ago and I'm staying clear of the lot of them. And when Bratton comes back, I'll stay clear of him."

Wend was all ears. "You say his men came back from their ride with the Paxton Boys, but that Bratton wasn't with them?"

Frank shrugged his shoulders. "Yeah, Ezra McCord and Joe Finley rode back into town the day before yesterday. But Bratton didn't come with them. I heard that they were down in the tavern tellin' about what happened at Germantown. But that's all second hand, 'cause I wasn't there. Like I said, I'm avoiding the whole bunch of them."

Wend watched as McKenzie trudged down the hill to the village, limping visibly. The youth had a good walk ahead of him as the family farm was nearly a half-mile eastward along the valley road. But Wend's mind was on what he had said about Bratton. He thought about the possibilities of what the waggoner was up to. Wend knew that Matt had to pick up his rebuilt wagon from the wheelwright's shop. But that wouldn't take days—he could have been back in Sherman Mill right on the heels of his two cronies. Bratton's absence could be explained by the simple need for him to make legitimate cargo runs. After all, he had essentially been tied up for several weeks riding with the Paxton Boys, and he undoubtedly needed to tend his business to replace his lost earnings. But Wend also wondered if he was driving his team and wagon down the Great Wagon Road to take up a mission for Grenough—perhaps moving the contents of the underground storehouse in York to the new site in the Shippensburg area. Then he thought about the tavern maid Colly and hoped she would keep her promise to send him word if Bratton showed up in York.

* * *

It was four days later that Bratton returned to Sherman Mill. Early in the morning, after tending the horses, Wend walked to his workshop. He had plenty of work to keep him busy. He was working on a new rifle for Washburn's Tavern and a backlog of repair work had accumulated as soon as the residents of the valley found out that he was back in town. As he walked toward the shop, he looked down into the village and saw that Matt Bratton's large Conestoga wagon was parked beside the blacksmith shop, its bright blue bed and yellow wheels standing out in contrast to the gloom of morning twilight. Obviously Bratton had arrived the previous evening.

Wend stood looking at the wagon and worked out Bratton's timing. If Bratton had left Carlisle six or seven days ago, he could have been in York two days later. If it took a day for loading the wagon, Bratton could have delivered the contents of the underground storehouse to the new hiding place in the vicinity of Shippensburg within two days. Then he could easily have unloaded the wagon and made it back to Sherman Mill in another two. So that scenario fit if Bratton had been acting on Grenough's behalf on this trip. But Wend shrugged his shoulders and walked into his shop, thinking that there was no proof: The waggoner could also simply have been carrying out legitimate freight jobs in the same time frame.

An hour later, The Cat entered the workshop. He prowled cautiously around the room, as if checking for potential enemies. Wend said, "For God's sake, Cat, come up and get your milk." He had brought a small bowl from Patricia's kitchen. In fact, The Cat was somewhat late this morning, for he usually arrived right after Wend came in for work. Wend speculated that he had had a busy night of hunting.

The Cat took Wend's meaning, and jumped up onto his workbench, where the milk bowl had been put in its usual place. He leaned over and sniffed at the milk. Finally determining that it was satisfactory to his taste, he daintily lapped at the liquid, periodically stopping to lick his lips. When he had finished, he laid down on the edge of the workbench, leisurely cleaning and grooming himself. Finally, he yawned deeply and curled up for his morning nap, as befitted a mighty hunter home from a busy night of stalking and combats.

* * *

Later, in mid-afternoon, Wend was hunched over his workbench checking out the lock and vent hole of a fowling piece which had been brought in because the customer said it constantly misfired. Then his concentration was interrupted when he heard the steps of someone walking though the lean-to and looked up to see the hulking figure of Matt Bratton standing in the doorway and glancing curiously around the shop.

As far as Wend could remember, the waggoner had never been in the shop before. He wondered what had brought him up from the village. But he didn't have long to wait.

"Dutchman, I've got something important to say to you and you better listen close." Bratton took two steps into the shop and stood towering over Wend.

Wend stood up and took a step back to give himself more room. "Well, I'm listening, Bratton."

"I'm here to give you a warning. A real serious warning that you better take to heart."

Wend quickly thought: *Has Grenough sent him here with a warning for me to stay away from his property or to threaten me physically?* Then he realized: *If that's what Bratton is about to say, Grenough is admitting that he and the waggoner are in cahoots and that he has something to hide. Why would he take such overt action?* But he didn't have to wait long to find out Bratton's message.

"I heard you was seen with Peggy at The Walking Horse tavern down in Carlisle. Sittin' together at the same table for lunch, smiling at each other, and having a powerful serious conversation. That don't sit well with me, Dutchman. It don't sit well at all. She's betrothed to me and I ain't going to sit still while you try to move in on her."

Wend couldn't believe what he was hearing. He laughed out loud. "Is *that* what this is about, Bratton? You're seriously threatening me over a lunch Peggy and I had at a public tavern in Carlisle?"

"You're damn right that's what this is about."

"For God's sake, Bratton. We had just worked together to save Ellen's life; Ellen McCartie, your future sister-in-law. We had traveled all night over the mountain and Peggy had spent all morning without sleep or breakfast, helping Doc Highsmith while he worked on Ellen. I simply took Peggy to lunch because she was famished and didn't have any money along to buy a meal herself. And all we were talking about was a highland girl who I knew during Bouquet's campaign." Wend shook his head. "You're out of your mind if you think anything was going on between us."

"Listen, Eckert. I've had you figured out from the very first. You've had your eyes on Peggy ever since you came to the valley in '59. So I'm warning you now: Keep your hands off her, or I'll permanently mess up that face of yours that all the girls in the valley seem to take such a fancy to."

Wend couldn't stop from laughing. "My God, you're serious. How could you ever think I had any intentions toward Peggy? Lord above, Bratton, I just spent seven months with the army trying to find a girl from Philadelphia. And as for the girls around here, they all seem to think that Elizabeth McClay has me in her power. And the whole valley knows that I haven't spent any time courting girls in the four years since I arrived."

"Don't try to wiggle out of this, Dutchman. You always got some smooth line. Just remember what I'm tellin' you, cause if I hear about somethin' like this again there won't be any more talkin'."

"Bratton, this is ridiculous. You could resolve the whole matter instantly by setting a date and marrying Peggy. You've been putting it off for years. If you're so worried, take action and be done with it. The fact that you haven't done that makes me wonder about your intentions."

Wend could see that the big man's anger blossom. His face was now bright red and he was breathing heavily. Then he seemed to explode.

"You know what, Eckert? I ain't waitin' for another time! I'm goin' to teach you a lesson right now!" He raised his fists and advanced toward Wend.

Wend took a step back and bumped into his rack of firelocks. He reached behind himself and grabbed one of the weapons. He grasped it by the barrel and swung it back like a club, ready to strike the big waggoner. "You take another step, Bratton, and I'll beat your head with this until your Pa has to come up here and carry you home. You got that? You better believe I'm serious!"

Now Bratton took a step backward. A sly grin came over his face and he dropped his fists. "Put that firelock down. This is just what I would have expected from you, Dutchman. I heard about how you jumped Lazarus Stewart and beat him with a pistol before he even had a chance to face you. Now, when I come at you ready to fight fair, you threaten me with a clubbed weapon. You're just yellow, and that's the plain truth."

"I don't care what's fair, Bratton. I'm going to defend myself in any way I can. And now I'm going to give you my own warning. If you ever threaten me again, I'll fix you proper with Peggy. I've traveled the Cumberland Valley enough to know how you behave on the road. If you ever try anything like this in the future, I'm going right to Peggy and I'll tell her about all the time you spend in Molly Reed's bed, down in Carlisle, when her husband isn't around, or about how you came on to a certain tavern maid at The Proud Rooster near York. And I'll mention all the stories I've been told by tavern keepers about your other amorous adventures. That should set you up for some serious discussions with Miss McCartie about your future, don't you think?"

Bratton took a step back and stood silently looking at Wend, obviously considering what he had heard. But his face was redder than ever. "You bastard. You're a sniveling coward, who would rat on a man to his woman 'cause you ain't got the guts to face up to him proper-like." He stared at Wend for a long moment, breathing heavily. "I'll get you, Dutchman. Mark my words: One day I'm going to fix you permanent." With that, he turned on his heels and stocked out of the shop.

Wend lowered the firelock and was just starting to lose the tension in his body when he again heard steps outside the shop. He feared that Bratton's anger had exploded again and that he was on his way back to carry out his threat of violence. Wend raised the gun over his shoulder, ready to defend himself.

But it was not Bratton who appeared in the door. Instead, Donegal entered and then stopped stock-still when he saw Wend in his defensive stance.

The highlander smiled ironically. "Did I miss something? Are the Shawnees over-running Sherman Valley again? Or are you just acting out your memories of Bouquet's battle last summer?"

Wend told Donegal about Bratton's visit.

"Not to worry, lad. I feel that the day is coming when our dear Mr. Bratton will get his comeuppance. We Scots are fey, don't you know?"

Wend put the rifle back in the rack. "Before I answer that question, I need to know what the word 'fey' means Simon."

"It means we have a sense of the future, particularly when mayhem and death are in the offing." Donegal laughed. "And I get that feeling every time that monstrously nasty man is around."

Wend stared at his friend and then said, "I hope your feeling is about Bratton's fate, not someone else we know."

Donegal nodded and blessed himself. "Indeed, I hope you are right. However, it turns out that in that great wagon of his, the evil man was carrying a sack of mail for Sherman Valley. Mail that he picked up in Carlisle. So at least it can be said that he does some good for his neighbors."

Wend had returned to his bench and was fooling with the fowling piece's lock again. "I guess we can be thankful that Bratton has some use."

"Well, on this cold but otherwise fine day, my lad, it turns out that you can number yourself among the thankful."

Wend looked at the highlander. "What do you mean by that?"

"One of the letters he carried was for you. And I happen to have it here in my own fine hand, since I took the liberty of picking it up for you at the general store."

Wend was startled and excited. He was expecting no letters except from Colly. He turned to reach for the mail.

But Simon was determined to have some fun. He read from the folded paper, "It says on the outside that this letter happens to be from a certain Miss Colleen Allison, who resides in York, at a place called The Proud Rooster." He smiled broadly. "Don't I recall that you recently took a little wagon trip, in the dead of winter, to the likes of Shippensburg and York, which you made clear to all your friends was for no more purpose than to look at iron furnaces? And I clearly remember you denying to the end of the day that it had anything to do with any young lasses. Oh, yes, I clearly heard you saying that!"

Wend answered. "That was correct when I said it. But certain things just developed."

Donegal threw back his head and laughed. "They do indeed! Especially for you, Wend, me lad! Joshua has it right about you, when he says that women like to drape themselves over your body." He looked down at the letter again. "As for you, my fine friend, you just have to hope that Miss Elizabeth McClay of Sherman Valley doesn't find out about Miss Colleen Allison of York. There will be the devil to pay and you'll have to do some fine answering to her if she does."

Wend grabbed the packet from Donegal's hand. Then he had a thought: "I don't suppose you would be the one to tell her, would you?"

Donegal drew himself up in indignation. "Me? I'm the soul of discretion." Then he smiled. "Of course, I can't be held responsible if something was to slip out when I've had a little rum or whiskey in me stomach. A man's mind gets befuddled and he is 'na able to control his mouth at times like that."

Wend shook his head. "Simon, you are a bastard. I should have made you go back to Scotland with the rest of the 77th. Now get out of here and let me get some work done. It's late enough in the day and I've lost a lot of time dealing with Bratton."

The Scotsman left and Wend could hear him giggling and laughing to himself as he walked toward the house. Undoubtedly Donegal would find a way to let the news "slip" out sometime during the course of the day, probably at supper that very night, thus making Wend the subject of all discussion for long minutes afterward.

Wend sat down and opened the letter. What he read drove from his mind all worry of being embarrassed at supper.

The Proud Rooster
York
February 22nd 1764

Dear Mr. Eckert,

My name is Edith Harrow and I'm writing this letter for Colly Allison. I'm supposed to say that the waggoner Matt Bratton, who you told Colly about, was here in the tavern yesterday, and it was clear he was working for Mr. Grenough. He stayed one day only, and in the evening he said something to another guest about picking up a load of goods here in York and taking them to Shippensburg. Colly said that would have meaning to you. Colly also told me to tell you she hopes you find business down here again, because she likes taking payment from you. She said that would also mean something special to you.

Now that's all she told me to write to you. But I'm writing something now she didn't want me to tell you. I can do that because she don't have her letters and don't know what I'm writing. The truth is you got her into a lot of trouble and pain. The night that man Bratton was here, he and the red haired man who came after you when you was staying here caught her out back while she was getting firewood off the pile. They dragged her into the woods far enough so no one could hear what was going on. Then they threatened her if she didn't tell them what she knew about you and if you had told her anything about why you were down here. When she wouldn't say nothing, they beat her on the face. She's wearing black marks around her eyes from that. Then each of them had their way with her while the other one held her down. They said they was teaching her a lesson.

I'd say you owe a lot to Colly for keeping her mouth closed and taking the worst those men could offer. She's a tough women and she was back at work today. And she still says she hopes you come see her again. But as for me, I hope you never show your face around here anymore, cause the truth is all you done is cause her big trouble.

The letter was signed in crude letters,

Colleen Allison

Wend stood up from the bench. He paced around the room in frustration and anger. He remembered the warm pleasure of the night spent with Colly and the girl's feisty courage in taking his part against Irwin and Reilly. Permeating those memories was guilt for getting her involved in his problems. Finally, letter in hand, he walked out under the lean-to roof and stared down at the blacksmith shop in the village. Bratton was plainly visible, working on the canvas covered farm wagon which he used to provide freight service between Sherman Mill and Carlisle. With him was Ezra McCord, who had taken over the driving duties from Frank McKenzie. The two men were laughing and joking as they worked. A surge of white-hot rage flowed through every part of Wend's body as he pictured the image of Bratton, pants down, forcing himself on Colly while Reilly held her. At that moment he wanted to storm down the hill and tear Bratton limb from limb. He even thought about getting a rifle and putting a ball through the waggoner's head. But then his steely self-control took over, for he knew that he must save his revenge on Bratton until a more appropriate time. Before he could take care of the waggoner, he had to figure out an effective plan to destroy Grenough and all of his men. Revenge on Bratton would have to be part of the larger scheme. And it must be done in a way that didn't land Wend on a gallows or in prison.

* * *

Wend went back to his bench but found the turmoil in his mind made it impossible to work. He realized that he needed some time to think and reflect on what the day's events had revealed. So he found himself taking the path down to his refuge spot on the banks of the creek. It was a collection of scattered large rocks which enclosed a grassy area. The spot was shielded from view by high bushes. Wend thought of it as his personal "nest" and visited when he needed to divorce himself from the larger world and be alone with his thoughts. As he walked down the path, The Cat scurried past him and led the way, determined to be the first to their destination.

He arrived to find that the evening was cold but the sky was clear and the sun was setting with great beauty, shades of red, orange, and copper spreading across the western sky. Wend sat down on one of the large rocks, crossing his arms and hunching his shoulders against the growing chill. He stared at the sunset, its colors reflected in the rippling creek water. Despite the disturbing events which had swirled around him during the day, his thoughts first strayed to Abigail Gibson, for over the years he had often dreamed about her when at this spot. Out there beyond the western mountain ridges and the Allegheny River, in a little village on Slippery Rock Creek, Abigail lived and labored. He tried to visualize what she might be doing at this very instant. Was she in front of a fire, preparing the evening meal for her family? Maybe, as she stirred the kettle, she was enjoying a quiet conversation with the oldest of her children, the little boy she and Wend had conceived in the tiny cabin beneath Fort Loudoun. Or perhaps she was sitting before the cook fire cuddling her little girl in her arms. Or was she laughing and joking with other women of the village as they worked? Did she even still think of herself as Abigail, the lawyer's daughter from Philadelphia, or in her mind had she completely become Orenda, the Mingo wife of the war captain Wolf Claw?

Wend shook off the unanswerable questions about the Philadelphia girl which he knew would haunt him now and then for the rest of his life. Instead, he forced himself to think about Grenough's syndicate and a way to destroy it. After hearing the words of influential men like John Armstrong and

Henry Bouquet, it was clear beyond any reasonable doubt that the trader was respected far too much for Wend to successfully take any legal action against him. In fact, there was little hard evidence that could be presented. Wend knew that he would be thrown out of any magistrate's office and made into a laughingstock if he tried that route. Moreover, if he unsuccessfully pressed charges, he would be marked as the logical suspect if he subsequently resorted to physical violence against Grenough or any part of his organization. A chill far stronger than the winter cold went through him with the realization that he had no option but to carry out a private war of vengeance to the death. And he must do it in a way that there would be no direct evidence against him.

He had spent some time working through different options during the long hours of the wagon trip back from York. It was clear that he must start with an attack on the frontier trading operations. So he had to find out where Mathews and Crowley would rendezvous with war parties for their trading. That was where Matt Bratton became an important part of his plans. If he understood the setup correctly, Bratton would be hauling the goods out to some remote location beyond the most settled areas of the colony and then, in a secluded cove, he would meet with the two traders and transfer the war goods to their pack horses. The question would be where, and the only way to find that out would be to follow Bratton. He expected that in late April or early May, when the snows had ended, the waggoner would leave Sherman Mill with his Conestoga wagon. He would probably spread some cover story about having a long distance cargo job, perhaps out to Fort Bedford. Wend would try to covertly trail him to the meeting site and then take the traders under long range rifle fire before they could get to their meeting with the first war party.

There was only one major defect in his plan. There would be at least two traders and Bratton at the meeting point. He would need to carry at least three rifles to do the job in one round of shooting. He could sling one rifle over his shoulder and balance a second across his pommel. But the third was a problem. He had to work out a way to do that; probably he would have to take two horses and pack at least one rifle on the second horse.

Another important decision had to be made. He could not deny that having one or two more men with him would be of immeasurable help. It would make the searching and handling of horses much easier. Moreover, he would have someone to hand him loaded rifles after each shot or perhaps do some of the shooting. He knew that Baird and Donegal were the perfect men for the job. But he could not convince himself to share his knowledge or his plans with either of them, at least as things stood at the present. Joshua had once worked for Grenough in the legitimate trading business before the war and considered him a friend. Furthermore, the scout admired Grenough for his knowledge of the frontier and tribal politics. And Donegal didn't really have a stake in Wend's problem. At any rate, he didn't feel that he had the right to ask either of them to jeopardize their lives or freedom if things went badly. *No, Wend thought, there's no choice: I will have to do the job by myself.*

Wend found himself frustrated because he had not been able to think of a realistic plan to destroy Grenough himself. So far, he had only worked out a means of killing the lowest level of the trader's organization. Even if his attack was successful, Grenough could easily replace working level flunkies like Mathews, Crowley, and Bratton in short order. They were as expendable as Kinnear and Flemming had been. Clearly, he must work out a way of taking out the core of the outlaw syndicate—Irwin, Reilly, and Grenough himself.

Eventually, the sun touched the western horizon and the growing cold permeated Wend's bones. He picked himself up and, escorted by his furry consort, climbed the path back up to the Carnahan farmstead.

Part III

The Legend of the Dutchman

April – June 1764

CHAPTER ELEVEN
Matters of the Heart

In early March, the people of Sherman Valley began to receive copies of the Pennsylvania Gazette with stories which covered the outcome of what had come to be called the Paxton Boys Insurrection. Wend read all of the articles with great care for he not only wanted to understand the outcome, he wanted to search for any discussion of Grenough's role in the resolution.

The Gazette's articles made it clear that the approach of the marchers, reported to number more than 600, had caused terror and pandemonium in Philadelphia. The 'peaceful' Quakers, who had long been unwilling to provide any kind of military assistance for the border towns, or even authorize an official government supported militia, were suddenly prepared to take arms in defense of their own dwellings. In a few days, a militia battalion of nine companies, largely made up of Quakers whose religion ostensibly forbade armed action, was formed to protect the city and the Moravian Indians from the border men. Strangely, many of the newly consecrated militia men somehow came armed with firelocks of their own. In addition, the governor and colonial assembly did with the Moravian Indians what Reverend Elder had futilely requested for the Conestogas—they ordered all of them shepherded from their exposed villages to the safety of a vacant army barracks in the heart of Philadelphia. Then, as Price Irwin had told Wend at The Proud Rooster, they had the Moravians sent to New York under armed guard.

By mid February the Ulster marchers reached the town of Germantown, on the outskirts of Philadelphia, where they encamped while trying to decide how to proceed. Reading between the lines of the news stories, Wend guessed that their bluster and martial ardor had cooled by the time that the occasion for real action was imminent and the existence of an armed opposition became known. For their part, the colonial assembly, faced with the threat of 600 armed men a few miles away from their meeting hall, dispatched a deputation of four men, led by Benjamin Franklin, to negotiate a peaceful settlement.

Then Wend found a newspaper passage that drew his rapt attention. After describing the composition of the negotiating deputation, the Gazette added the following: "Dr. Franklin also accepted the advisory services proffered by Mr. Richard Grenough, the prominent western merchant and trader, who is a resident of York. Mr. Grenough has much experience dealing with the Ulster-Scot people who form the core of the gathering at Germantown. He is also greatly informed on matters of the border area and Indian affairs. The Gazette has been informed by competent authority that Mr. Grenough will be acting as the colony's Indian Commissioner during the impending expedition against the Ohio tribes involved in the current uprising, which is to be led by Colonel Henry Bouquet of the Royal American Regiment."

A later edition of the newspaper told the story of the negotiations. The result was an agreement that had several elements. First, the colonial assembly would provide military assistance for the defense of the backcountry by forming a provincial battalion to man the forts. They also agreed to gather supplies, wagons, and livestock to support Bouquet in his march on the Ohio Indians. Finally, and most important to the Ulster-Scots, they would consider ways to allow the settlements to have more representation in the assembly. For their part, the Paxton Boys agreed to disperse and they shortly rode back to their settlements.

Wend read and re-read the stories and studied the words of the agreement as published in the Gazette. It soon became clear to him that the agreement had offered nothing concrete to the marchers that the colony wasn't already being pressured to do by the British government. The exception was the offer to consider representation for the border counties. But, reading carefully, Wend noted that the agreement simply said that the proposal would be put before the assembly and that there was no guarantee of action. Wend smiled to himself: The agreement had the characteristic signs of manipulation by the wily Dr. Franklin. Long ago, when his family lived in Lancaster, he had heard his father talk about how Franklin always seemed to manage events to his own advantage or to that of the authorities for whom he was working. And in this case, Wend was sure that the good doctor and Grenough had connived to craft a document which promised much and delivered little. In fact, it would serve the interests of both men. Franklin wanted the insurrection defused with the minimal cost to the government: That would burnish his credentials as a negotiator. Grenough's game was necessarily more complex:

He wanted the Paxton Boys to think of him as supporting them against the government and in their defense against the Indians; but he also wanted to garner the appreciation of the governor for helping to mediate an agreement.

On a cold March night after news of the outcome of the Paxton Boys march had arrived in Sherman Mill, Wend and Paul Carnahan sat by the hearth in the great room. Wend asked the minister for his opinion about the import of the events on the colony and the relations of the Ulster-Scots with the government.

The reverend clearly had been mulling that very question, for he responded after only a few seconds hesitation. "The truth is the Penn's have only themselves to blame for the Paxton problem, Wend; they made a Devil's Bargain with the Ulster people. They invited them to migrate into the colony and arranged for cheap land, knowing that they would arm, organize, and defend themselves if a threat arose from the tribes and the French. The Ulster settlements formed a shield for the eastern part of the colony at virtually no cost to the government. And just as important, the Quakers could maintain clean hands as pacifists—*they* weren't engaged in the dirty business of warfare and killing. It all worked very well in the French war and during minor Indian raids which followed. But this massive tribal uprising, with attacks across a broad area, hundreds of people killed, and the constant threat of massacre hanging over every farmstead and village, has driven the border people to distraction. I believe that the underlying compact between the Ulster people and the colony's government has been fractured forever now. There are deep currents stirring out here in the border country."

Wend asked, "*Currents stirring*? What do you mean by that?'

"The Ulster and other settlers have had a taste of making their own decisions and have come to understand that when trouble comes, they are on their own. They'll no longer quietly accept much control from Philadelphia." He paused again. "Mind you, there will be increasing friction in the future and far less patience with the government out here."

Wend asked bitterly, "And what of the Conestogas? They were caught in the middle between the Ulster and the government, and ended up paying the ultimate price!"

Carnahan looked up at Wend, a grim blackness in his eyes. "Yes, Wend, you've raised an important point: In my mind, the governor and the assembly have as much blood on their hands for that as Lazarus Stewart, Bratton, and all those other men who participated in the actual murders. Had the Penns formed a properly organized militia, commanded and disciplined by officers

217

appointed by the colony and had they listened to Reverend Elder's warning, the Conestogas would be as safe as the Moravians are now." The reverend's faced tensed, and he stared silently into the fire.

Wend studied Carnahan's visage. He could see anguish written large—his muscles tightened, his jaw set hard—and suspected the man was seeing an image of Molly, the little Conestoga girl who had died in his arms.

As Paul's silence persisted, Wend got up and stoked the fire; he sought to change the subject as a way of distracting the reverend from his memories of the bloody work house.

"Say, I've got some news, which I picked up talking to Colonel Bouquet in Carlisle on my way back from York."

"News? What kind of news?"

Wend told Carnahan about the army troops which would be maintained in the colonies and the new taxes being proposed by Parliament.

Carnahan abruptly sat straight up in his chair. "Good God! What are they thinking about over there?" He put his hand to his chin. "That's the last thing we need now, on top of all this unrest out here."

Wend was surprised. "What do you mean, Paul? I don't like the idea of new taxes, but it all seems logical and appropriate to me."

Carnahan stared at Wend for a moment. Then he grimaced and shook his head. "That's the German in you speaking. You've been here amongst the Ulster for five years, Wend. You talk and dress like us, but once in a while that German blood affects your thinking. You aren't quite Ulster yet!"

Wend laughed. "Face it, Paul; I'm never going to be completely Ulster, much as you try to make me. But I don't understand, Reverend. As Bouquet said, the army must be financed in some way. It just makes sense."

Carnahan smiled. "What can I say to make you understand the likely reaction of people around here?" He paused and thought about what he wanted to say. "Look, my experience is that the Germans back in Lancaster and further east have an abiding respect for authority and the government in general. They tend to keep their heads down, mind their businesses and their farms, and accommodate themselves to government rulings, even when they're not really happy about them. That's why the Penn's were delighted to have them settle here. Forgive me, but you're reacting just like those Germans back east. But I can tell you, when the Ulster-Scots, and probably a lot of other colonists, hear about the size of the army which will be garrisoned here and about the new taxes to support it, the first reaction is going to be a seething anger."

Wend shrugged. "I hadn't thought of all that."

Paul waved his hand at Wend. "Well think of this: We just finished talking about how the people here in the settlements are fed up with control from Philadelphia. Now they'll get word that England is going to be soaking them for money they can't spare to pay for troops they don't want. Add that all together and it's a formula for increased friction and maybe outright resistance. I could be wrong, but we may come to think of the Paxton Boys' defiance as mild in comparison to what results from these new Crown decisions."

Wend was frustrated. He had tried to take Carnahan's mind off of the slaughter in the workhouse, but what he thought would simply be interesting news had turned out to agitate the reverend even more. He decided to move on to a less contentious subject. "Paul, I've got something else to discuss with you."

Carnahan looked up. "Something else—what do you mean? Have you picked up more bad news in your travels?"

Wend smiled. "No, this is more personal: It's along the lines of you being the reverend of Sherman Valley and tending to your flock."

Carnahan's face brightened. "So quit leading me on and tell me what it's all about."

"It concerns Tom Marsh and several of the young people in the valley." Wend sat down in a chair next to the reverend. "Marsh is very depressed since the explosion at the mill."

"Are you surprised by that? I know it put him behind in his plans to expand and he's losing money until he can get it operating again."

"But there's something else you might not know: He and Hank had a big argument. Marsh blames his son for the mistake which caused the explosion. And what really disturbed him was that Hank told him, at the height of their exchange, that he doesn't want to stay in the milling business. He wants to become a farmer."

Carnahan put his hand to his chin. "I see what you mean. Marsh has always bragged about how smart Hank is and talked about him taking over the mill. That would hit him hard."

"Beyond that, Reverend, Hank and Ellen McCartie have fallen in love."

"Give me credit for having eyes, Wend."

"Well, Marsh blames the romance for distracting Hank from his work and thinks that Ellen is influencing him to leave the mill. The truth is, he has forbidden Hank to court Ellen."

"So I can now assume that Hank and Ellen are in deep despair?"

"Of course," Wend nodded. "They're seventeen and sixteen year olds in love. I know exactly how that feels—I spent four years and a military campaign working through that. But anyway, they're asking me to talk to Marsh on their behalf."

Carnahan looked over at Wend with humor in his eyes. "Oh? And how did you get in the middle of this?"

"Ellen and I have always been good friends and our closeness became strengthened by the death of Johnny Donaldson. So, before the explosion, she asked me to help convince Marsh to let Hank start farming part of the old Donaldson place, once Marsh bought it. In fact, I did some preliminary talking with Tom, just to lay the ground work, but hadn't actually told him that Hank wanted to be a farmer."

"I see. So, having gotten yourself in the middle of all this, why are you coming to me now?"

"Because it's too big for me to handle on my own. I can talk to Tom on fairly equal terms in matters of business. But on family and personal things like this, I've realized that I'm just too young. It needs a man more his age." Wend smiled. "And if that man were his minister it wouldn't hurt."

Carnahan raised an eyebrow. "Perhaps you can take a lesson from this situation. It often happens that when you get involved with other people's personal problems, things get out of hand. You end up with everybody mad at you or at least disappointed with whatever you do."

Wend said, "All right, Reverend, I take your meaning."

Carnahan looked into the fire. "Actually, I'm glad you brought this to me. I have noticed Tom's moroseness. I've been looking for a way to approach him and tactfully discuss the situation. But what you've said puts things in a more complex and urgent light."

Wend said, "You don't know the whole of it yet, Reverend. There's another complication. It involves Frank McKenzie."

"Well, you really have got yourself deep into this, haven't you, Wend? Let me guess: Is young McKenzie challenging Hank for Ellen's favors?"

Wend laughed. "No, it's not that kind of complication. The truth is, he is worried about what he's going to do with his life. He can't be a waggoner, like he was planning on, because of the gunshot wound to his leg. He's got a permanent limp and can't handle walking all day alongside a Conestoga. So he's planning on being a farmer. But he can't afford to buy land. So I put the idea into his head that, once Marsh does build his sawmill, he might try to make a deal with him to log-out the Donaldson land in exchange for getting title to enough of it for a farm."

Carnahan thought for a moment, then looked at Wend and nodded. "You're right; there might be a deal there. Marsh will buy the land dirt cheap for taxes and it would cost him more to hire someone to do the logging than giving Frank some acreage." Then Carnahan laughed, and said in words dripping with irony, "So let me understand your tangled idea: You want me to go down to Marsh and somehow, through my powers of ministerial persuasion, convince him to let Hank marry Ellen, become a farmer, and then also give McKenzie a shot at some of the Donaldson land?" He shook his head, and said jokingly, "Yes, that's a just a minor job for a minister. It ought to take no more than ten minutes and then Tom and I can retire to McCartie's and celebrate the brilliance of the deal over a round of ale."

Wend shook his head. "I understand that it sounds like a lot to ask. And the fact is, it wouldn't work out if that were all there was to it." Wend marshaled his thoughts, then continued, "It still needs some work. The first thing Marsh is going to say to you is, *If I let Hank go farm the Donaldson place, who is going to help me around the mill?*"

Carnahan nodded. "Yes, that's a good point; Edward is too young to take over the work that Hank's been doing."

Wend said, "I saw that problem, but couldn't figure out how to get around it. It would undoubtedly keep Marsh from letting Hank take up farming." Wend paused, and looked at Carnahan. "So I put another twist into the proposal: What if Frank McKenzie became apprenticed to Marsh and started learning the milling trade? After a year or so, he could do a lot of the work that Hank does and then Hank could move on to farming."

Carnahan looked at Wend sharply. "Look, I thought you said McKenzie wanted to become a *farmer?*"

"Yes, but that's mainly because he can't think of anything else to do. The truth is, he's a pretty smart fellow—used to working on his own with Bratton's wagon—so he ought to be able to pick up the job of running a mill rapidly. And his stiff leg wouldn't be much of a handicap in the mill. In fact, it would be even less of a problem than if he was a farmer."

"You've got it all figured out, don't you Wend?" Carnahan looked at Wend, laughed, and shook his head. "Have you talked to McKenzie about becoming a miller? Does he like the idea?"

Wend shook his head. "No, I just thought of that angle earlier today. But it does make the whole deal work."

Carnahan agreed. "It would—provided we were able to get both Marsh and McKenzie to agree." He thought for a long time, again staring into the fire. Then he said. "Look, this isn't going to be settled by one meeting with Marsh. I have to start a continuing conversation with him, first trying to get him out of his sadness. Once that's done, I can start to talk with him about Hank's future. It's going to take a long time." He looked over at Wend. "And don't go talking to McKenzie about working in the mill until I tell you. We don't want to get his hopes up prematurely and it is going to take me a while to bring Marsh around to the idea of taking on outside help at the mill."

* * *

After the conversation with Carnahan, Wend lit a lantern and retired to his room. He was relieved at having talked over both the Paxton Boys Insurrection and Marsh's situation with the reverend.

As he sat on his bed, he looked at his dresser and saw a clipping which he had saved from an issue of the Gazette. It was the undoubtedly the most intriguing article he had read in the papers recently: A story about the role played by the 77th Highlanders in the Paxton Boys affair. Wend had cut it out from the paper to keep it as a memento of his time with the highlanders. Now, in the flickering light of the candle, he re-read the clipping.

The story reported how the colonial authorities, not satisfied that simply putting the Moravians in Philadelphia barracks would be sufficient protection, had appealed to General Gage in New York to move the Indians to barracks in New York under a military escort. Gage replied by ordering the remnants of the 77th, which happened to be in Philadelphia on their way to New York, to convoy the Moravians northward. So, Captain James Robertson and his men, having fought the hostile tribes for seven years, now performed their last official army duty as the shield of a band of peaceful, Christian Indians. And defending them was no easy matter. Even in the most eastern parts of Pennsylvania and New Jersey there was fierce anger at all Indians after the news of the depredations of the Ohio tribes over the summer. As they marched north, the people of many towns and villages rioted against the Moravians, threatening to attack them. Ironically, the news story said that more than once the 77th had to fix bayonets against white men to protect the Christian Indians.

As he read, Wend was gripped by a strong kinship with these highlanders that he had marched and fought alongside for many months: In his mind he could picture the thin figure of Robertson standing in front of the ranks, sword in hand, determined to do his duty, strange and unexpected as it might seem. He could visualize Sergeant McCulloch and McKirdy and all the others standing in line, ready with leveled muskets, the same fierce look on their faces as he had seen at Bushy Run. And he knew that somewhere near at hand Esther McCulloch and the other women and children had stood, watching their men carry out this last duty for the crown.

Wend felt a tug at his heart, realizing that he was nearly as close to these people as he was to anyone in Sherman Mill. Indeed, they were like family and he had deep regret that because of the mission to the Ohio with Stirling he had not been able to bid farewell to them.

Wend shed his clothes, blew out the candle, and settled down to sleep, memories of the highlanders and Bushy Run still crowding his mind. At first sleep was hard to find, but eventually he felt a sense of relaxation flow over his body and drive out the tension of the day. Slowly he drifted off to slumber.

But sometime in the night his mind roused itself and he began to dream. It started with the highlanders and he found himself marching with the men of Robertson's light company of the 77th along a forest track, which he vaguely recognized as Forbes Road. Corporal McTavish was playing the pipes, which Wend knew was foolish, because he was in the Black Watch and didn't belong with them. But Donald McKirdy was keeping the cadence with his drum and that was as should be, except that he was in Captain McDonald's company, not Robertson's. Behind them Wend could hear the voices of the 77th's camp followers. Loudest among them was the brassy voice of Esther McCulloch and she seemed to be giving someone a piece of her mind, which was entirely normal and proper, and somehow the sound of her gave Wend great comfort.

Eventually he noticed that Mary Fraser was walking beside him. She was swinging along with the easy gait of a veteran soldier, dressed in the improvised marching outfit which Wend had seen her in so often: Red highlander's jacket covering a white shirt, a long skirt sewed together from two kilts, scuffed soldier's shoes, and a highland bonnet covering her beautiful auburn hair. Shoulder straps supported a pack and a haversack hung from her side. In her hand she carried a wooden staff made from a sapling. She was wearing the pewter jewelry that Wend had taken for her from the body of a Shawnee warrior: The oval earrings dangled from her ear lobes and the nose ring was suspended on a chain around her neck. Above them a brilliant sun showered them with golden light.

Wend turned to her and said, "I'm sorry I wasn't there when you died. I shouldn't have listened to Chaplin Ferguson. I should have gone to Colonel

Bouquet and got permission to remain behind with you when Stirling's company left for the Ohio Country."

Mary looked at him with that ingratiating smile which had captivated the entire battalion. "Nonsense, Wend. You made me a woman, a happy woman. And I told you myself that you had to go find out what happened to Abigail."

He shook his head. "No, no, I can't get over feeling ashamed that I left you alone to die. I'll never forgive myself for not finding a way to spend those last hours with you."

Then she said something which puzzled Wend. "Don't you know that I'm not dead? Can't you sense that I'm still with you?"

"Yes, I do feel very close to you sometimes. But I know it can't be real, for your body lies in the cold ground outside Fort Pitt."

The girl laughed at him. "No, Wend, listen to me. I am very near to you and always will be. All you have to do is follow your heart and you'll find me where I belong."

Those words brought Wend awake in a state of shock. He sat up in bed and felt sweat on his forehead. The dream had been frighteningly real and the feeling of Mary's presence still enveloped him. But moonlight was flowing in through his window, all was still, and he could clearly see that he was alone. He pulled the covers off and put his feet on the cold floor. He felt himself shaking slightly at the intense experience. Then he remembered Mary's last words in the dream: *Follow your heart and you'll find me where I belong.*

He puzzled over those words for a long time, sitting in the moonlight, with his hands holding his head, but he could make no sense of them. Finally, he lay back down and pulled the covers over himself. After a while, he fell into a fitful, dreamless sleep which lasted until the gloom of false dawn.

* * *

Peggy McCarty knelt at the side of Sherman Creek, her face over the water. The cool April morning breeze blew the loose ends of the straps which held her apron in place, and the chill made the girl visibly shiver. Then, as Wend watched, she wretched for the third time in a row, the vomit spewing into the water.

Wend could see it all quite clearly from his "nest" among the boulders and bushes along the bank of the stream. He had come down the path from his shop at the top of the hill, a mug of tea in his hand, to enjoy the bright sunlight of the spring morning before starting work. He had only been there a couple of minutes when he saw Peggy come running upstream from the village, glancing back several times as if to see if anybody was watching her. Then she had sunk to her knees at a spot about twenty yards downstream from him and almost immediately started to be sick.

Wend drank the rest of his tea and then put the mug down on a rock beside him. As he watched, the girl gagged again but nothing came out. Acting on impulse, Wend left his nest and walked along the bank until he was beside Peggy.

The raven haired girl looked up, surprised at his presence. "What are you doing here, Wend? You shouldn't sneak up on people like that!" There was embarrassment and anger in her words.

Wend didn't say anything. Instead he pulled out a cloth from his pocket, checked to make sure it was clean and then went to one knee to soak it in the creek water. "Here, you need to clean your mouth. And there's some of the vomit on your apron front."

Peggy took the cloth, wiped her face and then brushed the front of her apron.

"Is Bratton the father, Peggy?"

Her head snapped around, a look of fright on her face. "What do you mean, Wend? That's an impudent question to ask a girl. What could possibly make you think I'm with child?"

"Come on, Peggy. I watched my mother when she got sick carrying my brother, Bernd. And she did the same thing with Elise, my little sister. You've got the woman's sickness which comes in the morning and that means you have been impregnated."

Peggy looked up at him with defiance, her mouth pursed tightly. He thought for a moment she was getting ready to burst out into a tirade against him. Instead, she broke down and started sobbing.

Wend repeated his question. "Bratton *is* the father, isn't he?"

Peggy nodded her head. "I *think* so."

Wend thought for a moment, then going way out on a limb, asked, "But you can't be sure, can you?" He paused for a moment and said very gently, "There *have* been others, haven't there? Other men—out there in the stable— like that peddler you were with when I saw you that night in February?"

She looked at him with horror in her eyes. Peggy put her hands over her face and her tears increased, punctuated by sobs which shook her whole body. "Oh, God, Wend, I'm ruined. What's to become of me?"

"Does Matt know about this?"

"I told him last night." She broke out into tears again, accompanied by a near wail.

Wend could picture it all now. "Let me see if I can guess: You told him about the child and demanded that you two get married, like he's been promising. And then he refused. Is that close?"

"Wend, Matt and I have been together for over four years. We're supposed to be betrothed. I figured that we could get married right away, since everyone is expecting that anyway. So no one would have given much thought to my being pregnant soon after the wedding." She paused and wiped tears from her face. "But when I told him, he just stared at me for a moment. Then he laughed. He laughed right in my face! He called me a tart; a tart and a whore. He denied the child was his and said he wasn't raising someone else's brat."

"So, what are you going to do? How far along are you?"

"I just became really sure in the last few days. I don't know what I'm going to do. But I can't stay here and I have to have a plan before I start to show." Peggy smothered a sob. "Oh, God, I feel so ashamed. And the worst part is that Matt is right; I have been a tart." She looked up at Wend, a look of angst on her face. "My parents will be so disgraced if this gets out." Peggy dried the last of her tears. She put on a stiff face, stood up, and squared her shoulders. "But I will decide on something, some place to go. And sooner or later I'll have to tell my parents."

She thought of something and turned to him with an urgent expression. "You won't tell anyone about this, will you? Or about that night with the peddler when you saw me leave the stable? Oh please, Wend, I beg you, please keep this all a secret!"

Wend felt a wave of sympathy wash over him. "Of course I won't say anything: What kind of person do you think I am?" Then he had a thought. "Actually, Peggy, I might be able to help you."

"A way to help me? What do you mean?"

Wend said, "There's a widow I know who lives alone down in Carlisle. Here name is Alice Downey. She takes in borders and might be able to shelter you." Wend saw interest and hope grow in Peggy's face. "Your parents would have to pay her some rent and board, but that would at least get you out of the valley and away from the scrutiny of people here. While you were in Carlisle, you could figure out something to do after you had the baby. God knows, any tavern keeper would take you on."

Peggy considered for a moment, looking down into the running water. "Oh, Wend, do you think you could convince her? That would give me some time. And you're right that I might find a place to work after the baby came."

Wend said, "I have to take a new rifle down to Washburn's Tavern soon. I'll talk to her while I'm in Carlisle. How would that be?"

Peggy nodded. "I would be very grateful." She turned to Wend, a look of puzzlement on her face. "Wend, why are you doing this? I'm Bratton's girl, or at least I was. After all the things he's said and done against you, why are you helping me?"

"I'm helping you *because* you were Bratton's girl. He's made you a victim, just like he has so many others." He reflected a moment and the right words came to mind. They were her own words, spoken on that June night long ago when Ayika had given birth, the night she had been mad at him for deciding to leave the valley to scout for Bouquet's expedition. "I know how to help my friends and neighbors. It's the right thing to do. I know how to show loyalty to people of the valley."

Peggy blushed, then looked up at him quickly, and he knew that she remembered that night. She reached over and put her hand on his arm. "I said those words to hurt you because I was scared and didn't want you to leave. But I've regretted them ever since. Peddlers and other travelers have come to the tavern and told stories about what you did at Bushy Run. Most people in the valley are proud of you, Wend." She paused a moment. "And of course, I'm grateful for what you did to save Ellen."

Peggy looked back toward the village and said, "I have to get back to the tavern before they miss me. But you've given me hope."

Wend watched as she walked back along the creek, deep in thought, her arms crossed in front of her and looking down at the ground, just as she had the night that Ayika's baby had come.

* * *

The day after Wend had discovered Peggy McCartie' pregnancy, he and Donegal stood beside his workshop. Donegal had nailed a wooden target on a tree at a man's height and was practicing throwing his knife.

When they had first returned to Sherman Mill in January, the Scot had initially taken up residence as Wend's roommate in the main house. The men had spent the winter building him a lean-to shack attached to one side of the stable and he had moved in during March. The highlander had taken up working the Carnahans' farmland with Franklin in order to learn the skills he would need to tend his own land, when he eventually claimed his land grant. Meanwhile, he made plans to travel and scout for the place where he would eventually settle, while using the Carnahan farmstead as his base.

Donegal, like most highland soldiers, was an expert in using all manner of blades. He still routinely practiced with his broadsword, dagger, and throwing knife. He modestly admitted to being better than most at knife throwing.

Knife throwing was something that Wend had never learned and he found Donegal's practice intriguing. He had asked Donegal to explain the particulars of the art.

"The key," he told Wend, "Is knowing how many turns your thrown knife will make over a given distance. Then you have to place yourself at a distance where the point will end up in your target."

Donegal went to the tree and then paced carefully back about ten steps. He quickly turned and whipped the knife toward the tree. It rotated several times and ended up stuck right in the center of the target.

"Very impressive, Simon. So how far can you be away and still hit a target? There has to be a limit."

"Now, my fine lad, you should know after spendin' all this time marching with me, that I'm a man of few limits."

Wend laughed. "I can think of several of your limits right off the top of my head. Regardless, there is some distance beyond which you're thrown knife won't be effective."

"Well, the longest I've done to date is about thirty feet."

"So show me, Simon." Wend laughed again. "Make me a believer."

"Ah, laddie, you're on." The highlander paced off about thirty feet. Then he stopped and stared down at the village. "Well, it looks like our great friend Mr. Bratton is taking advantage of this fine April weather to make a freighting run."

Wend turned and looked down at the blacksmith shop. Bratton was in the process of hitching a six horse team to his Conestoga wagon. That grabbed Wend's attention immediately. Was this the trip that would mean the start of Grenough's spring trading campaign? Would Bratton be heading for Shippensburg and the secret storehouse of war goods? Then Wend thought, *It's only early April—there could still be heavy snows before full spring and the season of reliably dry roads arrived.* He had to find out how long Bratton planned to be gone. If it was only a short time, he could relax. But if he was putting out word that he would be on a long trip, Wend would have to gather up his kit, rifles, and make haste to catch up with Bratton. He reflected that he had a day or two to find out, for he could quickly overtake the slow moving wagon on the Great Wagon Road.

Suddenly he was recalled from his reverie by Donegal. "Hey, lad, are you going to watch me? You're the one who wanted to see me hit the target at thirty feet."

"Sorry, Simon. Go ahead and show me your stuff."

Donegal said, "You got to understand, at this distance, it's 'na just the number of turns you got to worry about. You also got to think about the arc of the knife's flight. With the size and weight of my knife, it has quite an arc."

He reared back and heaved the knife at the target with great energy. It hit the oval mark near the top and the blade sank deeply into the wood.

Donegal put his hands on his hips and looked at the knife. "A wee bit high, but I think it would have done the job, don't you, lad?"

"It would indeed, Simon. I'd not want to be your target."

CHAPTER TWELVE

War Party

Two days after his discovery of Peggy McCarty's pregnancy, Wend walked through the pre-dawn dusk to the stable, intent on feeding and grooming the mare and his team. It was a blustery spring morning; the trees and bushes moving and rustling with each gust of wind. He held a candle lantern with one hand and carried a small pot of tea in his other. He could hear the horses moving around in their stalls and Wend thought that they were a little spooked by the noise of the wind. As he entered, they all looked round at him and the mare gave him a whinny of welcome and stamped her front hoof. He fed them their morning oats and gave the mare a good rubdown, talking to her as he worked. His presence seemed to quiet the animals, who contentedly munched their feed as he groomed each of the horses.

With the horse chores finished, Wend picked up the lantern and teapot and walked over to his workshop. The new rifle, all but finished, lay on his bench where he had left it the previous evening. He had test fired it the day before and checked the sights on his range. He was satisfied with its performance. Now he must only take care of a few cosmetic tasks, inscribe his name and the sequential number which he placed on the barrel of all his firearms, and it would be ready for delivery. And since Matt Bratton had left the day before, that was important for he must also be on his way if he was to catch up with and trail the waggoner.

The Cat came in within a few seconds of his own arrival. Wend was about to greet him when he heard the sound of a horse whinnying. He was startled to realize that it was not from one of the animals in the barn, but that the sound came from further away; somewhere down by the creek or perhaps at McCartie's. Then he heard the mare reply from the stable. He was contemplating the meaning of the exchange when he suddenly noticed that The Cat had frozen where he stood, his back arched and his tail straight up in the air, and was staring at the rear of the workshop. Wend felt the hairs rise on the back of his neck and a weird, tingling feeling course through him. He snapped his head around to see where The Cat's eyes were focused.

And he looked directly into the eyes of a Mingo warrior, in full paint, sitting on his haunches in the deep shadows at the rear of the workshop, a patterned blanket over his shoulders and a rifle cradled in his arms.

Wend throttled the fear he felt rising inside and grabbed the new rifle from the workbench to use as a club.

The Indian took no action, but remained stolidly in the same crouching position against the rear wall. Then a broad smile slowly spread across his countenance, his teeth showing white against the paint on his face. "Calm down, Wend, I'm not planning to scalp you. But I do have to admit that thick mane of yours, even with the rear part missing, would look nice hanging from the trophy rack back at the village."

Wend lowered his clubbed rifle and stared at the warrior in shock. "Charlie?" He repeated quietly, "Charlie Sawak?"

"The very same, Wend. Although they call me White Eyes back at the village. But the elders are trying to decide on a better name for me."

Wend sighed and the anxiety flowed out of him. He turned and laid the rifle back on the bench. Then suddenly a thought came to him. He turned to Charlie and grinned. "How's Rose doing?"

Charlie stood up and smiled again. "So you figured that out, did you?" He leaned his rifle up against the wall. "She's doing just fine. Taking to Mingo life like she was born to it."

The source of the strange horse's whinny became clear to Wend. "You've got a horse tied up down in the woods, don't you?"

Charlie nodded. "Same old horse from my cart. He ain't that much of an animal, but he serves the purpose."

Wend said, "That explains why my animals were so skittish this morning. I should have sensed it was more than just the wind that was stirring them up." Wend sat down in his workbench chair and motioned for Charlie to take the other chair. "Well, tell me about your new life."

Charlie remained standing. "We can talk about that later, Wend. I'm not here for social reasons. We have some business to transact and I'm not wearing this paint just to impress you."

"All right, Charlie. Have some tea and tell me about what's on your mind."

Charlie gratefully gulped the warm drink, then looked up at Wend. "You were right—dead right—about the whole Grenough thing, Wend. He's the major supplier of powder, lead, guns, steel knives, and other things the Indians need to fight the war. The tribes deal with a red-headed man named Reilly, but chiefs in the Ohio country know he's just the front for Grenough. Right now, there's lots of argument going on among the leaders of different tribes and among different bands within the tribes. Some want to continue the rebellion, others are for peace. But those bands which want to continue fighting are in desperate need of munitions. They used up most of what they had on raids and at Bouquet's battle last summer, and much of what remained during the winter hunt." He thought for a moment. "Reilly has been spreading the word that traders named Mathews and Crowley will be ready to do some big trading soon. In fact, just a few days from now. Because of the amount of goods they plan to trade, they're planning to do it at a spot in the hills just north of Lyttleton. There are several parties of Indians—mostly Shawnees and Delawares—traveling east to meet with them."

Wend decided to draw his friend out. "So what are you leading up to, Charlie?"

"Isn't that pretty obvious? We can intercept Grenough's men and pay them their due."

Wend said quietly, "Precisely what do you mean, 'Pay them their due'?"

"I mean kill them and destroy their goods." Charlie stared at Wend. "Why are you acting so hesitant, Wend? Just a few months ago, in the seat of my cart, you vowed to me that you would take care of Grenough and his men yourself if the authorities wouldn't do it." Charlie paused. "Now we have the chance."

Wend paused a moment and looked at his friend. "Look, there's something I don't quite understand, Charlie. Despite our friendship, the fact is you're on the other side now. Why do you want to stop traders from providing war goods to the tribes?"

"The village of Mingoes I'm living with contains mostly Chief John Logan's relatives. You know he favors peace with the white men and hasn't taken part in this uprising. The leaders have decided to sit out the raids this summer and attend peace talks with Bouquet when his expedition arrives. And personally, my grudge is with the men who killed the Conestogas, not all white men." He thought for a moment, then continued, "My people recognize the righteousness of revenge, and we both have enough reason for vengeance in the case of these men. They had an undeniable role in the massacre of my people and Grenough's men had a role in the death of your family! This is no time for you to waver; I came all this way counting on you to help."

Wend relented and put his hand on Charlie's shoulder. "All right, my friend, I just wanted to understand your motives and make sure that you were really committed to the bloody work which we face. For a long time you were skeptical about my suspicions."

"For God's sake Wend, that all changed at the Lancaster workhouse. The men of Grenough's conspiracy must die!"

Wend nodded and sighed deeply. "Yes, they must. And frankly, I'm glad you're here, because if you hadn't come, I was going to have to do it all by myself." He smiled at Charlie. "Now, do you know where the rendezvous is, my painted friend?"

"Generally, and I have a description of certain landmarks in the area. But I didn't get the full details; I was afraid to ask too many questions. I was counting on you to help find the place."

Wend looked up at Charlie, another question on his mind. "How did you manage to break away from your village for so long? Wouldn't your long trip raise questions?"

Charlie shrugged. "Actually, I more or less told them the truth. I said that I had an act of vengeance to perform against an old enemy—against someone who had wronged my family. They could understand that. I just didn't tell them the identity of my enemy. And besides, they knew I would be back—I was leaving Rose with them."

Wend thought for a moment. In identifying the trading site as being north of Lyttleton, Charlie had provided him with information that would make their search much easier. And they wouldn't have to follow Bratton, as Wend had planned. "We don't have to find the exact trading site, Charlie. Bratton left here with his wagon two days ago. He's going to pick up the supplies somewhere in the southern part of Cumberland Valley near Shippensburg. Then he'll freight them to a meeting with Mathews and his partner in order to transfer to pack horses. He'll have to use Forbes' Road. We can go across country and enter the Path Valley from a northern direction. We'll intercept Bratton on the road north of Fort Loudoun. In essence, he'll come to us. Then we'll follow him to the place where he will meet with the traders. When that happens, we can get all three of them at once."

Charlie smiled broadly. "Now that's a good plan. I knew I could count on you! When do we get started?"

Wend paced the shop, his mind racing. "We still have more planning to do. I need to have a logical reason for leaving, to avoid suspicion after this is all over." Then he looked over at the work bench. "Actually, the reason's right

233

there. I'm supposed to go down to Carlisle to deliver this rifle to Washburn's. Everyone is expecting me to leave soon anyway. And it's perfect cover, because after we've finished, I'll actually take the rifle to the tavern. Lot's of people will know I was there."

Charlie nodded. "It all makes sense. When do we leave?"

"You go now, before the village wakes up. I don't want anyone discovering you or that nag of yours. And I'll leave tomorrow after I've had a chance to get my kit together. Moreover, it would look suspicious if I just picked up and left today without advance warning to my family."

"So where do I go?"

"I assume you came by way of the New Path from Aughwick?'

"True enough."

"All right, go back to the first big ridge at the end of the valley. There's an old Indian shelter site there, just off the trail."

"Yeah, I saw the trail mark on the tree on my way here. You want me to wait for you there?"

"Yes—you've been traveling steadily for days. Your horse can use the rest, because we're going to be riding overland through rough country. I'll be there tomorrow afternoon at the latest." He walked over and inspected Charlie's rifle. "This is the rifle I gave you. Is it still in good shape?"

"As good as the day you gave it to me."

Wend walked over to his rifle rack and selected one of his own firelocks. "Here, take this with you along with the one you've got. We're going to need at all the firepower we can get."

Charlie wrapped his blanket more tightly around himself and picked up both rifles.

Wend thought of something else. "Hey Charlie, wait a minute. Before you leave here, wipe all that paint off your body and your face. And I'm going to go get you some of my old clothes to wear. We don't want you looking like a hostile if you're seen by somebody while we're traveling. They'll call out the militia to come after us."

A half-hour later, dressed in a set of Wend's old clothes and a floppy hat, Charlie was ready to travel. He looked down at himself. "Wend, couldn't you have found something a bit more stylish?"

"You're perfect now, Charlie. Except for the sharp nose of yours, you look like any back country Ulster traveler."

"All right, I'm on my way and I'll wait for you. We Mingoes learn how to be very patient." Then a crooked smile came over his face. "But we also get hungry. And after months of eating Indian provisions, I'm dying for some good old home-cooked white man's food, seasoned with real spices and herbs. Do you think you could manage to smuggle some of that out to me when you come to the campsite?"

* * *

Wend pointed down into the narrow Path Valley. "Charlie, that's Forbes Road you can see running right through the middle of the bottom land. It comes up from Fort Loudoun and pretty much parallels the course of Conococheague Creek." Then he motioned across the valley to a spot on the Tuscarora Mountains which formed the other wall of the valley. "Look sharp and you can see where the road turns westward and climbs toward the gap. The Burnt Cabins and Fort Lyttleton are on the other side of the ridges."

The two stood on an outcropping of rock on the western side of Conococheague Ridge, the mountain which formed the boundary between the Cumberland and Path valleys. They had found this point of observation in the late afternoon after two days of hard riding from the Indian campsite in Sherman Valley.

"If we camp right here, we can keep the road under constant observation and there's no way that Bratton can get to his meeting point with the traders without us sighting his wagon. I figure that they plan to do the transfer of goods somewhere up in the Tuscarora's or just on the other side. That's remote enough that no one will chance upon their work. Undoubtedly the place designated for trading with the war parties will be somewhere westward of that, up in the next set of ridges north of Lyttleton, which can be reached only by pack trains traveling on narrow trails."

Charlie nodded. "Yes, that would generally agree with the location that I heard people describing." He looked down into the valley in front of them. "But if you're right about Bratton, we don't need to worry about that. We'll stop the traders before they ever get there."

Wend thought for a moment and responded, "If I've calculated correctly, Bratton should be coming through here sometime tomorrow, probably in the afternoon. But we should start keeping a sharp watch after dawn tomorrow."

They made camp in a sheltered spot behind the outcropping. The rocks prevented the light of their small fire from being visible down in the valley. For supper they heated some of the provisions that Wend had brought along and finished the meal off with warm tea. Then Wend took a small jug of whiskey out of his saddlebag and held it out to Charlie. "If I remember correctly, you'll really appreciate this!"

Wend was surprised by his friend's reaction. Instead of the expected smile, the sight of the jug elicited a stern frown. Charlie sat staring at the jug as if it were poison. Wend asked, "Charlie, what's the matter? You've always been appreciative of good border whiskey or rum!"

"Wend, I've sworn off liquor. I haven't had any since I left Lancaster."

"Charlie, I can't believe what I'm hearing. I've seen you drink anything you could get your hands on in taverns from Carlisle to Paxton, particularly if someone else was paying."

"Yes, that's true. But I've been in the Ohio Country among the Indians for four months now. Even in that short time I've seen what liquor does to them. Wend, even the best of the men seem to have no ability to resist it. And it is destroying them."

Wend stared into the fire a moment. "I had never thought of that."

Charlie nodded. "The wisest of the tribal leaders understand. Neolin, known as The Profit, advocates complete abstinence from liquor. He says that after the tribes defeat the white men and drive them away, they must discard all the things the Europeans have introduced to the tribes. We must live the way our forebears did. And the most important thing to be cast out is the rum and whiskey which steals the Indians' brains."

Wend looked at his friend. "That's probably a good idea for White Eyes, the Mingo warrior. But can't my old friend Charlie Sawak make an exception tonight and share a drink with me?" He placed the jug on the ground between them. "We have a lot to catch up on, Charlie, and tomorrow we're going into battle."

Sawak hesitated a moment, then a smile crept over his face. "Now that I think about it, Wend, you are absolutely right. There are occasions when rules have to be broken." He reached down and picked up the jug, and took a long pull. Then he looked at his friend, and asked, "By the way, how did you know that Rose came with me to the Ohio Country?"

Wend explained to Charlie about seeing the magistrate's handbill at Harris' Ferry and talking with the wounded Frank McKenzie to find out about Bratton's pursuit and Charlie's ambush. Then he told how he and the others had traced his journey along the Susquehanna to the crossing point.

Charlie looked at Wend with gratitude. "You are a good friend. Not many people would have done that. I'll always respect you for your concern."

Wend said, "One thing I've been curious about. How did it go fording the river?"

Charlie shook his head. "It was almost unbearably cold. And the raft has devilishly hard to control in the current. The fact is, we barely made it. Rose was leading the horse and I had straps tied to the back of the raft so that I could keep it from dragging downriver. But it still nearly upset several times."

Wend asked, "Where was Rose wounded?"

"You figured that out, too?" He shook his head in amazement. "She was lucky. The ball just grazed her arm, tearing out some flesh between the elbow and shoulder. Anyway, Rose was still able to lead the horse. But when we were only about a quarter of the way across, she stepped into a hole and fell. I was about to let go of the raft to help her. That would have been a disaster, because we probably would have lost everything. But she was able to hold on to the horse's lead line and get up on her own. She was completely soaked and immediately began shivering uncontrollably. We made it to one of the larger islands, which actually had some soil over the rocks and a few trees, and camped overnight with a small fire. I built it in the shelter of a couple of big rocks, and kept it small, but I was still worried someone would see the glow or our smoke. Even with the fire, Rose couldn't get rid of the chill she had taken in the river. She shook all night and I hugged her to try to keep her warm."

Wend reflected, "Well, obviously you made it across the rest of the river."

"We left the island at the very first light; since the sun hadn't provided any heat during the night, the water was even more frigid than before. But finally we made it to the west bank. I got our stuff off the raft and was able to rig a makeshift pack saddle for the horse from bits of the raft and saplings from the woods. I lashed it together with rope and the straps from the harness. Then, with our stuff loaded on the horse, we headed up Sherman Valley. At first we stayed on the wagon track. But I was worried people would see us and, about the time we got north of Croghan's Gap, we cut what I recognized was the New Path. Joshua had told me that it would take us all the way to Aughwick."

"We figured you had traveled that way and that you would cross the Allegheny at Kittanning."

"Yes, and we got some help. When we were nearly at the western end of Sherman Valley, we had an unexpected encounter. And it turned out to be very lucky for us." He stopped talking and looked at Wend with a broad smile. "We ran into Chief John Logan."

Wend stared in surprise. "John Logan, the Mingo chief?"

Charlie laughed at Wend's astonishment. "The very same. He was on a hunting trip and camping with his wife along the trail."

Wend knew about Logan, although he had never seen him. And because of Abigail's captivity, he had garnered every bit of information he could get on the Mingo tribe, mostly things that Joshua had told him. The Mingoes were essentially an artificial tribe, more a collection of semi-independent bands and villages linked only by barely remembered Iroquois roots and the remnants of a common language. In the mid-to-late 1600's, the Delawares and Iroquois confederation of nations had fought a series of wars, ending with victory by the Iroquois. The conquered Delawares were forced to refer to themselves as "The Women" and endure control by their conquerors from the north. To ensure that control, the Iroquois sent groups of emissaries, mostly from the Seneca tribe, to live among the Delaware and report their compliance with the terms of the peace. After generations, these groups evolved into the Mingo. But the tribe itself recognized no overall chief. Logan's father, also called John, had been the sachem of a group of Mingoes in central Pennsylvania, and principally because of location, was designated by the Iroquois confederation to deal with the Europeans in the colony. Pennsylvania's governors and other officials, not understanding the structure of the Mingoes, had assumed that the elder John Logan was the overall chief of the tribe rather than merely an Iroquois ambassador. His son John had assumed the mantle after the death of his father. But by that time, there was little ambassadorial work to be done, because most of the Delawares, and in fact, Logan's own band of Mingoes, had moved west to the Ohio Country.

John Logan, like his father, retained his friendship for the Pennsylvania government. So he and his immediate family continued to live and enjoy life in the central part of the colony, first in Sherman Valley and then in the vicinity of old Fort Granville, miles to the north of Aughwick. He had taken no part in the current uprising and Joshua believed he had actually used his diminished influence to try to tamp down the ardor for war among the Mingo.

Wend asked, "Did you stay with Logan for a while?"

"Just overnight. His wife cleaned and dressed Rose's wound. They gave us more provisions, which was a great help. But most important, Logan gave us a small piece of wampum which would identify us as his friends to his relatives in the Ohio Country and then told us how to find their village. He said they would welcome us—so that gave me peace of mind, for now we had a place to head for."

Wend asked, "How did he react to hearing about the massacre of the Conestogas?"

"Here's the surprise, Wend. He had already heard about it. I asked him how, and he jut said he had his ways. He said he was glad I had gotten away, because he had heard that everybody had died. He was happy that there would still be Conestoga blood among the Ohio tribes."

"So you ended up living in the village Logan mentioned?"

"Yes, but we had another big problem getting there." He looked at Wend with a sly smile. "And we met your girl along the way."

"My God, you saw Abigail?"

"Yes. We crossed the Allegheny with the help of the Delawares at Kittanning. We rode across in a canoe and they swam the horse across. Then we took the path along Slippery Rock Creek, as Logan had described. But that's when we ran into the problem that I told you about: Rose got sick. It was undoubtedly from her getting soaked in the Susquehanna. She had been sniffling and sneezing ever since then and it got worse as we went on. The day after we landed on the west bank of the Allegheny, she could hardly breath; it was hard for her to walk. On the second night in the Ohio Country, we were in camp along the creek and she began going between sweating and chills. I felt her forehead and she was hot and clammy. I was scared to death. She wasn't any better in the morning, but we didn't have any choice but to press on; by now, I had to support Rose as she walked. Logan had told us there were several villages along the creek, so I was hoping desperately that we would find one." He gathered his thoughts. "Finally, we came to a little village nestled in a looping bend of the creek."

Wend was feeling rising excitement. "Let me guess: It was surrounded by ridges which formed a snug cove, a swath of pine trees behind it, and fields nestled between the village and the hills."

Charlie nodded. "That's right! Well, we got to the edge of the village and I had to put Rose down. She was virtually unconscious. I shouted for help several times, then I tried to wipe the sweat from her face. A group of men and boys came out to look us over. One of them, realizing Rose was sick, shouted some orders and they gently carried her to the center of the village, near the fire ring. I bent over Rose again; she was all flushed and now she was shivering uncontrollably. The Indian men stood around in a circle, looking down at us."

"I can't tell you how upset I was; then, from behind the crowd of Mingoes I heard a female voice say quietly, 'Here, let me look at her.' Suddenly all the men and boys drew back as if one."

"I looked up to see a blond angel standing there. She had golden hair pulled back into a long braid which went down her back and the deepest blue, piercing eyes I've ever seen. It was like they could look into your very soul." He thought for a few moments. "She was dressed in an undyed, light colored shift, belted at the waist. It had almost no ornamentation, but she did have a string of beads around her neck. After standing there looking down at Rose for a few seconds, she knelt down beside her, felt her forehead, and bent over to listen to her breathing. Then she looked up at me and said, 'I'm called Orenda and I do the doctoring here.' She looked down at Rose again, then back to me and put her hand on my arm. 'Your woman has lung fever. Liquid is collecting in her lung. Soon she won't be able to breath at all. We need to work fast.' Then she spoke quickly to the men, and they carried Rose to a tiny hut on the outskirts of the village."

Wend said, "Your description is just like I saw her when I was there in early November with the army diplomatic mission."

Charlie continued, "I was in shock at first, but soon realized that it was your girl from what you had told me about her. Anyway, Abigail put Rose in that little hut, and then she boiled a mix of water and herbs over a small fire, filling the hut with an aromatic vapor. That helped Rose breath easier. She tended her for several days and nights like that. Then she started feeding her soup and other soft things. She really knew what to do, and on the seventh day Rose was on her way to recovery."

"Did you tell her that you knew me?" Wend asked.

"Of course—then it was her turn to be shocked. After that she showed me your son, Wend. He looks like you with the brown hair and blue eyes." Charlie stared at Wend for a moment. "She asked me to tell her everything I could about you. So I explained how you had helped out with the Conestogas and had helped me get away."

Wend sat looking into the fire, conjuring up a picture of Abigail and the boy from his memory.

Charlie laughed. "She also told me about what happened when you came to the village with the army and took your family's scalps back." He punched Wend in the ribs and giggled. "Hello, Mr. Scalp Stealer."

"I've heard that's what they call me."

"Well, the name ain't meant to flatter you. No way! And I don't recommend you visit the Ohio Country any time soon, 'cause all the villages know about you; any young buck would be glad to take your scalp and brag about it around his village council fire. And Wolf Claw's village is shamed in the eyes of other Mingo bands because they let you get away with taking all those scalps. But while they hate you, they also respect your skill for the way you shot those traders out on the Allegheny. Taken together, it means you are a marked man with the reputation of being a dangerous enemy."

"I'm not planning to visit the Ohio Country any time soon. How long did you stay at Abigail's village, Charlie?"

"We stayed there about two weeks after Rose got out of the medical hut. We got to be pretty good friends with Abigail and some of the other people. She and Rose got on real well; I think Abigail was glad to have another English girl to talk with for a while. She gave Rose a lot of tips on how to behave and blend in with the Indians. Toward the end, there was some discussion of us joining the village. But Wolf Claw had different ideas. For some reason he took to disliking me. And I have to say, the feeling was mutual. He's an arrogant bastard."

Wend thought about that. "Yes, I'm sure he is. I suspect he was afraid you would eventually become a rival for leadership."

Charlie made a face and shrugged his shoulders. "You could be right. Anyway, after two weeks Rose was in good health and we went on our way. We eventually found the village of Logan's people. It's down a little southwest of the Kuskuskies villages, which are on the Beaver River. When I showed them the wampum, they took us in with open arms. Like most Mingo villages, they can always use more people and we soon felt like the place was home."

* * *

When the sun was full up the next day the two men rotated watches on the outcropping, looking for the appearance of Bratton's wagon. Wend watched for the first few hours, relieved by Charlie in the middle of the morning. Then, when the Conestoga took over, he went down to their campsite to prepare the rifles for action.

Wend was satisfied that they had the perfect armament for their mission: He had made all three of the rifles with his own hands and they were functionally identical in design. He had brought his own rifle; the very first one he had ever built on his own. He had lost it to Wolf Claw in the massacre on Forbes Road, and then he had recovered it on the battlefield at Bushy Run where the Mingo war captain had dropped it. Wend had totally reconditioned it at the Fort Pitt armory. The second rifle was Charlie's, which Wend had carried during the Bouquet expedition and given to the Conestoga after the massacre in Lancaster. The final firelock was the one he had just completed for display at Washburn's in Carlisle. Each had barrels of the same bore, about twenty percent smaller than the average Pennsylvania rifle. That would make for a flatter trajectory in flight, a highly desirable attribute for long range shooting. Each rifle also had the same type of double-trigger lock, with a set trigger in the rear and firing trigger in front. And Wend had fired and adjusted the sights of each on his own range.

Wend drew the loads from all three of the rifles. Then he cleaned the barrels. After looking into Charlie's, he called up to his friend on the observation rock. "Hey, I thought you said you had been keeping this clean and oiled."

There was a long silence from Charlie. "I did the best I could, given the conditions. And the oil you gave me ran out a long time ago. Try to find the right kind of gun oil in the Ohio Country, particularly now that trading isn't allowed 'cause of the war! The Indians use some kind of oil they make up from animals."

Wend laughed. "I'm glad I decided to look at your rifle. But I'll clean and oil the barrel now. We need it to be in top shape."

Wend carefully reloaded the rifles to the standard that he used when shooting in contests. He had made up twelve loads of the finest quality powder, each measured to the identical quantity and each in a paper container. He had also brought along twelve balls which had been carefully filed and polished to ensure they were perfect spheres. His patches were fine silk which he had made of fabric purchased from a seamstress. When he was finished, and had primed the weapons' pans, he was sure that the firelocks would shoot as similar as any three in the world.

He finished just in time. As he was working on the last rifle, Charlie called down, "Hey, I see a wagon coming!"

Wend scrambled up to the overlook. He shaded his eyes and looked down to the south where Charlie pointed. He stared for a long minute. "That looks like his wagon." He mused, "Bratton must have been camping last night somewhere near Loudoun itself to be here this early."

Charlie stared at the wagon. "There's something different about that rig."

Wend again swept his eyes over the Conestoga wagon. Then he had it. "Bratton's got it hitched with eight horses instead of the usual six."

Charlie looked sharply, then nodded. "You're right. Now why would he do that?"

Wend thought about seeing the wagon being rebuilt in the wheelwright's shop at Carlisle.

"He's got an extra heavy load in that wagon. He needs the additional horses to get up the mountain slopes. That's the only answer."

They packed up in a hurry and loaded their horses. They were ready to move by the time the wagon passed their position and Wend was able to confirm that it was Bratton.

After Bratton had made the turn and started up the road to the gap, the wagon soon disappeared under the canopy of trees. Wend and Charlie carefully descended the mountain and set off up the road in pursuit.

As they started up the western ridge, Wend said, "We'll ride until we are a couple of hundred yards behind him. After that, I figure we'll spend most of our time leading the horses because the wagon is going to be moving slowly on these steep roads." He smiled and said, "And I'll have to watch my mare very carefully. She's a real flirt: If we get too close to Bratton, she's liable to start whinnying at his team."

* * *

The pass through the Tuscarora Mountains involved crossing several ridges which were lower than the surrounding peaks. There were many switchbacks used to make the grade acceptable for wagons. Bratton and the pack train made their rendezvous in a shallow valley after the first of the ridges.

Wend and Charlie were able to watch from cover. The pack animals had been tethered in a little cove beside the road and Bratton stopped the wagon adjacent to the clearing. They could see him talking with Mathews and Crowley.

Charlie asked, "How did the pack train get here? We didn't see them come up the road."

Wend answered, "I believe they came across the mountains directly from Shippensburg using the old Frankstown Trail. It's very rough and steep at various points; Joshua and I traveled it last year on foot while leading a column of soldiers to Bedford. But the pack train could use it if the animals didn't have any kind of a load, which is exactly the case. And there would be little chance of anyone seeing them. So it looks like they came out a day or two ago and have been camping here among the ridges."

They watched as the two traders got the pack horses ready for travel. There were twenty pack animals in total. Wend had expected all three men to start loading the pack horses from the wagon at this point. But to his surprise,

Mathews and Crowley each took a string of ten pack horses and started up the road though the pass. Bratton followed in the wagon.

Charlie spoke up. "Hey, what's going on? Why are they all going forward together instead of transferring the load right here?"

Wend shook his head. "I don't know. Perhaps they feel that this place isn't secure enough to move the goods to the horses. But for whatever reason, it's clear they're going to a more westward location."

The Conestoga shook his head. "Seems strange to me."

Then Wend got it straight in his head. "No, it makes sense, Charlie. It fits with Bratton having a heavy load and needing eight horses. He's got enough goods in there for Mathews and Crowley to trade with several war parties. He's going to park the wagon in a secure cove and act like a forward store house. They'll take only the goods they need for each trading session, to keep the loads light enough to get up steep trails into the mountains. Then they'll come back to give Bratton the pelts they've collected and to pick up more supplies to service the next war party."

Charlie nodded. "My God, Grenough's got this all figured out, doesn't he?"

"Yes, whatever else he may be, he's a clever organizer. You have to respect him for that." Wend thought for a second, "All we can do is follow them and watch what happens. There might be a place right on the road where we will have a clear field of fire to attack."

The caravan slowly moved over the next ridge and down into another small valley. Then they started climbing another ridge, which Wend realized was the last before they came down into the flatland above Burnt Cabins and Fort Pitt. The two pursuers stalked them as they moved along the switchbacks.

Finally, as they neared the crest, Wend stopped and looked out from the edge of the wagon track. "Charlie, this is the spot."

"What, you mean the place to attack?"

"Yes. Look, we're on the first leg of a long switchback which takes them to the very crest. They're about 250 yards ahead of us. After they make the sharp turn at the end of this leg, they'll come back toward us, but at a slightly higher level, across that gorge below us."

Charlie looked at the other leg of the switchback, then down at the gorge. "I see what you mean."

"Well, as they go up that leg of the switchback toward the crest, they'll come right in front of us, moving very slowly, and there's a clear field of fire to that section of the road, with no trees or bushes obscuring our view. It will easy for me to get a good bead on each of them in turn."

"But, Wend, for God's sake! It's at least two hundred yards across the gorge to the road over there. That will take some shooting!"

"Charlie, I can hit them; I've practiced on my range at this distance. And if we don't do it here, I don't know when we'll get this clear a shot. Once they get down into the flatlands it will be harder to follow them undetected. Wherever they're headed for may be a more difficult place for us to ambush them in safety for ourselves. No, we have to do it now."

They tied the horses to some trees at the side of the road. Wend found a good log at the edge of the road which was of the right size to use as a shooting support and was surrounded by some bushes to provide cover for them. Then, working together quickly and carefully, they prepared for the attack. Wend lay down with a rifle braced over the log, and Charlie knelt beside him with the other two.

Wend sighted along the barrel of his firelock, swinging it along the road opposite them. He said, "Yes, this is going to work well." He looked at Charlie and said, "I'll be shooting very rapidly. You keep feeding me the rifles as I reach for them. After my second shot—and you give me the third rifle—start reloading the first one as fast as you can, in case I miss someone."

Wend checked the priming in his rifle and Charlie did the same with the other two.

Then suddenly Wend felt Charlie's hand on his face. Startled, he asked, "What are you doing?"

"I'm putting paint on your face." Quickly Charlie used a finger to put a stripe of black paint on Wend's forehead and then one down his nose. Then he put two small stripes under each eye, one black and one red.

After he finished painting Wend, he applied similar war paint to himself.

Then Charlie said, in low but determined words, "This is the last war party of the Conestoga. It is fitting that we look the part."

They lay there together in readiness for several minutes. Then Charlie said softly, "Look, they're making the turn and starting to come toward us."

Wend saw that Mathews was leading with his string of horses, Crowley next, and then Bratton with his wagon. Mathews would be his first target and then he would move rightward to the remaining two in sequence.

He felt a great calm descending over him as the men approached. He whispered to Charlie, "We've got them. The man with the white hair is Gray Mathews, the one who knocked Donegal out at the door to the workhouse." He smiled at his friend. "All three of those men participated in the slaughter of the Conestoga. And now they're dead men who simply don't know it yet. And if I do my job right, they'll never know what hit them."

Charlie was silent for a moment, then said bitterly, "Death will come too easy for them, when you think about how they butchered my people with knives and hatchets."

Wend nodded. He spent a few seconds pulling himself into the shell of total concentration that he had conditioned himself to use in contests and when confronted with difficult shots. Then he pulled the cock back on his lock and sighted along his rifle, taking a steady bead on the head of Gray Mathews. When the trader was nearly opposite him, Wend pulled the sett trigger. Then he moved his finger to the firing trigger, waiting for the perfect moment to send the man to oblivion.

Suddenly the silence, and Wend's concentration, was broken by the sound of a horse loudly whinnying from behind him.

Charlie pushed himself up on his elbow and looked toward their horses. Then he swore. "Damn! That mare of yours has sighted the pack train and is calling out to the horses!"

Wend fought to keep his composure. In low tones, he said, "Ignore it: Stay still and quiet, Charlie."

As Wend looked along his sights, Mathews pulled up his horse and stared in their general direction. Then his mount pranced in excitement and answered the mare. Mathews sawed on the reins to quiet the animal.

The mare answered loudly from behind them, her call echoing through the surrounding hills.

Wend gritted his teeth in frustration. Mathews was moving so much that it was impossible to keep the rifle steady on him. Then the mare whinnied again and other horses in the pack train began to move around in excitement. Wend could see that Crawley and Bratton were now also looking toward where he and Charlie lay in hiding. *The situation was spiraling out of control! Soon the traders would spot them among the bushes!*

Wend felt drops of sweat forming around his hatband. But with a mighty effort of self-control, he steeled himself to quell the rising sense of panic. In a few seconds he had managed to force himself back into the shell of concentration. He thought, *If only Mathews' horse stands quiet for a second I can still make this shot. Then I'll try to deal with the others as best I can.*

Suddenly Mathews' horse stopped moving for an instant. Wend quickly took a deep breath and squeezed his firing trigger. The crack of the shot echoed through the forest.

246

CHAPTER THIRTEEN
Retribution

Wend stood by Sherman Creek in his "nest", watching the water flow past. A warm breeze, feeling more like late May than late April, was causing a slight movement of the trees and bushes. The afternoon sun imparted a pleasant warmth on his neck and shoulders. Wend sat down and kept watch downstream. It was the day after he had arrived back from Carlisle after delivering the rifle to Washburn's tavern. He sat among the bushes for about twenty minutes and then saw Peggy making her way along the side of the creek toward him. He had stopped by the tavern an hour before and quietly asked her to meet him by the stream. He stood up so she could see him and waved at her. She smiled and hurried toward where he stood.

"Pa wasn't happy about my leaving. Things are real busy today. But I told him all the smoke was bothering me and I had to get away for a little while."

Wend motioned her to one of the large rocks and then he sat down beside her. He could see right away that she was agitated; she clasped her hands and rubbed them together incessantly as she waited for him to speak. He paused for a moment to properly phrase what he had to say.

But Peggy impatiently spoke up before he was ready to talk. "I've been so nervous waiting for you to get back. Did you talk to the widow?"

Wend looked at her. "No, Peggy, I didn't." He watched as surprise, then puzzlement, and finally disappointment come over her face.

Then she spoke in a voice that was tinged with anger. "But Wend, you promised! I was counting on you! It gave me hope and I've thought of nothing else since you left. How could you let me down?" She put her hands to her face and Wend thought she was about to cry. She looked up and asked, "Are you trying to punish me because of the way I've behaved to you?"

"Peggy, I didn't talk to the widow because I thought of a better plan; something which will solve your whole problem. And once I thought of the idea, I didn't want to tell the widow or anyone else about your condition."

The look of puzzlement again came over her face. "What plan could be better than a way for me to get out of town and have my baby where no one here would know of my shame?"

Wend decided just to put it directly to her. "Peggy, we could get married. That would solve your problem completely."

She looked at him in shock, her mouth open. "What? Did I hear you right?"

Wend suppressed an urge to giggle at the expression on her face and he hurried to say the rest of what he had planned. "There's a lot of logic to it, Peggy. We've both had bad luck in love. In your case, after nearly five years, Bratton betrayed the affection you gave him. I've loved two girls; now one is married to a Mingo, the other is dead." He paused and looked into her eyes. "We're both twenty; the right time to start a family. And if we got married soon there wouldn't be much speculation about the timing of your child's birth." He paused a moment. "There would be even less if we moved away from Sherman Valley after the wedding. You've talked about wanting to go somewhere else. And just as you once said, I could probably do better in my trade at a busier place than Sherman Mill."

Peggy, still in shock, slowly shook her head and then looked at him. She put her hand on his arm. "Wend, I don't understand. How could you want to marry me? After all that Matt has done to you? And why in the world would you want to live with his child? Wouldn't you be filled with hate every time you looked at it?"

Wend smiled, took her hand and squeezed it. "Peggy, a child is a child. And we're not sure that it is Bratton's. I pledge to you that I'll raise your baby as my own, whoever the father might have been. Every child deserves a father and I think that what happens in the home shapes what they become as much or more than who happened to be the sire." Wend thought to himself: *Besides, if a Mingo warrior can raise my son as his own, I can at least show the same charity to Bratton's offspring.*

Peggy started to cry. "But Wend, there's something else. I've been such a tart. There have been many other men; I took money and gifts from them. How could you forget that? How could you live with me after that?"

"Well, I've slept with three women. Does that tarnish me? And at any rate, we've both done things we aren't proud about. At our advanced age, we should be practical." Wend smiled at her. "And besides, I may have a reputation for concealing my emotions, but I'd be a liar if I didn't admit that I see the same beauty in you as other men."

She looked at him and said, "But you've never shown the slightest interest in me."

Wend looked into her eyes. "That all changed on top of North Mountain, Peggy, the night we took Ellen to the doctor. In that moment when we stood together after we had fixed the wagon wheel, I looked at you beside me with your windblown hair and felt a surge of admiration and affection for you, and that feeling has never left me."

Peggy hesitated a moment, then smiled. "Yes, I felt the same thing. I felt so close to you at that instant that I wanted to put my arms around you. But the moment passed and we had to get on with the trip." She bit her lip and continued, "Then, when we had lunch at The Walking Horse, it seemed so proper and comfortable for us to be together that I haven't been able to get that out of my mind."

Wend squeezed her hand again. "Peggy, you are an incredibly attractive woman and I've thought about what it would be like to be in bed with you, just like every other man in this valley." He watched as she blushed at the compliment, then he looked directly into her eyes, because he wanted to make sure she understood his sincerity. "But there's something else: Out in the Ohio Country, after Abigail told me she wouldn't leave the Mingo, I had to think about what kind of woman attracted me. And I realized that I admire intelligent, strong willed, independent women who know how to take care of themselves. And that describes you as much as any girl I've known."

Peggy began to sob. She stared out onto the flowing water, then turned to him. "Wend, the truth is that I've been attracted to you since you came to Sherman Mill. But I couldn't bring myself to believe you would ever feel anything toward me. You were so obsessed with that Philadelphia girl and you never showed the least interest in any other woman. But after that moment on North Mountain, I began to hope."

"Peggy, I spent a lot of time thinking while I was away on this last trip, and finally realized that you were in love with me. I should have known it earlier, from the way you got mad at me when you found out I was leaving to go with Colonel Bouquet. And Ellen all but told me you were in love with me back in January. But then, I've always had trouble understanding girls."

Peggy shook her head. "Wend, there's more to it than that. There's something else you need to know: The truth is, I'm the reason that Matt has had it in for you all these years. Shortly after you got here, I mentioned that I thought you were handsome and that the boys of the valley could take a lesson from you about how to pursue their trades." She looked into the distance. "Matt reared up in incredible fury and asked how I could admire some stupid Dutchman like you. He raised his hand, like he was going to hit me, but then he thought better of it. After that, he never had a good thing to say about you and took every chance to make things hard for you."

Wend shrugged his shoulders. "It doesn't matter. That's all over now—we're free of Bratton." He put his left arm around her shoulders, and took her hand with his right. "So let me ask you formally. Peggy McCartie, I think we would make a wonderful couple and have a good life together. Will you marry me? And will you raise my children, starting with the one in your womb now?"

Peggy sat for a moment looking at the creek. A single loud sob convulsed her body. She wiped the tears away from her eyes, then turned to Wend, put her arms around his shoulders, and pressed her body against his. "Oh, God, Wend, of course I will. And I'll make you the best wife a man could wish for."

* * *

Wend sat at his workbench a few days after Peggy McCartie had agreed to become his wife. The word of the unexpected engagement was ricocheting around Sherman Valley with the impact of a loose canon ball on a rolling ship, particularly since few had known that Peggy and Matt Bratton were no longer together. The McCartie family was busily making plans for the wedding, at which Reverend Carnahan would naturally officiate. The people of the valley were buzzing about the prospect of watching Matt Bratton's reaction when he returned to Sherman Valley. Of course, no one was sure exactly when that would be.

Before Wend lay a disassembled rifle lock, which required a new frizzen and replacement of one of the springs. Wend was sorting through a box containing springs of different sizes, looking for a match to the old one. As he worked, Wend became aware of the sound of a horse and cart approaching at a fast pace down the wagon track from the west. It came to an abrupt halt outside his workshop and in a few seconds he looked up to see Elizabeth McClay standing in the shop doorway.

She leaned against the doorjamb with her arms crossed in front of her. Clearly, the girl wasn't in a good mood. "I told my mother I was coming to town to look at some dress material at the store. But I really came here to see you. Is what people are saying about you and Peggy McCartie true?"

Wend stood up and took off his work apron. "What did you hear?"

"A day laborer working on our farm told Pa you and she are going to get married. And in just a few days from now."

"Yes, that's true."

"I thought you had more sense than that, Wend Eckert. You're supposed to be so smart." She gritted her teeth and shook her head. "But it turns out that you're just like all the other men in the valley who have eyes only for dear Miss McCartie when she sashays around that tavern common room, flaunting her body. You couldn't even wait a decent time after she broke up with Matt Bratton to put in your bid. But I can see why she agreed to marry you right away—she knows you're the most successful tradesman in the valley. She knew how to set herself up right good."

Wend said, "Aren't you being a little harsh on her, Elizabeth?"

"Harsh? I haven't even got started. There are other things I could say—like all those rumors the other girls whisper about her making a whore of herself to traveling men at the tavern."

Wend took a step toward the girl. "That's enough, Elizabeth. I can see you are upset. But don't take it out on Peggy."

"You're right, Wend Eckert! My greatest disdain is for *you*. I've given you my favors and affection for the last four years. And made it clear I was ready to offer you everything I had, and don't deny that you know what I mean by that!" She clasped her hands into fists at her sides. "We could have made a good life together, with a good home and all the children you wanted. Instead you run after that cheap tart!"

"Elizabeth, you're a nice girl and we've been friends since I came to the valley. Our families have been close and there's no doubt that has often thrown us together. We've had some good times at village fairs and I've sat with you at church a couple of times, but I'm not aware of having made any advance which went beyond friendship."

"That's right, Wend Eckert, you haven't. But have you ever really looked at me? Can't you see that I'm no longer a child? I'm grown up and you can bet other men have noticed it. If you had looked at me as a woman, maybe you wouldn't be so hot to chase after Peggy McCartie like a dog going after some bitch in heat. And that's all that this marriage is about."

Wend shook his head. "Now Elizabeth, there is much more to it than that. But I'm not going to talk about my feelings right now. You're the one who has to think about the future; there are plenty of boys here in the valley who can give you what you want, particularly the one thing which I can't, which is a feeling of true love."

"Think about my future? What future? You've humiliated me before all the young people in the valley. I'm a laughing-stock and can't show my face in front of all my friends."

"Don't try to blame me for your embarrassment, Elizabeth. I'm not the one who has spread the word about us being a couple. You've got to take that on your own shoulders." He paused and said as sincerely as he could, "Besides, you are a beautiful and intelligent woman. I have heard many men say that and I've no doubt you'll soon have suitors calling on you."

Elizabeth turned a deep red and he could see the muscles in her face working hard. He expected her to lash out with more angry words, but instead she started to sob and then turned on her heel and ran out of the shop.

Wend followed Elizabeth out the door to see her climbing back into her cart and wiping tears from her eyes. She grabbed the reins and then looked down at him.

"Well, you've made your decision, Wend. And now you are going to have to live with it; live with it the rest of your life! I'm telling you right here, by marrying that whore you've let yourself in for more trouble than you can imagine! Before it's over, you're going to regret giving up a woman who knows how to love her man and treat him right. And when you find that out, don't you come crawling back to me! I'm not going to be the one to console you!"

She angrily slapped the reins on the horse's back and drove the cart off at a rapid clip down the track back toward the McClay farm.

As Wend stood watching her go, he suddenly became aware of the sound of hooves close behind him. Surprised, he turned around to see Sheriff Dunning climbing down from his horse. In the village below, Wend could see that six or seven other men were dismounting from their horses in McCartie's stableyard.

Dunning looked after the cart. He had a crooked smile on his face. "Wend, what did you do to get such a fine lookin' young lady so mad at you and go driving off in such a fired-up huff? If I was a young man like you, I'd go runnin' after her right away." He offered Wend his reins. "Here, lad, you want to take my horse? I ain't got any business which can't wait till you settle up with the girl."

Wend shook his head and looked back at the cart. "Thanks, Sheriff, but I have no reason to go after her. There's nothing I could say which would change the way she feels right now. Only time will heal her anger." Then he turned back to Dunning. "It's been a long time, Sheriff: What are you doing up in this part of the country?"

"My men and I have been riding a patrol along the road between here and Carlisle. Looking for any sign of war parties—this is the time of year when they might start to show up." He tied the reins to one of the lean-to support posts. "But I was figuring to kill two birds with one stone, Wend. I wanted to have a talk with you about something which has come up in the last few days."

Wend waved the sheriff to a seat on one of the benches. He reached to a shelf, and pulled out a jug of ale and two mugs. "Have a drink, Sheriff?"

Dunning nodded. "Don't mind if I do. It's a long ride up from Carlisle." The sheriff put the mug to his mouth and took a long pull.

Wend poured himself some of the liquid and sat down. "So what did you want to talk about, Sheriff?"

"Well, Wend, an interesting thing has come up. About a week ago, a messenger rode in from out by Lyttleton. Fellow named Dan Carmichael; he does a lot of courier and scouting work for the army, same as Joshua Baird. I think you know him?"

Wend said, "Sure, I met him last year during the expedition to Fort Pitt. And I bumped into him in Shippensburg, back in February."

Dunning nodded. "Anyway, he had an intriguing piece of news. It seems that a farmer up by Burnt Cabins was out in his field one day in mid-April and saw a pillar of smoke in the mountains to the east of his place. At first he thought it was a war party raid on a homestead. But then he realized that there weren't any farms in that direction. So he and some neighbors rode to check it out."

Wend listened raptly. But he knew what was coming.

The sheriff took another sip, and then continued. "Soon they found the source of the smoke. There had been a fire on the side of a large ridge, just below a section of Forbes' Road. It was an incredible scene. A whole area of the hillside had been blackened. And in the middle of the fire area was the burnt out remnants of a big Conestoga freight wagon. Now mind you, not much of it was left, just enough unburned parts to tell it was once a wagon. They were spread over the hillside, like maybe it had been blown apart by an explosion. The men said they found one of the wheels thrown maybe thirty yards away from the wagon box. There were also the remains of horse packs; perhaps twenty of them, all burned out like the wagon. They also found the bodies of several horses, which looked like they had stampeded over the side of the hill, hurt themselves, and been caught in the fire. There was a bunch more horses wandering around in the woods, all wearing the remnants of pack or wagon harness. It looked like someone had cut the straps and freed the horses."

The sheriff looked directly at Wend. "But I'm getting ahead of myself. On the hillside, the farmers also saw pieces of powder kegs, melted lead, and a passel of iron knife blades lying around in the ashes. There was also a bunch of hatchet heads which had been blown out of the wagon. Some of them were even imbedded in trees by the force of the explosion."

Wend remarked casually, "That must have been a very powerful explosion."

Dunning nodded. "No doubt, no doubt at all. But the most interesting thing they discovered was the bodies of two men, scorched up pretty bad. They examined the corpses and realized it didn't matter much that they were burnt. The truth is, those men didn't feel nothin' of the fire because they were dead before the flames hit them. Each one had the hole from a rifle ball right through his head, neat as you please."

Wend felt he had to show some curiosity. "So what do you figure about these two men?"

"Oh, I think it's pretty clear, Eckert. They were outlaw traders trying to take war goods to the Indians. In fact, the men who found the bodies tied them over horses and hauled them down to Fort Lyttleton. And Daniel Carmichael was there. He allowed as how he knew the men; they were named Mathews and Crowley. Dan said they been trading on the border for years."

Wend screwed up his face as if he was in deep thought. "Say, Sheriff, aren't those the two who were in Carlisle with Matt Bratton last January stirring up men to ride on the Moravians and Philadelphia with the Paxton Boys? The ones at that meeting where Donegal and I saw you?"

The sheriff raised an eyebrow at Wend and put his mug down. "Now that you mention it, that's true. I hadn't thought of that till you reminded me."

There was a prolonged silence as the sheriff thought about what Wend had said.

After a few seconds he picked up his narrative. "But the most interesting thing about the whole incident was the way those two men died. Carmichael and the farmers rode back up to the burned out hillside and walked around trying to figure exactly how it all happened. Now Dan is sure that the two men were shot while on horseback up on the road and they fell down the hillside. Probably that's when part of the pack train stampeded and went down the hill. He's just as convinced that the wagon was rolled down after the team had been cut free. But at any rate, he said there was only one place he found where those men could have been shot from." Dunning cocked his head and looked at Wend. "From a spot down the hill and across a gorge; maybe 200 or 225 yards away. It was the only spot with a clear enough field of fire. Carmichael said whoever done it must have been a hell of a long range marksman." The sheriff paused again.

Wend nodded, "If he shot at that range, he certainly knew what he was doing."

"Yes he would indeed." The sheriff stared at Wend meaningfully. "And in fact, Dan found tracks and dung for two or three horses right around that area where the shootin' would have been done. So he thinks the rifleman shot the two men from there, then he and whoever was with him rode up and ran the wagon down the hill, cut the packs off the uninjured horses and threw them down, and burned the whole mess."

Wend offered Dunning another drink. "Sure, I'll have more, that's good stuff, Eckert." He held out his cup and Wend filled it. "Now there's only one thing we ain't too sure about: What happened to the waggoner? He seems to have just disappeared. Only thing Dan could figure was that he saw the other two men get shot, and was able to run away into the bush before the shooter could get him."

Wend took a sip of his own drink. Keeping his voice as calm as he could manage, he asked, "So why are you making a point of telling me all of this, sheriff?"

Dunning sipped his ale and raised a finger. "Just the thing I was going to bring up, Eckert. It seems that Richard Grenough has been making the rounds of the taverns in Carlisle, spreading the word that you are known to have a personal grudge against Indian traders for having something to do with the death of your family. He's reminding everybody about the story of how you shot those other traders, Kinnear and Flemming, out on the Allegheny last year. He's also been pointing out what a good shot you are; he's got some story of seeing you shoot a tiny little target out from between Joshua Baird's legs at seventy paces in Bedford. And he's tactfully suggesting that you could be the shooter in this case." Dunning looked down at his mug. "Even without Grenough's accusations, most people in Carlisle figure you are one of the few people this side of the Susquehanna with the eye and skill to make those shots."

Wend put on his most impassive face. "So are you here to formally accuse me and make an arrest, sheriff?"

"Oh, Lord no, Eckert. No one—not even Grenough—has made formal charges against you *yet*. In fact, there hasn't been any real investigation. I just wanted you to know what's being said." He smiled. "In fact, truth be told, most people in town think that if you did it, you are something of a hero. They're quite happy that a pair of outlaw traders has been eliminated. The trouble is that Grenough and a couple of his friends are pushing me to make an official investigation and check out your whereabouts when all this happened."

"Wait a minute, sheriff; there seems to a bit of a mystery here. If most people recognize that stopping a couple of rogue traders was a good idea, why is Grenough pushing for an investigation to find the killer or killers? And shouldn't he be real happy that some of his competition in the trading business has been eliminated? Haven't you wondered what makes him so interested in finding the shooter?"

The sheriff considered his words for a moment and smiled. Wend could see that Dunning understood the implications of the point he was making. "Well, matter of fact, Grenough has that angle covered. He says we just can't have people taking the law into their own hands, shooting traders because they happen to *think* they are supplying the Indians. There are plenty of honest traders, including men working for him, who are supplying goods to the settlements. He makes the point that there's a legal system in place to take care of outlaws." Dunning looked at Wend and raised an eyebrow. "He does have a point there, doesn't he?"

Wend stood up and stocked around the lean-to, anger welling up in him. "Well sheriff, let's think about this situation. Two outlaws—obviously trading with the enemy—were killed, and influential people are trying to have the person who did it—whoever that might be—arrested. Mind you sheriff, I'm not admitting I had anything to do with the incident. But now think about this: A pack of Paxton men ruthlessly killed twenty peaceful Conestogas a few months ago and nobody has made a move to arrest, let alone punish, any of those men. Where's the legal system and justice there, Mr. Dunning?"

The sheriff leaned back in his seat, a broad smile on his face. "Now that's a very good point, Eckert. A damn good point! But I have to say, it is very rhetorical, lad. The question would make a good debate between lawyers."

Dunning put his empty cup on the bench and stood up. "But from a practical point, I came here to talk to you in a friendly way. Let's face it: Grenough has a lot of influence with magistrates and government officials all the way back to the governor himself. The fact is, John Armstrong told me the governor owes Grenough a favor after he helped deal with the Paxton Boys' demands. If he keeps up the pressure, he could force a formal investigation of you. But to tell you the truth, like most of the people around here, I'm glad those two traders are dead, and I would hate to see anyone's life ruined by being charged with their demise."

Wend looked directly in Dunning's eyes. "Nor would I, sheriff."

Dunning smiled. "So we agree. Now I have a suggestion. It might be a good idea for you to be out of the colony before somebody forces me to start investigating. That would be easiest on all of us."

Wend stared at the sheriff, his mind moving rapidly. "All right, sheriff, thank you for the warning. I'll think about it."

Dunning nodded and put a hand on Wend's shoulder. "Think *real* hard about it, lad. I believe I got maybe ten days or a fortnight before Grenough can force something. Seems to me you ought to be gone before then."

* * *

Two hours after the sheriff's visit, Wend walked over to the house for supper. Everyone else was already there, gathered in the great room; Carnahan, Patricia, Joshua, and Donegal. They were discussing something in quiet tones. The children were already busy eating at a small table in the kitchen.

Wend walked into the room and suddenly everyone stopped talking and looked up at him.

Joshua broke the silence. "Hey, Wend, I just got back from down in the village. I spent some time talking with John Dunning and his men." He looked around at the others. "It seems you are the major topic of conversation down in Carlisle."

Wend silently cursed to himself; he should have realized that if Dunning had talked to him, his men would be repeating the story down at the tavern. He decided to play for time. "What were they saying about me?"

Joshua laughed and pointed at him. "Ha! Put that stone face of yours away, Wend. This ain't the time to play cagy with us. They said our mutual friends Mathews and Crowley were found lying out as varmint food in the mountains north of Lyttleton, surrounded by a copious amount of burned out powder, lead, trade guns, and knife blades. And the wager is you are the one who put them there." He lifted an eyebrow. "Is there somethin' you just might want to tell your friends?"

Carnahan took his hand off his chin to speak. "I wondered about how long it took you to deliver that rifle down to Washburn's; you were gone at least three times longer than usual."

Joshua nodded his head. "Yeah, I thought about that too, but I just figured he was spending some time and money with the girls in one of those bawdy houses down on the west end of town."

Patricia stamped her foot in outrage. "Joshua, I don't want any of that kind of talk here in this house!" She blushed and said, "Besides, Wend wouldn't do anything like that."

Wend smiled at Patricia. "Thank you for your confidence in me, Patricia."

Donegal said quietly. "He still has 'na answered the question. Did you take those two skunks down, lad?"

Wend looked around at the people whom he considered his family and realized he couldn't hide the truth from them. So, in as few words as possible, he told them the story. First he explained his belief that Grenough, Bratton, and the two outlaw traders were all working together and the impossibility of getting the government to take action against Grenough. He described his visits to Shippensburg and York, and his encounter with Irwin and Reilly. Then he explained how Charlie had returned with the information which confirmed his suspicions and with the plan to resupply the Indians. He described how the two of them had intercepted Bratton's wagon, followed him to the rendezvous with the traders, and then attacked them on the long switchback.

His audience had listened with rapt attention when he told them of how the mare had alerted Mathews, Crowley, and Bratton to the fact that they were not alone. Wend had been able to hit Mathews in the moment when his horse had quieted. But then the sound of the shot and the sight of the gray-haired trader falling to the ground had spooked all the horses of the pack train. The first string of ten horses had begun bucking, and then the leading four animals lost their footing and went over the side of the gorge, screaming in fright as they fell to their death. For a moment, Crowley had stared, frozen in shock, at the plight of his compatriot and the pandemonium which had overwhelmed the horses. Then he quickly recovered and jumped down from his mount. But his delay had enabled Wend to take a loaded rifle from

Charlie's hands and make a snap shot which dropped Crowley in the brief moments when he stood beside his horse.

The real problem had come when Bratton, alerted by the shots and disintegration of the pack train, had dropped his reins, ducked under the wagon, and then bolted for the woods by the road. Wend had fired a desperation shot at him as he disappeared into the bush, and thought he had hit him, but when they got there, he had vanished. They had not taken the time to pursue him, but instead concentrated on burning the wagon, with all its goods, and then the packsaddles from the horses which hadn't stampeded.

Then he told how Charlie had bade him farewell and he had journeyed to Carlisle and put the new rifle on display in Washburn's.

When he had finished, he looked around at the faces of his friends, who still watched him in silence. For the first time, he felt a touch of shame at what he had done. "So I guess some people will call it murder and say that I have cast a shadow on the house of a minister. Undoubtedly I was naïve in thinking that no one would connect me with the shooting. I'm sorry, Reverend."

Carnahan was silent for a long moment, the hand back up on his chin. Then he slowly shook his head. "Murder? Shame on this house? Some might say that, but I wouldn't be one of them. No sir! What I just heard was the story of a war party; an act of war against enemies of the border settlements and Sherman Valley itself. How many Indian raiding parties won't have the powder and lead to carry out attacks this spring? How many lives have been saved by the death of those two men?"

But Joshua leaned forward in his chair, a look of concentration and puzzlement on his face. "I have no doubt that Mathews and Crowley was dealin' with the Indians. And nothing surprises me about Bratton. But it's hard for me to credit what you said about Grenough, Wend. I've known the man for over fifteen years; I've spent days traveling with him and sharing campfires, and I've never known him to be false to his friends or the colony."

Wend was frustrated. "For God's sake, I found an underground store of powder on his estate. He had a supply of hatchet heads made in Shippensburg, many of which were in the wagon we destroyed. What more proof do you want?"

Joshua obstinately shook his head. "I got it in my mind that maybe Mathews and Crowley was pullin' the wool over Grenough's eyes and was workin' on their own. Maybe they was actually stealin' from his supplies for their own benefit."

"But Joshua, what about Irwin and Reilly? They work directly for Grenough and I heard them talking about him in a way which confirmed that he knew what was going on."

"Yeah, Wend, I know what you *think* you heard. But I'm thinkin' they may have been in a conspiracy with Mathews and Crowley to operate behind Grenough's back. I never trusted that shifty fellow Irwin since we met him out at Bedford. Maybe he's the bastard behind the whole thing." Joshua shook his head. "I'm going to have to see direct proof that Grenough is behind all this."

Carnahan spoke up. "Listen, this is not the time to argue about Grenough's role. That can be worked out later. What we do know is that Wend caught and attacked three men who were undeniably in the act of supplying the tribes and killed at least two of them. Now we have to figure out how he's going avoid any misguided consequences originated by the government." He looked sternly at Joshua. "I think we can all agree on that."

Joshua was silent for a long moment. Then he smiled slyly. "Yeah, that's all fine, Reverend. There's no disputin' we got to protect Wend, not for a minute. We'll set aside the accusations he's making against Richard." He turned and said to Wend: "But Donegal and I still got a serious beef with you! After all the time we spent together on the march, all the fights we been in, after us all being there at the Conestoga massacre, what made you think to leave us out of a fine war-hunt like you put on? The fact is, you screwed up: If all four of us had been there, we not only would have killed those traders, we would have gotten Bratton for sure! Damn, Wend! I thought we were friends!"

Then Donegal chimed in: "Yeah, and you did in Mathews without even giving me a shot at him. You knew I had big plans for him after what he did to me in Lancaster!"

Suddenly, the tension in the room evaporated and all five of them laughed at what Joshua and Donegal had said.

Then Wend related what the sheriff had said about the pressures being exerted for an investigation. "So, I guess I'll have to make preparations and plan to leave right after the wedding."

Carnahan asked, "Where will you go?"

Wend had been thinking about that since the sheriff's departure. "Virginia, I guess. I've heard about many new settlements being started in the central valley; lots of people are moving down that way." He looked at Baird and Donegal. 'Do you remember that big waggoner we met at Fort Bedford?"

Joshua nodded. "Yeah, the one we helped win back his money with your shootin'."

Wend said, "That's the one: His name is Daniel Morgan. Well, he lives near a town called Winchester, in the northern part of the valley. He told me that the area is growing and he'd help out if I ever wanted to move down there. I never thought I'd find the necessity of taking him up on his offer. So I think we'll head for that town, at least to start out and get our bearings. And with that many people moving into the area, there has to be a good market for firelocks."

Joshua nodded. He looked over at Donegal. "What do you say, Simon? Why don't we help Wend get packed up and then escort him and his bride down to Virginia? It'll be an interesting trip for us, and this ain't the time for him to be making a journey alone, what with the threat of war parties."

Donegal smiled. "Count me in. We'll all be on the road again, just like the days scouting for Bouquet. And I can check out what the land's like in that colony."

Wend felt gratitude at their offer. He had frankly been feeling somewhat fearful at the prospect of traveling all that distance by himself. "I would greatly appreciate your company!"

Paul had been silent, reflecting on something. "Hugh Mercer just moved down to Virginia—to a place called Fredericksburg. I knew him well; he was a captain on the Kittanning expedition, then he was in command at Fort Pitt when it was being built. You would have met him, Wend, if your family had made it to the fort in 1759. I'll write you a letter of introduction; then you'll know at least one person in that colony."

Patricia stomped her foot, attracting their attention. "You men really get to me." She turned to Wend. "Aren't you forgetting something? You're still thinking like a single man. All this talk of what *you* are going to do! But have you forgotten that you are to be married in a few days' time? Shouldn't you be discussing this with a certain young lady? Do you think she doesn't have the right to be in on your future and hers?" She crossed her arms in front of her chest. "You had better get down to the tavern and talk to Peggy about leaving Sherman Mill and going to Virginia!"

* * *

A day after Sheriff Dunning's visit, Wend was in his shop, finishing up some repair work and thinking about how to efficiently pack up his tools and equipment, when Hank Marsh appeared at the door. He was dressed in his work apron and, as usual during the day, covered in mill dust. But he had an exuberant smile across his face, which was a change from the dour look he had been wearing ever since the explosion.

"Hi, Wend! I've got some news."

Wend could see that the youth was fairly bursting with excitement. He asked, "And what could that be, Hank?"

"My Pa's going to let me take up farming!"

"Seriously? How did that happen, Hank?"

"Reverend Carnahan's been talking with him. For a long time, I guess." He screwed up his face for a moment, then continued. "Anyway, last night Pa came back from the tavern and took me into his office. We had a long talk, like we ain't had for years—maybe never, now that I think about it, Wend. But in the end he said if I was really sure about taking up farming, he would give me a piece of the Donaldson place, including the homestead land and all the buildings that are still standing. "

Wend nodded. "That's marvelous, Hank. When is this going to happen?"

"In a year, maybe, whenever Pa's got enough capital built up to start work on the sawmill. Then, when I move out to the farm, my first job will be to start supplying him with good timber. I'll be in charge of logging all that land that's still in forest and getting the wood to the sawmill."

Wend said, "Well, it sounds like you've gotten everything you wanted."

A cloud came over Hank's face. "Yeah, but there's a catch. Pa says I can't leave until we find someone—an older person than little Edward—to become an apprentice in my place. I can leave only when he's trained to replace me."

Wend smiled mentally, for he could clearly see Paul Carnahan's influence at work. "Is that a problem?"

"Yeah, it is. Think about it Wend: It will have to be someone old enough to be responsible, and someone who wanted to spend all the time in a mill." He made a puzzled face. "Can you think of anyone here in the valley who would want that job?"

Wend shrugged his shoulders. "I'm sure it wouldn't be that hard. What about one of the day laborers who live in the cabins down from the general store? Someone like that might jump at the chance."

"Are you kidding, Wend? We didn't even consider them because they're all ne'er-do-wells, and they're mostly too old. They're farm hands 'cause they don't have the initiative to start out on their own."

Wend played like he was taken aback. "I guess you're right, Hank." He put his hand to his chin liking he was considering the problem deeply. Finally he said, "Say, what about Frank McKenzie?"

"Frank McKenzie? He's one of Bratton's gang. Or he was 'till he got shot-up. And he's helping farm his own Pa's land."

Wend looked very thoughtful. "You know, he's been staying clear of Bratton ever since he got back from that doctor's place in Carlisle. And he was smart enough to work on his own as a freight waggoner for Bratton. He had to do calculations for charging customers and maintain that wagon while Bratton wasn't around, which has pretty much been all the time."

Hank nodded. "You do have a point there. But would he want to work in a mill?"

Wend said, "Well, I had a conversation with him. He knows that he won't get his Pa's farm and he told me that he's trying to figure out what he's going to do. Maybe you ought to talk to him. He might be your way out of the mill."

"Yeah, I might just do that. Thanks for mentioning that, Wend." Hank turned to go, clearly deep in thought about McKenzie. Then he abruptly stopped and turned around. "Say, Wend, I almost forgot the main reason I came up here. I wanted to tell you that Matt Bratton is back in the village."

"Oh, he is? Why did you think it was so important to tell me?"

"Come on Wend—don't put on that blank face of yours. Every one wants to see how he is going to react to you and Peggy getting married."

Wend shrugged. "Actually, he decided he didn't want to marry Peggy. So he shouldn't care that we're getting together."

Hank laughed outright. "If you really believe that Wend, you're the only one in the valley who does. After all the trouble he's given you over the years, he isn't going to take it lightly." Then he continued, "But there's even bigger news. Bratton came back riding with Ezra McCord in the small freight wagon last night. He was bedraggled looking and he hurt his leg, so he limps pretty bad."

Wend thought to himself: *So I did put a ball into him as he bolted for the bush.*

Then Hank said, "And there's more news. It seems that Bratton lost his Conestoga wagon! He lost it in a card game down at Shippensburg. That's what his mother told Susan McCartie when they were both down in the general store this morning."

Wend asked, "Did she say anything about how he injured his leg?"

"Yes. She said that he fell down the stairs at the same tavern where he lost at cards."

Wend had to work hard to keep from laughing. "He must have been pretty drunk."

Hank grinned, "Yeah, that's what my Pa said! But the word is the leg's so bad it will take weeks for it to get back to normal. And he's going to be working with his Pa at the blacksmith shop until he can handle a wagon again."

* * *

Two days after Bratton's return, Wend, Joshua, and Donegal walked down to the tavern in the late afternoon to have a drink. They entered the common room to find that only three patrons were present. Peggy and Ellen were busy making preparations for the evening trade. The aroma of cooking meat wafted from the kitchen and Wend could hear Donovan and Susan talking as they worked. Joshua and Donegal went to the bar, where they ordered whiskey and struck up a conversation with Ellen. Wend sat down in the corner table—the one so often used by Bratton and his band of cronies—and Peggy joined him. She sat down and gave him a quick kiss on his cheek.

She was totally focused on arrangements for the wedding. "I can't believe it's only a few days away, Wend. Mother and I have almost finished making my dress. And I've sent out invitations to the people we want to have at the wedding, which is practically every one in the valley." She looked sharply at Wend. "Everyone but Matt and his friends." After the wedding, we'll all come down here. Pa will have tables and a counter all set up outside, just like we do for the shooting contests, and there'll be dancing until the late hours under torchlight!"

Wend had never seen Peggy look more beautiful. She seemed to be literally glowing with excitement. All her shame over the baby seemed to have been washed away.

The night of the sheriff's visit, he had confessed to Peggy about his role in the attack on the traders. Then, cautioning her to confidentiality, he had explained Bratton's part in the Grenough conspiracy. He had worried how she would take the news, but she reacted in the same way as Carnahan and the others. She had hugged him and said, "Why Wend, you have probably saved many families from attack. You should have no regrets." Moreover, she had immediately understood the need for them to leave the colony. After a brief discussion, she had readily agreed that Virginia or other southern colonies offered the best opportunity because their settlements were expanding and would offer a market for Wend's services. Of course, it was no surprise to Wend that she welcomed the idea of leaving Sherman Mill.

Now as they sat at the table, he held her hand as they discussed their plans. "We'll leave the day after the wedding, in time enough to make Carlisle by nightfall." They would be traveling in two wagons—a covered farm wagon for their personal possessions, few as they were, and the trusty old tool wagon with Wend's trade supplies and equipment. He pointed to the two men at the bar. "Joshua will ride point for us on horseback and Donegal will drive the tool wagon. Can you have the wagon all packed by then?"

Peggy considered his words and was about to speak when the tavern door swung open. Bratton, accompanied by McCord and Finley, entered talking boisterously. It was obvious to Wend that they had already been drinking, probably having shared a jug down at the blacksmith shop. They reflexively turned toward the corner table but stopped abruptly when they saw Wend and Peggy.

Bratton smiled to his companions, and loudly commented, "Well, it looks like the Dutchman has taken our table. Maybe he figures it goes with the girl." Then, limping heavily, he led the group to the other side of the common room where they took a table by the fireplace and started to talk and laugh loudly.

Peggy looked at Ellen, who nodded slightly and then walked over to take the Bratton group's order. Donegal and Joshua stared at their drinks casually, but Wend could see they were alert to the tension which had gripped the room.

Peggy felt it also, for she began to rapidly squeeze Wend's hand. She leaned over to whisper, "Perhaps I should get father to tell Matt that he's not welcome here?"

Wend shook his head. "It's clear this is an act of bravado. He's lost a lot of prestige around the valley and he's trying to regain some of it by showing he's not afraid to come in here. Telling him to leave would just lead to trouble. In fact, he may be looking for an excuse. Let's sit here and mind our business. Maybe if we ignore them, they'll feel they've made their point and leave after a drink."

But soon it became clear that Wend's hope was futile. Bratton's gang became louder and increasingly obnoxious. Then they began making references to Wend and Peggy. Somebody loudly said something about an "Indian lover" and the group turned to look over at Wend. Another voice could be heard talking about "the whore", and the word echoed around the room. Wend looked at Peggy and saw that she was staring into the distance and had turned bright red.

Wend thought, *He's baiting me: He wants to publically humiliate us so that Peggy and I will be under a cloud. And they've made a despicable insult to Peggy, which he knows that I can't ignore.*

The other patrons were looking nervously at Bratton and then over at Wend to see his reaction.

Wend looked over at Bratton's table. The burley man had swung around in his chair so that he was scowling directly at their table. His challenge was unmistakable.

Cold anger grew within Wend. He stood up, forced a wide a smile onto his face, and called over to Bratton's table in the calmest voice he could manage. "I can see that you gentleman are having a great deal of fun. But you are disturbing the tavern. And you are using language which shouldn't be spoken in front of ladies. I think it's time to quiet down and enjoy your drinks and also apologize to the two girls in here for the coarseness of your words."

Bratton eyed his drink while he thought about a response. Then he looked at his companions slyly and spoke loudly without bothering to turn and face Wend. "I don't see how tellin' the truth is disturbing anyone. Let's see: We called you an Indian lover, and I don't see anything wrong with that. It's common knowledge that you were over in Lancaster providing comfort to those double dealing Conestogas last December. Every right-thinking man rode to put an end to them." Heads nodded and there were mutterings of, "You got that right, Matt." Another voice said, "Hell, he didn't even stay around here to help defend the valley last summer. He rode off with the redcoats on his own business."

Bratton nodded to his cronies. "And as far as the girl is concerned, the Dutchman here is content with what others have used and left behind."

There were laughs all around Bratton's table.

Wend heard Peggy suck in her breath. Wend was momentarily stunned by the grossness of Bratton's comment. In the silence which followed, the waggoner finally turned to face Wend. "I'll say it again, Dutchman. You're marrying a whore who's been the pickin's of every peddler with a few coins in his pocket to pay for her services. Now what have you got to say about that?"

A string of pictures flashed through Wend's mind: Matt Bratton bullying men who could not stand up to him; Bratton taking advantage of women throughout the Cumberland Valley; Bratton carrying war supplies to hostile war parties; Bratton as part of the hatchet wielding mob which had killed the Conestogas; Bratton raping Colly Allison. And now, this blatant attempt to destroy Peggy's reputation. For one of the few times in his life, Wend Eckert lost control of himself.

A fury spread over him. "You bastard, you've left nothing but a trail of cowardice behind you! You don't have the guts to own up to what you've done to a woman; you murdered helpless Christian Indians; we both know you have caused death and misery all along the border. It's time someone serves you with what you deserve!"

Matt Bratton rolled his head back and laughed loudly. "Oh, lord! The Dutchman, of all people, is going to teach me a lesson. Even with my bum leg you're no match for me! You haven't got a pistol or a clubbed rifle in your hand now. Let's get started; this is going to be fun and well overdue!" He rose from his chair and laughed again to his cronies.

The other patrons jumped up from their tables and took refuge at the bar.

Wend had no intention of fighting Bratton fairly. Almost without thought, he picked up a stool from one of the tables and flung it at the waggoner. Bratton, still laughing and looking at his compatriots, didn't see it coming until it was too late to dodge and the stool hit him square in the face. Wend, in his fury, had flung it with such force that any lesser man would have been knocked off his feet or at least off balance. As it was, Bratton was able to maintain his footing, but he was momentarily stunned, standing tall beside his table.

Wend knew only one tactic for taking down a man in a brawl—the one he had improvised against Corporal McKirdy of the 77th during the fight over Mary Fraser at Fort Ligonier. He lowered himself into a tight crouch, spread his arms wide, and launched himself against Bratton. With his feet pumping as hard as he could manage, he smacked his head into the waggoner's stomach, snapped his arms under the man's thighs, and pulled upward with every bit of strength he could muster. With a groan, Bratton went over onto his back, and his head banged against a pile of split logs in front of the fire place. For the second time in a few moments the big man was stunned, his eyes glazed and staring at the ceiling.

Wend jumped onto Bratton's chest and began to pummel the waggoner's face with his fists. Then he realized he had a much better weapon at hand. He reached forward and got his hands on one of the split logs. He started to club Bratton on the head with the piece of wood. Instead of abating, his fury grew with every swing. Soon the waggoner's face was a bloody pulp and he realized the man was either senseless or nearly so. Wend stood up, a foot on either side of Bratton's chest, got a good two-handed hold on one end of the log, and raised it above his head to drive the other end straight down into Bratton's face as if he were driving a spike into the ground. At that moment he fully intended to kill Matt Bratton.

Suddenly a pair of arms reached around his, preventing him from landing the blow. He looked to see Joshua's face next to him, a look of amusement on his countenance. "Hey Eckert, seeing as the sheriff already has you under suspicion of murder, you might just want to leave this piece of shit alive."

Wend felt his frenzy fading and realized Baird was right. He looked over to see Donegal standing over the table where Bratton's friends sat, his dagger held menacingly in his right hand. The highlander had a demonic grin on his face and said, "By now, lads, you should have figured out that the real hard cases in this tavern are the three of us what marched with Bouquet and fought real warriors—'na you cowardly scum who used your hatchets to murder Conestoga women and children. So why don't you be good little boys now? Pick up your friend and take him to his sainted mother so that she can tend his bruises."

Bratton's friends looked around at Donegal, Joshua and Wend, then down at Bratton's bloody and motionless form. Without a word they slowly rose from the table and walked over to the fireplace, where they picked up the waggoner's limp body and carried it out the door. After their departure, Wend dropped the log and the highlander replaced the dagger in his belt.

Donegal said, "Charming set of fellows, they are. But I don't think they'll be visiting this common room any time soon." He cast a glance at Wend. "Well, you've sure learned the lesson about how to finish a fight since that night in Ligonier. Corporal McKirdy will never know how lucky he was!"

Baird had walked over to the bar. He picked up his drink, took a gulp, then turned around and said, "You may not realize it Wend, but you made some permanent-like changes in Bratton's face. From what I could make out through the blood, its got a whole new shape. I'll wager he's not going to have much luck with the ladies from here on out."

Wend, still breathing heavily, turned to see that Peggy had come over to him. She looked him over, reached up and brushed his hair back in place. "You haven't got any marks on you, Wend. It happened so fast, Matt couldn't lay a hand on you. That's something I never thought I'd live to see."

268

Wend took her in his arms and looked into her eyes. "What's important is that you are all right. He said some brutal things about you. He meant his words to permanently scar you, Peggy. I couldn't let that stand."

Peggy wiped a tear from her eye, and tucked her head against his chest. "Wend, I'm fine. I do have some scars, but the fact is I gave them to myself, and I'm tough enough to live with them. Like most scars, they'll fade over time. But Wend, no woman has ever had a more gallant defender."

CHAPTER FOURTEEN
The Dark Princess

Wend Eckert was so nervous about getting married that he remembered few details of his own wedding ceremony. In fact, his participation was mechanical and trancelike. Afterward, he mentioned it to some of the men who had been there; they all laughed and agreed that was the best way to live through getting hitched. Tom Marsh slapped him on the back and said, "Weddings are all about women, lad. They hardly notice that the man is there, long as he's cleaned up and says 'I do' at the right time."

The little church was full to overflowing, for nearly everyone in the valley had come to see this marriage, so sudden and unexpected, of Peggy McCartie and The Dutchman. The ceremony itself was uneventful, save for the smiles of amusement and murmurs of surprise which ran around the room when Reverend Carnahan pronounced Wend's full name for the first time anyone in the valley had heard it, "Wendelmar Johann Eckert".

Wend heard Joshua's laugh from the rear of the church, then the scout repeated the word in a tone of disbelief, "Wendelmar?", and everyone giggled again.

Wend felt himself blushing, but Peggy pressed his arm, smiled up at him and whispered, "It's all right, I like it Wend."

That afternoon the open area in front of McCartie's Tavern was the scene of as joyous a party as anyone could remember. A group of men played their violins with great spirit—if not perfect harmony— and it seemed that every man in Sherman Valley wanted to dance with Peggy Eckert. The bride was in her element, happily entertaining each partner. Joshua and Donegal stood by the bar, regaling the men with tales of Bouquet's expedition and the fight at Bushy Run, and from what Wend heard of it, the stories were benefiting from some grand and imaginative embellishments. Those women who were not dancing stood and sat in groups, talking and laughing. Across the wagon track, a gang of the younger boys skipped stones in the mill pond, watched by a gaggle of giggling girls. As he looked around, Wend realized that this was the first opportunity that the people of the valley had had for a social gathering since the start of the uprising and everyone wanted to cling to the lightheartedness of the moment.

He was particularly warmed to see the number of times Hank Marsh and Ellen McCartie were dance partners and the gleam in the miller's son's eye as he looked at the girl. As he watched the two of them step to the music, Tom Marsh himself, drink in hand, came up to stand beside Wend.

"They do make a fine couple, don't they?" He smiled at Wend.

Wend answered, "They do indeed. The kind this valley needs."

The miller shook his head. "You know, Hank is rather adamant that he doesn't want to be a miller; for some reason I can't fathom, he wants to be a farmer."

Wend, suppressing the urge to laugh, nodded and said, "I guess it's not that unusual for sons to break away from their fathers' trade. They want to strike out in their own direction."

"I'm coming to accept that. Anyway, I've been talking with young Frank McKenzie about coming into the mill as an apprentice. He seems eager for the opportunity. If he can learn the job fast enough, I'll be able to let Hank have part of the Donaldson place pretty soon. I'm breaking it up into three smaller farms and he said he wanted the section around the old homestead." Marsh inclined his head toward the couple. "If things keep going on like this, I'll make it a wedding present."

Wend thought: *So, Ellen may just get to live with her husband and raise a family on the old Donaldson farm after all.*

Later, Wend saw Franklin and Ayika watching the celebration from seats at one of the tables. Ayika held her sleeping little boy, now almost a year old, in her arms. Seeing them alone in the midst of the crowd, Wend went over and sat down beside the couple. They visited for a few minutes with Ayika speaking in the halting English she had learned.

After a while, Ayika turned to Wend with a serious look in her eye and motioned toward Peggy as she danced. "Wend Eckert, you are a lucky man. She is put here for you by Manitou, the Master of the Earth. You sought a golden princess among the Mingo, thinking Orenda was for you," she said, using Abigail's tribal name. "But looking down on the land and his people, the Master knew the Mingo needed Orenda's magic more than you. So in his wisdom, he kept Orenda among the Mingo and gave you another princess to make you happy." She reached out and put her hand on his arm. "Since you could not have the golden princess, he sent you a dark princess, a woman of the earth. You love her and treat her well and I think she make you laugh in the night and give you strong children."

Wend could think of nothing to say; he nodded and smiled to Ayika, hoping her words would prove true.

There were a few people missing from the gathering. The McClay's were there, but Elizabeth had stayed home, obviously still nursing her anger and embarrassment. That made Wend sad, for he had hoped to make peace with her before leaving the valley. And not only were none of the Bratton family at the party, their house was dark and shuttered. The word was that the day after the tavern fight, they had hitched up a wagon and, with their injured son laying in the wagon bed, headed down the road to Carlisle.

As he mixed with the crowd, Wend looked around and saw that perhaps the only dour face in the assemblage was that of Donovan McCartie as he stood behind the counter. It had obviously come home to him that, with Peggy's marriage, he was not only losing a daughter but the tavern was losing its most customer-pleasing asset.

In the midst of all the happiness, Wend also had a sad spot in his heart. He had been working for days emptying the contents of his shop into the tool wagon and then loading baggage into the covered wagon. Most of that time, The Cat had been sitting on his haunches or laying down, observing Wend's progress. His tail had switched back and forth as he watched, a sure sign that he was disturbed about what he was seeing. Then, the morning of the marriage, The Cat had disappeared and though Wend searched the workshop and the stable, he never saw him again before they left Sherman Mill.

* * *

Their little caravan made it into Carlisle at dusk the next day. They parked the two wagons in Washburn's courtyard and got stalls for all the animals in his stable. After the horses were cared for, Baird and Donegal walked down to Alice Downey's where they would spend the night.

A surprised George Washburn greeted them inside the common room. Wend introduced Peggy and noticed the tavern keeper could hardly take his eyes off her as he explained they had just been married. While they talked, it came to Wend that he would have to get used to men being taken with his wife's beauty. Washburn arranged for Wend and Peggy to have his best guest room and led them up the stairs himself.

After Washburn left, Peggy walked around the room inspecting it with the eye of a professional tavern keeper. "The furniture is good; better than anything we have. And his wife has a good eye for blending the colors on the curtains and the quilt." She ran her hand over a night table, looked at the floor underneath and then went and slightly shifted the chest at foot of the bed. She clucked her tongue at what she saw. "They need to spend more time cleaning; my Ma would never let us get away with dust like that." Then she stood in the middle of the room and nodded her approval. "But it's a nice room; a good place for us to spend our first night."

What with all the packing up to get ready to travel, they actually had spent the night of their wedding separately back in their own houses. So tonight would be their first one together in the same bed and Wend found himself growing increasingly nervous about the prospect.

When the couple went down for their evening meal, they found the common room crowded to capacity with diners and men at the bar. Washburn put on a nice supper for them, set up in a cozy corner at the rear of the room. The server brought out some tender roasted beef, potatoes and vegetables. Then the tavern keeper, with a flourish, presented them with a bottle of his best red wine. Peggy ate with relish and sipped the wine, but Wend couldn't find much of an appetite. He was acutely aware that many of the men in the room were casting surreptitious glances at Peggy. Finally it was time to ascend the stairs and, as they left, Wend couldn't shake the idea that all eyes in the common room were on them.

A maid had come in and turned down their bed. To Wend, it was an awkward moment and the nervousness which had been rising in him all evening suddenly overwhelmed him. He felt his neck and forehead breaking out in sweat.

He looked at Peggy and saw that she seemed to suffer from none of his agitation. She had already kicked off her slippers and was unpinning the small cap from her hair. She looked at him coyly. "Wend, please come over here and help me get out of my clothes."

Wend was startled and moved to comply. He said, "I'm sorry; I didn't realize that you would need help."

She laughed, "I don't *need* help, Wend; I *want* you to help." Peggy took his hands in hers and guided him in unfastening her gown. Then she reached down and, with a quick movement, dropped her petticoats to the floor.

Finally, with the hint of a flourish, she discarded her undergarments. For the first time, Wend saw her naked and found himself made breathless by the elegance of her body; the upturned breasts, the narrow waste, the long slim legs.

Wend was overcome by a thought: *Good God, no wonder men have been eager to pay for the use of her body.* And then he immediately felt shame for allowing the idea to cross his mind.

Now Peggy gave him a soft kiss, and with a smile, carefully began undressing him. First, she loosened his shirt and pulled it off his shoulders. She took a moment to look at his chest and then caressed him with her hands. And after a few seconds, Wend felt the beginning of arousal in his loins. In a few seconds more, Peggy slid her hands down to his waist and unfastened his breeches. That done, she guided him to a seat on the bed and went to her knees to take off his shoes and pull the breeches off his legs.

Peggy whispered, "Crawl under the covers." He obeyed, and in a heartbeat she was alongside him. She wrapped her arms around him and put her lips to his for a long embrace and at the same time pulled her body tight against his. He could feel the hardness of her nipples against his chest. Finally, she wrapped her right leg over him and used it to pull them even more tightly together. In an instant, Wend's arousal was complete and he could feel his manhood pressing against her. Peggy reached down and gently put her hand on it, which instantly stiffened him even further. He literally ached to enter her.

But he knew that he must ask the question which had been puzzling him for days and he silently cursed his own ignorance. "Peggy, I want to make love to you so much. But I don't know about these kinds of things; are you sure it is all right for us to do this while you are pregnant?"

He could see her smile in the flickering candlelight. Then she giggled, almost to herself. "Oh, my sweet, wonderful Wend! So brave and competent and self-reliant about manly things and so naïve about a little thing like this! Of course it's all right my love, and if you don't take me right now, I shall be a very disappointed woman. And you don't want that to happen on our first night!"

Wend rose up and entered her and Peggy wrapped both of those long legs around him. He began a rhythmic movement and she accentuated it with the writhing of her body in synchronization with his motion. Soon she began to moan, first quietly and then louder, and a frenzy seemed to take over her body. Peggy gasped, "Yes, yes, Wend, yes! Wend tried to discipline himself to extend her pleasure, but almost immediately he exploded into her. As he did so, Peggy seized him even more tightly, her nails digging into his back, as if to push as much of him into her as possible.

Finally, he heard her sigh and felt her body relax. He could feel the perspiration mingling on their bodies as they held each other. He kissed Peggy again and she returned it with a hard pressure on his mouth.

They held each other, not saying anything for many long minutes. Peggy moved her hand through his hair and kissed him repeatedly. She smiled at him and whispered, "Now I feel well and truly married."

Wend told her how beautiful she looked, laying there in dim light. "I'm a lucky man to be married to you, Mrs. Eckert."

In a few more minutes, Wend began to feel weary. The lovemaking and the labors of the day's travel started to have an effect on him and he drifted off. But suddenly Peggy was shaking him awake. He looked up to see that she was standing by the bed and had put on a dressing gown and slippers. "Wend, get up and come with me, right now!"

Wend felt sudden alarm. "But why, Peggy? What's happening?"

Her voice was stern, almost like he remembered his mother's when she chastised him in his youth. "You're a married man now; it's time you learned to listen to your wife. Get up, put your breeches and shirt on, and come with me."

Bewildered, Wend did what his wife told him. By the time he was dressed, she was standing by the door with a candle lantern and a blanket in her hand. When he joined her, she handed him the blanket and led him out into the hall and toward the back of the tavern. She said, almost to herself, "There has to be a stairway here; every tavern has a back way out." In a second she had found the steps and started downward.

Wend could think of nothing to say, so he just followed her down the stairway, which as she had predicted, ended right at the back of the building. Once they were on the ground outside, she looked out into the courtyard, to be sure there was no one about, and then she started to lead him over toward the stable.

Suddenly she stopped and put her hand on Wend. "I saw something move. Over there under your tool wagon!"

Wend took the lantern and held it high; a pair of eyes looked out for a moment, then disappeared. "It's nothing but some little night animal; a rat or fox, Peggy; looking for food here around the tavern. It won't bother us."

Peggy nodded and continued walking. When they got to the stable, she motioned for Wend to open the door.

They entered the stable and the mare looked around with sleepy eyes, and then, seeing Wend, gave him a snort of welcome. Peggy took the lantern and held it high to illuminate the interior and soon found what she was looking for. She led Wend over to a pile of hay in the corner and spread the blanket out over it. She turned to him with an impish smile and whispered: "You didn't really think you were going to get away with making love to me just once on our first night together? She set the lantern on a wooden chest and said, "We're going to do it out here in the stable, just like a couple of kids sneaking away from their families!" Wend, now fully wakened by the coolness of the air in the courtyard, couldn't keep from laughing, and Peggy sank into the hay and pulled him down with her.

Their second love making was much more deliberate as they took time to fully explore each other's bodies. But Wend soon felt the passion build in him and Peggy also began to move with increasing desire. In a few minutes, with her help, he was again aroused and inside her. This time he found he was able to hold himself in control much longer, moving back and forth until her frantic movements and moans left no doubt that she was truly ready for him. She shuddered at great length as he accelerated his motion and released his seed into her. When he finally relaxed, she ran her hands through his hair and he could see that she had a look of happiness and satisfaction in her eyes.

Wend lay back in the hay and Peggy curled up in his arms, her head on his chest. They lay there for long moments. He looked around the stable in the light of the candle and felt very grateful that she had thought of this change of scene and the excitement it had generated. Then, while he was still deep in thought, she patted him on his arm. "Wend, are you awake?" He looked over at her and said lazily, "Yes, Peggy. What do you want?"

She hugged him, and started to speak in a very serious, almost hard tone of voice. "Wend, I brought you out here for a reason. I've been around men all my life and I've learned a lot about them. Men always marry the nicest girl they can find; a good girl they know will keep their home and raise their children. But after a while, they get bored with the good girl; all the excitement goes out of the marriage. So then they look around for a bad girl, to recapture some of the excitement they had in their youth. They visit bawdy houses or spend time with a willing girl in a tavern stable somewhere—just like this. Or, if they're rich, they take on a mistress."

Wend kissed her. "Come on, Peggy. I'll never be untrue."

She laughed. "I *know* you won't, because I won't let you! I'm telling you now that I intend to be both for you. During the days, I'll work hard to make your home as warm and welcoming as you could want and be a good mother for our children. But in our bed at night, I'll be as bad a girl as any man could desire. You're never going to want to go looking for another bad girl."

Peggy pushed herself up to her knees and straddled Wend as he lay in the pile of hay. He realized that he had never seen her look more enticing. The flickering candle light highlighted the fine features of her face. The long black hair, released from its day-time constraints, tumbled partially over one eye and then down over her shoulders. The nipples of her exquisite breasts were very close to his face. She looked down on him with a mischievous expression. "And now I'm going to show you what I mean."

She reached down and wrapped both her hands around Wend's cock.

He looked up at her, realizing now that she intended to make love again. He felt panic rising in him, fearing that he couldn't manage to satisfy her. "Peggy, tonight's been incredible! But you've exhausted me. I can't do it again; not right away!"

Peggy laughed, "Don't be silly. You only think you're done. Just lay back and relax. Let me do the work." She put his hands on her breasts and then for long minutes massaged the inside of his thighs and all around his genitals. Wend soon began to feel pleasure growing, and, to his amazement, he started to feel the signs of arousal. Then Peggy again took hold of his member with both hands and began to caress it with a regular rhythm. Wend felt himself beginning to harden. As Peggy sensed the stiffening, she tightened her hold on it and stroked more rapidly and violently. Presently, to Wend's great disbelief, she had created a full erection. Then, satisfied with his stiffness, she took him inside her and began a slow up and down movement. Wend saw a determined look on her face as she methodically moved her body to achieve the result she desired.

In the next minutes, Wend came to understand the true meaning of the word "ecstasy." Peggy steadily increased the rhythmic movement of her body until he began to shudder and moan uncontrollably with delight. Twice she brought him to the maximum level of frenzy, but just as he thought he must reach climax, she suddenly slowed her motion to prevent him from finishing. On the third time, she brought him to full completion. His whole body quivered, his arms flailed wildly, and he was unable to prevent himself from shouting out loud with the overwhelming, exquisitely painful pleasure as he expelled into her. Peggy grinned and bent down on top of him. She put her hands over his mouth to muffle the last of his shouts as she giggled wildly in satisfaction at what she had accomplished. "You're going to wake everyone over in the tavern!" When he had regained his composure, she took her hands off his mouth and crushed her lips against his. She rose slightly, and whispered, "Now, Mr. Eckert, I believe you are justified in feeling exhausted."

Peggy slid down beside him again, her face and body glistening with perspiration from her efforts. She started speaking again, this time in a soft voice, and he realized she was now thinking of something besides lovemaking. "Wend, it's wonderful that you've put us up in a nice tavern for tonight, our first night together. But I know we are going to have some hard times ahead of us getting started. We're going to be poor, and, when we get to Virginia, we will probably have to live in a lean-to or shack for a time until we can get a proper cabin built. I know that you'll need for me to work in the fields for a while and I'm willing to do that. But believe this: I love you, your gentleness, and your respect for me. And even if you don't really love me now, I know we will grow together, get through the thin times, and we'll make a go of this."

Wend could feel tears rolling down Peggy's cheeks. He was disarmed by her honesty and her profession of love for him, and her readiness to live in poverty until they could get on their feet. But he knew it was time to relieve her of some of the anxiety about their future.

"Peggy, I have to tell you something that I can't keep secret from my wife."

She looked up at him, concern and puzzlement in her eyes. "Whatever it is, Wend, I don't care. We'll work out any problems together."

"No, Peggy, it's not a problem. It's sort of the opposite. I've been waiting for the proper time to tell you this. The truth is, we're not actually poor. We have money. Nobody would call us rich, but if we manage things well, we have enough to buy some land, build a decent house from milled lumber, construct a workshop, and keep ourselves going until I can build up my business in Virginia." He looked down and could see that her eyes had opened wide in astonishment.

Peggy stared up at him in disbelief, her mouth wide open. Then she asked in a quavering voice, "We really have that much money?"

Wend nodded. "Enough to get started."

She seemed almost dazed. "My God, we'll be nearly like gentry."

Wend shook his head. "I doubt if the true gentry would think of us that way. Most of the money comes from the sale of my parent's house, land, and furniture before we left Lancaster. It was in a barrel with a false bottom and I saved it from the massacre site. And of course, I've been putting aside everything I could from my business since then."

Finally she said, "My God, I knew you had some money from your trade, but I never dreamed of anything like this. No one in the valley realized you had a store of money. It's going to take me some time to get used to this, Wend."

Wend looked at his wife, and felt a glow inside at having been able to make her happy. "Well, Mrs. Eckert, I think it's time we stopped playing kids out here in the stable. Let's go back to the tavern and enjoy the rest of the night in the comfort of our fine bed."

* * *

The next morning Wend descended to Washburn's common room. The sun was well up, providing good illumination for the big room through the windows. Several guests were at tables working on their breakfast and Wend could hear Washburn and his staff banging around in the kitchen. He leaned up against the counter and ordered tea from a serving girl.

Wend had several errands to perform before they left Carlisle and was late in getting started. After the exertions of the night, he had had more trouble than usual getting himself awake. And then as he had been dressing, Peggy had wakened and insisted on helping him with his hair. "You do such a good job hiding the bare spot; I need to learn how to arrange it." She had him sit down in a chair while she fussed with brush, comb, and hair bands for him. As she worked, they talked about plans for the day and it had became a very intimate moment for them.

As Wend reflected, Washburn walked out from the kitchen. "Ah, Eckert. I trust everything went well last night! Did you find everything satisfactory with your room?"

Wend nodded. "All very fine, George. My wife thought the room was lovely."

Washburn nodded and went about his work arranging things under the counter. Wend looked up at his display rifle which rested on its pegs on the wall behind the bar. He realized this was a good time to perform his first errand. Wend said, in a matter of fact tone, "Well, George, we'll be leaving later today. After I finish my tea, I'm going to go ahead and take down that rifle and put it in my wagon. It'll be a good example of my work when we get set up in Virginia."

Washburn abruptly straightened up, stared at the rifle and then at Wend. A look of dismay came over his face. He stood silently for a moment, then walked over to the other end of the counter, opened a drawer, and counted out a handful of coins. He brought them over to Wend. "Lad, I'm not allowing that rifle to leave this room. Here's twice the price you're asking for it, and then some!" He pressed the money into Wend's hand.

Wend looked at Washburn. 'I don't understand; why are you doing this?"

Washburn laughed and shook his head. "That's money well spent! Having an Eckert Rifle on my wall has brought me in more trade in the last ten days than I can measure. I'd be loath to accuse you of anything, lad, but everyone in town is convinced you are the one who put an end to those traders up in the mountains north of Lyttleton. Particularly with Richard Grenough himself spreading the word that you had the motive. And they all want to see a rifle like the one which was used to do the job!"

"The truth is, lad, you've become something of a legend here in the county. First, soldiers and waggoners who were at Bushy Run came back and told tales about your scouting and marksmanship. And then old Dan Carmichael came in, tellin' the story about how somebody shot those traders at over 200 yards distance and destroyed all their contraband before it could get to the tribes. And just a day before you arrived, a man came down from Sherman Mill with a story about you fighting and walloping Matthew Bratton, the man known as the biggest brawler in Cumberland County. Finally, you arrive in town with Peggy McCartie as your wife. Many people know she was Bratton's girl, so, on top of everything else, people figure you took her away from him."

Wend felt himself blushing. "Come on, George. Aren't you laying it on a little thick?"

"Did you see all the people we had in here last evening? When word got out you were staying at the tavern I had my best day in a year. They were all here to see The Dutchman and his wife."

Wend was at a loss for words. He looked up at the firelock on the wall and thought: *I wonder what George would say if he knew that was one of the rifles Charlie and I actually used for the job?"*

Wend looked down at the money Washburn had given him. "All right, George. I was counting on that firearm for my stock, but you can have it. You've helped me many times over the years."

Wend put the coins in a pocket and swallowed the last of his tea. He was just putting the cup down when he saw Washburn gulp and stare wide-eyed in the direction of the door.

Wend turned to see Richard Grenough, resplendent in tailored suite, calf length leather boots, and beaver hat walk up to the counter and stand not three feet away. He leaned his decorative walking stick with its brass head against the side of the counter.

Grenough looked around and saw Wend. He stopped for a moment, recognition springing into his eyes, and then turned to Washburn. "A cup of tea, if you please George." He looked back to Wend. "Well, if I live and die, it's Mr. Wend Eckert, the scout and gunsmith. I heard last night that I might encounter you here in Washburn's."

The innkeeper set a cup of tea before the trader. Grenough spooned a little sugar into the liquid and then looked at Wend again. "You know, Mr. Eckert, we first met right here in Henry Bouquet's office last July. I had never heard of you before that day. But ever since, you're name seems to pop up regularly in my life, or at least in conversation."

Wend felt a knot forming in his stomach, but he was determined not to be cowed. "How's that, Mr. Grenough?"

Grenough said, "Oh, yes. Indeed it does. There was a lot of talk about what you did at Henry's battle out at Bushy Run last summer. There are stories one hears of you making long-range shots at some Indians who were harassing the column just after the battle was over."

Wend noted the man's use of Bouquet's first name and realized it was Grenough's way of showing his familiarity with a man of power in the colony.

"And of course, Mr. Eckert, I watched you display impressive shooting skills out at Fort Bedford last December. That was at a much shorter range, but under some very difficult conditions."

Wend wondered what Grenough was working up to.

The merchant pointed up at the wall behind the counter. "At Bushy Run, were you using a rifle similar to that one?"

Wend nodded. "Yes. As you may know, I specialize in first rate rifles with bores about twenty percent smaller than most. It makes for a flatter flight of the ball, which is useful at long ranges."

Grenough smiled. "Indeed, I'm sure you know your business." Then he said, "Well, it happens that a pair of traders named Mathews and Crowley was recently found dead up in the mountains north of the Great Cove. Most people believe they were preparing to trade with the hostile tribes. And along the same line, I remember you telling Henry last July that you thought there was some well-financed conspiracy to provide war supplies to the Indians. Am I not correct?"

"Yes, now that I think of it, I did mention that to the colonel while you were present." Wend grinned at Grenough. "And I think that idea has been born out by events. Clearly, the tribes were so much better supplied with powder, lead, and other materials necessary for war than anyone thought they would be." He shook his head. "Undoubtedly that permitted them to sustain their campaign against border settlements and the forts along Forbes Road."

The older man picked up his tea and looked at Wend over the brim as he prepared to take another sip. When he responded, he pointedly ignored Wend's jibe about war supplies. "Returning to the main point of our discussion, Mr. Eckert, supposedly these fellows Mathews and Crowley were shot at something like 200 yards." He raised his eyebrows. "I assume one of your rifles would have been suitable for that kind of work?"

Washburn, hearing Grenough's question, turned pale, snapped a worried look at Wend, and then hurried off to the other end of the bar.

Wend forced himself to smile and to take a long moment to answer, as if he were seriously weighing Grenough's question. "Well, I'm not familiar with all the details of that situation, but certainly I believe one of my rifles would be a good choice. But in any case, the man using the weapon would have to be an accomplished marksman."

"Of course, Eckert, of course." Grenough said tersely, then smiled broadly at Wend. "It would have to be someone with skills precisely similar to yours." Then he squinted at Wend for a second and grinned slyly. "I hear you are leaving the colony, Mr. Eckert. Moving to Virginia, I believe. Is that true?"

"Well, let's just say that I'm leaving the colony. Moving south, but I'm not sure where I'll find the best situation." Wend felt a roguish impulse come over him. "But you know, Mr. Grenough, I'm of German stock. And we Germans are a very neat people. I'm sure you've spent enough time in Lancaster to see how tidy all our people keep their farms and homesteads. Almost to a fault, we seem obsessed with searching out and fixing loose ends."

Grenough nodded hesitantly, not sure where Wend was going. "We'll, yes, I would have to admit that the German farms around Lancaster are very well kept, indeed."

"Yes, as my father always said, one should never leave a job before tying up all the loose ends. Anything else would be sloppy work. And I live by that in my trade; it's essential to achieving the quality my customers deserve." Wend paused and made sure that his eyes and those of Grenough's were locked. "And I'm very unhappy that I'll be leaving a couple of loose ends behind me here in Pennsylvania." He smiled again. "But I've promised myself that someday I'll find a way to get back and finish the job."

The big, well dressed business man held his eyes on Wend, while he slowly, deliberately put his empty cup on the counter and then carefully adjusted his waistcoat. Finally he nodded at Wend and smiled very tightly. "Well, Mr. Eckert, I wish you luck in finishing what you believe needs to be done. However, in my experience, sometimes it is best to leave well enough alone. I've heard it said that an artist can ruin a painting by making one brush stroke too many." Grenough stared at Wend for a long moment. "In any case, when you are ready to tie up those loose ends, I assure you that I will be pleased to be at your service in any way I can."

Grenough's eyes drilled into Wend for what seemed an eternity before he turned and nodded to Washburn. Then he picked up his walking stick, turned on his heal and left the tavern.

Wend kept his eyes on the man as he strode off down the street. As he watched, Washburn came back and stood across the counter from Wend. "Lad, after the way you taunted that man, it's a damn good thing you'll be on your way today."

Wend turned to Washburn. "Grenough's the one who has to worry. Now he knows my intentions and that he has reason to be looking over his shoulder." He smiled to tavern keeper. "George, please have someone take a tray of tea and biscuits up to my wife."

* * *

Wend finished picking up the supplies and other items he had ordered by mid-morning. He had hitched up the covered wagon and used it to make his rounds, so when the errands were done he pulled it up in the street at the front of Washburn's Tavern, ready to load their baggage from the room. He waved at Baird and Donegal, who were in the courtyard, hitching up the other team to the tool wagon. Joshua had already saddled up his riding horse and had it tied to a hitching post. Wend's mare would be tied behind the tool wagon for today's journey, which would take them to Shippensburg.

Wend had just climbed down from the wagon when he heard a voice behind him.

"Hello, Mr. Eckert. Good to see you again!"

Wend turned to see that Doctor Highsmith stood alongside the wagon, a broad smile on his face. "Good morning, Doctor. I'm glad to see you, sir."

"Well, my lad, it is quite a coincidence encountering you. It turns out that I've been doctoring another of your friends from Sherman Valley. Another person you've referred to me for treatment."

Wend was perplexed. "Who might that be?"

"Why, his name's Matt Bratton. His parents brought him down in a wagon some days ago." The doctor laughed and winked. "Although, from my conversation with the Bratton's, I understand that your method of referral was not particularly cordial."

"Doctor, Bratton is no friend of mine. What condition is he in now?"

"At first he was in and out of consciousness. He often talked wildly, saying nonsensical things, even when he seemed to be awake. He has undoubtedly suffered at least temporary damage to his brain. I have no way of telling if any of it is permanent." The doctor paused, then continued, "Physically, he is on the mend. However, his face has been permanently distorted. His left cheek-bone has been shattered and will never match the right side, his nose cartilage is squashed, and he is missing all his front teeth. He's going to have to live with scars all over his face."

Wend shrugged his shoulders. "I did lose my self-control. But frankly, I can't say that I'm sorry."

Highsmith smirked. "I assure you that the feeling is more than reciprocated. In his dreams poor Mr. Bratton was shouting obscenities at you which would do credit to the berth-deck sailors on my old ship. And he seems to have developed an overwhelming desire to visit retribution on you."

Wend said, "I can imagine." Then he asked, "Is Bratton still under your care?"

"No, Eckert. As a matter of fact, his parents took him away yesterday. I wasn't happy about that. I would have liked to have had more time to observe him, particularly considering the mental aspect. And then, of course, there was the gunshot wound in his leg."

Wend was all ears. "You say that he had a gun wound?"

"Oh, yes indeed. I discovered that when examining him. It is in the upper thigh area of his left leg. It was older than his other injuries and had been treated in a very crude manner. Someone had amateurishly dug out the ball and made quite a mess of the job. The wound is ugly and it was too late for me to do anything to help; there will always be a nasty scar there."

Wend thought for a moment. "Well, it seems that Bratton will be busy nursing his wounds for a while and not in any condition to travel on his own."

Highsmith nodded. "Yes, he'll be under the care of his mother for quite some time." Then his face brightened. "But I understand that you have recently been married."

"Yes, as a matter of fact, you'll be surprised to learn that I just married Peggy McCartie, Ellen's sister.'"

"Surprised? No, not at all. My good wife confidently informed me that it was going to happen right after you and the lovely Miss McCartie brought Ellen to my office back in February."

Wend was shocked. "She *what*?"

"Yes. She said she immediately saw that you both were infatuated with each other and that it was only a matter of time."

Wend shook his head. "How can that be? I didn't figure out that I was in love with her for long after that."

Highsmith grinned. "It is one of the mysteries of life that women can sense these things instinctively, Eckert. They communicate in different ways than we men do."

"Well, there must be something to what you say. Ellen hinted months ago that Peggy and I would get together. But, the fact of the matter is, I must admit that I've never been able to recognize when a woman is interested in me."

"Lad, face it: The man is always the last to know." Highsmith turned and patted his hand on the side of the wagon bed. "The word around town is that you are leaving Pennsylvania," he smiled conspiratorially, "And that your departure is a matter of some urgency."

Wend smiled at the doctor. "Let's just say that circumstances make my departure from the colony at this time very convenient to a number of people."

"Indeed. At the very least, it's probably a fortunate thing that you'll be gone before Mr. Bratton regains his good health."

Wend laughed heartily. "That's for sure, Doctor Highsmith!"

Highsmith touched two fingers of his right hand to his tri-cornered hat in a form of salute. "Goodbye, Wend Eckert, and, as we say in the naval service, I wish you fair winds and favorable seas in your journey." He smiled broadly. "Indeed, lad, I am going to miss you!"

Highsmith turned and strolled off in the direction of his office. As Wend watched him go, he noted that the doctor moved with the rolling gate of a veteran sailor.

Wend turned back to business. He walked over and drew a bucket of water for his team from Washburn's trough and carried it out to the horses. He was holding it for Joe to drink when he idly looked up Market Street, which was bustling with conveyances and foot traffic. As he watched, a group of three women carrying shopping baskets came out of a store about half a block away and turned to walk away from him to the eastward. They were talking and laughing as they walked. He noticed one of them was very young, wiry in build, and had auburn hair. Wend couldn't shrug off the feeling that she looked familiar. Then he felt a tug at his heart as it hit him: Naturally, she reminded him of Mary! The way she carried herself, the bounce in her step as she walked along; it was like seeing her ghost. But then he shook off the feeling. Of course it *couldn't* be her. Watching the group walk away, he came to a realization: *All my life, every time I see some young, thin, red-headed girl at a distance, I'm going to think of Mary, just the way I will be reminded of Abigail upon seeing a tall blond girl. In a sense, I will always be living with ghosts.*

As he was recovering from the momentary shock of seeing the auburn-haired girl, Peggy came out from the tavern. She was dressed for the road in a broad-brimmed man's hat and some old clothes that he had seen her wearing many times around Sherman Mill. Yet after their lovemaking in the tavern stable, he knew he could never see her in the same light again. Suddenly he remembered Ayika's words two days ago about Peggy making him "laugh in the night" and realized how soon the Mingo woman's predication had come true. While he was thinking that over, Peggy glanced over at him and smiled, and a flood of affection overwhelmed him as he remembered her smiling down at him in the hay on the stable floor.

CHAPTER FIFTEEN
The Road South

They rolled the wagons into the grassy field between Fort Loudoun and Conococheague Creek in the late afternoon on the third day after leaving Carlisle. Wend was surprised to see that the fort was now garrisoned by highlanders of the 42nd. A half company was completing drill in front of the fort as they arrived and Wend recognized the young ensign who was drilling them and several of the marching soldiers.

They were busily setting up camp near the stream when a corporal walked over from the fort. Wend thought he looked familiar and then realized it was McTavish, the piper who had been with them in Lieutenant Campbell's flying column to relieve Fort Ligonier in the first days of the uprising. He brought a message from the fort's commander.

"Captain McDonald presents his compliments, and requests that you call on him, Mr. Eckert. He was up on the firing platform and saw your wagons come in."

Wend thought for a moment. "Is this the same Captain McDonald who was in the 77th?"

McTavish nodded. "The very same; he purchased a commission in the 42nd after the 77th was disbanded and now he's in command here. He says to come on over for a while and have a drink on him. He also says to bring those scoundrels Baird and Donegal along."

They finished setting up camp and then left Peggy alone to prepare the evening meal. She laughed at them. "Yes, you boys go have a drink and swap lies with your army friends. That'll keep you out of my way while I make our meal. But don't go losing track of time. You'd best be back by the time my stew is ready. I don't want to be sitting here all alone in the dark with a pot of food and no one to eat it."

As they entered the fort, Wend felt a tide of nostalgia sweep over him, spurred by the familiar sounds and smells of an army establishment. Soldiers who they had marched with on Bouquet's expedition waved at the three of them and called out their names. He could hear men jocularly laughing and shouting at each other in one of the barracks huts. A squad sat together in front of another hut, smoking pipes, cleaning their gear, and mending clothing. Three women in ragged gowns stood gossiping around a fire as they prepared rations for their men. At the end of one of the huts, a couple of boys were on their knees playing a game in the dirt while a little girl carrying a doll watched them.

Captain Charles MacDonald sat at his desk in the small headquarters building puzzling over some paperwork. A clerk announced the three former scouts and he immediately jumped up to greet them heartily. "Gentlemen, am I glad to see you! My company has spent the whole bloody winter and spring in this forlorn place and our only excitement is when army convoys and travelers like you come through." He rose, and walked over to a sideboard, and poured drinks for all of them.

He held up his glass. "Here's to the old 77th Highlanders, gentlemen."

Donegal said, "I'll drink to that anytime, sir." Wend and Joshua joined in that sentiment and all three took a hearty sip.

MacDonald turned to Wend. "Eckert, I'm especially glad to see you. In all the confusion after the end of the battle near Bushy Run and the urgency of escorting the civilians out of Fort Pitt, I never got the chance to fully show my gratitude to you for saving my life during the charge." He shook his head and glanced around at his listeners. "I can't forget how I looked up from my knees after dealing with one of those savages and there was another swinging his hatchet over my head: I *knew* it was the end. Then suddenly the Indian's head exploded in blood and he collapsed on top of me. Later, in camp at Bushy Run Station, McKirdy told me what an incredible pistol shot you had made."

Wend shrugged his shoulders. "Sir, you thanked me personally the very next morning."

"Yes, but now I have an appropriate memento for you." He reached in a drawer. "This is my personal gorget, marked with my name and the insignia of the 77th, which I wore around my neck on the day of the battle. Keep it in memory of that day and as a symbol of my pledge that I will always be indebted to you for my life."

Wend could feel himself blushing as he accepted the silver gorget on its ribbon. "I thank you greatly, sir."

The captain laughed. "And as far as any of us who served in the regiment are concerned, you'll always be a member of the 77th. As of now, you're a highlander by the brotherhood of battle!"

Donegal's face brightened. "With respect, sir, I'll cheerfully second that. Perhaps we could seal it with another glass of your fine whiskey, sir?"

MacDonald laughed. "Aha! Now there's the Corporal Donegal I've known for seven years! First in line when the liquor ration is being doled out. All right, lads, let me charge you're cups and we'll drink to Eckert's fine shooting."

As they were sipping the whiskey, McDonald's face lit up. "All this talk about the old regiment reminds me—I got a letter from Captain Robertson that he posted just before they sailed for Scotland. It provided some news on the last mission of the 77th." He reached into a desk drawer.

McDonald scanned the letter, then began to summarize its contents, which related how the regiment had escorted the Moravians from Philadelphia to the very edge of New York harbor. Wend and the others listened politely, for they already knew much of what it said from the Pennsylvania Gazette article which Wend had saved.

McDonald looked around at his three visitors. "But the most intriguing thing is what Robertson says at the end. It turns out that, once they got all the Moravians to Perth Amboy in New Jersey, the governor of New York sent word that he would not permit the Indians to enter his colony. He demanded that the entire lot be sent back to Philadelphia." He looked around at his guests. "You can only imagine the disappointment that those Indians felt and their fear of being returned to Pennsylvania. Now here is what's interesting: Robertson says that a great bond had developed between his men and the Moravians after all the travails they had encountered along the way and all the times the soldiers had had to defend them. The highlanders consoled and hugged the Indians when the decision was announced. Some of our hard-bitten veterans actually wept at the plight of the Moravians. Then a company of the 60th came to escort the Indians back south and the 77th marched off to take their transport home."

McDonald looked up from the letter. "Rather ironic, don't you think? After fighting the tribes for all these years, the lads performed their last official duty as the shield of a band of Indians." He shook his head. "And Robertson says that watching those poor souls being marched off back to Philadelphia was the most frustrating thing that has happened to him in all his years of service."

Donegal spoke up. "With all respect, sir, but ain't that the way it always is? The army is trapped in the middle of all the politics and you never know what you'll be doing next."

McDonald smiled and nodded slowly. "Indeed, Donegal that's the truth. All you can do is follow the orders of the day."

The captain looked down at his desk, in silent reflection. Then he looked up and said, "So, where are you three heading?"

Wend explained the purpose of their journey and McDonald asked, "Does that mean you won't be joining us for Bouquet's expedition to the Muskingum this summer? Damn! I was rather looking forward to you scouting for us again."

Wend shook his head. "I'll be busy, setting up my home and trade, Captain. And these two are going to stay and help for a while."

McDonald held up his hand. "Well, it's still a shame you won't be around for the finish of the campaign." Then an idea came to him. "By the way, who was that young lady riding with you in your wagon. I saw her in my long glass, and if I may say, she was a delight to behold."

Wend smiled at the captain's words. "Well, sir, that's my wife, Peggy. We were married a few days ago. I guess that's another good reason I won't be on this year's campaign!"

McDonald smiled broadly. "Congratulations Eckert! Well, there's a reason for another drink! He walked over to the sideboard and topped off all their glasses. Then a cloud came over his face, and he turned to Wend. "Though I must admit, Eckert, that I am a little puzzled. After last year's campaign, I always thought you and Mary Fraser would end up together."

Now the three others looked at each other in puzzlement. After a few seconds Wend said, "Well, sir, that would indeed have been the case. I was very much in love with her. But, of course, she died last year at Fort Pitt. I guess maybe you missed that because you were away so much escorting supply convoys and patrolling Forbes Road following the battle."

A look of embarrassment came over the captain's face. He shook his head. "My God, Eckert, I thought you knew! I don't know how to tell you this: Mary Fraser *didn't* die."

Joshua stared at Wend, a look of shock and dismay on his face.

Donegal said. "Good God, sir! The lass is alive?"

MacDonald glanced at Donegal and nodded, then turned back to Wend. "Yes, Mary was indeed near death, but Esther McCulloch fought the grim reaper tooth and nail! That woman—My God, you know how obstinate and insubordinate she can be—literally badgered Surgeon Munro into rather a bold action. She demanded that he cut into that wound of Mary's, to inspect it and see why it was mortifying. At first, he flat out refused; he said that kind of work was unprecedented and beyond his skill as a simple army surgeon. But Esther kept after him, saying it couldn't hurt anything since Mary was dying anyway. So a day after you left for the Ohio Country with Stirling, they plied her with whiskey and gave her a piece of leather to bite on. And then, with Mrs. McCulloch and one of the officers' wives holding her down, Munro cut the wound open, right at the center of the mortification. Esther said the pain must have been excruciating, but Mary was as brave as any man when the surgeon started cutting. Munro probed around in there and damned if a piece of dirty cloth wadding didn't come out."

Donegal exclaimed, "The devil you say!"

The captain nodded. "Quite right, Corporal. The surgeon said it must have been left in there after being used to soak up the blood when they operated at Bushy Run; they probably missed it in the darkness. It was contaminating the wound and keeping her from recovering all that time. So then he cleaned out the wound, cleansed it the best he could with alcohol, and sewed her up again. And in a few days she was up and around. She fully recovered and they sent her east with the 77th when they marched out. But then Chaplin Ferguson arranged for her to stay in the colonies as a nurse with the 42nd."

McDonald took a sip of his drink and looked around at all three of them. "Right now, she's up at Carlisle Encampment."

Wend had felt a hand clutching at his heart as McDonald told them Mary's story and now he suddenly felt the room closing in around him. *Mary is alive!* He thought: *God in Heaven, why have you done this to me? First you took my family from me, then Abigail, and now you have allowed events to put Mary Fraser beyond my reach. Are you playing with me, or is this some test of my faith?*

McDonald, embarrassed and seeking to change the subject, started talking about the upcoming campaign against the tribes in the Ohio Country. "Well, it's fortunate you three came by here now. A few weeks later and you would have missed us. We'll be leaving to march west, where Bouquet will be gathering his forces. A provincial company will be coming in to relieve us here."

Baird, noting Wend's discomfort, took the opportunity to finish the conversation. "Well, sir, it's been good seeing you again. And your fine liquor was surely welcome after the dust of the road. But we'll be having a long day tomorrow, crossing the mountain and all. We need to get back to our camp, and at any rate Mrs. Eckert will have supper waiting."

McDonald looked sharply at Joshua. "You're going over the mountains, instead of directly south from here? That seems rather out of your way."

Joshua shook his head in resignation. "Yes, but Wend here wants to clean up his family's graves before we leave Pennsylvania. So we'll take Forbes Road over the mountains to the gravesite at the base of Sideling Hill. Then we'll continue on to Bedford and take the road south from there to Cumberland."

After a few more pleasantries, they walked out through the fort's gate. Wend took a few steps, then went over and leaned for support against the stockade wall, feeling weak from the shock of McDonald's news.

The other two gathered around him. Donegal put his hand on Wend's shoulder. "Lord, son, what are you going to do? Little Mary is only forty miles from here."

Wend looked at his two friends. "That's not the worst of it, Simon. I saw Mary; I saw her on the day we left Carlisle! She and some other women came out of a shop and walked away from me on Market Street—toward the fort. I thought I was just seeing another girl who looked like her, but by God, now I'm sure it was her!"

Joshua just shook his head in disbelief at the turn of events.

Wend thought for a moment, a surge of regret rippling over him like a river. Suddenly he remembered his dream of several months ago and Mary's words: "Follow your heart and you will find me where I belong." His mind was in turmoil; then it dawned on him: The phrase meant that she would be with the army at a fort somewhere. *My God, had Mary somehow been able to communicate with him through the medium of a dream?*

He said, "I should have done more to find out what happened to her; I should have taken time to seek out people from the army and find out what occurred after we left with Stirling. But we were so sure she was dead, it didn't even cross my mind." His brain was galloping like a horse out of control. "My God, she must think that I didn't care enough about her to find out, or to come after her. She probably doesn't know that I thought she was dead."

Baird shook his head. "You're blaming yourself too much, lad. None of us thought she was alive. And she's smart enough to know that you would have come for her if you thought there was any chance she survived. Besides, she probably thought that you had rescued Abigail and was with her."

Donegal grabbed Wend's arm. "Come on, lad. Let's go back into the fort. McDonald will give us a quill, paper, and ink. You can at least write her a note so she'll know what happened. It will give her, and you, some peace of mind."

Wend thought a moment, and then shook his head. "No, Simon. That would just make things worse. What do I write: 'My Dear, I'll love you forever, but the fact that I'm married to another woman won't let us be together?' That would just open the wound further."

"So what are you going to do?" Joshua asked.

"Nothing: There's nothing to do but carry on with the life I've made for myself. It was my decision to marry Peggy and I'm going to make her the best husband I can. It would be dishonorable to do anything else. And God knows she's making every effort to be a good wife to me."

Donegal swore. "Life is sure playing more tricks on you than any man deserves."

They walked back to their camp to find Peggy standing in front of the cook fire, tending her stew. But she was not lacking for company. A gaggle of admiring young highlanders stood around her, laughing as she joked and kidded with them. Peggy was glowing with the pleasure of the soldiers' attention, for all the world like she was back in her father's tavern entertaining the men of Sherman Valley.

Wend recognized some of the soldiers and several shouted out greetings to them by name as they arrived at the fire. Donegal spoke to them in Gaelic. After a few moments, the highlanders said their goodbyes and trooped off back to the fort. Peggy pushed her hair back in place and said, "Those were nice boys. I think they were just happy to see a woman. But I didn't understand half of what they were saying in that highland language!"

Wend put his arm around her. "A difference of language has never kept men from keeping company with a beautiful woman." Then he looked at the stewpot. "Do you need any help getting our meal ready?"

"Are you joking? Those soldiers were more than ready to help me. They brought me wood and water. Anything I needed!" She looked at him. "Did you boys have a good time with the captain?"

There was a moment of silence as Wend thought how to answer. Both Joshua and Donegal stared at him, waiting to see what he would say. Finally he said, "Sure—we talked about the campaign last year and people we all knew."

Peggy put her hand on Wend's arm. "Well, I wasn't sure. You three all looked so serious walking across the field toward us. I almost thought you had gotten bad news." Then she turned and bent over the cooking pot. "If you're ready, let's get on with the meal. I have a feeling you all are going to want to get to bed early tonight."

Wend looked down at her, saw how happy she was, and knew that he would never do anything to take the joy from her eyes.

* * *

After leaving Fort Loudoun, they made slow progress going up the Path Valley and crossing the mountains. It was mid-morning of the second day when the little caravan reached the ambush site where Mathews and Crawley had died. They stopped the wagons and all four of the travelers gathered to look down at the black, burned-out swath of destruction on the side of the hill below the switchback. Wend noted that everything useful had been salvaged by the local settlers and mused that Grenough's hatchet heads and knife blades were undoubtedly already in use on farms around Burnt Cabins, Lyttleton, and down in the Great Cove. The only distinguishable remains were scorched fragments of Bratton's wagon and the bones of some of the horses, which had by this time been picked clean by birds and varmints.

Wend pointed out the spot where he and Charlie had lain to make his shots and explained some details of how the two of them had fired the wagon and sent it on its way down the hill. But they didn't tarry long, for their goal was to make Fort Lyttleton by the end of the day and it was clear that everyone felt a sense of foreboding at the spot.

It was a just about an hour later that Joshua, riding point, abruptly turned and rode back to the wagons and waved them to a stop. He pulled up his horse and motioned for Donegal to come up from his seat on the tool wagon.

When they were all gathered, he announced, "I got to tell you: Somebody's behind us on the road; just out of sight."

Wend asked, "How do you know? It's thickly wooded here—how could you tell from up front?"

"I was up on that rise just ahead; I pulled up and looked back and saw flocks of birds rising from the trees which had branches above the road as someone moved along."

Peggy said, "It could be another wagon traveling the road."

Donegal thought for a moment. "Or it could be a war party trailing us, waiting for the right time for an ambush; but I think it's a little early in the season for that."

294

Joshua nodded. "Yeah, it could be a lot of things—I just wanted to let you all know. Keep an eye out, look back when we come to turns; you might catch sight of something."

Donegal shrugged his shoulders and looked at Wend. "I've had that Scotsman's fey feeling ever since we left that ambush spot up in the gap."

Wend shook his head and was about to say what was on everybody's mind; that it could be someone from Grenough's ring stalking them. It was lucky that he moved his head, because suddenly there was the buzz of a rifle ball and Wend's hat flew off and landed on Peggy. An instant later they heard the sharp report of the gun itself.

Peggy screamed.

Wend grabbed Peggy and pulled her off the wagon and into the brush on the opposite side of the wagon from the direction of the shot. Just then another shot rang out and the ball hit the wagon seat they had just vacated.

Baird and Donegal instantaneously joined them.

Donegal said, "I think somebody is trying for a little revenge, lad."

Baird said laconically, "It's good they ain't as fine a shot as you, Eckert."

Wend gritted his teeth. "It has to be Grenough, or more likely, some of his men."

Joshua said, "Yeah, those shots were so close together that there has to be at least two of them. The firing came from that long hill across the road." He paused to think a moment, then said, "You take care of your bride Wend; Donegal and I will hunt down whoever is up there.

Wend shook his head. "No, that's not the answer Joshua. Think about it: You'll be at a disadvantage with that bum leg. And besides, we don't know how many men are out there. We can't leave the wagons and Peggy guarded by only one person. It makes more sense for me to go after whoever's on the hill—and besides, I'm the one they're after. You two take the wagons and find a sheltered cove off the road where you can protect Peggy. Wait there for me to rejoin you."

Peggy exclaimed, "That's crazy, Wend! You'll get killed. Why don't we hide on this side of the horses and lead them by their bridles until the wagons are over the next hill and then drive off as fast as we can."

Wend hugged Peggy. "That won't work. They'd just jump on their horses and set up another ambush. We must take care of them here. Peggy, believe in me. I will be back."

Without giving anyone a chance to say anything further, Wend grabbed his rifle and pistols from the wagon. Then he ran around the back of the wagon and dashed across the road. Another shot rang out and the ball kicked up dirt just behind him. Then he was across and into the bush. From his cover, he stopped to assess the situation. Wend realized that his chances would be nil if he simply headed for the top of the hill to find the shooters. He decided that a better option would be to first find the horses, which had to be somewhere near the road. Then he could stock the attackers or possibly set up an ambush for them when they returned to their mounts. So he moved silently through the forest, paralleling the road.

He soon found the horses. Wend actually smelled them first, for they had deposited some dung. Then he heard them as they moved around and one snorted. He crept forward until he had the animals in sight. There were two of them, tied to trees. Now he knew the strength of the enemy. He also knew that both men were still up on the ridge.

Wend stopped to think for a few minutes. The attackers had seen him leave the wagons. They were laying in wait for him to come to them, probably figuring that he would try to work his way directly to the crest using the best cover he could find. So he reckoned that he was now in a good position to approach them from a direction they wouldn't expect.

Moving stealthily, he made his way upward. In a few moments he got lucky, for he found signs of the men moving through the woods; crushed grass, tracks on mossy ground, and disturbed underbrush. So he knew he was on the right track.

A few minutes later, he saw some movement ahead of him. Creeping even more cautiously, he soon caught sight of Shane Reilly—kneeling, rifle in hand, in ambush behind a log. The redhead was just short of the crest of the hill and had a good view of the road below. Wend looked down the hill and was relieved to see that Joshua and Donegal had done what he had asked; the wagons were gone from their earlier position on the road. He could see that Reilly was visually searching the hill below him, obviously looking for Wend's approach.

Reilly was only thirty yards away from Wend, so it would be an easy shot. He leveled his rifle at the man, sighting in at the base of his skull. He squeezed the trigger, but at that very moment Reilly rose to a crouch to shift his position; Wend's shot echoed through the forest and the ball hit Reilly's hip. The trader fell on his side, clutched his hip, and simultaneously let out a loud yelp of pain.

Wend feverishly went to work reloading his rifle while keeping an eye on Reilly as the man writhed in pain. He was clearly in no position to attempt to fire back at Wend.

He was almost finished when he heard a soft noise behind him. Wend looked up just as a he was struck a blow on the back of his head and the world went black.

* * *

Wend awakened to find water dripping over his face. He looked up to see Price Irwin standing over him holding a water bottle, a broad smile on his face. Wend realized he was sitting against a tree with his hands tied behind him. He looked around and saw that Reilly was sitting with his back braced up against the same log where he had originally sighted him.

Irwin was in a positively jovial mood. "Well, Eckert, my lad, how are you feeling now? Got a bit of a headache, have you? But then, being hit with a pistol barrel will do that to you. At least you had a good long sleep while I tended to Shane's wound."

Wend felt anger at himself. "So you two set a trap for me. And I walked right into it."

Irwin laughed. "Yes, and I thought you were supposed to be the great woodsman, Eckert. But our little ambush worked out marvelously well."

Reilly swore. "Shit, Price, it would have worked a damn sight better if you had hit him before he shot me in the side."

Irwin said to his compatriot, "Sorry, Shane, but things never work out exactly as you plan them." He winked at Wend. "I think our friend here would agree with that!"

Wend refused to play along with Irwin's little game of fake joviality. "Why didn't you finish me when I was out, Irwin? What are you going to do with me?"

"Oh, indeed it's death for you, son. And right in this very spot. And very appropriate, don't you think, being only a couple of miles from where you did in our mates?" Irwin exchanged a grin with Reilly. "But, more to the point, Mr. Grenough insisted that, if I had the chance, I give you a personal message from him before we sent you to your rewards."

"And what would that message be?"

"Mr. Grenough said to tell you that, 'You took one brush stroke too many' and that 'He had no intention of being a loose end for anybody.' He said for me to tell it to you *exactly* that way and that you would understand." Irwin pulled a great horse pistol from his belt. "Did that all make sense to you, my fine lad?"

Wend stared at the pistol and thought: *So this is how it all ends.* Then he mentally apologized to his father: *I'm sorry that I failed to finish what I pledged to do; to take vengeance on all the men who destroyed our family.*

Wend Eckert looked up into the eyes of Price Irwin and said what he knew would be his last words. "I've got Grenough's message. You can tell him that I'll deal with him in Hell. Now do what you have to do and be damned to you."

Irwin grinned from ear to ear and pointed the pistol directly at Wend's eyes. He was amazed at how large the bore looked just six inches from his face.

As Irwin cocked the pistol he said, "I can't tell you how much I'm going to enjoy this, Eckert."

Then Wend heard a barely audible swishing sound. Suddenly a thrown knife, moving so fast that he could barely see it, drove into the left side of Irwin's neck and the point instantly emerged on the other side. The tip ended up projecting about an inch from the side of the man's neck. Irwin's eyes widened in surprise and his mouth opened into a perfect oval. A great spurt of blood began pumping out of his neck where the knife had entered, much of it splattering over Wend. Clearly an artery had been slit wide open. Price Irwin dropped the pistol in Wend's lap and fell over on his side. He was dead in moments, the blood staining the ground under him.

Shane Reilly grabbed his own pistol from his belt, cocked it and aimed in the direction the knife had come from. But before he could pull the trigger, a shot sounded and blood erupted from his shoulder. He dropped his pistol and looked down in shock at the wound.

Donegal emerged from the woods, followed by Joshua, whose rifle was still smoking.

Donegal reached down, grabbed the top of Irwin's head with his right hand and pulled his knife from the man's neck with his left. "Now, lad, don't you ever be doubting my skill at throwing the knife again."

The highlander reached down and cut Wend's hands free.

Joshua walked over to where Reilly sat and kicked the pistol away from him. Then he grinned wolfishly at Wend. "Ha! Ever since Bushy Run you and other smart-ass people been tellin' me I was over the hill and that my leg was gonna put me in a rockin' chair on the front porch. Ha! Even my own sister was saying I couldn't scout or hunt no more. Well, I tell you it weren't no crippled old man who found the trail and climbed up here in time to keep that asshole Irwin from puttin' a ball between your eyes. Ha! Crippled indeed!"

Wend, rubbing his hands to get circulation back, smiled in amusement. "Joshua, I never said you were over the hill, I just said you had to take care with that leg. But there's something more important right now. How long were you out there listening in the bush? Did you hear what Irwin said about Grenough?"

Joshua said, "Yeah, we heard. So I guess I got to admit that what you said about Richard was right. I wouldn't have believed it if I hadn't heard it from his man's own lips. But, yessir, there ain't no doubt about it now." He looked over at Wend. "But don't distract me: There's something even more important; something I hope you learned up here."

Wend stood up. "What's that, Joshua?"

"You gotta stop thinkin' you can do everything yourself! You've been goin' around cuttin' your friends out of what you got on your mind. You did it when we was followin' that Conestoga Indian up on the Susquehanna, you done it on your trip down to Shippensburg and York, and you did it when you went on that little war party to kill them traders, at that spot not more than a few miles back there on the road." He motioned with his thumb back toward the pass. "You don't let your friends in on things till there ain't no other choice. You keep that up, it's goin' to get you killed one day, just like it almost did right here. Yeah, I hope you learned your lesson."

Donegal nodded at Wend with a tight smile and said, "Joshua's got it right, lad. You better take what he said to heart."

Suddenly Wend thought of something. "My God, where's Peggy? You two left her all alone!"

Donegal laughed. "And it's damn lucky you are that we did. Coming up here and getting you out of trouble was a two man job." He winked at Joshua. "Don't worry, lad. We just took the wagons over the next hill and put them into a little closed-off clearing. Peggy's sitting in cover behind some bushes with two loaded pistols and a knife. And knowing that woman, any man who comes into that clearing has got more trouble than he can handle facin' him."

Joshua said, "Besides, it was Peggy herself who demanded we come up here after you. She allowed as how she weren't about to be no widow woman just a week after gettin' married."

Wend nodded. Then he walked over to where Shane Reilly sat, blood oozing from both of his wounds. The red-headed trader looked up at Wend, breathing heavily. His face was creased in pain. But he summoned up a last act of defiance. "All right Eckert, I know when my time has come. Finish me off with that pistol, if you got the guts to do it face-to-face instead of with a rifle at two hundred yards."

"Yes, Reilly, I've got the guts to do it face-to-face. But I've got a question to ask you first. Do you remember a tavern maid at The Proud Rooster named Colly Allison?"

"Oh, yeah. I remember her. Little auburn-haired pug nosed bitch. She'd spread her legs if she liked your looks or you made her the right offer. Sure, I remember her. Why?"

Wend's face tightened into his steely, unreadable look. "You remember the day you and Matt Bratton took her back into the pine grove behind the tavern and had your way with her, one after the other? Do you, Shane?"

"Yeah, and I'll bet she does too." He forced a crooked smile. "She's gonna' remember that day for the rest of her life."

Wend said, "I'm glad you remember, because this is for her."

He snatched the knife out of the sheath under his left shoulder and without any hesitation reached down and drove the eight inch blade upward right to the hilt into Reilly's genitals and groin.

Reilly let out a shrill, high-pitched screech and flopped over onto his belly, writhing in agony. His arms and legs flailed as if he was trying to crawl away from the pain, but he had too little strength left to actually move himself. At the same time he continuously shrieked in agony.

All three of the other men stood staring calmly at Reilly's death throes. Blood pooled up between his legs.

Wend picked up some dry leaves, wiped off the blade of his knife, and slid it back into the sheath.

Joshua began reloading his rifle. As he worked, he continued to watch Reilly and said, in a conversational tone, "Wend, you are indeed takin' a cruel turn in your advancing age."

Donegal cocked his head and added, "You're right, Joshua; I've been watching the lad become nastier and nastier over the last year." Then he motioned toward Reilly and observed, "You know, I would say that we are seeing the perfect example of the old saying, 'Squealing like a stabbed pig'."

Presently Reilly groaned one last time and expired. Wend went over, kicked the body to make sure he was finished, and said, "I promised myself I'd take revenge on Bratton and him for the way they treated that girl. She helped me at a time when I needed it most."

Joshua nodded. "Well, you done that for sure. But now, we got a problem. We got to decide what we're goin' to do with these carcasses."

Donegal shrugged. "Leave them lying here for the varmints. They don't deserve anything more."

Joshua shook his head. "Naw, we got to put them underground. Otherwise, some passerby will sight the vultures circling and come up to see what's attracting them. If word gets around, somebody may connect it with us. We'll have to get shovels from the tool wagon and dig graves, though I hate to waste the effort on these two snakes."

Wend smiled broadly and shook his head. Joshua's words had triggered a full-blown idea in his mind. "No, we aren't going to do any burying here. I'm going to take care of them myself. All I need for you to do is help me get them down the hill and lash them onto their horses."

Donegal looked askance at Wend. "What have you got going on in that crafty mind of yours?"

Wend looked at his two friends. "Joshua's right: These men *are* snakes. I'm going to take them up to the crest of Sideling Hill and put them in a place where they'll spend eternity with slimy serpents of their own kind and nobody will ever discover their bones."

Smiles of understanding spread across the faces of the other two men.

Wend said, "You two take Peggy and the wagons to Fort Lyttleton. I'll meet you there late tonight."

* * *

It was late morning by the time they reached the grave site of Wend's family at the base of Sideling Hill. They had spent the previous night at Lyttleton and then departed in the gloom of false dawn.

Wend had brought along a scythe and a pair of long-handled axes; that made the task of clearing brush off of the graves much easier than when he, Joshua, and Donegal had done it with knives and hatchets during Bouquet's expedition. Donegal and Wend did most of the work while Joshua tended the animals since his leg kept him from doing much bending. Even Peggy helped, getting down on her knees and pulling weeds from the top of the graves themselves.

Wend took down the remains of the stick crosses which had been erected by Robertson's men back in 1759. Then, with a shovel from the tool wagon, he dug one big hole at the head of his father's grave and dug a smaller hole over Magistrate Gibson's resting place. It was hard work, what with all the roots and stones, but eventually he got both of them to the depth he wanted. Then he pulled a canvas bag out of the covered wagon and walked to the hole at his father's grave. He took out the five scalps of his family, including his own, and carefully placed them in the hole. Then he walked over to the other hole and did the same with Magistrate Gibson's hair. Finally, he and Donegal went over to the rear of the covered wagon and lowered the tailgate. Working together, they unloaded the grave marker which he had ordered from a stonecutter in Carlisle. All the names of his family were inscribed on its face. Picking up the stone, and the one he had also ordered for Gibson, had been the major errand he had accomplished on the last morning in Carlisle.

They placed the gravestones into the two holes and then wedged them securely with rocks before filling in the dirt. When they had finished, Wend stood back to take in the scene. He was satisfied that he had done as much as possible to create a fitting memorial. The weeds and grass might grow up, but the stones would last indefinitely. The forest's relentless growth would not be able to destroy the memory of his family.

They gathered around, and, with Peggy on his arm, Wend read several of his mother's favorite passages from the bible. Thoughts of his family weighed heavy on his mind as he read, but he was surprised to find that no tears came. He thought to himself: *Maybe enough time has passed, and enough has happened, so that I can get on with my life and building a family of my own.*

When he finished, there was a prolonged silence among the four of them. Peggy read the names engraved on the stone marker out loud and thought for a moment. Then she squeezed his arm, and whispered, "Wend, if it's a boy, let's name him Bernd Johann, after your brother and Pa. And if it's a girl, let's call her Elise Mary, after your sister and Mother."

Wend looked at his wife warmly, grateful for her thoughtfulness. "I would very much like that, Mrs. Eckert."

Wend looked up at the sun. It was time to move on. "Joshua, why don't you ride with Peggy in the front wagon for a time? I'll ride point. Your horse needs a rest and the mare could use some exercise." As the others got ready to move out, Wend pulled his saddle out of the tool wagon and placed it on the mare's back. She nuzzled him with pleasure at the prospect of running free of the wagon.

Soon they were ready to go. Wend shouted to Joshua: "We've done everything we can here; let's roll the wagons."

Baird didn't answer. Instead, he simply cracked the whip over the team and started the covered wagon up the long, winding slope toward the crest of Sideling Hill. Donegal followed with the tool wagon.

Wend waited behind for one final moment alone with his family and stood by holding the mare's reins as the wagons departed. Then, out of the corner of his eye, he thought he saw something move at the rear of the tool wagon, disturbing the tarp which covered the bed. Doubting his eyes, he looked more closely. As he watched, a gray head and two paws appeared above the tailgate. To Wend's surprise, The Cat looked out, his front paws resting on the top of the tailgate, and surveyed the countryside with all the aplomb of a lord glancing out from his gilded carriage.

Wend felt a surge of exhilaration at seeing that his old friend was with them. He realized that it must have been none other than The Cat that he and Peggy had seen looking out from underneath the wagons that night in the courtyard at Washburn's.

Wend glanced up at the blue sky visible through the gap in the forest canopy and felt the warm afternoon sun bathing his face. He swung up into the saddle and the mare pranced with anticipation and impatience. The horse's eagerness was infectious and transmitted a sense of excitement to him. It occurred to Wend that at this moment he was more content and joyous than at any time since disaster had struck five years ago at this very spot. The shadow of loss and grief which had been hanging over him and dominating his actions had passed and at last his life was on a course of his own choosing. He dug his heels into the mare's side and she came easily to the gallop, climbing the incline in swift, powerful strides and rapidly overtaking the two laboring wagons. He doffed his hat with a flourish to Peggy as they swept past the covered wagon and she waved back and laughed with delight at the sight of the racing mare and rider.

Wend Eckert, the Dutchman of Sherman Valley, slapped his hat back on his head, waved his arm up the hill toward the crest, and shouted back to his wife and Joshua: "Let's go to Virginia!"

THE END OF CONESTOGA WINTER

AUTHOR'S NOTES

AND ACKNOWLEDGEMENTS

The initial novel in the Wend Eckert series, *Forbes Road*, was written to tell the story of Colonel Henry Bouquet's expedition to lift the Ohio Country tribes' siege of Fort Pitt following the outbreak of Pontiac's War. In conducting research for that story, it became clear to me that the civil turbulence in the border areas of Pennsylvania which resulted from the war was a fascinating story in its own right. To steal a phrase from the late Paul Harvey, the massacre of the Conestoga Indians and the subsequent Paxton Boys Insurrection constitute "The Rest of the Story." But more than that, they mark the first signs in Pennsylvania of the dissatisfaction with government which grew into the fury which sparked the American Revolution.

The paragraphs below discuss the treatment, in *Conestoga Winter,* of various aspects of history which are directly described or referred to in the narrative. Also, as is my practice, I've endeavored to alert the reader to instances where departures from strict historical accuracy have been made to advance the fictional storyline.

Daniel Morgan at Bedford. During the general period of this novel, Morgan was indeed operating as proprietor of a freighting company. In fact, in later years he loved to call himself, "The Old Waggoner." I've not been able to discover any research on specific trips he made or the limits of the geographic area which he served. Given the needs of the British military campaign for logistical support, and the fact that contract waggoners were used, it is not beyond the realm of possibility that Morgan and his merry men could have been at Bedford when Wend and his friends passed through on their way home from Fort Pitt. On the other hand, it is a matter of record that Morgan loved to show off the scars on his back from the lashing he received during the Braddock campaign.

Longrifle Marksmanship. The shooting contest at Bedford wherein Wend shoots a scrap of wood from between Joshua's legs is derived from incidents which have been reported in several published first-hand reports. There is an eyewitness letter from a writer in Lancaster who observed two brothers from Captain Michael Cresep's Maryland rifle company performing the same trick in August, 1775 as the company was on its way to join the revolutionary forces besieging Boston. The company was stopping overnight and put on a show for the residents which also included other shooting demonstrations. A good account is presented in *The Kentucky Rifle* (John G. W. Dillin, George Shumway Publisher, 1967, Chap 14).

Susquehannock/Conestoga Indian Tribe. In antiquity, the Susquehannock Indians were very populous and powerful, their lands centered in the Susquehanna basin of Pennsylvania and the northern areas of Maryland and Virginia. Susquehannock villages were reported on the banks of the upper Chesapeake and on the Potomac River. Captain John Smith of Jamestown saw Susquehannocks in 1608 and described them as having a tall and robust stature. Estimates of their numbers range from 2000 to 7000 at the time of European contact. However, due to a series of defeats in warfare with other tribes and European settlers, coupled with the effects of disease, by the late part of the century the tribe had shrunk to no more than 300 members and had come under the domination of the Iroquois Confederation. As of 1677 the survivors were living in a single village near Lancaster, Pennsylvania which would come to be called Conestoga Town. Pennsylvanians thus came to call the residents *Conestoga Indians.* In 1701 the tribal leaders signed a treaty with William Penn which gave the Conestogas special protections and ratified their rights to the land surrounding their village. There is very little explanation available as to why the tribe dwindled so rapidly to twenty-some members by 1763. It appears that, over time, some Conestogas did indeed move west and join the villages of other tribes (Probably Mingo/Seneca) in the Ohio Country or the Iroquois lands to the north. It is also known that some residents left Conestoga Town to work and live on local farms. One couple, identified simply as Michael and Martha, survived the massacre in this way and are buried on the lands which once was the farm of Christian Hershey (Yes, part of *that* Hershey family) where they lived and worked. I personally believe that, over the years following the treaty, young Conestogas, witnessing stagnation at Conestoga Town, chose assimilation into other tribes or into white culture as the path to a more vital and prosperous future.

The Derivation of Charlie Sawak. As they say in movie credits, the character Charlie Sawak was "suggested" by a Conestoga named Will Sock. As with Charlie, Will was a young adult member of the tribe who traveled throughout the Susquehanna area, sometimes selling craft goods made by his fellow Conestogas. But there the resemblance ends. Will Sock appears to have been a rather aggressive, in-your-face type character whose words and actions gave the enemies of the tribe ammunition for moving against Conestoga Town and its inhabitants. It was rumored that he threatened a blacksmith with physical violence for refusing to fix his hatchet, was seen consorting with war parties from the Ohio Country, and that he was among a group which killed an Indian named Chagrea from another peaceful tribe. These rumors have never been substantiated and are discounted by modern historians. However, there is credible evidence that at one point he traveled west to visit with Senecas or Mingoes in the Ohio Country. Some contemporaries claimed that the attack on the work house in Lancaster started as an attempt to take Will Sock prisoner and then got out of hand. In any case, he died with his tribal compatriots in the second massacre. As readers will have noted, our Charlie Sawak had a modicum of formal education, the amiable and outgoing personality of a salesman, and was more of a lover than a fighter. Until the massacre of the tribe, he harbored a desire to eventually blend in with the European culture, as I believe many of the younger Conestogas had already done.

Leadership of the Conestoga Massacres. The leadership of the two attacks is not documented, and in fact there is no firm knowledge of the men who composed the raiding parties. It is clear that many people knew the identities of the attackers, but that a widespread conspiracy of silence was in effect among the Ulster-Scots to protect the raiders from government legal action. However, some accounts do identify Mathew Smith as the likely leader of the massacre at Conestoga Town and Lazarus Stewart as the leader of the later attack on the work house in Lancaster. Stewart was indeed the commander of one of the two Paxton militia companies. Clearly, Governor John Penn was convinced that Stewart had a major role in the attacks and did order him relieved of duties in the Paxton Militia as described in the manuscript. For simplification of the narrative, I have used Stewart as the leader of both attacks. History shows that Stewart was an aggressive militia leader and a fierce enemy of the remaining Indians who lived to the east of the Susquehanna River. He ultimately was killed during the revolution leading militia in a fight with loyalist troops from Connecticut who were attempting to take possession of Pennsylvania's Wyoming Valley.

Role of Reverend John Elder. Historical treatment of Reverend Elder in the Conestoga incident varies from defender of the tribe to unindicted conspirator in their demise, depending on the writer and the era in which the writing occurred. In his own time Elder was revered by the Ulster-Scots residents as the minister of one of the earliest Presbyterian congregations in the border region. He must be given due credit for organizing the Paxton Militia during the French and Indian War and in some cases actually going into the field, firelock in hand, to lead operations in defense of the settlers. Nineteenth century accounts of the Conestoga massacre took him at his word and lauded him for actively trying to prevent attacks on the Indians. In fact, most researchers do portray him as sending the warning letter to the governor requesting that the Conestogas be moved to protective custody in Philadelphia. Also, some narratives indicate that he tried to reason with the second group of raiders to stop them from riding to Lancaster for the assault on the workhouse. However, some modern researchers suspect that from the beginning he was well aware of the plans to attack the Conestogas and tacitly gave his blessing to the undertaking. We'll probably never learn the exact extent of his involvement. My approach has been to take a middle ground, portraying him as being overwhelmed by the outpouring of anger by Paxton residents and, convinced that nothing he could do would stop their attack, simply allowing it to happen. Note that Elder's ride with Reverend Carnahan in an ostensible attempt to head off the Paxton men at Conestoga Town and provide assistance to survivors at the work house is purely fictional. Placing him there with the principal characters was a device to dramatize the events and introduce Elder and the Paxton militia organization into the narrative at the proper time.

Military Forces in Colonial America. For the most part, the military structure in the colonies consisted of three levels. At the top were British regular army units. As Bouquet pointed out to Wend in Chapter Nine, until Braddock's expedition of 1755 there were only a few far-flung independent companies of British infantry. One of these joined with George Washington's Virginia troops at the Battle of Great Meadows (Fort Necessity). Subsequent to the start of the French and Indian War, there were always a significant number of British infantry battalions in the colonies. During the interregnum between the end of Pontiac's Rebellion and the outbreak of the revolution, there was an authorized strength of approximately 10,000 troops in a planned fifteen battalions.

At the second level were the provincial regiments. These were formally enlisted, but temporary, units of troops formed by the colonies to supplement the British foot regiments. They were usually raised in times of emergency and the troops enlisted for a set time frame, typically a year. They were provided uniforms, weapons, pay, and subsistence by the colonies, supplemented by funds and material support from the mother country. Washington's Virginia Regiment (Later expanded to two battalions) was perhaps the best known example of this type organization during the French and Indian War era. Under duress from both the British government and settlers, Pennsylvania did form the Pennsylvania Regiment during the French and Indian War. Although it evolved through several structural iterations, the regiment ultimately consisted of three battalions. Elements of the regiment marched as part of General Forbes' expedition to capture the Forks of the Ohio in 1758. The regiment was disbanded at the conclusion of the French war, but was in fact re-established in 1764 for use in the latter stages of Pontiac's War.

The third level of the military establishment was the militia. Most colonies had some sort of official militia organization. For example, Virginia's was based on the county structure, with an officer of the colony called "The County Lieutenant" who administered the local militia units and reported to the colony's central government. However, because of the pacifism integral to the Quaker religion, Pennsylvania did not have a government controlled militia establishment. Benjamin Franklin did organize a surrogate independent militia network in the face of a threatened Indian uprising in 1747. This organization was called "The Associators" and became dormant once the immediate threat abated.

Subsequently the void was filled in the border areas by private, locally established militias which were not normally sanctioned by the colonial government. However, after the outbreak of Pontiac's War, pressure from the settlers in the border country forced the Pennsylvania government to officially adopt the ad hoc militia and recognize their officers. As one would expect, the discipline and effectiveness of these units varied widely. At one end of the spectrum were well organized units, led by experienced warfighters with some actual military background, usually gained in provincial units. Two of the most well known were the previously discussed Paxton Militia and the Black Boys Militia which was centered in the Conococheague region to the south. The Paxton Militia consisted of two companies led by Stewart and Asher Clayton, both of whom had some formal military experience. The

Black Boys militia was led by a certain James Smith, who attained legendary status among colonials. Smith had been captured by the Indians while a laborer helping to construct Braddock's Road in 1755 and escaped after about a year. He organized and trained his men to fight Indian style; when in the field on patrol they painted themselves black and otherwise dressed like tribal warriors. In 1765, Smith and the Black Boys were at the center of an insurrection protesting the renewal of Crown sanctioned trade with the Ohio tribes. Subsequently Smith went on to become a well respected colonel in the revolutionary army. At the other end of the spectrum were loosely structured self-defense units akin to an armed version of modern neighborhood watch organizations. These were generally most viable in defense of private forts or fortified houses during the extremis of a war party raid. In both *Forbes Road* and *Conestoga Winter* I have included the fictional Sherman Valley militia company as part of the Paxton organization to facilitate Wend's interactions with John Elder, Lazarus Stewart, and Clayton Asher.

Iron-Making Furnaces. The existence of an ironworks in Shippensburg is fiction, but the description of the iron making equipment and process is representative of a typical production facility. And, in fact, the Codorus Furnace north of York was being constructed in 1764 by a consortium led by Robert Bennet (*Bennett* in some articles); it commenced operations in 1765. The actual Codorus furnace, or stack, still exists in Hellam Township, having been rebuilt several times. Colonial Pennsylvania had a thriving iron making business, which had existed since Thomas Rutter built the first iron works in 1716. These metal production establishments employed as many as 70 men, and, as described in the manuscript, often formed substantial villages called "Iron Plantations" in colonial times. The preponderance of these establishments were located in rural areas due to the need to be near production resources such as unlimited wood for charcoal and ore deposits. Some produced only iron for sale to forges while others incorporated both iron production and forges to create wrought iron at the same location. Our modern media, where it has chosen to produce stories about the frontier, mostly highlights the woodsmen living in isolated cabins or farmers working the land. But the fact is that very close on the heels of this first wave of settlers were tradesmen like Wend and industrialists such as gristmill operators and iron makers. Their story, important as it was to development, has rarely been told.

Useful References. Much of my research for this novel was done in parallel with the development of the *Forbes Road* manuscript. When I started in the late 1990's, the only widely published account of the Conestoga murders and the Paxton Boys march on Philadelphia was in the second volume of Francis Parkman's *The Conspiracy of Pontiac* (Originally published in 1851; my reprint version was published by Bison Books/University of Nebraska Press, in 1994). This manuscript is particularly useful because it presents a concise outline of the events; moreover it also reflects both the views and prejudices of a 19th century writer and, in appendices, the written statements and sentiments of people who were alive at the time of the actual events. Another vintage reference is Donald A. Cadzow's *Archaeological Studies of The Susquehannock Indians of Pennsylvania* (Pennsylvania Historical Commission, 1936). Used copies can be obtained through online book sellers, and the book contains a fairly detailed and very useful summary of the tribe's history from the advent of European settlers until the massacre. Professor Kevin Kenny's *Peaceable Kingdom Lost: The Paxton boys and the Destruction of William Penn's Holy Experiment* (Oxford University Press, 2009) is a well researched and thoughtful academic level interpretation of the cultural background of Pennsylvania and the violent events of 1763-1764. *Massacre of the Conestogas: On the Trail of the Paxton Boys in Lancaster County* by Jack Brubaker (The History Press, Charleston, SC, 2010) is a workmanlike, focused, and very readable account of the massacre and the aftermath. I greatly appreciated the detail presented and I am indebted to the author for his account of the burial of the Conestoga remains, on which I largely depended for my retelling.

For the sections related to iron manufacture, I relied on several online sources, visits to actual sites, and an old, but remarkably thorough book entitled, *Pennsylvania Iron Manufacture in the Eighteenth Century* by Arthur C. Bining, (Originally published through the Pennsylvania Historical and Museum Commission, 1938, reprint by Augustus M. Kelley Publishers, New York, 1970). Many on-line sites were useful, but the Centre County Historical Society's multipage description and illustration of iron-making at Centre Furnace, including explanation of furnace operations, worker identification and responsibilities, and a glossary of furnace/forge vocabulary was superb (www.centrecountyhistory.org/iron/ironmaking).

A very timely and illuminating book for my research was Judith Ridner's *A Town In-Between: Carlisle, Pennsylvania and The Early Mid-Atlantic Interior*

(University of Pennsylvania Press, 2010). Particularly relevant were the chapters regarding the early development and layout of the town.

Acknowledgements. I have many people to thank for helping in the production of this second volume of Wend Eckert's adventures. Bryant White extended permission for use of his painting, *Time of War*, for the cover of *Conestoga Winter* and another of his paintings, *The Gunsmith*, for promotional activity. His portfolio of historical art can be viewed online at www. whitehistoricart.com. Numerous others helped directly with the writing and review of the manuscript. Chief among them is my wife Cathy, who diligently reads every word and is in charge of advising me when I'm in danger of jumping the shark with any plotline or in the actions of characters. My son, Michael Shade, read the entire first draft in one weekend, and as he always does, provided insightful comments which led to improvements in the story. I am indebted to Major John Chapman, USMC (Ret) who provided his usual excellent services in being the first outside reader to critique the draft. Above all, I am particularly grateful to the many readers who have purchased *Forbes Road* and have taken the time to communicate their reactions directly to me by letter or email through the www.forbesroadbook.com website. The effort you have made to provide general feedback and suggestions for further research and plot development have been extremely useful and personally gratifying.

Robert J. Shade
February, 2013

Made in the USA
Middletown, DE
02 April 2019